She turned the handle and, with her heart thumping in her chest, made her way along the short passageway to the parlour. She pushed open the door and gasped. There, sitting in her chair with his feet on the fender was the man she'd last seen almost four years ago: her husband, Freddie Ellis.

Standing just over five foot eight, he was taller than most local-born men, many of whom struggled to match Kate's five foot four. He was dressed in a well-fitted houndstooth jacket and matching trousers, and his tall crowned hat was placed on the table beside him. With hazel eyes and a full head of dark brown hair combed back so that it skimmed his collar Freddie was a man women looked twice at. Kate herself had thought him the most handsome man in the world when she'd first set eyes on him.

He stood up and, with an expression she once thought endearing, said, 'Hello, Kate.'

'Who is it, Mam?' Joe whispered, shaking her skirt.

The urge to scream rose up inside her but somehow Kate held it in. 'Ella, Joe, this is your father.'

Jean Fullerton was born in the East End within the sound of the Bow Bells. She is a trained nurse and has three daughters. Her first novel, *No Cure for Love*, won the Harry Bowling Prize, and her second novel, *A Glimpse at Happiness*, was shortlisted for the RNA Romantic Novel of the Year award.

By Jean Fullerton

No Cure for Love
A Glimpse at Happiness
Perhaps Tomorrow
Hold on to Hope

Hold on to Hope

JEAN FULLERTON

An Orion paperback

First published in Great Britain in 2012
by Orion
This paperback edition published in 2012
by Orion Books,
an imprint of The Orion Publishing Group Ltd,
Orion House, 5 Upper Saint Martin's Lane,
London WC2H 9EA

An Hachette UK company

A CIP catalogue record for this book
is available from the British Library.

Typeset by Input Data Systems Ltd,
Bridgwater, Somerset

Printed in Great Britain by
CPI Group (UK) Ltd, Croydon, CR0 4YY

The Orion Publishing Group's policy is to use papers that
are natural, renewable and recyclable products and
made from wood grown in sustainable forests. The logging
and manufacturing processes are expected to conform to
the environmental regulations of the country of origin.

www.orionbooks.co.uk

To Hannah, Nathan, Sarah and Imogen.

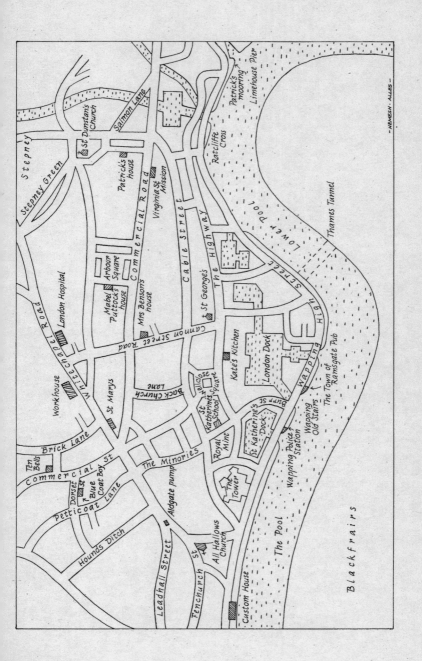

Chapter One

Kate Ellis tucked the wayward strand of blonde hair behind her ear and handed over the bowl of steaming stew to the next customer.

'There you go. That'll be threepence, please. And just take a cuppa.' She nodded at Sally, her assistant standing beside her and pouring tea into a dozen or so mugs.

The docker handed her the money and Kate pulled out the drawer under the counter, slipped the cash into the well-worn copper section then shut the drawer. She wiped the sweat from her forehead with the back of her hand. There might be icicles hanging from the crane arms in the docks but the chop house was steamy as a laundry.

Kate's Kitchen sat on St George's Highway about a mile east of Smithfield on the corner of Neptune Street and was situated at the rough end of Wapping and Shadwell's main thoroughfare. Her eating house drew trade from the old St Katharine's church area and the tobacco docks as well as the port offices around the Royal Mint.

The shop took up most of the downstairs part of the property and allowed Kate a small parlour, accessed from behind the counter and through the back door. The room had a fireplace and a set of narrow wooden steps leading to the two rooms above, where she and her children slept. The backyard contained the privy and the chicken coop. The derelict stable formed the back wall.

Many of the local traders were having brash new windows fitted, made up of a single sheet of glass; Kate kept her front window with its traditional small panes. She felt that they helped to give the shop a homely feel, along with the clean, bright paintwork and red-chequered curtains.

'How're you doing, Sally?' Kate asked.

'I'll have to brew another pot in a mo' but I'll squeeze another couple of mugs out of this one first,' Sally replied.

'Good. The next batch of pies should be ready in a minute.' Kate squeezed behind her assistant to reach the oven.

Sally's husband, Will, was a long-time drinking pal of Kate's brother Patrick. He had been a lighterman on the river until his boat collided with a Woolwich steam packet on its way upriver three years ago which crushed his arm. As soon as Patrick told Kate of Sally's circumstances she had offered her work.

Although there was barely room to accommodate both women, she and Sally had developed an uncanny knack of avoiding bumping into each other as they dished up dozens of hot dinners and poured gallons of sweet tea.

'I thought your Joe would be back by now,' Sally said, sliding the dirty plates stacked on the end of the marble counter into the enamel sink.

'So did I,' Kate replied, pouring custard on to two bowls of jam pudding.

On cue, the parlour door opened and Kate turned to see her son Joe standing in the doorway.

As usual, and despite Kate combing it into order that morning, Joe's hair now flew off in all directions. There was a smear of mud on his right cheek and both socks had lost their fight with gravity and were bunched just above the tops of his boots. Despite eating what seemed to be his own body weight in food each day, Joe remained stick thin, probably because he burnt up so much energy tearing around the streets.

'I thought I told you to come back at noon,' Kate said, picking up the tea towel.

Joe found space behind the counter and grabbed a wooden spoon. 'Sorry, Mam, but me and Sammy were playing soldiers.' He swished his improvised sword back and forth. 'We was fighting off cannibals, like the ones Uncle Pat told us about.'

The corner of Kate's mouth lifted. 'And I'll have to have a word with my brother about his tall tales.'

'But it's true,' Joe protested as he parried an imaginary enemy. The spoon pinged against a mug, setting it wobbling.

'I'll have that,' Kate took the spoon from him, 'before my china ends up shattered on the floor.'

Joe surrendered his sword and lolled against the counter. 'What's for dinner?' he asked, gathering a fingerful of custard from the side of the jug and popping it into his mouth.

'Nothing until you've nipped these around to the trade door at Murphy's Wharf,' Kate said, picking up a basket filled with wrapped pies that had been kept warm beside the stove.

Joe stuck out his lower lip. 'Oh, Maaaam.'

'It won't take you a moment and I'll have your plate ready when you get back.' She tousled his fair hair. 'There'll be an extra dollop of jam if you're quick.'

Joe grinned, showing a shadow of his father's easy charm, before scooping up the basket and dodging between the tables.

'And don't drop the money on the way back!'

The bell over the door jingled as Joe dashed out, almost knocking Ruben Krowsky, one of the coffee sellers, flying.

Ruben stamped his feet on the coconut mat and unwound his scarf as clinging wisps of river fog evaporated in the warmth of the shop.

'Afternoon, Ruben,' Kate called over the heads of the other customers.

'And to you, dear lady,' the old man replied, as he reached the counter. 'I see your Joe's full of beans today.'

Kate laughed. 'Isn't he always?'

'And how is my lovely Ella? Working hard at her lessons?'

A little bubble of pride started in Kate's chest. 'She's grand! She got a special commendation from her teacher last week for her neat handwriting.'

'Did she?' Ruben said, approvingly.

'She did. And of course Joe will be going to St Katharine's after Christmas.'

'Already?'

'Well, he's six in May.'

'Six! It only seems yesterday he started walking.'

Kate laughed. 'Joe's long given up walking in favour of running.'

'A truer word was never spoken.' Ruben's long face creased into a smile. 'I know I've said it before but you don't look old enough to be their ma.'

'Go away with you,' Kate replied, feeling her face grow warm.

Ruben put a fingerless-gloved hand on his chest. 'As Jehovah is my witness! You can't be a day older than my Sadie and she's only twenty-four in January.'

'Ah well then, I have a couple of years on her,' Kate replied. 'How's Hester?'

He shook his head dolefully. 'Oy. Not good. She's been coughing all night, fit to wake the dead.'

'I'm sorry to hear that.' She took a plate from the stack on the end of the counter. 'Stew or pie?'

'Pie, I think.'

Kate picked up a tea towel, opened the oven and manoeuvred a steak and onion pie onto the plate. She scooped up a generous portion of mashed potato alongside it then ladled gravy over both. 'That should warm your cockles,' she said, handing it to him.

'I hope so! It's cold enough to freeze the blood in a poor man's veins. I shouldn't wonder if we don't see ice floating on the river soon like it did back in '49. Do you remember?'

'How could I forget,' Kate replied, smiling at him. 'That's when we first met.'

A fatherly expression stole over Ruben's face. 'Ah yes. I can still see you now with baby in one arm, a basket hooked over the other and selling pies at the dock gates.'

'And you gave me a mug of coffee and let me warm Ella by your stove,' Kate replied, softly.

Ruben looked amazed. 'Did I?'

She smiled. 'You know you did. Now, Ruben, I think there's a space or two at the back. And also,' she picked up one of the wrapped pies from the back of the hotplate, 'put it on your stove to keep it warm for later.'

Ruben put his hand up. 'No, I couldn't—'

'Sure you can, for Hester.'

He took the parcel and tucked it in his pocket. 'Thank you and a blessing on your house.' Picking out a knife and fork from the tub on the counter, he made his way between the tables to the rear of the shop.

The bell tinkled again and Joe dashed back in.

'That was quick,' Kate said, wiping her hands on her apron and reaching for a bowl.

'That's cos I'm the fastest runner in the street,' Joe told her, his eyes fixed on the ladle as it filled the dish with mutton stew.

Kate took the money from him and then handed him his dinner. 'Go and keep old Ruben company.'

Cradling his stew in his hand, Joe made his way between the men seated around the dozen tables to where the old coffee seller was eating his dinner.

Knowing that the end-of-lunch bells would soon ring, most of Kate's customers were mopping up the last drops of gravy and preparing to go back to work. And sure enough, within half an hour the last few stragglers were gone, leaving only a couple of street traders sipping coffee at the back. Joe finished his dinner and Kate got him to help sort the cutlery to keep him occupied. As she wiped down the last table, her daughter Ella walked in.

Although she wouldn't turn seven until April, Ella was already half a head taller than many of her classmates who were two years older. With bright blue eyes and two long blonde plaits bouncing down her back, she looked very much as Kate had done twenty years before. The cold had put a sparkle in her eyes and pink on her cheeks.

She was dressed in the uniform at St Katharine's School, a navy button-up dress, a white pinafore and a dark blue calf-length coat. Well, the coat should have been calf-length but it, like the dress and pinafore, was almost up to her knees and would have to be replaced before the next school year.

'You're out early,' Kate said, putting the last plate on top of the stack.

'The boiler went out so Miss Wainwright called Mr Delaney in to look at it. After he played about with it for a bit, it started smoking and filled the classrooms. Mr Rudd had to close the school.'

The two teachers did their best to keep St Katharine's going but since the old headmaster Mr Gardener died a year ago, the school seemed to be going to rack and ruin. Perhaps, instead of sending Joe there in January, she should apply for a place in the Green Coat School in Norbiton Road just off Salmon's Lane. She had to find a good place for him as without a proper school certificate there was no hope of either of them securing an apprenticeship or an office job. She had heard that St Katharine's school guardians were interviewing someone to replace the old headmaster so maybe she'd wait a couple of weeks before making a final decision.

'Sally, do you think you can finish off here while I go and put my orders in for next week?' Kate asked, untying her apron.

'Sure thing, Mrs E,' Sally replied.

'In fact,' Kate glanced at the darkening sky through the window, 'I doubt in this weather you'll get many more in so as soon as the last few have left, you can lock up. And take the last couple of pies yourself.'

Sally's pale face lifted into a smile. 'Thank you very much, Mrs E. That should do Will and the boys just right for their supper.'

'And make sure you take one for yourself,' Kate added, thinking Sally could do with putting a bit of meat on her bones.

Sally's two older lads were already working on the river but they only brought home boys' wages so Kate made sure there was always a bit of something left over.

'I will,' Sally replied, putting another handful of dishes in the sink. 'And I'll set the pot to soak before I go. What do you want me to do with the leftover bread?'

'Just leave it. I'll make some bread pudding with half of it and take the rest to the mission when I get back. There should be enough stew left to feed a few more poor souls.'

Kate collected her coat and bonnet from behind the parlour door. 'Joe, Ella, do you want to come with me to Watney Market?'

'Yes, Ma,' Ella said, rewinding her scarf around her head.

Joe jumped off the stool behind the counter and dashed around. 'Can we have a ha'penny to spend in the sweetshop?'

'I think I might just find a farthing or two for you both. Now get your coat, Joe, and we'll be off.'

As Kate had hoped, the stallholders were selling off their fresh produce cheap rather than have it spoiled by the frost overnight. After giving next week's order to the butcher and grocer, Kate loaded up her basket and dropped in two oranges for an after-supper treat. When they started home, the lamplighters were already at the top of their long ladders, bringing to life the lamps dotted along the main thoroughfare. They could hear the faint hiss of the gas as they passed underneath.

The fog along the highway was so thick that she and the children could hardly see across the road. Taking the long way to avoid the sailors outside the seamen's mission, Kate hurried on. She'd left a pie for their supper on the table and it wouldn't take long to heat it while she brewed a cuppa for them all. Then, when the children were tucked into bed, she could set the meat simmering for tomorrow and darn Joe's socks yet again.

Going around to the back of the shop, Kate lifted the gate latch and ushered the children into the yard. The chickens, snug in their coop, clucked and cooed as Kate closed the gates behind her.

She pulled her key out to open the back door but found it already unlocked. Her brows pulled together. She had been into the yard to gather eggs before dinner and was sure she'd locked it after her.

She turned the handle and, with her heart thumping in her chest, made her way along the short passageway to the parlour. She pushed open the door and gasped. There, sitting in her chair with his feet on the fender was the man she'd last seen almost four years ago: her husband, Freddie Ellis.

Standing just over five foot eight, he was taller than most local-born men, many of whom struggled to match Kate's five foot four. He was dressed in a well-fitted houndstooth jacket and matching trousers, and his tall crowned hat was placed on the table beside him. With hazel eyes and a full head of dark brown hair combed back so that it skimmed his collar Freddie was a man women looked twice at. Kate herself had thought him the most handsome man in the world when she'd first set eyes on him.

He stood up and, with an expression she once thought endearing, said, 'Hello, Kate.'

'Who is it, Mam?' Joe whispered, shaking her skirt.

The urge to scream rose up inside her but somehow Kate held it in. 'Ella, Joe, this is your father.'

Ella took a step closer to her and stared wide-eyed at Freddie.

Joe rushed forward. 'I'm Joe and I'm five and almost as tall as Ella and she's six!' He stretched up to his tiptoes.

Freddie crouched down until his face was level with Joe's. 'So you're my Joe?' His gaze ran slowly over his son's face. 'Why ain't you just the replica of me when I was a lad? But are you a scrapper like me?'

Joe raised his fists in front of his face. Freddie looked impressed. He touched Joe's small white knuckles with his scarred ones. 'You've got you dabs just—'

'Children, go to your room,' Kate cut in.

Ella gave her a father an apprehensive look and headed for the door.

Joe's shoulders slumped. 'But, Mam . . .'

Kate glared him. Defiance flickered briefly across Joe's face but then he followed his sister, dragging his feet all the way. The door clicked shut.

Kate glared at Freddie, who gave her a cocky grin and sat down again.

'I must say you've got a nice little place here,' he said, slowly looking around. 'I 'ope you don't mind I got myself a bite to eat.'

Kate glanced at the empty plate where their supper had been. 'What do you want?'

'Who says I want anything?'

Kate regarded him coolly. 'You always do.'

'Ain't you going to ask me where I've been?'

Kate shrugged. 'Why should I care? Millbank or Pentonville. One prison's much the same as another.'

Freddie sneered. 'I suppose cos I ain't been around for a while you'd hope I was dead and buried somewhere.'

Kate didn't answer.

Resentment flashed across Freddie's face before he smiled and with slow deliberation rested his feet back on the fender. 'So this your place then?' he asked, putting his hands behind his head and leaning back.

'No.'

'Pity. Whose is it then?'

'None of your business.'

Freddie jumped up and loomed over Kate who had to stop herself gagging as the stench of stale sweat and beer wafted over her. 'Got yourself a man then, have you?'

Forcing herself not to step back, Kate met his gaze coolly. 'I haven't forgotten my marriage vows – even if you did the moment the ink was dry. My brother owns the shop and I run it for him. If you must know.'

Freddie laughed. 'I should have known it. I should have guessed good old Pat would set you up. Your fucking Paddy family were always thick as thieves.'

Kate clenched her fists by her sides. 'My brother wouldn't see me and my children starve, if that's what you mean. Now, I've no notion as to why you've decided to turn up after four years, and I care even less. So I'll thank you to be on your way—'

His hand shot out and grasped her throat. His eyes ran slowly over her face. 'You always did look your best with a temper on you,' he said in a heavy voice.

Kate tried to twist out of his grip but he pressed his thumb into her windpipe. She let her arms fall to her sides. Looking at her husband's half-closed eyes and loose, moist lips, a shiver of disgust ran through her. At least he wouldn't kiss her. He never did.

Freddie pressed her back against the kitchen table and rammed his knee between her legs.

'If you ain't got yourself another man yet, you must be panting for it.' He grabbed her breast and squeezed it painfully. 'You always were a good handful.'

He pulled up her skirts and thrust his hand between her legs. 'Let me see how much you've missed me.'

As his fingers poked painfully into her, Kate's stomach heaved. She forced it down and moulded herself into him.

'Oh, Freddie,' she murmured.

He laughed, gripping her hair and forcing her head back. 'I knew you wouldn't say no to a bit of 'ow's-your-father,' he said, fumbling with her bodice buttons. 'You never could.'

His hand left her throat and tore the front of her gown open. He yanked the flimsy chemise aside and ran his tongue over her breast, leaving a damp trail.

Kate reached out, grabbed the heavy metal pie dish and smashed the rim into his ear. As Freddie arched back and clutched his head, Kate jerked her knee into his crotch. He let go of her and doubled over, clutching the front of his trousers.

'You fucking bitch,' he croaked, then vomited over his boots.

Kate shoved him back. 'Get out!'

Freddie staggered to his feet. 'I'll stay if I want. You're my wife and what's yours belongs to me. That's what the law says.'

'Call the law then! I'm sure the local coppers'll be glad to know you're back in the area.' Kate strode to the back door and threw it open. 'Go on then. If you're quick you'll catch Sergeant Bell on the corner of Pennington Street checking the patrols.'

Cradling his injured genitals Freddie stumbled into the shop. There was a crash as the cash drawer hit the floor. He reappeared, knocking aside a stool and trampling her knitting underfoot. As he reached the back door, he turned.

'You may have got the drop on me this time, you cow, but right's right and as your lawfully wedded husband, this,' he held up his fist holding the day's takings, 'is mine, so don't think you've seen the back of me.'

He shoved her hard-earned money into his pocket and, nearly tripping over himself, staggered out the back door.

Kate shut the door and stood frozen. Her heart was pounding and when her knees threatened to give way, she sank on to a chair. Staring blindly, she rebuttoned her bodice with shaking fingers.

Yes, she remembered the winter of '49. In that bitter December six years ago Freddie moved out of the home she'd made for them and in with his trollop. Left alone with a hungry child and another in her belly, she spent her last shilling on a bag of flour, a knob of fat and a couple of pounds of beef, which she'd used to bake her first two dozen pies to sell at the dock gates.

The following March, six weeks before Joe came into the world, Freddie was sent down for eighteen months in Coldbath Fields for receiving stolen goods. He'd come back to bother her again just when Ella had learnt to tie her bootlaces. Shortly after, he was arrested and sentenced to another two years for aggravated burglary. When he didn't turn up after his release a year ago, Kate implored the Virgin Mary, for her children's sake as well as her own, that she would never have to set eyes on Freddie Ellis again. It seemed her prayers had gone unanswered.

Chapter Two

Captain Jonathan Quinn of the Coldstream Guards marched past the adjutant's desk to the window for the third time in ten minutes. He'd been ordered to present himself to the colonel at three o'clock sharp, which he did – thirty minutes ago.

The Main Guard, the guardhouse running between the Conqueror's White Tower and the Wakefield Tower, wasn't the worst place he'd been summoned to for a dressing-down. If pushed, he'd say that that honour would go to the commander's tent, shot through and splattered with gore, beside the Hariawala. On that occasion he'd been threatened with a flogging for refusing to lead his men to certain death into the guns of the Sikh army. Although this interview wasn't to upbraid him for insubordination to an incompetent senior officer, Jonathan knew it would be just as hostile.

Pulling down the front of his red dress tunic, he clasped his hands behind his back and resumed his study of the squad being drilled on Tower Green.

The lieutenant sitting behind the desk coughed and Jonathan turned.

'I'm certain the colonel won't be much longer, Captain,' the young man said.

'I'm sure,' Jonathan replied in a tone that implied otherwise. He tilted his head. 'It's Parnell, isn't it?'

The soldier jumped to his feet and saluted. 'Yes, sir.'

'Stand easy.'

Parnell's shoulders relaxed. 'It's good of you to remember me, sir.'

Jonathan looked him over. 'It was a while ago, I grant you, and you've grown a ...' He pointed to his top lip. 'But I never forget a man who has served under me.'

The lieutenant smoothed his waxed moustache. 'Yes, sir. We've both changed a bit since our stint in Alexandra in '46.' His gaze flickered to the eyepatch covering the mangled socket of Jonathan's left eye.

'Just so,' he replied, forcing himself not to adjust its position.

Parnell stood to attention again. 'I hope you'll pardon me for mentioning it but the regiment, every man jack of 'em, is right proud of your actions on the Heights of Alma, sir.'

'I did no more than my duty.'

'Maybe so, but everyone in the garrison knows there would have been a dozen more widows if you hadn't done it so well,' Parnell replied.

'Lieutenant!' bellowed a voice from the other side of the oak door.

The adjutant dashed over and opened it. He snapped to attention. 'Yes, sir.'

'Is Captain Quinn there?' the colonel's gruff voice shouted from inside the room.

'Yes, sir.'

'Then send him in, God damn you. They're expecting me at Horse Guard's at five.'

Parnell gave another crisp salute and stood back. Jonathan pulled down the front of his jacket again, adjusted his scarlet sash and marched into his commanding officer's study.

As he expected, the regiment's senior officer was sitting behind the long mahogany desk studying a pile of letters with a pen in his right hand and a large brandy in his left. Framed on the wall behind him his predecessors, wearing uniforms, wigs, and shouldering arms from bygone ages, stared down at him in silent splendour. On the dresser over by the window lay unfurled maps and a pile of unread despatches with their blood-red seals still intact.

Jonathan double-stepped to attention and saluted. 'Captain Quinn, reporting as ordered, sir.'

The colonel threw down the pen and looked up. His bloodshot eyes narrowed as he grasped a letter from the top of the heap.

'Tell me, Captain Quinn, what is this pile of horse shit?'

Jonathan regarded him coolly. 'My resignation.'

'Damn you,' the colonel forced out through clenched teeth. 'I can see that. But why?'

'I thought I had made my reasons clear.'

'Did you? Did you indeed?'

The colonel held his gaze for a second or two then pulled out his monocle and glanced over Jonathan's letter again. 'You can't expect me to send this up to the Colonel-in-Chief.'

'Why not, sir?'

'Because you describe your commanding officer as an "incompetent fool",' he replied, as if explaining to a child.

'He is, sir.'

'Good God, man!' he said, as the monocle fell from his eye. 'He is also the Duke of Cambridge. The Queen's cousin.'

'Well then, he's an incompetent *royal* fool, sir.'

The colonel slammed his fist down on the desk and the inkwell rattled. 'And what of the regiment, blast you? Have you forgotten your family connection to the Guards?

'No, sir, but my resignation stands.'

The colonel glared at Jonathan and muttered a series of unintelligible oaths from under his moustache.

'Look,' he said, resting his elbows on the desktop and steepling his fingers in front of him. 'Let's forget I'm your commanding officer for a moment and let me talk to you as your father.'

Jonathan regarded him levelly.

'I know you've been though the mill losing your ...' he tapped under his left eye. 'But it's not reason enough to throw away a promising career. I mean to say, there's hardly an officer in Horse Guard's who hasn't had a bit shot off in some battle somewhere.' He laughed. 'Look at old Dog Meat Huntley. He had a leg hacked off at Waterloo, lost three fingers to a dodgy grenade in Ghuznee and his ear bitten off by a horse at Moodkee and he's still serving Queen and county as Provost Marshall of equipment and supplies.'

Jonathan raised an eyebrow. 'Well, sir, that probably explains why the men in Sebastopol haven't got their winter uniforms yet.'

Irritation flashed across the colonel's face. 'It's that sort of impertinent quip that's given you the reputation as an agitator.' He fixed Jonathan with the look that had scattered Frenchmen, Hindu Kush tribesmen and junior ranks alike. 'Our ancestor and your namesake, Sir Jonathan Quinn, marched south with General Monck two hundred years ago. We Quinns have served in this regiment ever since and now you're going to turn your back on your obligations because you've had an eye shot out.'

'Have you *read* my letter, Father?'

'Of course I have. Well, the first couple of lines before my dyspepsia prevented me from reading further.'

'Had you'd read it in full, you would know that I'm not resigning because of my *eye*. I'm resigning before I'm *court-martialled* for—'

'Court-martialled!'

'—for refusing to lead any more good men to their slaughter on the orders of some short-sighted buffoon of a general who can't tell his left from his right.'

An unhealthy colour mottled his father's cheeks. 'That's no way to talk about Lord Raglan. He is our most experienced and capable field marshal.'

'Tell that to the widows of the Light Brigade.'

They glared at each other and then his father jammed his monocle back under his brow and chewed his moustache. 'And what has Miss Davenport to say about all this? I assume you've told her of your crackbrained idea.'

'I have. She was naturally a little shocked but I'm certain she'll come around,' Jonathan said, remembering the look of horror on Louisa's face. 'She and her mother are in the country visiting family at the moment, so she has time to get used to the idea.'

His father looked him over, then threw the letter into the elephant-foot waste bin beside his desk. 'Well, she might come around but I won't. I will not accept it. Do you hear? I won't. You're dismissed.' He picked up the pen and shuffled the pile of papers in front of him.

A small pulse started in Jonathan's temple. 'I'm afraid you have no choice, sir,' he said, in a flat voice. 'Under the Queen's army order governing the Purchase and Relinquishing of Commissions, section twenty, subsection—'

His father's face flushed again and this time his eyes bulged, too. 'Don't quote army regulations to me! I was fighting under them while you were still wearing a bum-rag.' He stood up and planted his thick-set hands on the table. 'Now hear this, Jonathan. I don't give a hell-roasting damn about your opinion of the high command, army regulations, your poxy men or your bloody missing eye, but I will not have a my son dishonour me and the family's name. And I'll tell you this' – he leant forward until his nose was just inches from Jonathan's – 'you can dress up your reasons for throwing away a promising career any way you like but I'll tell you what I call it: *cowardice*.'

Jonathan's jaw clenched as he fought the urge to grab his father by the lapels and haul him over the desk. Somehow, despite his pounding temper clouding his thoughts, he kept his arms by his sides. He matched his father's enraged expression for a moment then stood to attention and saluted. He turned and marched to the door.

'Quinn!'

Jonathan turned.

'How dare you turn your back on your commanding officer!' His father jabbed a finger at him. 'This will earn you a week in the guardhouse.'

Jonathan gave him an icy look. 'I'm not turning my back on you as my colonel. I'm turning my back on you as my *father*.' He saluted again. 'Good day, sir!'

Jonathan burst out of the office and took the stairs two at a time in order to put as much distance between him and his father as possible. He marched back through the Tower's precinct.

He automatically returned the salutes of the guards on duty as he passed under the Byward Tower then continued to the Middle. The sergeant leading the patrol down from the residential quarters took one look at his face and brought his troop to immediate attention. Jonathan forced out a 'very good, Sergeant' as he stormed past. Even the captain of the soldier posted at the final guardhouse gave him a wary look as Jonathan checked himself out. He marched over the drawbridge and, leaving London's oldest castle behind him, started up the road towards Tower Hill.

Coward! Jonathan thought. *He was damn lucky I didn't* ... He drew a deep breath and forced his mind and pulse to slow.

With his boots crunching over the flint cobbles, Jonathan passed the newly built Tower ticket office, the Inland Revenue building and the row of taverns and eating houses that were already filled with soldiers from the garrison.

His father's flushed face loomed back into his mind as Jonathan pushed his way through a group of spotty delivery boys who jumped aside.

A woman with dirty brown hair piled haphazardly on to her head stepped in front of him. She was wearing a tatty gown, rouged lips and a willing smile.

'Well, aren't you the handsome captain, then.' She swept her gaze over him and then caught sight of his expression. 'Begging your pardon, sir,' she said, as she scuttled back to her friends.

The argument with his father still rolling around in his head, Jonathan continued at route-march pace for twenty minutes.

'Wotcha self, General.'

Jonathan stepped back as a laden wagon skimmed past him. He looked around, puzzled as he tried to get his bearings. It didn't look like Leadenhall.

The broad thoroughfare he was standing in had shops clustered together on both sides of the street. Each vied with the other to attract customers with artistically arranged window displays or gravity-defying pavement displays. The usual traders of butchers, greengrocers and drapers were interspersed with others such as rope manufactures, watch and chronometer makers and one shop with the sign 'J. Salmon, world-famous ship's biscuit bakers', written in bold type across the window. Even though it was almost dark, there was still a constant stream of drays in both directions, the horses on one cart with the noses almost touching the backboard of the wagon in front. There was also a number of public houses; he counted five within view. He glanced up at the St George's High Street sign.

He gave a short laugh. *You bloody clot, you've walked right passed the Minories.*

A gust of icy wind cut through him and Jonathan realised that in his eagerness to get away from his father, he'd left his greatcoat behind.

He looked around in the wintry light and spotted a chop house on the other side of the road. The windows were steamed up, like all the other shops, but the bright paintwork and draped curtains made it seem homely and welcoming.

Kate's Kitchen, Jonathan mused. *No doubt the coffee tastes like dirty dishwater but . . .*

Dodging between the wagons and sidestepping the horse droppings and rotting vegetables, he crossed the road. Pushing open the door, he ducked to avoid knocking his head as he stepped in.

A couple of the dockers sitting around the tables gave him the once-over and then returned to their mugs of tea. Jonathan made his way to the counter.

The shop had a low beamed ceiling and a bare wooden floor but it was newly swept. The tables were of various sizes and makes yet they were all scrubbed clean. The work surface was also spotless as were the two piles of plates and the dozen china mugs stacked on it. Jonathan leant back, rested his elbows against the worktop and waited for the proprietor to appear.

He'd have a cup of whatever passed for coffee here and then head back. He had a train to Colchester to catch in the morning and no matter what his father said, once he'd handed in his equipment at the end of the week, he would be a civilian again.

Jonathan heard a door open behind him. He turned.

Standing behind the counter and looking up at him with a welcoming smile stood a young woman with cornsilk-coloured hair swept into a soft swirl on her head. She had a broad forehead, a small but defined chin and high cheekbones. Her sage-green gown showed signs of wear but it tucked into every curve of her body.

'Good evening, Captain, what would you like?' she asked, the smile on her full lips growing wider.

'A coffee, if I may,' he replied. He leant across the counter and smiled back at her. 'With plenty of sugar.'

As the captain's gaze ran over her, Kate's heart fluttered in a way it hadn't done since she first fell for Freddie. She cut the feeling short. She wasn't foolish enough to be stopped in her tracks by a man in uniform.

That said, she couldn't help but notice he stood a little over six feet tall and filled out the shoulders of his jacket to their full capacity. He was clean-shaven and his neatly trimmed hair was dark brown. His eyepatch drew her attention but didn't hold it as the strong angular nose, blunt chin and square jaw demanded their fair share, as did the admiring expression in his remaining hazel eye.

Kate turned to the stack of cups and reminded herself where being dazzled by a handsome face had got her last time.

'I'm guessing you'll like it strong, sir,' she said, spooning a heaped measure of coffee from the earthenware jar.

'Please,' he replied, behind her.

She felt her cheeks grow warm. *This is ridiculous*, she thought, filling the percolator with water and putting it back on the stove.

Why was she so flustered? It wasn't as if a day went past without some docker, stevedore or porter trying to sweet-talk her as he ordered his meal. And wasn't this soldier doing just that? He had probably done the same to every woman he'd come across since he started shaving.

She looked coolly at him. 'It'll just be a moment.'

'I'm in no hurry.'

'Would you like a slice to go with it, sir?' she asked, nodding at the fruit cake under the glass cover.

'Please, it looks tempting,' he replied, not even glancing at the cake.

Kate cut a slice and eased it into a small plate. 'That will be a penny for the coffee and ha'penny for the cake,' she said, handing it to him.

He fished a couple of coins out of his pocket and slid them across the counter. Kate gave him his change.

'Are you posted in the garrison?' she asked, as she poured the coffee into one of her larger mugs.

He shook his head and a thick fringe of hair fell over his forehead. 'I'm stationed at Colchester,' he said, combing it back with his fingers. 'I'm only here for today – catching the train back tomorrow.'

'That's a bit of a journey for one day, if you don't mind me saying,' Kate replied.

A wry smile spread over his face. 'Colonel's orders.'

Kate made a play of wiping the counter. 'That sounds serious.'

An odd expression flitted across the captain's face. 'It was.' He gripped the mug.

'Be careful, sir. It might be a little hot still,' Kate said.

'I'm used to drinking it near scalding. Sometimes on patrol it was the only thing that kept me from freezing.' He took a sip. 'Perfect. Just like the wallah in Bangalore used to make.' He took a bite of cake. '*This* is delicious. Did you make it?'

'I did,' Kate said, only just stopping herself from falling for such an obvious bit of flattery.

She turned and busied herself behind the counter. As she tidied the plates and bowls ready for the end-of-day rush, she couldn't help but catch a glimpse of his red coat out of the corner of her eye. And when she turned, she found him still studying her.

He popped the last chunk of cake into his mouth and licked his thumb. 'That's the best I've tasted since I can't remember when.'

'Thank you,' Kate replied. 'It's a pity you won't be here to sample tomorrow's madeira.'

'Who knows, maybe I'll pass this way again sometime.' He threw back the last mouthful of coffee and put the cup down. 'Good day.'

He turned and strode across the shop. Kate stared after him and listened as the bell tinkled a couple of times to mark his departure.

Sally came back and put the dirty dishes on the counter. 'Cor, it would certainly add a bit of spark to the place if he dropped by now and again,' she said, gazing dreamily at the door.

Kate laughed. 'Well, don't get yourself too keen. He's not likely to.'

Sally sighed and went back to the customers' side of the shop. Kate picked up the captain's empty plate and mug and thrust them into the water.

Yes, the good-looking captain would indeed add a bit of spark but she didn't need it. Spark in a man dazzled your eyes and muddled your brain. Spark coupled with a handsome face and gravelly voice made you do things you shouldn't ought to and that you lived to regret. She'd been fooled once before but she was older and wiser now and wouldn't be led into that trap again, especially not by a well-spoken toff in an expensively tailored uniform.

Chapter Three

Aggie Wilcox's gaze idly traced the patch of damp on the ceiling as the bells of Christ Church Spitalfields chimed four o'clock across the road. The attic room in Moody's common lodging house was a far cry from the Retreat, the discreet establishment for gentlemen just off Bloomsbury Square, but a girl had to live. She turned her head and looked at the heavily built man sprawled across the bed beside her. With receding sandy hair, a pot belly and quivery jowls, Tom bore a striking resemblance to the cattle he drove to London each week for slaughter.

Carefully, without bouncing the straw-stuffed mattress, Aggie slid off the bed. Sitting on the edge of the only chair in the room, she lifted her skirt and wiped between her legs with her petticoat. She hadn't conceived since the old crone, who looked after the girls in the brothel, hooked the last unwelcome infant out of her six years before, but she couldn't be too careful.

Tom farted and muttered something before his breathing returned to a regular rhythm. Aggie eased herself from the chair and, avoiding the squeaky floorboard, tiptoed to his jacket hanging at the end of the bed. She fumbled through his pockets and found a tobacco pouch, a flint box and a handkerchief. There was a small T stitched in the corner, no doubt embroidered by his wife for a birthday or anniversary. It wasn't much, but she might get a penny for it at the pawnbrokers. She opened the drawstring and took a wodge of tobacco, twisted it in the handkerchief, then tucked it inside her bodice. She put the pouch and metal box back and searched the other pocket. Pulling out a handful of coins, Aggie held them in the fading light streaming in from the window. Seventeen shillings and three-pence. Not bad for half a dozen mangy cows.

Her fingers itched to take one of the crowns that sat twinkling among the dull pennies but even after a skinful of ale he would notice if one of them went missing. It had been taking a similar risk that had almost been the undoing of her and she wasn't going to make that stupid mistake again. Besides, if she got shot of Tom soon she could probably catch herself another clodhopper or two before sunset. She selected a sixpence and a couple of coppers, tucked them in her skirt pocket and then slid the rest back.

Tom coughed and blinked awake. He sat up, ran his dirt-caked hands over his face and shook himself like a tawny mongrel. 'I must have dropped right off.'

Aggie put her hands behind her back and swayed provocatively. 'I ain't surprised, you old tomcat, you.'

He got off the bed, leaving mud on the threadbare counterpane where his heels had rested.

'I bet you say that to all the men,' he said, rebuttoning his flies.

Aggie looked downcast and she sidled over to him, coiling her arm around his. 'Course I do, but' – she gave him a sideways glance – 'I don't always mean it.'

He laughed and rummaged in his pocket, giving her a florin. 'For my favourite girl. I'll be back next week.'

Aggie looked up at him and her lower lip trembled slightly. 'I might not be here next week. Not if the landlord throws me and me poor old mother out on the streets.'

Tom's bushy brows pulled together. 'Now, now, duck, you know I'm happy to pay a bit more than the going rate but I gave you an extra shilling last time. I can't keep—'

'I know you did and,' she forced a tear, 'you've paid me fair and square for your jiggy. I ain't asking you for more. I've got my pride, you know. You'll just have to find another special girl to make you happy next time you come to market.'

Tom scratched his head. 'Won't the local church help? After all, your pa was a parson.'

Aggie shook her head. 'Ma won't allow me to go begging them for a penny. Not after the way the bishop treated her.'

'Perhaps your landlord would let you stay if you gave him half what you owe him,' Tom said.

'And how would I buy my ma her medicine if I did? It's the only thing that dulls the pain.'

'Well I . . .'

Aggie walked her fingers up his arm. 'He's a terribly wicked man, is my landlord. And even if my old ma weren't on her last breath – which I swear she is – he'd still throw us out.' She pressed her groin into his. 'Couldn't you find it in your heart to spare a bob or two?'

'I don't kn—'

Aggie ran the palm of her hand down the front of his trousers. 'I *am* your special girl, aren't I?'

Tom swallowed and fumbled in his pocket again. 'If you promise to be in the Ten Bells waiting for me ...'

Aggie caught him around the neck. 'I will and ...' she whispered something that the woman who'd embroidered his handkerchief would never in a thousand years consider doing.

Tom's eyes lit up. 'I could stay a while longer.'

Aggie picked up his coat and shoved it at him. 'Oh, sweetheart, I only wish I could.' She bundled him towards the door. 'But I have to get home to Mother.'

'But ... but ...'

Aggie closed the door and leant against it. There was silence for a moment then she heard the sound of his boots clomping down the stairs.

Aggie fastened her bodice, leaving the last four buttons open, and rearranged her grubby chemise over her breasts. She took out the few remaining pins in her red hair and held them in her mouth while she combed her fingers through it. Bending forward, she twirled it into a knot on the top of her head and secured it. She adjusted her cleavage and smoothed her skirt. It was her favourite gown – emerald green with a low-cut, tight-fitting top. It was just right for catching a man's eye and keeping his mind from worrying about the cost of her company.

Dancing across the floor to the window, Aggie studied her reflection in the dirty glass. She smiled and, judging Tom would be halfway to Minories station to catch his train by now, she left the room. She trotted down the rickety stairs, past the communal rooms with the coffin-like beds and into the entrance hall.

Isaac Ketch, the bully-boy who supervised the lodgers, was sitting with his feet up on the fender cleaning his teeth with the point of his knife. He looked up and grinned as she swept over to him.

'You made swift work of that yokel.' His eyes drifted down to her cleavage. 'You out for another?'

Aggie nodded. 'Keep the room free.' She adjusted the front of her gown again. 'I'm popping into the Blue Coat Boy for a couple before I catch another dick.'

She stepped out into Dorset Street and shielded her eyes against the hazy December light. The closely packed houses on either side seemed to lean towards each other and the sun only illuminated the cobbles briefly at sunrise and sunset. The rest of the time the squalid thoroughfare was left in shadow. The once-fine homes were now mainly lodging houses and outside each there was the usual collection of tatty individuals waiting for the superintendent to let them in for the night. As the working day had not yet ended, it was mainly barefooted women clutching babies and children, huddled together against the biting cold. Aggie pulled the edges of her velvet jacket together, thankful she'd had the foresight to snatch that from the peg before Madame Tootle threw her out.

It had been that jealous bitch Rosie Potter's fault, but she'd taken the smile off Rosie's face, literally, when she'd pressed her poxy moosh to the side of the stove-pipe boiler. She'd like to see the old madam try to wring ten shillings out of a punter now for an hour of Rosie.

Side-stepping the pungent slurry of human and animal waste, Aggie started down the street. A couple of navvies on the other side of the road looked her way as she passed but she'd have to steel herself with a gin or two before taking another punter up to Moody's loft. She'd entertained several clients a day at the Retreat but they had been gents who had appreciated her charm; now the men she had to endure hardly noticed her prettiness at all.

Shoving aside a couple of rag-tag kids who stood in her path, Aggie headed for the Blue Coat Boy. A couple of early customers propping up the bar glanced over as she sauntered in but soon returned to their drinks. At the far end of the pub in his usual place sat the man who could be the answer to her prayers: Ollie Mac, the leader of the Black Eagle Gang.

Well, in truth, the weasel-faced, balding leader of the Spitalfields gang was hardly a man to set a girl's pulse racing but if she could snare him her position would be secure. Of course, she had to get rid of the old sow he lived with: Lilly. That shouldn't be too difficult but if she were lucky she wouldn't have to do a thing if the sprog Lilly had stuffed up her skirt carried her to the grave in a few weeks.

Aggie sauntered over to the bar, her skirts sweeping a path through the damp sawdust. Mary, the fat barmaid, stopped polishing the glasses and came over.

'Gin,' Aggie said, twisting back and forth to check herself in the mirror behind the bar. 'And the good stuff. Not the pissing gut rot you usually serve.'

'And a good afternoon to you, Lady Muck,' Mary replied, uncorking a bottle from the back shelf.

Aggie threw a ha'penny on the counter and took the glass. She swallowed half the measure in one gulp, enjoying the sensation of the liquid burning as it passed down her throat and into the pit her stomach. Ollie Mac was talking with Stefan, the big Swede who acted as his muscle. They laughed and then Stefan moved away. Aggie pressed her lips together to bring the colour back and swayed over.

'Afternoon, Mr Mac,' she said breathily as she leant forward to show her cleavage to full advantage.

Ollie's eyes slid down to her opened bodice. 'Afternoon, Aggie. You're looking perky today. Can I get you another drink?'

'That's very kind of you.' She sat on the vacant chair next to him.

Ollie signalled to Mary. 'You been out turning tricks already?'

Aggie gave a throaty laugh. 'They're queuing up, Mr Mac.'

He sat back. Aggie pulled a small leather wallet from the bottom of her bodice and counted out the half a crown she'd earned that morning. 'That's this week's money, Mr Mac.'

Ollie chinked it in his hand a couple of times then slipped it in his pocket. 'That's what I like about you, Aggie. You pay on the nose and don't give me the excuses – like some I could mention.'

Aggie drew closer and rested her hand lightly on the top of his thigh. 'I hope that's not the only thing you like about me, Mr Mac.'

A spark of lust flashed in Ollie's eyes. 'It's not.' He reached across and fondled her breast.

Aggie giggled as his fingers delved beneath her bodice. She allowed him a free roam for a moment or two then drew back. 'Perhaps we shouldn't . . . not just yet,' she said. 'It can be dangerous to unsettle a breeding woman.' She placed her hand on the bare flesh above her breasts. 'And I'd *never* forgive myself if something happened to your Lilly.'

'You're all heart,' Ollie said.

Aggie stood up, then leant forward again and ran her finger along the line of his stubbly chin. 'And a whole lot more, for a man who treats me right.'

He chuckled then slapped her rear. 'Off you go before Lilly finds you here.'

Aggie straightened up and blew him an exaggerated kiss. She turned and, satisfied that his eyes were glued to her bottom, ambled towards the door.

Freddie walked out of the clothing warehouse behind Leman Street and turned to look at his reflection in the shop window. He adjusted the blood-coloured cravat and smoothed the lapels of his new black jacket. If he said it himself, not bad. He fixed the angle of his new billycock hat and walked towards Aldgate.

Leman Street was one of the main roads running north from the docks, and other than the fact that the Garrick had been rebuilt and was now grandly named the Albert and Garrick Royal Amphitheatre, the rest of the street looked very much as he remembered. There were a couple of new white-stoned offices with brass plates on their walls between the old soot-blackened shops. The road was packed with wagons and people going about their mid-morning business. Delivery carts piled high with furniture, hay and crates negotiated their way between the fly-pitch barrows selling the early catch from Billingsgate market half a mile away. The icy wind fluttered the bunting on the shop awnings and whirled the smoke from the coffee sellers and the hot-chestnut men's two-wheeled stoves. He crossed the road and, leaving the workaday bustle of Whitechapel High Street behind, entered the dark alleys at the south end of Spitalfields rookery. Within a few minutes Freddie had reached the front door of the Blue Coat Boy in Dorset Street. As the first flurry of snow settled on the shoulders of his new jacket, Freddie stepped into the warm bar.

Although there was hardly space in the bar to breathe, sitting at the back of the pub at a table in a well-defined space sat a slightly built, clean-shaven man with a large glass of brandy in his hand. He was flanked by two men; one with a mop of white-blond hair and the other with a shaven head.

At first glance you could have mistaken Ollie Mac as a clerk or a shop worker but, if you studied him more closely, you'd see that his herringbone suit was made to measure rather than from a warehouse rack, and that a diamond pin held his silk cravat in place. The brewery might own the Blue Coat Boy but it was Ollie Mac who ruled it. He looked up and studied Freddie for a second before a wide, crooked smile cut across his face, revealing a gold front tooth.

'Well stone the crows, Freddie Ellis,' he shouted slamming the palm of his thick-set hand on the table.

The bruiser sitting on Ollie's left looked up from honing his blade and rose to his feet. Stefan Magson's broad features clearly showed his Scandinavian ancestry. He had the look of a playful bull mastiff about him but the harsh glint in his ice-blue eyes warned you not to be fooled.

'Look what the cat dragged in,' he said and stomped towards Freddie.

He stopped in front of him and jabbed his fist within a hair's breadth of Freddie's cheek. Freddie dodged and punched back, missing Stefan's stubbly chin by the same margin. Stefan grinned and they air-sparred for a few moments as men nearby gave them anxious looks and moved away.

Stefan slapped Freddie on the back. 'Welcome home, you old bugger.'

'Mary!' Ollie bellowed as Freddie took the seat opposite him. 'Get me a bottle of my special to welcome back my long-lost friend.'

Freddie took the seat opposite Ollie. 'That's very kind of you, Mr Mac.'

Ollie waved Freddie's words aside and offered him a cigar from a leather holder. 'So, when did they let you back?'

'A couple of days ago,' Freddie replied.

'Where you been then?'

'Down on the coast; Portsmouth, to be exact. I got pally with a geezer in Millbank and promised to visit his missus when I got out. See how she was getting on, you know.'

Ollie nudged him and winked. 'And how was she getting on?'

Freddie grinned. 'A lot better after she hooked up with me. I got meself in with a little gang lifting stuff off the ship while she's working for the rent with the sailors on the dockside. I had a nice little racket going until she got herself in the family way. She tried to keep it hid but I caught her honking up one morning. Naturally I took her down to the local old woman to sort her out but she was too far gone and it twisted her insides or summink. Anyhow, that was the end of her. I hung about for a couple of months but then the fucking navy press gang started nosing about so I thought I'd come back to the Smoke.'

'You been down to see your bit of Irish skirt?' Ollie asked.

'I did and got a right earful.'

'She weren't happy to see you then?'

'No, she fucking wasn't. You should have seen her face when I walked in. If looks could kill, I'd be in my grave now. But I had the last laugh.' He smiled slyly. 'She's done all right for herself while I've been gone. Her poxy Mick brother's set her up in a chop house down the Highway so I took a couple of shillings from the till while I was there.'

Ollie laughed. 'What did she say?'

'Nuffink she could say. I'm her husband and what's hers is mine, ain't it?' He grinned. 'Of course, it didn't stop her looking at me like I was a lump of shit, but she'd better get used to it.'

'Listen up, lads,' Ollie said. 'If you want to keep your old lady in order you could do a lot worse than a lesson or two from this old fucker.' He punched Freddie lightly on his shoulder.

The men around him laughed. The barmaid arrived and set a fresh bottle of brandy and another glass on the table.

Ollie caught her around the waist and pulled her to him. 'See this chap here, Mary,' he said, pointing at Freddie with the damp end of his cigar. 'He's a hero. A bloody hero. So you treat him right.'

Mary gave Freddie a groin-tightening look. 'I'd like to, Mr Mac.'

Freddie gave her the smile that had got him in to and out of trouble more times than he could mention. She swept her eyes over him again then swayed back to the bar.

Ollie thumped the table again, sending the glasses jingling. 'I see you ain't lost your touch, or your style.' He flicked the lapels of Freddie's new jacket.

Freddie flicked an imaginary speck of dust off the sleeve. 'It's a start.'

Ollie filled their glasses. 'Pity you only got buttons at your wrists and not a couple of sparklers.' He flashed his gold cufflinks. 'But we'll soon sort that out now you're back.'

'I was hoping to hear you say that, Mr Mac.'

'I've got a quick job tomorrow night if you're in. Just an in-and-out and you'll be a guinea the richer by dawn. You in?'

'Need you ask?'

'Good. Meet Stefan at the back just before midnight and,' Ollie tapped the side of his nose, 'he'll see you right. Have another.' He refilled their glasses and leant forward. ''Ow's your little lad? I bet he's a right chip off the old block.'

Freddie grinned. 'He bloody is. He looks just like me when I was his age. Of course, she mollycoddles him but now I'm back I can keep an eye on him.'

Ollie's hard-bitten face took on a tender expression. 'My old woman's in the family way,' he said.

Freddie couldn't hide his surprise. 'I thought you said you weren't married.'

'I'm not, but I wouldn't remind Lilly of that because she knocked the last idiot who did into the middle of next week.' Ollie drained the last of the brandy into their glasses then waved the empty bottle at Mary.

Something flickered in the corner of Freddie's eye and he looked around. Leaning against the bar talking to a costermonger stood a young woman in a green gown with a matching velvet jacket. The cuffs and elbows showed wear and there were mud stains around the hem but she looked like a queen standing among the workmen in their drab-coloured clothes. Her red hair was whirled up in a high knot.

'Who's that?' Freddie asked, running his eyes slowly over the woman.

'Red Aggie. She pitched up about a month ago,' Ollie replied. 'She rents one of Moody's rooms during the day and lodges with Welsh Meg in Thawl Street the rest of the time.'

'Is she one of yours?'

Ollie took a sip of his drink. 'I look after her interests.'

Aggie let out a throaty laugh and looked their way. Ollie raised his glass to her and she laughed again.

Freddie's groin tightened. 'Are you and her . . .'

Ollie shook his head. 'My Lilly would rip her face and my balls off if I was but I can't say the thought ain't crossed my mind.'

Several thoughts crossed Freddie's mind. Usually he didn't have any truck with the local trollops. He didn't need to when there were lonely wives in every street. But Aggie seemed something different.

'Where's she from?' Freddie asked.

Ollie nudged him and grinned. 'Why don't you go and ask her?'

Aggie caught his eye. Freddie stood up. 'Thank you, Mr Mac. I believe I will.'

'Good evening, miss.'

Aggie turned and found herself looking at the man she'd seen sitting with Ollie.

'Yes.'

'Can I buy you a drink?' he said.

'A brandy, if you can afford it.'

He pulled a shilling from his pocket, holding it aloft to attract the barmaid's attention, and Aggie studied him more closely.

Although his suit was nowhere near the quality of Ollie's, it sat well on him. He had strong, clean-cut features and, in contrast to the working men around her, was clean-shaven, which also set him a notch above.

The barmaid came over.

'A brandy for the young lady, if you please,' he said and then turned back to her. 'I'm Freddie Ellis.'

'Agatha Wilcox,' she replied, as her drink arrived. 'Red Aggie to my friends.'

'Well, Aggie, you must be new around here because if you weren't I'd have noticed you long before now.' He handed her a glass and closed his fingers around hers briefly before letting go.

'I've come from up west,' Aggie replied, enjoying his frank admiration.

Freddie's eyes ran over her again. 'I can see that from your classy get-up.'

'I was a lady's maid and my father was a . . .'

She was just about to give him the 'my father was a clergyman and my dear old mother's ill' routine but she paused. The first question men usually asked was 'How much?' so Freddie Ellis's attention was a nice change. He hadn't flinched either when she'd asked for a brandy.

She took a sip of her brandy. 'So what do you do then, Freddie Ellis?'

He leant back on the counter. 'This and that.'

'What – for Mr Mac?'

'I'm one of his top men.'

'Is that so?'

He nodded.

'We'll how come I haven't seen you before either?' she asked suspiciously.

'I've been lying low. I can't tell you what but . . .' he winked. 'You know.'

Aggie took another sip of brandy and studied him over her glass. Of course he could be giving her a whole load of horse shit but . . .

The door from the upstairs rooms opened and Lilly waddled in, her jutting belly lifting the front of her skirt out of the spit and sawdust on the floor.

Fecking cow! Aggie thought as she smiled at Ollie Mac's heavily pregnant common-law wife.

Ollie stood up and pulled out a chair for Lilly, fussing around her like a mother hen until she finally squeezed her fat arse on the seat, then called for a stout for her.

It was clear that Aggie might tempt him to stray for a day or two but if Lilly found out . . . No. Although ousting Lilly would have been the quickest way to get back to where she belonged – on top – it was too dangerous. What she needed was a man who she could . . .

'Do you want another brandy?' Freddie asked.

Aggie turned and smiled. 'I don't mind if I do but, perhaps, somewhere else?'

Freddie slipped his arm around her waist. 'That's just what I was thinking. Have you got somewhere more private?'

'I've got a room nearby and a couple of glasses but nothing to put in them,' Aggie said, pressing herself into him.

Freddie smacked half a crown on the counter. 'Give's a bottle of brandy, Mary.' He grinned down at Aggie. 'That should help us get to know each other.'

'I should say,' Aggie replied, giving him the look that always earned her an extra shilling.

He hadn't mentioned money and she wasn't going to ask. After all, half a crown wasn't all she wanted out of Freddie Ellis.

Jonathan tipped the porter a couple of coins as he stepped on to the train.

'Quinn!'

Jonathan turned. Captain Reginald Braithwaite, his fellow officer and good friend, emerged from the clouds of steam and marched down the platform towards him.

Reggie had served with Jonathan in India, chasing tribesmen in the foothills of the Himalayas with barely any food and water. He had a thin but animated face and red-brown hair.

'I thought it was you,' Reggie said as he climbed into the compartment. 'On your way back to camp?'

'I am,' Jonathan replied, as the porter stowed his leather case in the luggage rack above. 'If I'd known you were in town, you could have saved me from a bloody dull supper in the mess last night. Where did you stay?'

'In Cavendish Square with my grandfather,' Reggie replied, heaving his own bag up alongside Jonathan's. 'And if I'd known you were around, you could have saved *me* from lukewarm pea soup, cold ham and bellowing down the table at my deaf old 'un throughout dinner.' He nudged Jonathan and winked. 'And we could have played a few hands at the Emperor's. I'm sure Madame Kitty would be pleased to see you again.'

He pulled out a cigar and offered it Jonathan, who shook his head. Reggie bit off the end and sat down.

'Of course, as a man of honour I should challenge you to a duel for stealing the lovely Kitty's affections away from me,' he said, out of the side of his mouth as he struck a Lucifer. 'And I would. In an instant. If I hadn't been smitten by the delectable Mademoiselle Marie.'

Jonathan laughed. 'Well, from now on you can keep both of them company, as I'm soon to be married.'

'So I heard, and to old Commander Davenport's daughter?'

'Indeed,' Jonathan replied.

Reggie's eyebrows rose. 'I heard she had her sights set on a major and nothing less.'

Jonathan smiled. The station master blew the whistle, a couple of doors slammed and then the train shunted out of Bishopsgate station.

Reggie drew on his cigar. 'So you told him, then?'

'I did.'

'What did he say?'

'Need you ask?'

Reggie blew a series of smoke rings. 'That bad?'

'He called me a coward. Among other things,' Jonathan replied, hearing the faint echo of his father's voice in his head.

'Well, you know I think you're a damn fool to chuck it all in—'

'You have mentioned it once or twice,' Jonathan cut in.

Reggie's pale eyes flickered over Jonathan's face. 'Yes, well, be that as it may – and even though I do think you're stark-staring mad – no one could ever accuse you of cowardice.'

Jonathan adjusted his eyepatch. 'He can bluster all he likes. My resignation is in and effective from the end of the month.'

Reggie drew on the cigar. 'That's just over a week away! Have you decided what you're going to do yet?'

Jonathan shook his head. 'I'm not certain. I toyed with the idea of sailing to Australia. You know, stake out some land, build a homestead.'

Reggie looked unconvinced. 'I know you're sick of the army, but good God, man, can't see you as a sheep farmer. And what would Miss Davenport say to that?'

Jonathan grinned. 'A great deal, I expect, and none of it easy on the ear, so I'll probably apply for a post in the East India Company. They're always crying out for men with experience as regional superintendents. Louise lived in Jaipur with her family until she was thirteen so I'm sure she'll be agreeable to the plan.' Jonathan glanced out at the neat houses of Bow as the train whizzed by then pulled out his hip flask and offered it to Reggie. 'Enough of me and my sorry tale of woe. What were you doing in London?'

'My grandfather summoned me last week,' Reggie said, taking a mouthful. 'It's to do with this blasted school he's patron of. It seems the old headmaster drank himself to death a year ago and the board of guardians haven't been able to find a replacement for him since.'

'What's that got to do with you?' Jonathan asked. 'Surely his solicitors would deal with that.'

'They would if he'd let them but he wants me to intervene personally. My great-grandfather made his fortune from investing in St Katharine Dock and when they cleared the slum around the old church, they had to relocate the school. The guardians asked him to be patron and my family has been responsible ever since.'

'I still don't see why you're involved,' Jonathan said, as the urban sprawl of east London gave way to the countryside of Wanstead and Forest Gate.

'Because dear old grandpa has a soft spot for St Katharine's and,' Reggie looked sheepish, 'I'm a tad fond of the crusty old bugger, so like to please him if I can.'

'Have you advertised?'

'Of course we have. Five weeks in *The Times*, no less, but the last headmaster had let standards slip so far that the handful of prospective candidates took one look at the place and withdrew their applications. Of course, the area the school's situated in doesn't help. It's next to the London docks. As you'll appreciate, there aren't many educated men willing to live and work in such a rough area.' Reggie's narrow face lit up. 'I know what—'

'No!'

'But I haven't asked you anything,' Reggie replied innocently.

Jonathan brows pulled tightly together. 'You don't have to and the answer is still no.' Reggie looked crestfallen. 'I'm sorry, old man, but the day I become a headmaster will be the day *The Times* announces my father's joined the navy.'

Chapter Four

Kate drew a curly swirl with the chalk at the bottom of her menu and then held it at arm's length to read it back.

Beef Pie and Mash 4½d
Meat Pie and Mash 3½d
Faggots, Mustard Pickle and Mash 4d
Saveloy and Pease Pudding 3d
Kidneys, Mash and Gravy 3d
Irish Stew 2d
Roast Spuds 1d
Jam Pudding 1½d with Custard 2d
Spotty Dick 2d with custard 2½d
Tea ¼d
Coffee ¾d

'That should have them queuing down the street tomorrow,' said Sally, as she collected the last of the empty cups from the back tables.

'Let's hope so,' Kate replied, propping up the menu in the window. 'You can leave those and get off if you like.'

'Thanks, Mrs E. Is your brother dropping by?' Sally asked as she slid the tray on to the counter.

Kate nodded. 'I'm surprised he's not here already.' She went to the window and wiped a hole in the condensation. 'It's a real pea-souper out there so I hope he's not been caught upriver,' she said, peering down the street as figures loomed in and out of the fog.

Patrick owned three barges and hauled coal up and down the river out of Limehouse. That was difficult enough on a clear day but with smoke belching from riverside factories mingling with the damp mist in a choking miasma, navigating home safely through the multitude of boats and barge traffic could be treacherous. Twice before, he'd hit a skiff and had to rescue the craft's owners from the murky water.

She straightened the curtains and then took the shutter handle out from its case under the window. She hooked the end into the long bracket, wound down the shutter, then pulled it down on the door.

Sally wrapped herself up in her coat and scarf. 'I'll pop into the butcher's and collect the suet on my way in tomorrow. Goodnight!' she called over her shoulder as she left.

Kate bolted the door behind her then blew out the lamps. When she went back into the parlour she found Ella sewing a dress for her doll and Joe sitting up at the table flipping through a picture book about farm animals. He looked up as she came in.

'Is Pa coming home tonight?' he asked, as he had every evening for the last four days.

Ella looked up wide-eyed from her task and bit her lip. Unfortunately, she understood a great deal more of what passed between her parents than Joe. She had also noticed the bruising around Kate's neck.

'Not tonight,' Kate replied, caressing his cheek softly.

Ella relaxed but Joe slumped over his book and rested his chin on his hands.

''S not fair,' he said, jutting out his bottom lip.

Kate ruffled her son's hair. 'Uncle Pat will be here soon, Joe, *and* it's almost Christmas.'

Joe perked up. 'Are we going to Uncle Pat's this year? And will there be plum pudding?'

'No, we'll be at Aunt Mattie's and *yes* there'll be plum pudding.' The children bobbed on their seats with excitement. 'Now clear away and start getting ready for bed. I'll take some warm water up for you both for a quick wash.'

Ella folded her work into Kate's sewing box and collected her nightdress from the fender in front of the fire where it had been hung to air. She disappeared upstairs.

'Maaaa, do I *have* to have a wash?' Joe asked, dragging his feet across the rag rug after his sister.

'I'll let you get away with a cat's lick tonight only because we're going to the baths tomorrow, but *brush your hair*!' she shouted after him as he dashed from the room.

Kate tidied the table and then took down her accounts and order books along with the inkwell and pens from the top shelf of the dresser. She set them on the table and had just found the right pages when there was a knock on the back door.

Kate went over and threw back the bolts. Patrick walked in, bringing a blast of icy air with him.

'Brrr ... it's good to be out of the cold,' he said, unwinding his scarf.

'I was getting worried,' Kate said, stretching up and kissing his chilly cheek. 'You sit and warm yourself and I'll fetch you a coffee.'

Kate's eldest brother Patrick favoured their long-dead father, and unlike Kate's fair tresses his hair was black, albeit with a few grey streaks running through it. Sailing his barge the length of the Thames and back each day had kept him trim and staved off the effects of his wife, Josie's, delicious home cooking.

She took his coat and hung it up alongside her own then went through to the shop where she'd left the percolator on the back of the range. She cut Patrick a slice of bread pudding to eat with his coffee in the parlour. Patrick was sitting at the table running his finger down the column of the shop's accounts.

'There you go,' she said, putting down the cup and plate at his elbow.

He looked up and smiled. 'Thanks, sis.' He looked at the ceiling. 'I don't want to alarm you but I think you've got a couple of elephants running about up there.'

Kate laughed and went to the bottom of the stairs. 'Come and say a quick hello to your uncle Pat,' she called up.

There was a thundering of feet as Joe and Ella appeared.

'Uncle Pat,' they shouted as they launched themselves at him. Patrick caught one in each arm and hugged them both.

'Are you behaving for your mother?'

'Yes, Uncle Pat,' they answered in unison.

He kissed them both. 'I'm glad to hear it.'

'Ma says Aunt Mattie is getting a Christmas tree,' Ella said, hugging him around the neck.

'Is she?' Patrick said in mock astonishment.

The children giggled.

'And this year it will be the best Christmas ever,' said Joe.

Patrick bounced him on his knee. 'And why's that?'

'Because Pa will be there,' Joe replied.

Patrick's jovial expression slipped a little as he looked over Joe's head at Kate.

Kate clapped her hands. 'Right, Uncle Pat's been at work all day and he has to do my books yet before he can go home, so kiss him goodnight.'

The children gave their uncle a peck on the cheek and then ran back upstairs. Kate went to the hall door.

'I'll be up in a while,' she called, without taking her eyes from Patrick's humourless face.

'So he's back,' he said, as she closed the door.

Kate nodded.

'When?'

'Four days ago.' She told him about the encounter with Freddie. 'I haven't seen him since.'

Patrick stared at her for a moment then stood up and turned to face the fire. He gripped the mantelshelf and stood motionless for several seconds then spun around.

'Bastard!' He slammed his hand on the table. 'I'd hoped to God after all this time that he'd be mouldering in his grave somewhere.'

Concern replaced his fury as his gaze flickered over Kate. 'Has he touched you or the children?'

'I'd swing for him myself first,' Kate replied. 'Ella was wary of him from the moment he walked in but he made a bit of a fuss of Joe and now he thinks it's wonderful to have his "*pa*" come home from "*sea*".'

'Sea?'

'That's where he said he'd been.'

Patrick looked her over again. 'What about you, Kate? Did he hurt you?'

'Not really.' Kate's hand went to her high-buttoned neckline.

Patrick hooked his finger into the top and pulled it down gently.

Pain cut across his face. 'Sweet Mary.' He gasped as he saw the marks made by Freddie's fingers.

Kate put her hand over his, thankful he couldn't see the bruise on her hip when she'd been shoved on the table. 'Patrick.'

He gathered her in his arms and kissed her forehead. 'I'm sorry, sis. I curse the day I made him do the right thing by you.'

Kate pushed him away. 'And if you hadn't, I'd never have had Joe,' she replied. 'And it shows we were right not to declare me as your partner in Kate's Kitchen. If I legally owned half instead of you fronting the whole business, he'd be able to get his hands on all the money you saved for us.' She bit her lip. 'I've taken to hiding the day's taking in a tin at the back of the grate so he can't get his hands on more than a couple of shillings. I know you've got a lot on your plate but perhaps you could take the money to the bank twice a week in future. Just to keep it out of his grasp. And I wouldn't fret too much, Pat. I doubt I'll have to suffer his company too often. He'll soon hook up with some floozy and disappear again.'

'Well, let's hope this time it's for good.' Patrick's expression hardened. 'Perhaps I'll take him for a one-way trip up the estuary.'

Kate gripped her brother's arm. 'Don't you go doing something stupid. It's not like the old days, you know. The police investigate bodies floating in the river now.'

'Then I'll make sure he's weighed down.'

'Promise me you won't, Pat. He's not worth it.'

Patrick's stubborn expression remained a few seconds longer and then he relaxed. 'All right, but he'd better not lay a finger on you or the children again. Coppers or no coppers, he'll find himself trussed up in the bottom of my boat on the outgoing tide.'

Ma tucked the blanket under the mattress then bent over him and kissed him. 'Goodnight, Joe,' she said, smoothing his hair off his forehead gently.

'Night, Ma,' he replied with a yawn.

She turned to Ella, whose bed was on the other side of the room. She gave her a peck on the cheek and then picked up the lamp and left the room, leaving the door half open. Joe listened to his mother's footsteps as she went down the stairs then he pulled the sheet up until it was firmly under his chin. He closed his eyes and was mulling over which of his marbles to offer Dicky Potter for his big green and brown one when his uncle Pat's booming laugh drifted up from the room below.

He turned his head and looked across at his sister. 'When do you think Pa will be back?'

'I don't know,' Ella said.

'Maybe he'll come tomorrow.'

'He might,' Ella replied, in a voice that said otherwise.

'He's just as I imagined him,' Joe said. 'Did you hear him say I had my dabs right? And how I looked like him?'

Ella didn't answer.

'I bet he's had so many adventures. Like fighting off wild natives and battling storms just like Uncle Pat did when he was at sea. I expect he'll tell me all about them when we go fishing.'

'What makes you think he'll take you anywhere?'

'Cos Uncle Nat takes Brian and Bert and Uncle Pat takes Mickey and Rob.' Joe gazed up at the ceiling and imagined himself with a fishing rod in his hand, dangling his feet over the edge of the canal with his father alongside him. 'And then Pa and me will stroll down the Highway or along the Waste to get some hot chestnuts.'

'I wouldn't count on it,' replied Ella.

Joe turned and glared at her. 'You're just jealous cos he didn't make a fuss of you.'

Again Ella didn't respond. In the dark Joe practised lifting one eyebrow without moving the other, the way his father had. 'Why do you think Uncle Patrick looked annoyed when I mentioned Pa?'

'Go to sleep, Joe.'

'I thought he'd be pleased Pa was back so he wouldn't have to go to the bank for Ma any more,' Joe continued. 'But he wasn't. He looked like he did that time he had to go and fetch Cousin Mickey from the police station after he was arrested for brawling.'

'You're too young to understand,' Ella replied, shifting in her bed and making the springs bong. 'I've got a spelling test tomorrow so stop talking and let me go to sleep.'

Joe studied the shape of his sister under the piles of blankets for a moment then poked his tongue out. He turned over and snuggled down.

It was all right for Ella, she had Ma to show her things and take her places but he didn't even have an older brother. He couldn't count the number of times Uncle Pat had taken him on his barge or he'd ridden alongside Uncle Nat on one of his coal wagons, but it wasn't the same. Although they played around and joked with him and called him a 'good lad' and 'top chap' they never looked at him in that special way they did when their eyes rested on their own sons.

But Pa had. And now he was back. It was almost too wonderful for Joe to take in all at once. Pa would put an end to Ella teasing and stop Ma treating him like a baby. And best of all, Smugger Black or Eddie Walters wouldn't be able to spread it around that his father was the rent man or the brush salesman because when they saw him and Freddie walking side by side, everyone would know who his father was and that he'd come home.

Joe's eyes fluttered closed and he yawned. His father was home and from now on everything would be different.

Jonathan leant on the polished bar of the officers' mess in Colchester barracks and stared into the bottom of his glass for a moment then threw back what remained of his drink. He picked up the bottle next to his elbow and tried to pour another but it was empty. He held it up.

'Same again,' he called to the steward hovering at the other end.

The young man hesitated briefly then took another bottle of brandy from the shelf behind him and brought it over.

'There you go, sir,' he said, uncorking it. 'And whose mess bill shall I—'

'Mine,' said a voice behind him.

Jonathan turned to find Reggie Braithwaite standing behind him.

'And bring another glass,' Reggie added.

'Very good, sir.' The steward set a glass beside the newly opened bottle and shot away.

Reggie poured himself a drink and then topped up Jonathan's. 'This is not like you, Quinn, wallowing in your cups. But I suppose it's understandable, drinking to forget it's your last day in the army.'

'It's not the army that's caused me to down a bottle of brandy, but this.' He dragged a crumpled letter from his pocket and slammed it on the table. 'It's from Louise. She broken off our engagement.'

'I'm sorry to hear that,' Reggie said softly. 'Did she say why?'

Jonathan gulped down a large mouthful and glared at the envelope with Louise's spidery handwriting. 'Pretty much what she said when I told her; that I've taken leave of my senses and that I'm selfishly throwing away our future happiness on a whim. I know it was a shock for her but I'd hoped that once she had time to get used to the idea she'd come around to my way of thinking, but it seems not. She further writes that as both her grandfathers served under Wellington, her father was decorated after the battle for Kabul and her three brothers are currently serving in the Sudan, Egypt and Singapore respectively, she can't imagine herself anything other than an officer's wife. She concludes by telling me that I've betrayed her trust and she never wants to see me again.'

He threw the last of his brandy down his throat, grabbed the bottle from Reggie and refilled his glass.

'And if that wasn't bad enough, in the same post I received a letter from the family's solicitors saying my allowance has been suspended until – and I quote – "I resume my duty to Queen and Country" and another from the East India Company informing me that because of the volatile situation with some of the northern tribesmen they aren't appointing any new regional commissions in the near future but they will keep my application on file.'

Reggie refilled his glass. 'That's damn bad luck.'

Jonathan emptied it in one.

'What will you do?' Reggie said.

'Swear off women for a start,' Jonathan replied, as an image of Louise, furious and tearful, loomed into his mind.

'Of course you are.'

'I bloody am. Well, at least letting them wheedle their way into my soul like I did with Louise. No, I shall be sensible about this whole damn marriage thing and pick a reasonable woman like old Ginger Ollerton did.'

'So you'll be looking for a woman like Ginger's wife, will you?' Reggie asked, barely keeping the amusement from his voice.

'Well, a little less bovine perhaps, but I'm done with letting myself be led down the path by a pretty face and sparkling eyes. A woman with a bit of money and a soft tongue will do me nicely,' he replied.

Reggie laughed. 'I'm sure it will but seriously, do you have any plans?'

'In the short term, go to my sister for a few days and then to London,' Jonathan continued. 'I have a little saved so I can find rooms in town and put out some feelers. In the long term there's still Australia, of course, but I'll have to go there to stake my claim and I really had my sights set on India, but after this,' he lifted Louise's letter again, 'I don't know. But I'll have to find something soon or I'll be living on the streets while I wait for the pen-pushers at East India House to contact me again.' He took another large measure of brandy. 'Women! I'm finished with them.'

'Well, I'll drink to that.' Reggie raised his glass. 'And the Queen!'

'The Queen,' repeated Jonathan.

'Of course, while you're searching for this sensible woman you could think about taking up my suggestion,' Reggie said, slowly.

Jonathan looked puzzled. 'What suggestion?'

'The headmaster's post at St Katharine's?' he said quietly.

Jonathan laughed. 'I told you, Reggie. You're barking up the wrong tree with that one. I'd be better off sailing on the next boat to Botany Bay.'

He started to raise his glass again but Reggie gripped his arm. 'I'm not asking you to bury yourself in east London for the rest of your life but it might give you a little breathing space. And what if you sail off on the first ship to Australia and then Louise changes her mind?'

Jonathan looked thoughtful. 'I suppose you have a point but it's the most ridiculous thing I've ever heard, even from you!'

'But it's perfect,' Reggie continued. 'You've got nothing planned and you'll be able to bash it into shape in a month or two.'

'But I don't know the first thing about being a headmaster,' Jonathan replied, wondering why he was even bothering to put up reasoned arguments against such a crackbrained notion.

'You've been to school, haven't you?'

'Of course, but—'

'Then copy all the bits you enjoyed and chuck out stuff you didn't,' Reggie cut in. 'It can't be much different from licking a company of raw recruits into shape and you've done that often enough.'

'But what about the girls?'

'You'll have a schoolmistress to order them.' He sat forward eagerly. 'Look, Jonathan. You've got no income and who knows how long it will be until the East India Company contact you, so here's the perfect, nay the providential, solution to both our problems.'

'That may be so but—'

'It will give you time to think instead of jumping at the first thing that comes to you. Plus, you'll be helping a brother-in-arms.'

Jonathan studied his friend's enthusiastic face. Him a school-master? In charge of a bunch of children and answerable to a com-mittee of do-gooders?

Reggie looked eagerly at him. 'Just go and see, Jonathan, that's all I ask.'

It was preposterous, absurd, and ludicrous. He'd be mad to agree. But . . .

He swallowed the last of his drink and put the glass down. 'All right, Reggie. I'll take a look – just a look – but I'm *not* promising anything.'

Kate shovelled another half-dozen large lumps of coal into the oven fire and lifted the teapot.

'Another cup?' she asked.

Mattie looked up and nodded.

'I hope Joe doesn't get too cold,' Kate said as she put the kettle on the range. 'It's freezing out there.'

'Boys don't feel the cold. My Bertie's the same,' Mattie replied.

'It's a pity you couldn't bring him today.'

'He wanted to come but the doctor said he was to stay in bed until his temperature was down. Plus he loves being looked after by Nathaniel's sister. With Brian helping his father in the yard and Beth at school he'd have her undivided attention.'

'And some extra little treats no doubt,' Kate said.

Mattie laughed and held up the line of green, yellow and red bunting triangles strung along a length of tape. 'What do you think?'

'I'd say you need to pin them higher than last year.' Kate laughed. 'Do you remember how Pat caught it with his shoulder and Nathaniel tangled the garlands around his legs when we played blind man's bluff?'

'They were more like a couple of nippers than grown men!'

'That they were. There wasn't this to-do about Christmas when we were children,' Kate said as she set a fresh cup of tea next to her sister. 'I remember going to church with Ma, of course, and a bit of something special for dinner, but Pa still went to work. Now the streets are deserted.'

'I know, and now there are presents and decorations and everyone sends Christmas cards,' Mattie said.

Kate returned to her chair, picked up one of the small sacks, rethreaded her needle then sewed the edges together.

Mattie measured off the next length of tape using her nose to her fingertip as a guide. 'Three yards should do it for the far wall, don't you think?'

Kate nodded. She bit off some cotton from the end of the little pocket and popped in a handful of candy twists. She tied the ribbon to fasten the top and held it up. 'They're not quite sugared almonds, I know, but I'm sure the children will enjoy finding them under the cushions.'

'I'm sure they will.' Mattie's eyes twinkled and a girlish smile lit her face. 'Oh, Kate, isn't it exciting we're having a tree?'

'It is! Just like the Queen!'

Mattie nodded. 'It's going to be such fun. I can't wait to see the children's faces when Nathaniel staggers in with it.'

Kate tucked a stray curl behind her ear. 'Are you sure you can manage having us all again?'

She looked down at her hands. 'You know I feel badly that I can't have you all here but I daren't, just in case . . .'

Mattie reached across and squeezed Kate's hand. 'I understand. We all do. Can you imagine what would happen if we were all tucking into our roast beef and Freddie strolled in?'

Kate could. And it wouldn't be peace and goodwill.

'Has he been back?' Mattie asked, taking a sip of tea.

'He swaggered in last week smelling of cheap perfume and drink just as I was closing up, of course.'

'What did you do?'

'Told him to sling his hook.'

'Did he?'

'Only after taking three shillings from the till.'

'Oh, Kate.'

Kate shrugged. 'What can I do? The law won't intervene. At least now with Patrick banking the takings twice a week and me hiding most of the money he can only take a couple of bob.'

'Well, I hope whatever liquor he bought with it chokes him,' Mattie said, crossing herself rapidly.

Kate heard the back door open. She glanced at Mattie who stared back with her needle motionless in her hand.

The parlour door crashed open and Freddie sauntered in. He was wearing a new brown-and-mustard striped suit and three days' worth of beard on his face.

Kate looked him over. 'Talk of the devil ...'

'... and he's sure to appear,' finished Mattie.

Freddie glanced from one to the other. 'Well, ain't this a luverly picture? And Mattie! Tis right grand to see you, so it is,' he said, mocking an Irish accent. 'I haven't seen you since I don't know when.'

'Four years,' Mattie replied. 'Surely you remember, Freddie. You came home drunk, as usual, and beat Kate senseless. I nursed her while my husband and brother had a *word* with you. I'm thinking you probably still have the scars.'

Freddie's friendly expression disappeared. 'And I see old Nat's keeping his end up.' His eyes slipped to her stomach. 'But then you fucking Paddies always did breed like rabbits.'

Kate stood and put her hands on her hips. 'What do you want?'

He picked up the last quarter of the Madeira cake she and Mattie had been enjoying and crammed it into his mouth.

'Where's Joe?'

'Why?'

'Cos I want to see him,' Freddie replied, spraying crumbs down his lapels.

'What about?'

'Never you fucking mind,' Freddie shouted. 'He's my boy, ain't he?'

'More's the pity,' muttered Mattie.

Freddie jabbed his finger at her. 'And *you* keep your nose out.'

Kate stepped in front of her sister. 'He's out playing.'

'When's he coming back?'

'In a couple of hours.'

Freddie glanced at the sky through the window. 'I ain't got the time to wait around. Tell him to meet me outside the Sword tomorrow at five.'

'I'll tell him no such thing,' Kate replied.

A snarl curled Freddie's top lip. 'Then I'll find him and tell him myself.' He stepped forward and loomed over her. 'And I'll tell you something else for free: you'll do as I say or the next time I have to find him I'll take him away – with me.'

Ice seemed to replace the blood in her veins but somehow Kate managed not to react. She fixed Freddie with a flint-like stare.

They glared at each other for a second or two and then he lowered his eyes. He shoved over the chair and lumbered into the shop. They heard the money drawer open and when Freddie came back he was jingling a handful of coins. 'I'm a bit short this week.' He winked and shoved the money in his pocket and strolled out.

Kate stared after him for a moment then slammed her hand on the table. 'God, I wish I'd listened to you, Mattie.'

Mattie stood up and put her arm around Kate's shoulders. 'You were young.'

'I wasn't too young to get myself into trouble,' Kate replied, still staring at the door.

Mattie kissed her on the cheek. 'He doesn't mean it. You know, about taking Joe.'

Kate turned and looked at her sister. 'He'd better not, for his sake.'

Chapter Five

Jonathan looked at the four people sitting opposite him on the other side of the long desk and wondered, yet again, why on earth he'd let Braithwaite talk him into such a ridiculous course of action and just how desperate the guardians were to even consider him.

He shouldn't have worried over his lack of experience: Mr Overton, chairman of the panel and vicar of St George's Church, knew even less about education than Jonathan. On the chairman's right sat Mr Puttock, the churchwarden, who had a limp handshake and an inability to look you in the eye for more than a few seconds.

On the other side sat the well-padded Mr Wendover, who'd almost shaken Jonathan's arm off when he greeted him and called him one of the 'Queen's heroes' but who'd had to be reminded twice of Jonathan's name.

The last person on the interview panel was an elderly woman introduced as Mrs Benson. In her pale blue day gown, feathered bonnet and kindly expression, she looked out of place beside the dark formality of the three men.

Mr Overton looked up at him. 'Well, your credentials are sound enough and Captain Braithwaite hints that because of your actions during the battle of Alma, you may be considered for the Queen's new gallantry medal.'

Jonathan resisted the urge to adjust his eyepatch. 'I did no more than my duty, sir.'

Mr Wendover chuckled, sending the gold chain across his paunch jingling. 'You'll need battle nerve if you're going to tackle the bigger boys at St Katharine's.'

Mr Overton shot him an irritated glance before turning his attention back to Jonathan.

'Well, we don't need to deliberate for too long over this matter, do we?' The vicar put Reggie's letter on top of the pile in front of him. 'As you know, the remuneration is £300 a year, paid quarterly. Accommodation is provided. You will be required to attend this church, which the school is attached to. You are directly answerable to the guardian board and they require a twice-yearly report, or more frequently if they feel necessary.' His jowls lifted into a munificent smile. 'Therefore, if there is nothing further, we would like to offer you the position of Headmaster at St Katharine's Found—'

Mrs Benson raised a gloved hand.

The vicar pursed his lips. 'Mrs Benson?'

'If I may, Mr Overton, I have a question for Captain Quinn before we conclude,' she said, quietly.

The vicar's cheeks puffed out for a second then he inclined his head towards her. 'Of course.'

Mrs Benson fixed Jonathan with her smoky-grey eyes. 'Captain Quinn, can you tell me of your most recent encounter with a child?'

'My dear lady,' began the vicar, 'I think Captain Quinn has—'

The old woman shot him a look worthy of any sergeant major and the vicar's mouth closed. She looked back at Jonathan.

He cleared his throat. 'Indeed, ma'am. On my journey to London I had the pleasure of sharing a train carriage with Mrs Farrow, the wife of the army surgeon at Colchester, and her young family. Although their nurse travelled with them, after an hour or so her two boys – spirited lads with strong opinions about the mutton pasties packed for lunch – started to squabble. By the time we reached Chelmsford they were on the brink of war. Their mother had her hands full tending to her little daughter and a babe-in-arms so, with her permission, I told Masters Cuthbert and Reginald the story of Jason and the Argonauts. It was a particular favourite of mine as a boy,' he explained to the old woman, whose eyes hadn't left his face. 'By the time we'd found the Golden Fleece, escaped the Hydra and avoided being crushed by the Clashing Rock, the train was pulling into Bishopsgate.' He cleared his throat. 'I didn't dwell on the Argonauts dealings with the women on Lemnos, given that the boys were ten and twelve.'

Mrs Benson's eyes twinkled. 'Naturally.'

Mr Overton shuffled the papers again. 'Thank you, Captain Quinn. I can't say I care for the more fanciful classic myself but it sounds a most interesting encounter. Now, have you any further questions, Mrs Benson?'

She shook her head, which caused her lace to flutter gently. Mr Overton straightened his papers and beamed at Jonathan. 'Well, then, it is my great pleasure to offer you the Headmastership of St Katharine's Foundation School.'

*

By the time Jonathan had taken his leave of the panel, the daylight had almost gone. Setting his hat at an angle over his left eye, he marched across the churchyard, and back on to St George's High Street. Jonathan tucked his cane under his arm and turned westwards towards the Kent and Essex Hotel where he was staying.

He sidestepped the barrels of pitch outside the chandler's and the boots strung from the awning of a pawnbroker. As he passed a public house with a worn picture of a Tudor rose swinging above the door, a lump of broken cork bounced through the mud towards him.

Jonathan stopped it with his foot as two scruffy-haired boys skidded to a stop in front of him. He kicked the broken ship's float back. The two lads touched their foreheads then stood back to let him past, their eyes wide with wonder at the patch over his left eye. Suddenly the bar door swung open and three sailors burst out.

The first one through the door, a squat individual with threadbare canvas trousers, a dirty jacket and weeks' worth of stubble, collided with the smaller one of the two boys and sent him sprawling into the gutter. The sailor staggered to regain his balance but his companions, dressed in the same dishevelled manner, pushed into him as they wheeled through the door and sent him crashing to the ground. He lurched upright and grabbed the boy as he tried to scramble away.

'I'll teach you to trip me up, you little bugger,' he said, dragging the child to his feet.

Jonathan caught the sailor's fist mid-air. 'It was your feet that sent you tumbling, not the boy.'

The sailor struggled against Jonathan's grip but it didn't budge. He cursed and released the child. Turning on Jonathan, his unfocused gaze flickered over his expensive suit and top hat.

'What's your game?' he asked, shoving him in the chest.

Although his hat tumbled off Jonathan stood his ground. A mocking smile spread across the sailor's face, revealing his remaining tobacco-stained teeth. 'Eh, come 'ere and have a look, Smugger. It's fucking Nelson.'

Smugger staggered over, his eyes swimming unsteadily for a moment before they focused on Jonathan. He gave him a salute that would have earned even a raw recruit a stint in the guardhouse.

'Yesss, ssssir, Admiral, surrr!' he spluttered.

Jonathan regarded them dispassionately.

The third sailor swaggered in front of Jonathan. 'Oi! Admiral! You looking for a bit of skirt?'

''E's looking for trouble, more like,' the first sailor replied, breathing a concoction of cheap spirit and decay into Jonathan's face.

Jonathan glanced at the two boys huddled together by the wall. 'Off you go, lads.'

The taller of the two boys disappeared around the corner but the lad sent sprawling by the sailor hesitated before shooting off across the main road, dodging between the wagons as he ran.

Jonathan stepped forward until he was almost nose to nose with the sailor. He tapped him on the shoulder with his cane. 'Step aside, chum.'

Smugger's jaw dropped and Mogg ground his teeth.

'Chum! I'll give you fucking chum.' He whipped out a twelve-inch knife from his belt and ran it across his tongue. 'When I'm finished with you, you one-eyed toff, you'll be blind.'

Smugger drew out an iron hook and the sailor on Jonathan's left disappeared from view behind the blackness of his eyepatch. Jonathan cursed and tried to sense the man's proximity while watching the two in front of him. He shifted his weight on to the balls of his feet and gripped his cane.

Mogg snarled then jabbed the knife at Jonathan's face. Jonathan jerked back as the razor-sharp blade passed within a whisker of his cheek. Sidestepping, Jonathan smashed the brass-knobbed handle of his cane against his attacker's temple. Mogg sank to the floor.

Jonathan slipped the concealed sword from his cane and thrust the empty scabbard backwards into what he prayed would be the breastbone of the man behind him, then he swiped his blade at Smugger.

The sailor screamed as the edge of the blade sliced across his forearm. He dropped the docker's hook and Jonathan spun around.

The sailor behind him was doubled over but had just about recovered from Jonathan's backward blow. Jonathan threw his cane aside as the man lunged at him. Jonathan smashed his fist squarely into his assailant's nose. There was a satisfying crunch and the man staggered back. Jonathan punched him again and he fell, with a small groan, across Mogg's unconscious body.

Jonathan turned again to face Smugger. His hand was clamped over his injured forearm but blood oozed through his fingers.

He spat on the floor. 'I'll do you, so I will, you bastard.'

He lurched forward and, snatching the long knife from the cobbles, slashed it in an arc through the space between them. Jonathan's blade whistled through the air and he jabbed the tip of it on to the sailor's Adam's apple. The knife clattered to the pavement as a small trickle of blood ran down from the point of the blade. Smugger retreated as Jonathan backed him against the pub wall. Police rattles sounded and five police officers ran along the road.

Jonathan gave the man at the point of his blade a sardonic smile. 'Next time, step aside, chum!' He released the sailor, who slumped forward.

'Are you all right, sir?' the police officer at the head of the patrol asked as he reached Jonathan.

'Yes, thank you, Sergeant.' Jonathan picked up his walking stick and slid the thin sword back inside.

'This lad here told us you were being murdered.' The officer drew forward the boy whom Jonathan had saved from a beating.

The lad had a smear of dirt across his cheeks but it was only a day's not a week's worth, and although his clothes were old, they were neatly patched. Unusually, he wore stout boots, and despite the policeman's large hand on his shoulder, stood tall.

Jonathan picked up his hat and dusted it off. 'I am indebted to you ...?'

'Joe Ellis.'

'Well, thank you, Master Ellis.'

Joe shrugged. ''S'all right but you want to be careful, mister. It ain't safe for outsiders to wander around here.'

'The lad's right, sir,' the police officer said. 'Strangers are easy pickings for ruffians.'

'Thank you for your warning, Constable. But as I have just been appointed headmaster of St Katharine's School, I won't be a stranger for very long.'

Joe looked astounded. 'Cor, the way you pinned that fella to the wall I thought you were a soldier or summink, not a *teacher*.'

'Now, now, laddie, show a bit of respect to your betters. Don't give this gentleman none of your cheek or you'll feel the weight of my hand,' the officer said.

'Thank you, officer.' Jonathan drew a silver threepenny piece from his pocket and handed it to the lad. 'Perhaps you'll find yourself a hot pie as a reward for your bravery.'

The lad's eyes lit up for a second then he closed his fist. 'Ta, mister.' He touched his forehead briefly then sped off.

'The nippers around here are cheeky little buggers,' the officer said as they watched Joe Ellis disappear around the corner. 'And with fingers like lightning when it comes to filching an apple from a stall. You'll have to wield that cane of yours something fierce to get them to take any notice. If you don't mind me saying so, it's the only thing most of them know. "Spare the rod and spoil the child," that's what old Mr Gardener, the previous headmaster – God rest his soul – used to say and he went through a switch a week to get the little sods to show some respect.'

'Perhaps so.' Jonathan glanced around.

The street seemed familiar for some reason. Then he realised why when he spotted the brightly painted woodwork and homely curtains of the chop house. It was the very same street that he'd found himself in on the day he'd stormed out of his father's office.

An image of the young woman with the striking blue eyes who served strong coffee and made delicious cakes floated into his mind.

Jonathan repositioned his hat. 'Thank you for your timely intervention, officer, but if there's nothing else I'll—'

'Begging your pardon, sir, but I shall need a full statement from you about the incident,' the officer said. 'That is, if you've no other pressing engagement.'

Jonathan sighed. 'Of course. Lead the way.'

By the time Joe rushed through the door his mother was at the table chopping cabbage while Ella sat scraping a couple of knobbly potatoes opposite. Mam looked up and smiled. 'I was just wondering where you were. Put the wood in the hole,' she said, nodding at the open door.

Joe closed it and removed his coat, hanging it on the crooked nail in the wall. 'You'll never guess what happened, Mam. Me and Tricky were just having a lark ...' He began, and then told her about the fight. 'And he had one eye—'

'One eye?' Ma asked, looking at him oddly.

'Yer, this one.' He pointed at his right eye. 'The other one was covered with a black patch. I thought he'd be for the slaughter so I ... I ran all the way down Wapping Lane, even with the stitch, and found a policeman. He and some others took the sailors away and the man gave me this!'

He held the coin aloft and it twinkled in the light from the tallow candles on the mantelshelf.

'I wouldn't flash that around too much, if you know what's good for you,' Ella said.

Joe's eyes narrowed. 'You're just jealous cos I've got something you ain't.'

Ella rolled her eyes like Ma did sometimes.

Ma got up and came over. She ruffled his hair. 'This teacher, what did he look—'

The door burst open and his father lumbered in. Ella jumped down from the table and went to stand by Ma.

'What do you want?' she asked.

His father staggered a little then righted himself. 'Want?' he shouted. 'I don't have to fucking *want* anything to walk into my own house.'

'It isn't your house, it's my brother's and you've been drinking,' Ma said, sharply.

'What's it to you?' Freddie looked around unfocused for a moment then his gaze rested on Joe. He swayed unsteadily towards him and grasped his narrow shoulders with a heavy hand. 'I've come to see my boy.'

'Pa! Pa!' Joe shouted, unable to hold his excitement inside any longer as he repeated the story again. '. . . And he gave me this.' He held up the coin for his father to see.

Freddie blinked a couple of times. 'You went and fetched the rozzers?'

'I did, or the man would have been murdered,' Joe replied, beaming up at his father.

Freddie belched noisily. 'I don't what no nabbers' nark for a son.'

Joe looked at the floor.

Freddie's expression remained severe for a second longer then he bent down in front of his son. 'Ain't you just the bravest little man?' he said, breathing sour spirit over him.

Joe turned to his mother, waiting for her to smile with pride, too, but she didn't.

'Well, now you've seen him, you can go,' she said stiffly.

Freddie let go of Joe and stumbled towards Kate. Ella tucked herself further behind her skirts but her ma didn't move.

'My brother was asking after you,' she said.

A furious expression spread across Freddie's face and he spun around and staggered back towards the door.

Joe ran after him. 'Don't go, Pa,' he said, grabbing at his coat.

Freddie stopped and clasped Joe's shoulders again. 'Don't worry, son. I'll come back to see you. After all, a man needs a son like you to look after his interests.' His father took the coin from Joe's hand and slipped it in his waistcoat pocket. He patted him on the head. 'Good lad.'

He kicked the back door open and disappeared. Joe stared down at his empty palm and tears stung the corners of his eyes.

'Come and have your supper, Joe,' Ma said softly, hugging Ella.

Joe slunk into a chair and folded his arms on the table. Ella slipped into the chair beside him and he felt her eyes on him. Although he dreaded seeing the smug look on his sister's face, Joe glanced across at her.

Oddly, she looked sad. She leant forward until her nose almost touched his. 'I told you not to flash it about.'

Chapter Six

Kate crossed herself and rose to her feet as the congregation around her started to file out of the pews. Ella followed her and began to put on her knitted gloves.

'Can I go and see Maisie, Ma?' she asked.

'Of course you can, and tell her mother I'll call in to see if she wants anything from the market tomorrow,' Kate replied, tucking her daughter's scarf around her collar a little tighter.

Joe jumped off the bench. 'And can I find Lenny?'

'Yes, but remember Auntie Mattie is expecting us so don't wander off. And watch where you're going,' she called after him as he nearly knocked Mrs Benson flying.

The old lady smiled fondly after him and, leaning heavily on her walking stick, made her way down the aisle.

'Such lovely children,' she said, as she came to a halt in front of Kate.

'Thank you, Mrs Benson, although spirited would be what I'd call them.'

Mrs Benson chuckled noiselessly, making the ostrich feather in her hat float. 'Happy children always have a touch of tomfoolery in them, as you did, if I remember rightly. And what about you, Kate?'

Kate put on a bright smile. 'Kate's Kitchen is doing grand business.'

'I'm pleased to hear that.' She touched Kate's arm lightly. 'Have you applied for a place at St Katharine's for Joseph yet?'

'No, not yet,' Kate replied, forcing herself to hold the old lady's unwavering gaze.

She had all but decided to make enquiries at the Greencoat School in Stepney, where Patrick and Josie sent their children, but as Mrs Benson's family had supported St Katharine's for years and she'd always been so kind to her, Kate didn't want to hurt her feelings.

'I wouldn't delay for much longer if I were you, Kate,' the older women replied. 'Once the news gets around about who the guardians have appointed as headmaster, there will be a clamour for places.'

'Who is it?'

Mrs Benson adjusted her bag over her arm. 'I'm not at liberty to divulge really until it's official, but suffice to say that he greatly impressed me, and the rest of the board. I have every reason to believe that by this time next year, St Katharine's will again rival Raine's for academic achievement.'

'Really?' Kate replied, unable to keep the surprise from her voice.

'Indeed. So I suggest you make an appointment to see Mr Overton as soon as possible. I wouldn't want a bright boy like your Joe to miss out. I'm sure you'll be impressed by St Katharine's new head-master when you meet him, Kate.'

'Thank you, Mrs Benson,' Kate said.

'Not at all.' Her face wrinkled into a girlish smile. 'I've always had a soft spot for your two. Such merry children. Good day, Kate, and give my regards to your mother.'

She turned and walked slowly towards the church door.

As Kate watched the older woman hobble down the aisle, pos-sibilities raced around in her head. She'd been raised as a Catholic and had attended Mass each week without fail until she married Freddie. But after the priest at the mission refused her communion because she'd married a protestant, Kate moved to St George's and had been a regular member of the congregation ever since. Freddie's family had a long association with the church, she had the children christened there and Ella was already a pupil so she should be able to get a letter of recommendation from Mr Overton without any problem. Perhaps she should send Joe to St Katharine's for a term or two at least.

After all, if Mrs Benson believed that the new headmaster could help turn St Katharine's around, then he must be a truly remarkable man and an exceptional teacher.

Jonathan wiped his mouth and placed his napkin on his empty breakfast plate. He took a sip from his cup of tea and then added another spoonful of sugar. Sitting back in his chair he looked over at the tea chests containing his unpacked books and correspondence in the corner of the room. They would have to stay as they were for a week or so yet, until the carpenter had fixed the shelves and repaired the leg on the roll-top desk.

Although the school board didn't require him to take up the post until the new year, Jonathan had decided to start as soon as possible. He wouldn't be paid until the end of the March but he had enough to keep body and soul together in the meantime. He'd made his decision and there was no reason to delay.

That was two weeks ago and the day before yesterday he'd settled his account at the Kent and Essex, packed his carpet bag and caught a cab from Whitechapel to Cartwright Street to take up residence.

The headmaster's house adjoined the school and was a good-sized family dwelling built sometime in the early 1700s. It consisted of a drawing room and dining room on the ground floor to the front of the house and a small morning room overlooking the handkerchief-sized garden to the rear. Jonathan had taken the largest of the three generously proportioned bedrooms upstairs. The kitchen and scullery occupied the sub-basement and Mr and Mrs Delaney, the live-in help provided by the board, lodged in the servants' quarters in the attic. Mr Delaney acted as both the odd-job man and groundsman, and his wife took care of the domestic duties and cooking.

The accommodation was furnished but with items so ancient and woodwormed that Jonathan had been forced to plunder his reserves to replace them.

There was a light knock and Mrs Delaney's rosy face appeared around the edge of the dining-room door. 'Would you like anything more, sir?'

'No, thank you. I've had enough to set me up for the day,' Jonathan replied.

Mrs Delaney waddled in, holding a tray and grimacing with each rolling step.

'Are you in pain, Mrs Delaney?' Jonathan asked.

She shook her head. 'You mustn't mind me, sir,' she said as she started collecting the breakfast dishes. 'It just the rheumatics. I am a martyr to them, so I am. But don't you worry. I'll set straight to cleaning out the back bedroom as you instructed.'

Jonathan pulled out his pocket watch. Eight thirty. Mr Delaney would be opening the school gates in a few moments so he needed to get to his position between the girls' and boys' entrances to welcome the pupils in.

He stood up and went into the hall. Mrs Delaney followed and helped him shrug on his coat.

'If you don't mind me saying so, Captain Quinn, this is a grand day for old St Katharine's.'

'Thank you, Mrs Delaney,' he replied. 'Now, I have to fetch the school Bible.'

Jonathan left the housekeeper in the hall and went into the sunlight-filled morning room. The walls were decorated with pale floral paper and it was where the mistress would have instructed her housekeeper and given her orders to tradesmen but as there was no lady of the house, Jonathan had designated it as his study.

He picked up the leather-bound book and caught sight of himself in the mirror on the wall. He stared at the black, unadorned jacket that had replaced the braided red tunic decorated with brass buttons. An ache for the easy camaraderie of the barrack room surged up so forcefully that he drew a breath. Perhaps his father and Louisa had been right and he was just throwing away his future for a redundant principle; resigning his commission hadn't stopped the butchery in the Crimea.

An image of the bloody remains of his men laid out in a barren square flashed into his mind. No doubt the obstinate, short-sighted generals and commanders would continue to launch futile attacks, costing thousands of lives. But Jonathan was determined to no longer take part in the carnage.

He studied his reflection for a few moments longer then tucked the Bible under his arm and marched out, in double-time, to his new life.

Freddie woke up with a start as the door slammed. He looked around disorientated and on guard but relaxed as he recognised the faded curtains and Aggie's gowns strewn over the furniture and floors. Her room was on the top floor of an old weaver's house in Trawl Street, just a stroll from the Blue Coat Boy. It had a small fire grate with a couple of coals glowing in it, which only just kept the room warm. There was one window that couldn't be opened and the drapes were strung on string. It wasn't a palace but then he and Aggie didn't need some swanky place.

The early morning sun streaking through the window stung his eyes and he blinked a couple of times to clear the sleep from his brain. He'd been up all night and was surprised Aggie wasn't still in bed when he'd got back at dawn.

'Look what the cat dragged in,' she said, taking off her coat and throwing it across the chair. It fell on the floor alongside a dirty plate, and an empty bottle rolled into the middle of the room.

Freddie swung his legs off the bed. 'Hello, sweetheart,' he said, smiling at her as he stood up.

Aggie put her hands on her hips and glared at him. 'Don't you "hello, sweetheart" me, Freddie Ellis. Where have you been for the past three days?'

'Out Essex way doing a job with the boys.'

Her lower lip started to tremble. 'Oh, Freddie, why didn't you tell me? I thought you'd gone skulking back to your Paddy wife.'

'Of course I didn't,' he replied. 'Where've you been?'

'Catching a bit of early trade at the market.' She threw a couple of shillings on the table. 'That should keep Ollie sweet until next week.'

Freddie pulled a silver locket dangling on a chain from his top pocket and held it aloft. 'Just to show I've been thinking about you,' he said, swinging it back and forth.

Aggie's eyes lit up. 'Give me,' she said, stretching out for it as she came towards him.

He held it up so she couldn't reach it. 'Don't I get summink, too?' He twisted his cheek towards her.

She gave him a peck on the cheek and Freddie relinquished the necklace into her hands.

He smiled as he watched her dance over to the mirror. Women were nags by nature but their fluttery little brains were easily distracted by a trinket.

'It's so pretty,' she said, slipping it over her head and admiring her reflection.

'Just like you,' he said, knowing that a bit of flannel did no harm either. He caught her around the waist. 'I thought perhaps after three days I might get more than just a smacker.'

She wriggled out of his arms. 'After disappearing like that you're lucky I ain't found myself another fella.'

'Don't be like that,' he said, catching her again. 'What could I do? Mr Mac's the boss.'

'You could have coughed up my money each week for a start,' Aggie replied, her eyes flickering to his diamond tie pin. 'I've had to work myself sore for two days to get his dosh.' She snuggled into him, rubbing her hip against his crotch. 'I thought you only wanted me to toot your flute.'

'Course I do,' he replied. 'But I ain't got the money to pay your protection as well as my own expenses.'

Aggie slid her arms around his neck and put her mouth close to his ear. 'But I wouldn't have to turn tricks if you were the boss, would I?' she whispered. 'After all, you're out there night after night taking all the risks while he sits at home with the fat cow and smelly brat of his, creaming off the profits. But just think, Freddie, if you were the top man you'd be the one sitting at home with your feet up while Stefan and the others are out grafting for you.'

An icy feeling started creeping up Freddie's spine. 'I don't know,

Aggie. It all sounds fine but if Ollie got wind of it I'd be cat's meat. Let's leave things be just for now.'

She shrugged. 'I'm sure you know best, Freddie. Even if you did get rid of Ollie there'd still be Stefan to deal with and no one would blame you being scared of—'

'I can take him,' he interrupted, trying not to think of the twelve-inch blade the big Swede kept tucked in his belt.

Aggie slid her hands up his shirt front and smiled adoringly at him. 'Of course you could and once you have, you'll be the one calling the shots, not Ollie Mac and fat Lilly.'

Freddie glanced around the tawdry room and thought of Ollie's plush parlour at the back of the Boy. She was right. He was the one out there in the cold and wet, dodging the coppers. It would be him who'd be sent down by the magistrate for seven to ten – not Ollie Mac. And what did he get for all his hard work? Whatever Ollie decided to bung him each Saturday, that's what.

He slipped his arm around Aggie's waist and pulled her against him. 'Don't worry, sweetheart. We'll have to play dumb for a bit but if Ollie thinks he can order my woman around then I'm going to show him different.'

'Oh, Freddie,' Aggie sighed. 'I'm so glad I'm your special gal. But, Freddie?' She slid her fingers under the front of his shirt and tickled his chest. 'Next time, bring me something gold.'

Chapter Seven

Jonathan reached forward and pulled the school ledger on the desk towards him. He might as well finish off last week's entries while he was waiting. He reread the week's records, crossed a couple of t's he'd missed and then wrote:

Friday 7th December 1855

38 scholars attended today and two children were absent with throat illness. Miss Wainwright's class were given an extended recreation period mid-morning so that the sweep could clear the obstruction from the flue and clear the smoke from the classroom. The object lesson today was The Fox for the older children and the names of the colours for the infants. The standard-one poem recited by the senior girl was 'God Made Them All.'

He signed his name at the bottom of last week's log, put his hands behind his head and leant back.

St Katharine's was a purpose-built single-storey rectangular building with a pitched roof. It had once faced the old medieval church of the same name but that had been swept away when the dock had been built some forty years before. Now there were only warehouses as neighbours.

The walls of the classroom had been painted a toneless grey so long ago that much of it had flaked off to expose the coarse brickwork underneath. A series of wax-coated posters depicting the kings and queens of England and a British man-of-war in full sail hung from the picture rail, like old regimental flags. Each print was so faded that even at a distance of three feet it was difficult to discern Elizabeth I from Charles II. Beside the tall teacher's desk stood an abacus and a hinged blackboard with more wood than pitch on the surface. Tucked in the corner was a cupboard where the slates and scribers were kept. The girls' end of the classroom looked much the same but with posters of native trees and flowers instead of military subjects.

There was a light knock. Jonathan adjusted his patch and called, 'Enter.'

The door opened and Miss Wainwright and Mr Rudd came in.

Leticia Wainwright was in her late thirties and on the skinny side of slender, which gave her features a pinched look. She was dressed as usual in an unadorned black gown, which drained the colour from her complexion. Mr Rudd, on the other hand, had a florid face and dressed in a crumpled hopsack suit, looking more like a down-at-heel shopkeeper than a teacher.

'Headmaster,' they said in unison.

Jonathan waved them in. 'Please sit.'

Miss Wainwright perched on the edge of her seat with her knees together while Mr Rudd stretched his neck out of his stiff collar and crossed his legs.

'Thank you for your prompt attendance.'

'Say nothing of it. After all, you are in command of our happy little family and we must obey. Must we not, Leticia?' Mr Rudd said.

'Oh, yes. We must obey,' echoed Miss Wainwright.

Mr Rudd dusted the chalk residue from his tweed trousers. 'Of course, if there is anything you think might improve with a bit of tinkering then—'

'I've read each and every one of Mr Gardener's reports from the last five years and found them – how can I put this charitably – wanting.'

Mr Rudd's assured smile slipped a little. 'I'm afraid the previous headmaster suffered bouts of ill health.'

Jonathan raised an eyebrow. 'So I understand from the empty brandy bottle I found tucked at the back of my desk drawer.'

Mr Rudd swallowed and Miss Wainwright studied her feet.

'As I did not know him, nor any burdens he carried, I shall not condemn him. We must put that behind us. But I have decided to make a few changes.' Jonathan took out half a dozen sheets of paper. 'As from next Monday, I will be reading God's word and leading morning prayer to both boys and girls together. To that end, I have asked Mr Delaney to draw back the central screen each day.'

'But it hasn't been moved for years,' Mr Rudd protested.

'You can hardly have an act of corporate worship without us all being in the same room,' Jonathan replied. 'Now, to the second item on my list.'

Miss Wainwright coughed. 'Forgive me for asking, Headmaster, but will this take long? I must get home to Mother.'

Jonathan raised an eyebrow. 'The school day ends at four o'clock. It is only five past three so you needn't worry about catching your omnibus *just* yet.' He returned to his notes. 'The second matter is that from Monday all pupils will follow the same curriculum. These are the subjects that will be included.' He handed a sheet of paper to each of them. 'The only variants will be that the girls will continue to learn needlework and the boys carpentry. The next item concerns the issue of uniforms, or should I say, the lack of uniform.'

Miss Wainwright's thin face screwed up. 'Forgive me, Headmaster, but this is a very poor area. Mothers send their children to school in what they can afford.'

'I am aware of that, Miss Wainwright, and so was Alderman Ferries, who some seventy years ago set aside a sum of a hundred pounds in his will to' – Jonathan ran his finger down his notes until he found the appropriate entry – ' "provide good, sound raiments for young persons attending St Katharine's School".' He looked up. 'Why do we have pupils wearing threadbare dresses and jackets while, according to my records, this fund hasn't been drawn on for almost nine years?'

Mr Rudd gave a light laugh. 'It's foolish, I know, but there's a boneheaded stubbornness among the locals to accept charity.'

'That is commendable, of course, but if the reputation of the school is to be reformed, I cannot have the children dressed as if they are pupils of a ragged school. I have approached Davison's, the outfitters on the Highway, and he has agreed to supply our pupils with discounted uniforms. The school will make good his losses from the alderman's funds.' He turned to the next page of his notes. 'And now to the question of the children's health.'

'It's shocking,' Miss Wainwright said.

'I agree, and will be asking the school nurse to resume her visit every month. I'm also in correspondence with Dr Munroe, the clinical director of the London Hospital, with a view to having all the children inoculated against smallpox. I also have plans for their diet but I'll advise you of those at a later date.'

'If I may say so, Headmaster, that is most charitable of you,' Miss Wainwright said, fluttering her pale eyelashes at him.

'Thank you. And now let us turn to the last matter on my list: discipline.' He pulled the punishment book over. 'I am somewhat concerned about . . . how can I put this?' He fixed the teachers with a steely gaze. 'The over-*enthusiastic* use of the cane.'

Mr Rudd ran his finger around the inside of his collar again. 'Some of the pupils come from belligerent and argumentative backgrounds and bring such behaviour into the classroom.'

'Indeed, but there doesn't seem to be a day without at least half a dozen names entered into the punishment book.' He tapped the page lightly with his finger. 'Henceforth, I alone will sanction corporal punishment. And I'm abolishing the dunce's hat.'

Mr Rudd sat forward. 'But how are we meant to control the class?'

Jonathan gave them a stern look. 'How do you think I got men to march day and night without food or water and charge into the enemies' guns?' They looked blank. 'By leadership, and that is how we are going to educate the children of this school. Through leadership. Do you understand?'

Mr Rudd and Miss Wainwright nodded.

'Good.' Jonathan stood up. 'According to the records, St Katharine's used to be a beacon for education and I am determined it will be once again.' He stood up. 'Thank you for your time. I'll see you on Monday.'

Mr Rudd and Miss Wainwright rose to their feet and left the office.

Jonathan fell back into his chair with a sigh. The scar around his eyes was itching so he took off his eyepatch and rubbed it. He closed his good eye and let his shoulders relax. Mr Rudd and Miss Wainwright hadn't put up as much opposition to his changes as he thought they might. Perhaps he would be able to turn the school's fortunes around sooner rather than later. Perhaps being the headmaster of St Katharine's wasn't going to be so bad after all and maybe next time he wrote to Captain Braithwaite, Jonathan would be a little more genuine in his thanks.

There was a knock on the door. 'Come,' he called, quickly readjusting his eyepatch.

The door squeaked open and then the lock clicked as it closed. Jonathan looked up.

Standing there was the young woman from the chop house. Next to her was the young lad he'd met a few weeks earlier outside the pub.

She looked astonished. '*You're* the new headmaster!'

'Yes.'

'Captain Quinn?'

'Yes.'

'But you're an army officer stationed in Colchester?'

'I resigned.'

'Oh.'

'A month ago,' he replied, annoyed that he was having trouble forming more than two words at a time.

'Oh.' She blinked and pulled herself together. 'Begging you pardon, sir, I . . . I'm Mrs Ellis and I have an appointment to talk about my son.'

'You're married?'

She looked cross. 'Of course.'

'I'm sorry, I didn't mean to imply . . .'

'I have a daughter, too. She is already a pupil and I've come to apply for a place for my son, Joe. You were expecting me, weren't you?'

'No . . . yes. I was but . . .' Jonathan took himself firmly in hand and rose to his feet. 'Please forgive me, Mrs Ellis; I'm just a little surprised to meet you again in these circumstances. Won't you please sit down?'

A little surprised! I should say, thought Kate as he drew the chair away from the desk.

'Please, take a seat.'

'Thank you, sir,' she said, feeling her colour rise under his unwavering stare.

She sat down and positioned Joe alongside her. Joe had whipped off his cap as Captain Quinn resumed his seat.

'It's good of you to see me and as I'm sure you're a busy man I'll try not to take up too much of your time, Captain Quinn,' she said, annoyed that her voice quivered.

He leant across the desk. 'Please, there's no hurry.'

Kate nodded. 'As I say, sir, I have come to apply for a place for my son, Joseph Patrick, who is five.'

Joe stepped forward, put his right arm across his middle and bowed.

'Good day, sir,' Joe said, in an oddly solemn voice.

'Well, now, this is an afternoon for surprises, is it not, Mrs Ellis? For not only do I have the pleasure of meeting you again,' his gaze ran over her and Kate's heart thumped, 'but also the brave lad who assisted me when I was set upon by ruffians.' He looked at Joe and smiled. 'Did he tell you of his valiant deed?'

She nodded. 'When he described the man he'd rescued, I wondered . . .' Her gaze flicked onto his patch. 'The way Joe told the tale it sounded like you needed little help.'

'British army training, Mrs Ellis. It has stood me in good stead on more than one occasion.'

Kate opened the drawstring bag on her wrist and pulled out a carefully folded sheet of paper. 'If you please, sir, this is the letter of recommendation from Mr Overton. I hope you find it all in order.'

Captain Quinn took it from her. Their fingers touched for the briefest moment and Kate pulled her hand away. He scrutinised the vicar's letter for a moment then looked up again.

'Your husband's family have a long connection with St George's church.' Captain Quinn raised an eyebrow. 'And I see that he attended St Katharine's school, too?'

'Yes, sir,' Kate replied.

In truth Freddie had spent more time out of school than in it but had left for good at twelve with just enough skills to make sense of an order book.

'Well, things have changed here, Mrs Ellis. I have instituted new rules, which I am sure will enhance the learning and welfare of our pupils. The children are required to wear the stipulated uniform, which must be kept in good order at all times. They must wear boots even in the summer. They must be clean and with their hair combed.'

'I understand,' Kate replied.

His expression softened and he smiled at her. 'I'm sure you will have no trouble meeting those requirements because, if I might say, your son is a credit to you – as I'm sure your daughter is also, Mrs Ellis.'

'Thank you, sir.'

There was a moment of awkward silence then he looked down distractedly at the papers.

He cleared his throat. 'I drill the children each morning and both girls and boys are taught the three Rs along with geography, history and nature studies. And they must attend each day without fail unless they are unwell.'

'I understand.'

'Very well.' He smiled. 'I have great pleasure in offering Master Ellis a place in St Katharine's school, when classes resume after the Christmas break.'

'I am most grateful, sir, I really am. And I can promise that Joe,' she tousled his hair, 'will be perfect a scholar. Won't you, Joe?'

Joe grinned and nodded.

Captain Quinn looked down at her with the same expression that had unsettled her from the moment he'd walked into the shop.

'You'll get a letter of confirmation in a week or two, Mrs Ellis.' They stared at each other for a moment then he took the quill from the inkwell.

'Of course.' Kate nudged Joe.

'Good day, sir,' Joe said.

Kate ushered him out of the door. She turned to say goodbye again but Captain Quinn didn't look up. She closed the door behind her.

As they walked into the deserted schoolyard the icy wind tugged at Kate's bonnet.

'Ma?' Joe asked.

'Yes.'

'Do you like Captain Quinn?'

'Oh, I can't say. I've only just met him,' Kate replied, feeling her cheeks glow again.

'I do,' said Joe. 'But I don't know why people call 'im Nelson.'

From the moment Mabel Puttock spotted Mrs Benson sitting in her usual pew on the other side of the aisle, she was exceedingly glad she'd decided to wear her new pink gown. Well, in truth, it wasn't the sight of the elderly widow that caught her attention but the man sitting alongside her.

All through the service, which seemed unusually long, she had found her eyes straying in his direction. Her father had been on the interview panel for the new headmaster so she knew well enough who he was but Papa had failed to mention that Captain Quinn was strikingly handsome.

Captain Quinn hadn't noticed her but by the way he responded to Mr Overton's liturgy, she could tell he was a true believer like herself. Even so, she could hardly wait for the service to end.

The organ struck up for the final hymn and the congregation rose to their feet. With her eyes on the crucifix and her prettiest expression on her face just in case, Mabel took up the refrain.

The sacristan procession led by the vicar filed out. As soon as the vestry door closed, the congregation sank to their knees again for private prayer. Quickly asking the Almighty to watch over her for another week, Mabel crossed herself and slid out of the pew.

Old Mrs Harris spotted her and lumbered towards her. *For goodness sake*, thought Mabel as she saw her take out a handkerchief and dab her eyes. *He was seventy-two and has been dead for six months.*

Turning her head, Mabel ducked behind a column and continued down the aisle. She stopped a discreet distance from Mrs Benson but made sure she was in her eye-line.

Mabel twirled a brown curl and straightened a couple of bows on her sleeve as she waited for Mrs Benson and Captain Quinn to finish their conversation with the vicar's wife. From under the brim of her bonnet she studied St Katharine's new headmaster. She'd thought him impressive at a distance but close up he was striking. Mrs Overton was pointing to the stained-glass window and explaining the history of the church. Captain Quinn looked up and Mabel edged forward and coughed lightly.

They turned and looked at her. 'Good morning, Mrs Benson. Mrs Overton.'

'And to you, Miss Puttock,' Mrs Overton replied.

'I thought Mr Overton's sermon was particularly fine this morning.' Mabel said.

'Why, thank you, Miss Puttock. Our attitude towards the deserving poor in these lax times is one of his favourite themes.' Her eyes flickered past Mabel. 'Oh! I've just spotted Mrs Lamb. Please excuse me, Mrs Benson. Captain Quinn.'

She hurried off and Mabel waited expectantly.

Mrs Benson smiled impishly at her. 'Good morning, Miss Puttock, you're looking very pretty today.' Mabel lowered her eyes modestly. 'I don't believe you've met Captain Quinn, our new headmaster.'

Mabel looked up. 'No, I'm afraid I haven't.'

'Captain Quinn, may I introduce Miss Puttock.'

He looked at her and Mabel's heart fluttered. 'It's a pleasure to meet you, Miss Puttock.'

Mabel gave him a dazzling smile. 'Captain Quinn. I've heard so much about you.'

'Please don't believe any of it.' He laughed and Mrs Benson did too.

Mabel frowned. 'But they were only good things, Captain Quinn.'

Mrs Benson slipped her arm in Mabel's. 'I'm sure they were.' She looked at Captain Quinn. 'Miss Puttock is one of my keenest parish workers. She helps with the infants' Sunday school, visits the poor to give them comfort and arranges the church flowers.' She smiled mischievously. 'And she will make someone a wonderful wife one day.'

Mabel blushed. 'It's most fortunate that you are here with Mrs Benson,' she said, looking shyly up at him from under her lashes, 'because I want to discuss the school's summer fair with her. It's only a few months away and I thought to celebrate our new headmaster we ought to make it a bit special. Perhaps with a military theme?'

'What a very good idea,' said Mrs Benson. 'What do you think, Captain Quinn?'

Mabel saw that his attention was taken by something at the other end of the church. She followed his gaze but could only see Mrs Ellis, the woman who ran the chop house. Her two children were milling about by the door.

Captain Quinn smiled apologetically. 'I'm sorry, Mrs Benson. I missed what you said.'

Mrs Benson shook her finger at him. 'If you don't pay attention, young man, you'll find yourself standing in the corner.' Mabel looked shocked but Captain Quinn just laughed. 'Miss Puttock suggested we give our humble school fair a military flavour to welcome you,' she repeated.

'That's a capital idea!'

'Perhaps,' Mabel fluttered her eyelashes again, 'as a returning hero, you would do us the honour of opening the fair for us.'

'You flatter me, Miss Puttock. But I would be delighted,' he said, smiling at her.

Mabel lowered her eyes as she felt her cheeks grow warm. 'Also, if you don't think me too bold, I would like to invite you to take tea with Mama and me one afternoon. Say perhaps next Wednesday at four o'clock?' she said, breathlessly.

His smile widened. 'That is very kind of you and I would be delighted. But now, if you would excuse me, ladies, I have a lunch date with a friend of mine: Captain Braithwaite.'

He gave them a bow and strolled back down the church towards the main doors. Mabel watched him until he walked out of the church.

'So what do you think of St Katharine's new headmaster, Mabel?' Mrs Benson asked when he was out of earshot.

'I think we are most fortunate to have a man such as Captain Quinn teaching the parish children.'

'And I imagine he must have looked splendid in his uniform. Don't you think?'

'Oh yes,' she replied as a surge of unmaidenly longing rose up in her. 'He must have looked splendid indeed.'

Chapter Eight

Ella and Joe stood in the middle of Davison's outfitters with their arms by their sides as Kate looked them over. Behind them and crammed into every nook and cranny were hats, shawls and bonnets of all shapes of sizes. Above their heads, brightly coloured dresses and petticoats hung like bunting from ceiling hooks while against the far wall stood row upon row of boots graded from small to large and tied together in pairs by their laces. On the left side of the shop men's suits were squashed together on a high rail while under them, in folded piles, were the serge trousers and rough fabric shirts worn by dock labourers and rivermen alike. Opposite were bales of serviceable fabric ready for the thrifty housewife to make clothes either for her own use or to sell. The front shop mainly sold new clothes and the back had two metal rails holding what was labelled 'quality second-hand attire'. The musky smell from these tingled Kate's nose as she studied her children.

Joe stood upright in a single-breasted, cut-down version of a man's ordinary jacket with cuffs almost covering his fingers. The trousers he was wearing would need to be turned up four inches to be the correct length. Ella stood beside him in a round-necked, blue-serge gown with her eyes mesmerised by detachable lace collars and spools of coloured ribbon displayed under the glass-top counter next to her.

Kate smiled and smoothed the front of Joe's jacket, noting that the seam of the sleeve cleared his shoulder by a good three inches.

She turned her attention to Ella. The bodice hung loosely over Ella's slender chest and there were four deep folds around the skirt that could be let out as required. Kate ran her hand gently over her daughter's cheek and wondered if she could spare a penny for a length of ribbon.

'There's years of wear in both sets,' Mrs Davison declared, folding her chubby arms across her imposing bosom.

'There's certainly enough growing room,' Kate replied. 'As long as you two don't shoot up again.'

Joe stretched one hand high above his head. 'I'm going to grow this tall.'

'Are you now,' the shopkeeper replied, an indulgent smile lightening her heavy features. She looked back at Kate. 'As I say, you'll not get a more durable set of school clothes for the same price anywhere.'

Kate checked the buttons at the back of Ella's dress and pulled the shoulder of Joe's jacket again. 'How much did you say?'

'Five shillings for the young lady's and seven and six for the lad's.'

Kate looked them over again and, although they were swamped by their clothes, a little bubble of pride swelled in her to see them looking so grand and grown up.

Kate fished into the drawstring bag on her wrist. 'I'll take them. If you could wrap them with the rest.'

Ella and Joe went behind the screen and changed as Kate counted out her money.

'You're the third mother in this week,' Mrs Davison said, pulling a length of brown paper from the roll-dispenser screwed to the counter top.

'Really?'

'Oh, yes, it's that new headmaster.' She closed one eye. 'He might only have one peeper but according to my sister, it don't miss a thing. She said that her boy has come on leaps and bounds in his letters and you can almost figure out his writing now.' Mrs Davison placed two hanks of wool and a spool of thread on to three yards of bleached calico. 'He drills the children first thing and they do jumping and running exercises too. And, would you believe it – he joins in, too. Strips off his coat and runs alongside them back and forth across the playground.' She chuckled. 'Could you imagine old Mr Gardener doing such a thing?'

No, Kate couldn't, but disturbingly she could only too easily picture Captain Quinn in his shirt.

Mrs Davison cut off a length of string to tie the parcel. 'I expect it's his military training. I heard from his housekeeper that he does exercises in the backyard with weights and dumbbells before breakfast each morning.'

Ella and Joe came back and handed their new clothes to the shopkeeper.

With a deft twist and turn, Mrs Davison tied everything together. 'There you go, young man,' she said, as she handed Joe the parcel. 'And don't swing it or your ma's shopping will be all over the road.'

Ella and Joe stepped out into the fading afternoon light. A couple of hansom cabs trotted past with their oil lamps already lit. Kate guided the children through the ironmonger's pavement display and stopped Joe just in time before he collided with the planks of oak and pine leaning against the wall of the timber merchants. The fresh scent of newly sawn wood mingled with the cloying smell from the oil merchant's vats and the heady smell of the forge down the alley. Kate paused as they reached Sawkin's fruiters. A young lad standing sentry in a buff apron that almost covered his toes sprang forward.

'Can I help you, missus?' he warbled.

Kate picked up an orange. 'How much?'

'A ha'penny each or three for a penny.'

Kate squeezed it. 'They're not very juicy, are they? I'll tell you what – you let me have three, for a farthing each, and I'll take them.'

'Done.' He handed the fruit to Ella.

Kate pulled open her purse to fish for the coins when someone stepped out in front of her.

'Good afternoon, Mrs Ellis.'

'Oh, Captain Quinn,' Kate managed to say as she stared up into his face. 'Good afternoon.'

He smiled and raised his hat. 'And Miss Ellis, whom Miss Wainwright tells me is a great help with the younger members of the class.' Ella bobbed a curtsy. 'And young Master Ellis.'

Joe bowed stiffly.

'And what have you been up to?' Captain Quinn asked.

'Ma's just bought us our new clothes for school,' Ella replied.

'And what do you think of them?'

'They're grand, just grand!'

'Mine are too big,' Joe chipped in.

A smile tugged at Captain Quinn's lips. 'Are they?'

'They are but the cap fits. Trick hasn't got a cap.'

'Trick?'

'He's my mate,' Joe explained. 'He hasn't got any boots neither. Mam, can I go and knock for him?' he asked, looking imploringly up at Kate.

Kate nodded and took the parcel from him. 'If you promise to keep your scarf on and watch out for the carts.'

Joe dashed off.

Captain Quinn watched him for a moment then looked at Kate with that familiar disconcerting stare.

'I'm just buying a couple of oranges for the children,' Kate said, unable to think of anything more sensible to say.

'So am I. For the school.'

'Oh, well,' Kate said, unable to take her eyes from him. 'I shouldn't keep you. I'm sure you're off somewhere important.'

'I am but which way are you going?' he asked.

'Towards the church.'

He smiled. 'As am I. Let's walk together. Perhaps I can carry that for you,' he said, glancing at the package she was carrying.

'That's very kind of you, sir, but there's really no need.'

'It's no trouble.' He hooked his finger in the loop of string and lifted the package out of her arms. They started along the pavement and Kate was suddenly conscious of just how tall he was and how drab her workaday clothes were alongside his tailored suit.

Several tradesmen standing in their shop doorways acknowledged Captain Quinn with a touch of their caps but looked oddly at her walking beside him.

Kate bit her lip and studied his profile hesitantly before she spoke. 'I hope you don't think I was being rude when we met last week, sir, but I was just shocked that it was you.'

'I was a little surprised myself.' His gaze ran over her. 'But I didn't think you were impolite at all.'

They stared at each other for a moment then Kate looked ahead.

'I trust you're settled in to the schoolhouse,' she said, in what she hoped was a conversational tone.

'I have,' he replied. 'I've still a couple of chests to unpack but after years of barracks and army food the schoolhouse and Mrs Delaney's cooking is very welcome.' They walked on for a bit in silence. 'And what does your husband do, Mrs Ellis?'

An unhappy lump settled across Kate's chest. 'He drives a wagon,' she replied, remembering Freddie's last honest job.

They carried on for a few more moments and then he stopped.

'I am afraid we must now part company.' He handed the parcel back to her. 'It's been a pleasure meeting you again.' He tipped his hat. 'Good day.'

'Good day, sir,' Kate replied.

His gaze ran over her again then he went through the church gates. Kate watched him make his way across the churchyard.

Ella slipped her hand in Kate's. 'Ma.'

Kate looked down at her daughter. 'Yes, my love?'

'Isn't it exciting having Captain Quinn as the new headmaster, what with him being a soldier and all?'

Kate smiled stiffly. It was exciting, but then so was Freddie when she'd first met him and she could very well do without it.

Jonathan marvelled at the vicar's ability to string out a straight-forward agenda item – the buying of a new broom – for Mr Delaney for a full twenty minutes. He could tell that Mrs Benson and Mr Puttock felt the same; the glazed look on their eyes betrayed them. They were all sitting at one end of the table and as close to the pot-bellied stove as they could get without igniting themselves.

As the vicar asked his warden yet again to explain the attributes of a hazel over hog's bristle, Jonathan shifted his position and struggled to keep his patience. Mrs Benson, swathed in furs, looked up and gave him a kindly smile. He took a deep breath and resigned himself to another ten minutes of mind-numbing tedium and his thoughts drifted back, yet again, to his meeting with Mrs Ellis.

Of course, he knew he should have simply greeted her and walked on but when her blue eyes fixed on him he could do no other than play the gallant. His gaze drifted up to the small stained-glass window in the apex of the room and he realised that the gold halo of St whoever was almost exactly the same colour as her hair.

Mr Overton's voice cut through his thoughts: 'So if you could arrange to purchase our caretaker a new broom, Mr Puttock, I'd be grateful. If we could now move on to Captain Quinn's report. Are there any comments?'

'Most enlightening,' Mrs Benson said.

Mr Puttock raised a bony finger. 'If I may?'

'Of course, sir,' Jonathan replied.

'While I approve wholeheartedly of the new regime of discipline you've introduced, I do wonder about the need for the great number of books you've bought since you arrived,' he said, holding up Jonathan's four-page report. 'Is it strictly necessary?'

'It is if you want the children to learn to read properly.'

'I feel I must agree with Mr Puttock,' the vicar said in his Sunday-sermon tone. 'They have the school Bibles. Generations have learnt their lessons using God's word.'

'As I did myself,' Jonathan said. 'But all the books in the school, including the Bibles, were in such a shocking condition that I had no choice but to donate them to the West African Missionary Society. However, as you can see in my report, I secured a very good discount from the wholesaler in Houndsditch who indicated he would give us the same favourable terms next time.'

The churchwarden's faced flushed. 'Next—'

'That was very enterprising of you, Captain Quinn,' Mrs Benson cut in. 'And I see you have bought the Little Scholars series. I read the favourable report in *The Times* about them. Did you see it, Mr Puttock?'

The churchwarden was wrong-footed. 'No. No, um, I haven't had a chance yet.' He adjusted his half-rimmed glasses and studied Jonathan's report again. 'Well, perhaps we can overlook the books, but maps and charts of African beasts?' He gave what can only be described as an oily smile. 'With all due respect, Captain Quinn, most of these children will never travel further than the River Lea. They'll have no need to know where China is. And if they want to look at a lion, they can stroll down to Jamrach's Animal Emporium and see what he has in stock. Don't you think, Mr Overton?'

'I must disagree with you, sir,' Jonathan cut in, in the tone that had put down more than one barrack-room rebellion. 'Apart from the fact that hundreds of local boys become sailors and make their way to the four corners of the globe, England needs an educated population if it is to capitalise on the new colonies and markets our merchants open up each day.' He fixed Mr Puttock with a steely look. 'Of which *China* and *Africa* are two of the most lucrative.'

Mrs Benson's lips twitched and the churchwarden's colour flared again but he didn't reply.

Mr Overton shuffled his papers. 'Mmmm. We'll let the matter rest but I would appreciate, Captain Quinn, if you would address any further requests for equipment to the board first. Now, if we could just review the pupils joining the school in January.'

The guardians drew out their lists.

'This all seems very encouraging,' Mr Overton said approvingly. 'We must be almost full.'

'There are three places left,' Jonathan said. 'And I am seeing two parents at the end of the week so I expect they will be gone very soon.'

The vicar beamed. 'Excellent.' He looked at his fellow guardians. 'I propose that we formally enter into the minutes our heartfelt thanks to Captain Quinn for his hard work.'

'I would like to second that,' Mrs Benson said, nodding in agreement.

Mr Puttock tapped the paper on the table in front of him. 'I notice you have given a place to the Ellis boy.'

'I did,' Jonathan said.

Mr Overton ran his eye over the list again and looked apprehensive.

'Of course, had we known there would be such a demand for places, I might not have given him a recommendation.'

'Why?' asked Jonathan.

'Because Mrs Ellis is a Catholic.'

Mrs Benson's soft white brows pulled together. 'Really, Mr Overton,' she said, sharply. 'I don't think we should hold that against her. The children attend the church each week without fail, which is more than can be said for some members of the congregation.'

The warden pursed his lips. 'Perhaps so, Mrs Benson, but you can't deny that the Ellis children come from bad blood.'

Jonathan's expression darkened. 'Mrs Ellis struck me as an exemplary mother. She may be poor but her children were clean and tidy with good manners and stout boots on their feet. I haven't met their father yet but he clearly provides for his family. I distinctly remember in your reference letter, Mr Overton, you stated that the family have a long association with St George's and that you would recommend him without hesitation.'

'Well, James Ellis, the children's great-grandfather, was church warden but ...'

'But Freddie Ellis, their father, hasn't been inside the church since he got married,' Mr Puttock chipped in. 'And then only because Kate Ellis's family forced him.' He chuckled. 'And that was a story that had tongues wagging for weeks.'

'It's sad to say but truly Freddie Ellis hasn't provided for his family from the moment he had them,' Mr Benson said quietly. 'It's Mrs Ellis who puts boots on their feet and food on the table. It's a pity he's back.'

'Back?'

'Two years at Her Majesty's pleasure for receiving stolen goods most recently, and four years before that for some other crime,' Mr Puttock replied. 'I'd keep an eye on your new books, if I were you, in case the Ellis lad takes after his father.'

Jonathan stared at them for a moment before speaking. 'Thank you for enlightening me,' he said, in a controlled tone. 'But I stand by my initial judgement of Mrs Ellis, who it seems has made the best of a difficult situation. She may be young but in my estimation she is a fine example of womanhood ... I mean motherhood,' he added quickly, forcing himself not to shift under Mrs Benson's unremitting stare.

There was a moment's silence and then Mr Overton cleared his throat. 'If there's nothing else it falls upon me to thank Captain

Quinn for his detailed and encouraging report. I call the meeting to a close.'

The vicar turned to talk to Mr Puttock, which gave Jonathan the opportunity to speak to Mrs Benson.

'May I offer to escort you to your carriage?' he asked.

'That is most gentlemanly of you, Captain Quinn,' she said, leaning on her cane and rising to her feet. The top of her head barely reached his shoulder. She adjusted her coat and Jonathan offered her his arm to lead her out of the vestry.

'It's a very long time since I had a handsome man escort me from a church,' she said.

Jonathan laughed. 'I was never that before and I certainly don't qualify now.'

Mrs Benson stopped in her tracks for a moment and held him back with surprising strength. 'That is for another to judge, Captain Quinn.'

'Your pardon,' Jonathan replied, as they began again along the path. 'May I ask you a question, Mrs Benson?'

'As long as it's not my age, you may,' she replied, leaning on his arm.

'At my interview you asked about my recent dealings with children. Why?'

'I wanted to know if you actually liked children. An important qualification for a headmaster, wouldn't you agree?'

Jonathan raised his eyebrows. 'I certainly would.'

'Now come on, young man. Get me to my carriage before this wind takes away what little breath I have.'

A moment later Jonathan was opening the door and helping her inside. She settled in and he placed the rug over her legs.

'Are you free Tuesday next at four o'clock, Captain Quinn?' she asked, as he closed the door.

'I am.'

'Then come to tea. I insist – and am too old to be argued with,' Mrs Benson said, her eyes dancing with amusement.

Jonathan smiled as he closed the door. 'I wouldn't dream of it.'

Joe blew on his hands and rubbed them together, wishing he'd remembered to pick up the knitted gloves his mother had left out for him that morning. He should have been home an hour ago but he didn't care. It was only three weeks until the best day of the year and he had to speak to his father about it.

The local bobby plodded towards Joe at his regulation three miles per hour and looked at him suspiciously but Joe kept his eyes on the faded door of the Old Rose and carried on until he was outside.

Ma would be furious if she found out that he'd gone into a pub alone but what else could he do? Pa hardly ever came to the house and when he did, Ma sent him packing. It wasn't fair. Not after Pa had been away for so long.

Joe pushed open the door and stepped into a fog of tobacco smoke and noise. With his eyes watering, Joe pushed between the drinkers and spotted his father lounging on the bar at the far end of the pub.

'Pa! Pa!'

Freddie looked around. 'Gawd luv us. If it ain't my Joe,' he said to the men surrounding him. He lifted Joe off his feet and sat him on the counter. 'What you doing here, son?'

'I came to find you, Pa,' Joe replied, grinning up at his father.

'See, didn't I tell you my boy was a chip off the old block?' Freddie said to the other men.

'He's a replica of you,' said one.

''E's a lad to be proud of, that's for sure,' said another.

Joe's chest swelled.

'Oi! Conny, fetch my boy a couple of mouthfuls,' Freddie called to the barmaid.

The roly-poly woman behind the bar blew him a kiss and filled a small mug. She handed it to Joe. 'There you go, ducks. That'll put 'airs on your chest.'

Joe peered down into the drink. There was dirty froth floating on the top along with specks of sawdust.

'Knock it back,' Freddie urged.

Joe closed his eyes and forced a mouthful of bitter liquid down.

'Does your ma know you're here?'

Joe shook his head.

'Good.' His father grinned at the men around him. 'See, he's learnt already not to tell a woman his business.'

The men laughed again. Freddie drained the last of his drink. 'Right, I'm off. Come on, Joe. I'll walk you home. I wouldn't want anything to happen to my boy, would I?'

By the time Joe got down from the counter, his father was already halfway to the door. Joe hurried after him and caught up with him outside the pub.

'I like your new suit, Pa,' he said, trying to mimic his father's rolling gait.

Freddie flicked an invisible speck of dirt off his left sleeve. 'It ain't bad, is it?'

'Pa, are you looking forward to Christmas?'

Freddie shrugged. 'I can't say I've given it much thought.'

'But Ma *has* told you we're all at Aunt Mattie's this year?' Joe asked. 'Last year Aunt Josie had a side of beef so big Uncle Pat had to cut it in half to get it on the plate. And there'll be pudding and jelly and custard and this year we're having a tree. With—'

'I don't know I'll be invited,' Freddie cut in.

'But why, Pa—'

'Hasn't your ma told you?' Freddie asked. Joe shook his head. 'Well, I used to work in your aunt Mattie's coal yard but then when your ma took a fancy to me your aunt Mattie turned against me. She told your uncle Pat a pack of lies and he came looking for a fight – but I gave him a right pasting instead. When he heard I was going to marry your ma he had the nerve to tell *me* I wasn't good enough for her.' Freddie's expression turned ugly. 'Him, his sisters and their bunch of sprogs are nothing but Irish tinkers, the lot of them.'

Joe's mind whirled. If Uncle Pat, Aunt Mattie and the rest of the family were Irish tinkers what about ... Joe stopped and looked down at his boots.

His father turned. 'What's up with you?'

'Am I an Irish tinker, too, Pa?'

Freddie scuffed his hand across Joe's head lightly, disturbing his hair. 'Don't be daft. You're my boy. I'll tell you what. Why don't I come to Christmas dinner and then you and me can tell your uncle Pat, aunt Mattie and uncle Nathaniel to fuck themselves?'

Joe laughed uneasily. 'So you'll come?'

'Course I will.'

He stood up and they walked on to the shop. Joe was about to cross the road when he noticed his father had come to a halt.

'Aren't you coming in, Pa?' Joe asked, looking up at his father hopefully.

'Not right now, boy. I have a bit of business to do.' Freddie hunkered down. 'Do you think you could do me a favour?' Joe nodded. 'Pop in and fetch me a couple of bob out of the till?'

'But ... but ...' Joe stammered.

'A shilling or two will do.' Freddie repositioned his hat, shoved his hands in his pockets and leant against the wall.

With his heart like a lump of lead in his chest, Joe crossed the road and slipped through the yard gates. Holding his breath, he crept into the house and down the hall to the parlour. He almost laughed with relief when he saw the room was empty. He dashed through and into the shop. Without pausing, he pulled open the drawer under the counter and grabbed a handful of coins. With his heart thundering in his chest Joe ran back through the house, out of the yard and to his father.

Freddie held out his hand and Joe dropped the money into his palm. Freddie's fingers closed around it and he shoved it in his pocket.

'As I said, a man needs a son to look after his interests.' He peeled himself off the wall.

'When will I see you, Pa?' Joe asked as his father walked away.

'Soon,' Freddie called over his shoulder.

'And you *will* come for Christmas?'

'Of course.'

Joe stared after him for a moment or two then he went back into the house, closing the door behind him.

'Is that you, Joe?' Kate called down the stairs.

'Yes, Ma.'

She came down the stairs and into the parlour. 'I told you to be back hours ago,' she said, looking furiously at him.

'I'm sorry, Ma.'

'You will be for making me worry. I was just about to start searching the streets.' She ran her fingers through his fringe. 'I'll get your supper but next time this happens, young man, you'll be going without it.'

Joe sat up at the table and his mother put a plate of mince and potatoes in front of him. 'Come upstairs when you've done and get ready for bed. Don't ask me if you can play outside – because the answer's no for a week.'

Joe forked up a mouthful of potato. It had been kept warm for so long that it was dry and the mince was crispy but he didn't mind. He didn't mind either that he'd been punished. Nothing troubled him now that he knew Pa was going to be with them for Christmas.

Chapter Nine

Jonathan took a mouthful of tea in an attempt to moisten the cake in his mouth. He looked appreciatively across at Mabel sitting next to her mother on the sofa.

'Delicious,' he said when he finally managed to swallow the last piece.

Mrs Puttock, who was a stouter replica of her daughter, simpered. 'Thank you, but you should be complimenting my darling Mabel. It was she who made the sponge.'

Mabel held up the silver teapot. 'Can I pour you another, Captain Quinn?'

'Please.' Jonathan handed her his cup.

'You have a lovely house, Mrs Puttock,' he said, glancing around at the red flock wallpaper, tassel-fringed drapes and thick lace curtains. 'And such an array of figurines in your display cabinets.'

'Mama is a collector of fine porcelain, along with other novelties.' Mabel indicated the dozen or so stuffed birds captured beneath a crystal dome on the sideboard.

Mrs Puttock gazed up at the framed photograph of her husband standing stiffly beside a potted aspidistra on the mantelshelf. 'I see it as my God-given duty to provide my dear Ernest with a refuge from the cares of the business world. After all, he is our provider and head of the household.'

'Your husband is a fortunate man,' Jonathan said, as Mabel handed him his second cup of tea.

Mrs Puttock patted her daughter's hand. 'And I have taught my dear daughter to follow my example. Have I not, my dear?'

Mabel lowered her eyes and a pretty blush spread across her cheeks. 'Yes, Mama.' She gave him a shy look from under her lashes.

'Well, it's clear by her excellent cake that she is a most apt pupil,' he said, thinking that the green of her gown would suit a fair-haired blonde better than Mabel's darker colouring.

'Would you like another slice?' Mrs Puttock asked.

Jonathan shook his head. 'Thank you, but no. I had a filling lunch.'

'So do you feel settled?' she then asked.

'I think I have my bearings and the measure of the area,' Jonathan replied.

'And what of the school?' asked Mabel.

'I think I have the measure of that, too. Although I fear I have a great deal of work to do to bring its reputation up to the standard it once had,' Jonathan replied.

'I have no doubt you will as I hear nothing but praise about the changes you've put into place,' said Mrs Puttock. 'Although I understand you are now teaching the girls arithmetic. Forgive me for asking, but is that wise?'

'Wise?'

'Well, I understand the female brain isn't designed to cope with such complexities,' she said anxiously.

Jonathan suppressed a smile. 'Let me assure you, Mrs Puttock, it is quite safe. After all, you use arithmetic every day for balancing your accounts, checking the tradesmen's bills or to measure out ingredients.'

Mrs Puttock nodded slowly. 'I do, but multiplication and—'

'Mama, I'm sure Captain Quinn knows what he's doing.'

Mrs Puttock glanced at her daughter then threw her hands in the air. 'Forgive me. Such things are beyond my comprehension.'

Mabel sighed prettily. 'It is such a dear little school and I'm very fond of it.'

Jonathan laughed. 'I'm sure you are. I'm very fond of my old school, too.'

'Oh, no, Captain,' Mrs Puttock cut in. 'Mabel went to Miss Cavendish's School for Young Ladies in Mitre Square, a small, select establishment that caters for girls with Mabel's sensitive nature. And we couldn't risk our dearest child picking up one of those dreadful diseases that the local children seem to be so prone to.'

'Of course,' Jonathan said.

Mrs Puttock took her daughter's hand to her lips. 'God chose to bless us only once but what more could we want,' She looked at him. 'Don't you agree?'

In truth, Mabel was a little slender for Jonathan's taste as he'd always preferred women with curves, like Kate Ellis, but Mabel had been gently brought up, by parents who clearly could deny her nothing. Added to which her undisguised adoration had gone a long way in taking the sting out of Louise's rejection.

Jonathan smiled. 'Indeed, I do.'

The blush returned to Mabel's cheeks.

Mrs Puttock placed her teacup in her saucer. 'I have often thought that had I not needed her at home, my daughter might have made a very good schoolmistress, until she married, of course.'

'I do so love children,' Mabel chipped in.

'I noticed and, if your mother can spare you, I would be most grateful if you could come to the school and help the girls with their samplers,' Jonathan said, smiling warmly at her.

She gave him a shy smile. 'It would be my pleasure.'

Jonathan glanced at the marble and gilt clock on the mantelpiece. 'This has been a most enjoyable visit, Mrs Puttock, but I am afraid I must get back to my duties.'

Mrs Puttock beamed at him. 'The pleasure has been all ours. Hasn't it, Mabel?'

'Yes,' she replied. 'I hope we will be able to entertain you again sometime.'

'Well it should be for me to reciprocate so I wonder, as we've become such friends, if you would like to accompany me to the concert at All Hallows by the Tower next Wednesday the 19th? The choir will be performing Handel's *Messiah* as part of their Christmas season. I hear they are very fine. And I include Mr Puttock in the invitation.'

'I'm afraid my husband is at a Vintners Guild meeting that night, but Mabel and I would be delighted to attend.' Mrs Puttock looked at her daughter, who nodded.

Jonathan stood up. 'Wonderful. I shall collect you at seven.' He smiled. 'And I'm sure we'll have a splendid time.'

Jonathan stared at the dead child lying on an old straw mattress against the wall and a lump formed in his throat. The youngster's mother had combed the boy's hair and dressed him in school clothes ready to receive those who wanted to pay their last respects. This was the third such visit Jonathan had made to a pupil's house in the last two weeks. Three days ago it was Millie Carroll who was carried to an early grave by a winter chill, and then Peter Williams and two of his siblings who died of whooping cough the week before. And now Danny Barber, the tousled-haired seven-year-old who had just mastered long division, was dead after catching lockjaw from playing barefooted on the shoreline.

Beside him stood his parents: Billy, a thick-set man with hands like shovels, and Dolly, a work-worn woman with red-rimmed eyes.

'Let me say again how very sorry I am,' Jonathan said, thinking that sifting through the carnage after a battle was easier than gazing on a dead child.

'Thank you. It was very good of you to come, Captain Quinn. Wasn't it, Dolly?'

'Yes,' she sniffed. 'Very good.'

'When is the funeral?'

'Tomorrow,' Billy replied. 'Just a simple affair. My brother's made a coffin and we shall carry him to the church ourselves.'

Dolly ran her finger down her son's cold cheek. 'It seems odd to see our Danny so still.' She started crying again. 'How many times did I tell him *not* to play in the mud at low tide?'

Billy put his arm around his wife's shoulders. 'Now, now, pet. Looking for the hows and whys of it won't bring him back. It's God's will and we must suffer it.' He pulled a handkerchief from his back pocket and blew his nose loudly.

The lump thickened in Jonathan's throat. 'I'll leave you to tend to your family, Mr Barber.'

Jonathan stepped out to the third-floor landing. The overpowering smell of boiled cabbage and human waste wafted up from below. Number forty Cable Street had once been an elegant house but those days had long gone and now the sounds of the numerous families crowded into the rooms below echoed around him.

He put his hat on and was just about to leave when Kate Ellis appeared at the bottom of the stairwell. She was wearing the same green gown that he'd first seen her in, and a shawl around her shoulders. She was carrying a blackened pot in her apron.

She looked up. 'Captain Quinn,' she said as she stopped in front of him. 'What are you doing here?'

'I came to pay my respects to Mr and Mrs Barber. Danny was a pupil at the school.'

'I know. It's heartbreaking. He was Joe's friend, too. I sat with poor Dolly yesterday while Bill made the arrangements.'

'I'm sure she appreciated that.'

'It's the least I could do. When a child's taken like that there's not a mother in the area who doesn't think it could have been hers.' She shifted the weight of the pot into one arm and crossed herself.

'Let me carry that for you,' he said, taking it from her.

'Be careful, it might be a little greasy, sir,' Kate said, watching the lid brush dangerously close to his expensive jacket.

He smiled. 'Where are you going?'

'To deliver to the Webbs at the top of the house.'

'Then lead the way.'

They climbed the flights of stairs and Kate knocked on the door. 'May I come in?'

'Of course you can, my dear,' a faint voice called back.

Jonathan opened the door for her and they walked in.

The stark, bare room had once been part of the servants' quarters. A small fireplace had been punched out of the main chimney stack and it was the only source of heat.

An old man wearing scruffy trousers and a jacket with frayed cuffs was poking life back into the handful of coal in the grate while an old woman lay under a faded patchwork counterpane pile that could have been mistaken for rags. Mr Webb turned as they entered.

'Kate, it's grand to see you,' he said, as a smile spread across his sunken lips. He looked over her head at Jonathan. 'And who is this fine fella?'

'This is Captain Quinn,' she replied. 'He's St Katharine's head-master.'

Jonathan put the dish on the table.

Mr Webb pulled his worn jacket across his chest and limped towards her. 'So this is the captain you were telling us about last week.'

Kate's eyes flickered to Jonathan. 'I mentioned the changes you've made at the school,' she explained hastily.

Mr Webb looked him over. 'So you fought at Alma?'

'I did,' Jonathan replied, oddly pleased that Kate had mentioned him at all.

'And your father's a colonel in the same regiment.'

Kate's cheeks reddened. 'Mrs Benson happened to mention it in church last week.'

'And now you're helping our lovely Kate by carrying our pot for her,' the old man said, his dark eyes twinkling.

'I was visiting the Barbers downstairs and we met on the landing,' he explained.

Mr Webb shook his head dolefully. 'That poor, poor woman.' He wagged his finger at Kate. 'Make sure your Ella and Joe don't go larking around in the mud.'

Kate shook her head as she unpacked the basket. 'How has Mrs Webb been today?'

'No better. I had to put her to bed a few hours ago. I carried on as best I could but the cold makes the canes so stiff, I only managed a couple.' He nodded towards the sheaves of willow and a small pile of latticed seats. 'Still, mustn't grumble, must we, Duch?' he said, raising his voice and giving his wife a jolly smile. 'Not when we have our pretty Kate to bring our supper.'

Mrs Webb struggled to match her husband's smile. 'Hello, my de—' A fit of coughing wracked her body.

Kate sped over to the table and poured some small beer from the jug into a chipped mug. She perched on the bedside as she gently helped the old woman drink.

'Be-begging yo-your pardon,' Mrs Webb said as her breathing steadied. 'It's the damp. It goes straight to me chest.'

'Say nothing of it,' Kate whispered.

Cupping a bowl of stew in his hands, Mr Webb went to the other side of the bed. 'There you go. This will set you right.' He fed his wife a spoonful then pulled out a square of muslin from his sleeve and wiped away a smear of gravy. Kate slid off the bed. 'I'll leave you to your supper.'

Mrs Webb reached out and scrabbled at the table beside her bed until she caught hold of a twist of paper. She offered it to Kate.

'For your little 'uns. It's only a couple of aniseed sticks,' she said, pressing them into Kate's hand.

'Oh, you shouldn't have,' Kate said.

Mr Webb fumbled in his waistcoat. 'I have a ha'pence somewhere.'

Kate held up her hand. 'And as I tell you each time, put it back in your pocket.'

The old man's face creased into a smile. 'God bless you and keep you, Kate.' He turned to Jonathan. 'I tell you, Captain, she's one in a million, so she is.'

Kate blushed. 'I'll see myself out. Don't let your supper get cold. Is there anything you want from the market tomorrow?'

'A new pair of eyes so I can finish that lot.' He nodded towards the wicker canes again. 'Duch is partial to a lamb's heart, so if you can get one for a ha'penny, I'll have it.'

'I'll see what I can do.'

'Good evening, Mr Webb, and I hope your wife soon feels better,' Jonathan said, walking to the door, which he opened for Kate.

'Won't the parish give them outside relief?' he asked as they reached the second floor.

'They would if Mr Webb asked. But he won't. He's a stubborn old goat.' She smiled fondly. 'But the truth is they'll be lucky to avoid the workhouse for much longer.'

'I'm sorry to hear that,' Jonathan said, opening the door for her and following her down the front steps.

He looked up at the darkening sky. 'It's getting late. Shall I walk you home?'

She shook her head. 'That's very kind of you, sir, but I'm sure you must have lots of things to do and the shop is just around the corner. I'll see you in church on Sunday.'

Jonathan tipped his hat to Kate and watched her walk away.

Kate pressed her forehead to the window and looked at the clock on the wall outside the instrument maker's down the street. Where was Sally? She always arrived at least half an hour before they opened at four and it wasn't like her to be late.

She gave a last glance along the street and then walked back behind the counter and stirred the stew. The pies were already heating in the oven and she'd set the potatoes to boil a little earlier, so other than heating the stew and stacking the bowls ready on the counter she could cope. She'd sent Ella to the market to fetch some sewing needles and thread from the haberdasher's so she could help when she returned but, even so, without Sally it would be a push to manage the teatime rush.

As she reached up to take the dishes down from the shelf the doorbell jingled. Kate glanced over her shoulder as Sally hurried in.

'I'm sorry I'm late, Mrs E,' Sally said as she closed the door behind her.

Kate turned and set the crockery down. 'I was just wondering where you— What's wrong?' she asked as she saw Sally's tear-stained face. 'It's not one of your boys, is it?'

Sally shook her head. 'It's my sister . . .'

She put her hands over her face and started sobbing. Kate came out from behind the counter and put her arms around Sally's shaking shoulders. 'Come, come,' she said, leading her to the table in the corner. 'Let me get you a cuppa and then you can tell me all about it.'

'That's kind of you but I'm already late and I don't want to hold you up further.'

'I've done the spuds and the pies are ready so you're not,' Kate replied, guiding her onto the chair. 'And besides I can't have you sobbing into my stew and making it salty, can I?'

Sally forced a little smile and sank onto the chair. Kate went back to the counter and poured them both a mug of tea from the large enamelled teapot. She spooned in two heaped teaspoons of sugar and took it back to Sally then sat down opposite.

'Now what's the matter with Bette?'

Sally cupped her hand around her drink. 'It's not really Bette, it's that bloody worthless husband of hers. He hasn't been home since Saturday but as he often disappears for a week or so she didn't think anything of it until she heard that he'd been seen boarding a ship in Hermitage Wharf with two heavy carpet bags and a woman on his arm. My Will went down to see what was going on and found that he, and someone listed as his wife, had sailed for New York the day before yesterday. And if that weren't bad enough the rent man came at dinner time and told her that the bastard hadn't paid the rent for two weeks and if she didn't have the money to pay him he was going to evict her and the kids. She didn't so she had to bundle up what she could and get out. She and the three young 'uns pitched up at our house two hours ago.' She pulled out her handkerchief and blew her nose. 'From the first moment I saw him I knew what he was like. I tried to warn her but would she listen? No, she bloody wouldn't and now look where it's landed her.'

Kate felt a twinge of sympathy as she remembered Mattie trying to do the same for her.

'What's going to happen to her and the children?'

'It's a bit of a squash in two rooms, but me mother would come back and haunt me if I let my sister and her kids go to the poor house so she's staying with us. Even though my Will's the night-watchman at the brewery Bette will have to find some work as we can't afford to feed four extra mouths.' Sally covered her face with her hands and sobbed quietly.

Kate studied the top of her head for a moment then spoke. 'I tell you what. I can't offer her more than a shilling a day but why doesn't your Bette come along and do a couple of hours for me?'

Sally looked up. 'That's very kind and I know you mean well, but we couldn't take charity,' she said, pulling herself together.

'And I'm not offering it,' Kate said firmly. 'I've been thinking for a while now I needed someone else in the shop to maybe clear the tables and wash up.' Sally looked dubious. 'Look, I don't need to tell you how we're rushed off our feet most days. See?' She nodded over Sally's head to the men already hanging about outside. 'They're already queuing.'

Sally glanced behind her. 'Well I suppose my Jenny could mind her kids for a couple of hours . . .'

Kate slapped her hand on the table. 'That's settled then. And, as there's no time like the present, bring her along with you tomorrow.' She stood up. 'And now we had better open up before they break the door down,' she said as one of her regulars cupped his hand on the door window and peered in.

Sally rose to her feet. 'Right you are,' she said, wiping her face with her palms.

Kate started towards the counter but Sally caught her arm. 'Thank you, Mrs Ellis,' she said softly.

Kate smiled.

Sally's dark eyes searched her face. 'Why are some men such bastards?' she asked, before going to turn the sign on the door around.

Why indeed, thought Kate, having asked herself the same question at least a hundred times in the last six years. But she'd learnt the hard way and she should keep that in mind next time Captain Quinn smiled at her.

Chapter Ten

When the last strains of the choir faded up to the rafters of All Saints' Church, Jonathan applauded as enthusiastically as the rest of the audience. He looked at Mabel sitting beside him.

Even though her voluptuous frilly pink dress reminded him of his sister's favourite doll, he couldn't deny that she was really rather pretty. She turned and smiled.

'That was wonderful,' Mabel said. 'Such fine singing and the choirboys at the front looked so adorable in their robes.'

'I'm glad you enjoyed it,' Jonathan said, as they rose to their feet. 'It's a pity your mother wasn't able to accompany you.'

'She has an ear for music and will be sad to have missed such a fine performance.'

'I hope she feels better soon,' Jonathan said.

A frown creased Mabel's brow. 'Poor Mama, she is a martyr to sick headaches but I gave her a double dose of her Gentlewomen's Patent Elixir before I left so I expect her to be fully recovered in the morning.'

They slowly made their way towards the door and bade the vicar goodnight. Stepping into the dark, Mabel pulled her fur collar around her ears as the chill December night nipped at them. Although it was nearly nine o'clock the gas lamps lining the street bathed the wintry scene in a mellow glow. Wisps of fog swirled about the legs of the people standing around the coffee and hot chestnut vendors.

As they reached the road Jonathan caught her arm. Mabel turned.

'Thank you for accompanying me this evening,' he said warmly.

'No, thank you for suggesting it,' she replied, her warm breath escaping in little puffs.

'I should call a cab before you get too chilled,' Jonathan said, glancing up and down the road.

Mabel put her hand on his arm. 'I'm not at all cold,' she said. 'Why don't we walk home, as it's not far? We could stroll along the river.'

'I'm happy to as it means I have the pleasure of your company for a little longer, but only if you are sure.'

He held out his arm. She took it and they continued. Jonathan measured his step to keep pace with her. With the granite splendour of the Tower of London to their left they strolled towards the river.

'It was good of your father to allow you to come to the concert without a chaperone,' he said.

'I don't suppose he would if it were anyone else,' Mabel replied, lifting her skirts to avoid a pile of horse manure. 'But he knows you'll make certain I'll come to no harm.'

'Indeed not.' Jonathan put his hand on his chest. 'I swear as an officer and a gentleman I would fight off marauding pirates, defeat heathen tribesman and overpower the Zulu King himself to return you safely home,' he said in a comically solemn tone.

Mabel giggled and then suddenly pointed past him towards the river. 'Oh, what's that? And why are all those people milling around?'

Jonathan looked at the huge three-masted ship illuminated by lamps hung from its rigging, and undulating in the swell of the incoming tide.

'That's the *Agamemnon*,' he replied. 'It the navy's first steam-powered warship. It has just brought troops back from Sebastopol.'

'Can we get closer?' Mabel asked.

'Of course.' Jonathan took her elbow, guiding her through the onlookers towards the road that ran between the river and the fortress's outer wall. He found her a space beside a cannon and then stood behind her.

'I don't think I've ever seen such a large ship,' she said, leaning over the railings.

'Three thousand tons,' Jonathan said, staring across the oily dark-ness of the river. 'I remember the first time I saw her, anchored mid-stream with all guns blazing at Sebastopol. And I was glad to see her too. My bandages had only been removed the day before. It had been cold there, too. Freezing, in fact. I remember how—'

'There's more space over there behind that tree,' Mabel said, standing on tiptoes and craning her neck.

'You might be better to stay here as the pavement looks uneven,' Jonathan replied.

Mabel gathered her skirts around her and started forward. Jon-athan suppressed his irritation and guided her through the press of people to the new vantage point.

Mabel stepped over a protruding root and beckoned him closer. 'This is much better.'

Jonathan followed her into the shadows.

'Look, can you see—'

Mabel screamed and pitched forward. Jonathan caught her and her arms flew around his neck. He set her on her feet and found himself holding her in an altogether too familiar a manner.

'Forgive me,' he said, trying to untangle himself.

Mabel put her hand on her forehead. 'Oh, Captain Quinn, I feel a little ...' she swayed and he caught her around the waist again. She rested her hands on his chest.

'Thank you. I'll be quite well in a few moments,' she said breathlessly, tilting her face up to his.

A prickly sensation crept up his spine. Jonathan looked over Mabel's head at Kate Ellis.

'I'm sorry. I heard a scream. I didn't mean to intrude,' she said, an odd expression on her face.

'Miss Puttock was just trying to find a better vantage point when she tripped,' he said, releasing Mabel and straightening up.

Kate smiled frostily. 'Of course. It was lucky you happened by.'

Mabel smoothed the fringing on her cape. 'Captain Quinn invited me to a choral recital and we have just had a most agreeable few hours together, have we not?' She looked up at him.

'Indeed,' he said, feeling Kate's eyes boring into him. 'Mrs Puttock was supposed to come also, but she's unwell. But what are you doing here, Mrs Ellis?'

'I brought Joe to see the ship,' she replied. 'Since you told the class about how you'd seen it in the Crimea he's been full of it, and seeing the excitement you stirred up in him I wanted to see the warship, too.'

They stared at each other uncomfortably.

Joe ran around the tree carrying a toffee apple. 'Ma, I got the biggest one on the stall.' He saw his headmaster and skidded to a stop. He stood to attention next to his mother.

Kate took her son's hand. 'Well, good evening to you, Captain. Miss Puttock.'

She led Joe away and Jonathan stared after her.

Mabel's voice cut across his thoughts. 'Jim is *such* a sweet boy.'

'Joe,' Jonathan corrected, feeling oddly uncomfortable.

Mabel's eyes narrowed a fraction and then she smiled. 'Of course, and he looks *so* like his father.'

Jonathan pushed Kate Ellis from his mind and offered Mabel his arm again.

'If you've fully recovered, Miss Puttock, perhaps we should continue.' Jonathan smiled at her. 'After all, I wouldn't want your father to think me unable to escort his daughter safely back and deny me your pleasant company on another occasion.'

As the sun disappeared behind the row of shops opposite, Jonathan climbed the white steps to number 83 Cannon Street Road and knocked on the huge imposing black-painted door. He turned and looked around. Mrs Benson's house seemed out of place among the busy shops. Its uncluttered whitewashed façade stood out in marked contrast to its neighbours, most of which had long since ceased to be homes and now had shops on the lower level with dwellings above. The painted placards advertising everything from soap to ship's tack sat like brash newcomers alongside the genteel grey-painted shutters of the upper floors. The door was soon opened and Jonathan was greeted by an aged servant dressed in a dark suit hanging loosely from his narrow shoulders.

'I'm Captain Quinn,' Jonathan said, stepping in. 'I believe Mrs Benson is expecting me.'

'Very good, sir,' the old man replied. He directed Jonathan to the side parlour door. 'Madam will join you shortly,' he wheezed, and left.

Mrs Benson's day room was well proportioned, with high ceilings and classical cornicing. It was decorated in sage-green striped wallpaper that had been the vogue some years before. An elaborate marble fireplace dominated the far wall. Unlike the current fashion of draping cloth over the surface, the crisp edge of the stone shelf was unadorned apart from a selection of china figurines of shepherdesses and dairymaids. Two large portraits hung on either side of the mirror above the fireplace. One was of a sea captain sitting with a small child on his lap and his wife behind him. The central figure, a buff-looking man in a double-breasted frock coat, sat proudly with a scene of tall-rigged merchant ships bobbing on the river as a backdrop.

The other painting was of a young man dressed in the same red jacket Jonathan had once put on each day for twelve years. The background this time was the purple-capped mountains of Kashmir, looking very much as Jonathan remembered them. The officer posed beside a hip-high Doric column with one hand resting lightly on the top and a torn Afghan tribal banner at his feet. He looked proudly out at the world with pale blue eyes similar to those of the child in the other portrait.

The door opened and Mrs Benson walked in, leaning heavily on her ebony cane. She was dressed in a watered-silk lavender gown with lace trimmings and a finely crocheted shawl. Little wisps of white hair had escaped from the cap tied under her chin, clinging to the lace edging like cobwebs to a leaf.

'Tell Jones to serve tea, Willamore,' she instructed her manservant, who bowed and closed the door behind him.

'You'll forgive me for keeping you waiting,' she said, holding out her hand to him. 'I don't move as fast as I used to.'

'Of course.' Jonathan took her hand and the power of her grip again surprised him.

'Please take a seat, Captain Quinn,' she said, settling herself into the chair by the fire.

Jonathan sank into a soft well-worn leather seat opposite and crossed his legs. There was a knock at the door and a woman who must have been as old as the manservant came in carrying a tray. Jonathan watched with trepidation as she tottered across the carpet. He was sure she would tumble over the fringes of the rug but she managed to set the tray on the low table between Jonathan and her mistress with only a small drop of milk escaping the jug.

'Thank you, Jones,' Mrs Benson said, pouring the tea. She handed a cup to Jonathan and picked up the cake knife. 'May I offer you a slice?'

'Please,' Jonathan replied, stirring sugar into his tea.

'This is wonderful,' he said, after swallowing the first mouthful of the buttery cake.

'Thank you. Jones always did have a light touch for such things. Now,' she said, making herself comfortable, 'tell me what you've been doing at St Katharine's that wasn't in the guardians' report. And don't worry' – she gave him a one of her mischievous looks – 'I won't tell tales out of school.'

Jonathan obliged. From the drill in the morning to how he made a point of saying goodbye personally to each child as they left in the afternoon, Jonathan told her of his daily routine.

'My goodness,' she said when he'd finished. 'And the oranges?'

'The navy has citrus as part of their rations and as I don't think even I will get the children to eat lemons or limes, I thought oranges best. Half of one each day should be enough. There was an article in the *Journal of Scientific Enquiry* proposing that fruit of all kinds is of benefit to the growing child.'

Mrs Benson's cup stopped midway to her lips. 'Indeed? And do you read other journals of such a serious nature?'

Jonathan laughed. 'No. But I do take the *Saturday Review, The Times* and *Punch*.'

'*Punch*!' Mrs Benson looked suitably horrified and then she laughed. 'Well, we all like a jolly story.'

The old woman studied him a little longer and then spoke again. 'And what of you, Captain Quinn? Your mother – is she still alive?'

'Sadly not. She died when I was seven.'

'I'm sorry to hear that. And your father is a colonel, I understand.'

'He is. We served the same regiment. There's been a Quinn in the Coldstream Guards since the Merry Monarch's time,' Jonathan said. He gave her a brief resumé of his family, omitting his falling-out with his father and his suspended allowance.

'And is there a special someone who's going to be a Mrs Quinn?'

'I did have hopes that I would be married by now, but it came to nothing and now with this . . .' He touched his eyepatch.

'Don't sell yourself short. I've seen several young women all of a flutter when you appear in church each Sunday. Miss Puttock in particular.'

Jonathan smiled politely. 'I confess I find Miss Puttock delightful.' The memory of Kate Ellis discovering him and Mabel behind the tree threatened to intrude again. Jonathan pushed it aside and stood up. He went over to the pictures above the fireplace. 'I was studying your fine portraits.'

The old woman gripped the arm of her seat and rose to her feet. She came and stood beside him. 'My father,' she said.

'And you on his knee,' Jonathan added.

A soft expression lit her face. 'I was his little darling,' she said, without taking her eyes from the image. 'Of course, he longed to have a son but after twelve infants that were either stillborn or died before their first birthday they had to be content with me. But a son couldn't have got into any more scrapes or stuck in any more trees than I did.'

Jonathan laughed as he tried to imagine the old women whose head barely reached his shoulder scampering among the branches. 'And this must be your son. He looks very much like you,' Jonathan said. 'Is he still in India?'

A pall of sadness settled over her. 'He is,' she replied. 'In the garrison graveyard at Lucknow.' She looked up at the portrait. 'He was my only one.'

'I'm so sorry,' Jonathan said. 'How did he die?'

'Stupidly,' she said, without rancour. 'Christopher had been leading a night patrol and they were ambushed. His men fought bravely and he sent a messenger back to the main patrol warning them there were rebels about. He pursued the tribesmen but lost the trail so they headed back. There had been a nasty incident a month before when a supply column had come under fire so the sentries, all young men, many of them fresh from training, were naturally on edge. When Christopher's patrol rode up the hillside in the half light of dawn, the guards thought it was rebels and opened fire.' Mrs Benson stretched out and rested her white wrinkled fingers on the bottom of the gilt frame and looked up. 'Thankfully, only one of the bullets found a target. Unfortunately, it was Christopher. His commander wrote that he was shot in the heart and died instantly.'

'I am sure that was so,' Jonathan replied, thinking how many times he'd written the same thing, regardless of the truth.

She gave him a tight smile. 'The Lord giveth and the Lord taketh away.' She looked back at her son's portrait. 'We had this painted the last time he was home on leave. It's very like him. I'm grateful that his father didn't live to hear the news. Gerald died in January 1838 and I received the letter from Christopher's commander on the seventh of March.' Her gaze flickered on to his eyepatch. 'Just one bullet.'

'I'm so sorry,' Jonathan said again.

Grief briefly cut across Mrs Benson's lined face and then she smiled up at him. 'I've enjoyed our talk, Captain. I hope you will come again. In fact, I would have invited you to join me for Christmas dinner but I expect you'll be spending the festivities with your family. I'll have to be content with entertaining you when you return.' She tilted her head. 'You know, you are much broader than Christopher, and darker, but you remind me of him in some ways. Perhaps it's the military bearing. I would have loved to see you in your uniform ... I'm sure Miss Puttock would have, too.'

Chapter Eleven

Jonathan stood between the boys' and girls' doorways and cast his gaze over the small walled playground at the side of the school. The thirty or so children stood in four rows with their hands behind their backs, looking ahead.

'Good morning, children,' he shouted, his warm breath turning to mist in the cold morning air.

'Good morning, sir,' thirty-four young voices shouted back.

'And a fine morning it is too, is it not, Miss Wainwright?' he asked the girls' schoolmistress who stood on his right.

Miss Wainwright gave him a girly smile. 'Yes indeed, Mr Quinn.'

'But cold,' Jonathan said, rubbing his hands together in an exaggerated manner. A couple of the children giggled. 'Right then, let's get warmed up and blow those cobwebs from our brains before we start the day. School! Quick march!' The boy at the head of the first column peeled off, followed by his classmates. 'Left right, left right,' called Jonathan. 'Let's warm ourselves up.' Boots crunched over the beaten earth. 'Pick up your feet, Walters,' he shouted at the young boy scraping his toecaps at the end of the line. 'The girls are marching better than you.'

Jonathan marched them around twice more then raised his hand. They stopped, re-formed their original lines and stood at ease with their hands behind their backs.

'That is a vast improvement on last week's drill,' he told them. The group of children stood a little taller.

'Miss Wainwright. Ladies first. Will you lead the girls in?'

'Certainly, Mr Quinn,' she replied, batting her almost invisible eyelashes at him.

The line of girls stood to attention and followed their teacher in an orderly fashion into the school.

Jonathan cast a sharp eye over the boys. They stood rigid under his inspection. He suppressed a smile. They wouldn't have passed muster on a parade ground but four weeks of morning drill was starting to bring the pupils of St Katharine's into line. Well, in the playground, at least; the other areas of the school would take considerably longer.

'Company!' he bellowed over the frosty schoolyard. He remembered how many times he'd called men to order on the parade ground, and to face the enemy with the word. 'Follow on. And no dawdling.'

The line of boys marched into the school with Jonathan bringing up the rear.

By the time Jonathan took up his position in front of them and picked up the school Bible, the children were already sitting in the rows of old rough-hewn benches.

'Today's lesson is from St Luke's Gospel, chapter eight, starting at verse five. "A sower went out to sow his seed ..."' Sitting with their backs ramrod straight the children listened attentively as Jonathan read the parable of the sower. 'He that hath ears to hear, let him hear,' he concluded closing the heavy book with a thump. He cast his gaze over the upturned faces. 'And remember to keep your ears open throughout your lessons today. Now let us pray.'

The large hand of the school clock in the far wall hit the VI at the bottom of the dial as Amen echoed around the room for the last time and the boys appointed to close the partition sprang into action.

Jonathan went to the blackboard to chalk up the first lesson. 'Potter and Lamb, please give out the slates,' he said to the monitors. 'And Logan ...' A lad sprawled across a desk at the back row looked up. 'Down here where Mr Rudd can see you.' He pointed at the vacant seat in the front row then finished writing the neat row of words.

He turned and addressed the class. 'The first lesson today is reading. For those of you who are paying attention' – he glared at two boys in the middle row elbowing each other who stopped immediately – 'I have written this week's words clearly on the board.' He tapped the chalk on the first line. 'The under-eights must learn the first three rows and any of the rows after if they can. The rest of you must master all thirty words for the test on Friday. I am leaving Mr Rudd to supervise you as I have matters that require my attention.'

He signalled to Mr Rudd, 'If you please, Mr Rudd.'

The young man picked up the pointer and tapped the board. 'D-o-g dog.'

'D-o-g dog,' repeated the class.

Jonathan left them to it and returned to his office. Mrs Delaney had already brought his morning coffee across and it sat in its usual place beside the inkwell with the saucer on top to keep it warm.

He took up the bookseller's catalogue and sat behind his desk. Taking a new sheet of paper he opened it on the page he'd dog-eared the day before and wrote his order.

Three dozen each of Vere Foster copy books and *Merry Multiplication*. Two copies of *Busy Hour A B C* for the younger children. An illustrated copy of *Child's Companion and Juvenile Instructor* for Miss Wainwright to read to the girls and *The Swiss Family Robinson*, with a map of the island, for the boys. He added two dozen slates and scribers to the list to replace the broken ones and then two quires of best writing paper with matching envelopes and a quart of best Indian ink for his own use.

He looked it over and totted up the cost. Seventeen shilling and ninepence! No doubt the guardians would have something to say about that, especially when they also saw the order he placed with the Society for the Propagation of Christian Knowledge for new Bibles; but no matter. They had appointed him to raise the standard and bring the school around and that was exactly what he was going to do.

He rolled the blotter across the sheet a couple of times then folded it and slid it into an envelope. He scribbled on the address and then reached for his coffee. He took a sip and pulled a face.

Perhaps he should send Mrs Delaney to Kate's Kitchen so Mrs Ellis could teach her how to make proper coffee. An image of Kate Ellis staring at him with Miss Puttock in his arms flashed into his mind once more. He shoved it away. Why should it niggle him that it was Kate Ellis who had found them together? He dismissed it. After all, it wasn't as if it mattered that Kate Ellis came upon him and Mabel in the shrubbery.

He picked up the letter and glanced out of the window. As the Royal Mail hadn't yet installed letter boxes anywhere in the area, Miss Wainwright usually posted any letter on her way home in the main office on Mile End Road. But as it was a pleasant afternoon for a stroll, perhaps he'd do it himself.

Kate plopped the last of the potatoes into the saucepan and scooped the peelings into the pail ready for the pig man to collect.

'You can go when you've finished, Bette,' Kate called across to the woman scrubbing the tables. 'And there's a bit of bread pudding left you can take with you.'

'I'm right thankful to you, Mrs E,' Bette replied, pausing for a moment and looking up.

Kate moved to fill the kettle and the doorbell jingled. She turned as Captain Quinn ducked his head and strode into the shop. He spotted her behind the counter and smiled. Before she could stop it, her heart did a little double step.

'Good afternoon, sir,' she said, trying to dispel the image of Mabel Puttock in his arms that seemed permanently lodged in her brain. 'Can I get you your usual?'

He removed his hat and ran his fingers through his hair. 'Please.'

He took a stool on the other side of the counter and smiled again. Kate busied herself with the percolator.

'Lovely day, isn't it?' he said.

'Yes it is,' she replied, not looking around.

'Miss Wainwright told me Ella did very well in her spelling test today.'

'Did she?'

'And I commend Joe on his drill.'

'I'm pleased to hear that.' Kate closed her eyes for a couple of seconds and turned. 'There you go, sir,' she said, brightly. 'One coffee; strong and sweet.'

He drew in a deep breath over the steaming cup and then took a sip. 'Marvellous, as always.' He swallowed another mouthful. 'Did the *Agamemnon* match up to Joe's expectations?'

'He talks of nothing else,' Kate replied. 'Did Miss Puttock enjoy her evening?'

'Yes, very much.'

'I'm pleased to hear it,' Kate said chirpily. 'She's a charming young woman.'

'Yes she is.' There was an awkward silence then Captain Quinn forced a laugh. 'I have to confess I was surprised to see you down by the river that evening.'

Kate didn't answer.

He laughed again. 'I suppose finding me and Miss Puttock behind the tree, it could have looked a little—'

'Fishy?'

His cup stopped halfway to his mouth and he frowned. 'I was going to say odd.'

Kate wiped the counter she'd cleaned only a moment before. 'I'm sure it's no business of mine what you were doing in the bushes with Miss Puttock.'

'I wasn't doing *anything* in the bushes with Miss Puttock. As

I explained quite clearly at the time, she fell and I caught her. It was all quite innocent.'

'Of course.'

'No, really,' he protested. 'I warned her the area was uneven but she wanted to get a better view of the ship and tripped.'

'So you say. But don't worry,' Kate said, trying not to thinking of them entwined together, 'I'm no gossip. I won't mention it to anyone.'

Captain Quinn looked very annoyed. 'I don't care if you tell the whole parish, Mrs Ellis, because there is *nothing* to tell. I only mention it because I'm here and I wouldn't want you to get the wrong impression of the situation, or me, for that matter.'

'Of course.' Kate forced a smile. 'I'm sure you wouldn't act improperly towards a young lady like Miss Puttock.'

'I certainly would not.' He finished his coffee. 'Well, I ought to head back to the school so I can't dawdle but I'm glad we cleared up that little misunderstanding. Good day, Mrs Ellis.'

'And good day to you too, sir,' Kate replied, wiping the surface for the third time.

He studied her for a moment then put on his hat and left.

Kate stared after him. It was none of her business what Captain Quinn was doing with Miss Puttock in the shadows. Besides which, Miss Puttock was a very nice young woman, if a little bossy and overbearing. Why wouldn't he set his sights on her with her refined ways and dowry? And anyhow, why should it matter to her? Even if she were free, she didn't imagine for one moment that someone from Captain Quinn's background would look twice at the likes of her. And she shouldn't let her foolish mind imagine that he called into Kate's Kitchen for anything more than a good cup of coffee.

But as much as she knew the truth of it, as she watched him march down the street, a grey cloud of unhappiness settled on her shoulders.

Chapter Twelve

Kate spooned up the last chunk of suet pudding and popped it in her mouth, enjoying the sharp taste of the plums as they mingled with sweet eggy custard. She looked around the table at her family. Well, 'table' was pushing it – the Nolan family were eating their Christmas dinner off a door propped up by Mattie's dining table at one end and a barrel at the other. It wasn't ideal, as the barrel was fractionally lower than the table so when someone leant on it everyone had to grab hold to stop it tipping. But to Kate's mind, with a sheet thrown over, it was grand as any.

Presiding over the table sat her brother-in-law, Nathaniel, dressed in his best suit with Mattie to his right. To his left sat Sarah, Kate's mother, wearing a new dress and her feather-like white hair drawn back under a small lawn cap and a shawl around her shoulders. She lived with Patrick and Josie and, despite gnarled knuckles and swollen knees, insisted on doing the family's washing and helping with the children. Beside her were Mattie and Nathaniel's four children: ten-year-old Brian, Beth, who was the same age as Ella, five-year-old Bertie, Joe's partner in crime, and baby Catherine, who was having an afternoon sleep on the sofa.

At the other end of the table sat Patrick, also in his Sunday best with Josie and their four children on his left. They had been blessed with Annie, a dark, slender sixteen-year-old; Mickey who at fourteen was so like his father he could have been his twin; Rob, an inquisitive ten-year-old; and Nell, a chirpy seven-year-old.

The table took up most of the floor space in the parlour and so it was a devil of a squash to get everyone around. Mattie had gathered all the chairs in the house but even so the boys were sitting on upended crates.

The magnificent feast that Kate, Mattie and Josie had spent all morning peeling, roasting and boiling had been totally demolished. Patrick had carved the joint of beef to its bones, the three tureens that had been piled high with roasted potatoes, cabbage and carrots were empty, as was the large jug with rivulets of gravy clinging to its sides. A few crumbs were all that remained of the plum duff.

Kate glanced at her son beside her, doggedly chopping his pudding with the edge of his spoon.

'Are you having a nice time?' she asked.

'Yes, Ma,' he replied, glancing at her and then returning to his task.

'We'll be opening the presents soon,' she continued encouragingly. 'What do you think you might get?'

He shrugged but didn't look up.

Patrick put his spoon in his bowl and leant back. 'I don't think I could eat another mouthful.'

Nathaniel wiped his mouth with his napkin. 'Me neither, but I could do with a top-up.' He held up his empty tankard.

'I'll join you,' Patrick said, rising to his feet and squeezing his way around the back to the keg of beer. He caught his two daughters, Annie and Nell, around the waist and tickled them as they tried to push him off.

Joe laughed along with everyone else but it seemed a little forced as his eyes followed his uncle's every movement.

'Give us a Christmas kiss and I'll let you go,' Patrick said. The girls gave him a peck on either cheek and he released them.

He picked up a spare tankard and filled it to the brim. 'There you go,' he said, handing it to his son Mickey. 'That'll put hairs on your chest. And you, Rob,' he nodded at his other son, 'can have a small one.'

'Can I have a small one, too, Pa?' Brian asked, looking pleadingly up at his father.

'I don't see why not, son,' Nathaniel replied. 'But don't gulp it or you'll go dizzy.'

Patrick filled another half tankard and passed it along the table to his nephew. 'I'll tell you, Nat, these lads of ours will be standing their rounds in the Town before we know it.'

Everyone laughed again but Joe looked down at his empty pudding bowl.

'Should we clear away?' Kate asked, stacking her bowl with Joe and Ella's.

Mattie nodded. 'And while we put the dishes to soak, the men can move the table.'

The family squeezed themselves out from behind the improvised table and the women and girls collected up the plates and cutlery. Nathaniel and Patrick took the door and crates into the garden and then the whole family returned to the parlour. The younger children sat on the rug in front of the tree, nudging and laughing as they tried to guess what they might get. The older girls sat side by side on the sofa and arranged their skirts while their brothers stood with their tankards and warmed the backs of their legs as their fathers often did.

Kate took the chair beside Sarah, who took her hand and patted it. 'I'm glad you and the young 'uns could come,' she said. 'After Mattie told me about the run-in with *him*, I thought he might try and stop you.'

'To be sure, Ma, wild horses couldn't keep me away,' Kate replied, leaning over and kissing her mother's wrinkled cheeks.

Her mother caught her in a tight, shaky embrace. 'When I think of your father, God rest his soul, and what a good and loving man he was, it fair breaks my heart to know you're tied to that pig. If only we'd known.' She released Kate and there were tears in her old eyes.

'Hush, Ma,' Kate said, giving her mother what she hoped was a reassuring smile.

Sarah pulled out her old worn rosary from beneath her clothes and kissed the crucifix. 'May sweet Mary forgive me but I pray every day for him to fall in the river.'

'Honestly, Ma!' Kate said, remembering her constant battle not to wish the same.

Sarah kissed the crucifix again. 'Mary, hear my prayer. And then send Kate a man to love her as he should.'

An image of Captain Quinn dressed in the sharply fitting suit he'd been wearing at church the week before flashed briefly into Kate's mind. *I wonder where he is spending Christmas day*, she thought.

Josie's voice cut through her thoughts. 'Can I join you?' she asked, pulling up a chair next to her mother-in-law. 'Your Joe's a bit quiet,' Josie said. 'He's not sickening for anything, is he?'

Kate forced a smile. 'No. He's just a bit overwhelmed by it all, I think.'

'Right, everyone,' Nathaniel shouted over the chatter. 'It's time to give out the presents, and my lovely wife, Mattie,' he held out his hand and she joined him by the tree, 'the apple of my eye,' there was a chorus of ohs and ahs, 'and the thorn in my side,' he said, earning himself a thump, 'will do the honours.'

Everyone clapped and the children shuffled expectantly. Mattie removed the little parcels from the tree and handed them out to the children. There were squeals of delight as the girls unwrapped lace collars, fine knitted stockings and coloured ribbons. The younger boys shouted approval as they tore the paper off wooden trains and soldiers. Patrick gave Mickey a new sailor's knife with a ten-inch blade while Annie was given a lace petticoat and kid gloves.

Annie thanked Kate for the yard of lace and Mickey said the socks she'd knitted him would keep his feet warm on the barge. Beth gave her a kiss for the hair ribbons and prompted by their mothers, Brian and Rob remembered to thank her for their sets of brass sailor buttons. Josie then gave out the adults' presents and after everyone had thanked everyone else for their gifts, Nathaniel clapped his hands.

'Now,' he said. 'I have a little something else, Pat, especially for you and me.' He pulled two sprigs of mistletoe out from behind his back. 'And I thought before we start the games we could put it to good use.'

Patrick laughed and took the twig from his brother-in-law then dodged through the children to Josie. She giggled as her husband held the branch over them and planted a kiss on her mouth. Ella and Beth put their hands over their mouths and giggled while Rob and Brian hooted and rolled their eyes.

'Now you, woman,' Nathaniel said, catching Mattie around her expanding waist.

He kissed her on the lips and then nuzzled her neck as their children jumped up and down and clapped. Mickey curled two fingers in his mouth and let out a shrill, two-note whistle.

'Oh, my word,' Sarah laughed and wiped her eyes.

Kate smiled and clapped her hands, then caught the look on her son's face. He was sitting alone, cross-legged on the rug with his new toy soldier resting on his knee. The light from above caught the hint of moisture in his saucer-wide eyes and his lower lip trembled as he watched his uncles and aunts kiss and cuddle.

A lump caught in Kate's throat and tears pinched the corners of her eyes as he looked across at her.

Jonathan counted the tick-tock of the clock and wondered if it was too late to walk to the Peahen and book a room for the night. Of course he wouldn't, for his sister Barbara's sake, but even her grand five-bedroom house at the St Peter's end of St Albans High Street was beginning to feel quite small with his father under the same roof.

'Would you like a piece, Jonathan?' Barbara pointed at the fruit cake with the silver server.

She was sitting between Jonathan and their father in the drawing room.

'If I may,' he replied.

'And for you, Papa?'

Colonel Quinn gave a curt nod without looking up from the roaring fire in the grate.

'Was Edmund any better when you took him his tea?' Jonathan asked.

She nodded. 'He is cooler to the touch. He hopes to join us again tomorrow.'

'Bah!' said his father. 'I marched for three days in a monsoon carrying a full pack and dodging natives' arrows when I was Edmund's age. He must have some weakness of the chest if he takes a chill after a light shower.'

'A light shower!' Barbara said. 'Edmund was drenched to the skin by the time you brought him back. It isn't a weak chest to blame for his fever but you for making him traipse around the countryside all afternoon.'

'We were *shooting*.'

'But in such weather! Why couldn't you have played chess or billiards or something?'

The colonel's gaze flickered on to Jonathan. 'I had need of some air.'

'I'm sure Edmund will be his old self by tomorrow, Barbara,' Jonathan said. 'He has to be as I have to redeem my honour after he beat me at chess the other day.'

'Honour,' grumbled their father.

'Father!' Barbara said, looking angrily at him.

He muttered something incomprehensible in reply.

Jonathan counted backwards slowly then turned to his sister. 'Will the children be down soon?'

'I've told Nurse to bring them after their tea,' Barbara replied.

'I can't believe how much Eddy has grown, nor how much he is like his father.'

'Now he is seven, Edmund has started looking at suitable schools for him. And of course Isaac is six in February,' she said, glowing with motherly pride.

'They are lively lads – full of energy. They all but ran me breathless playing ball with them yesterday,' Jonathan said.

Barbara laughed. 'I would have thought you were used to it now you have fifty children in your charge.'

'You must stay with me in the summer and we can take them to the zoological gardens,' Jonathan said.

'I'm sure they would enjoy that, and seeing you more often.'

Jonathan drank the rest of his tea and Barbara added hot water to the teapot.

'Will you be joining the hunt tomorrow, Father?' she asked.

The colonel looked around. 'Naturally! The Quinns have joined the St Stephen's day hunt for decades.' He glared at Jonathan. 'It's a family tradition. And *I'm* not one to throw over convention for a selfish whim.'

The fire crackled and the logs shifted as the silence hung in the air. Jonathan made a play of finishing his tea and carefully placed the cup back in the centre of the saucer.

'I must say, Barbara, I like the way you've decorated the room,' he said, indicating the dark red flowered wallpaper and heavy chenille, tasselled drapes. 'I'm afraid my current living quarters are very plain by comparison.'

'All it needs is a woman's t—'

'I hear Louise Davenport has become engaged to Major Cruickshank,' their father cut in.

'Yes, Captain Braithwaite told me the news in his last letter,' Jonathan replied evenly.

The news of Louise's engagement didn't sting Jonathan as much as it might have done a month or two back. Annoyingly that wasn't because of his growing friendship with Mabel Puttock but because he seemed to have developed a ridiculous fixation on Kate Ellis, fired, no doubt, by his bachelor lifestyle.

The colonel snorted. 'I'll wager his family are cock-a-hoop that young Willy's caught himself an heiress.'

'I'm sure they are,' Jonathan said. 'I wrote to Louise sending her and her fiancé my best wishes.'

His father's face mottled. 'Did you? Did you indeed!' He stood up and jabbed his finger at Jonathan. 'She would never have looked twice at old Twister Cruickshank's chinless son if you'd done your duty and ripped up that resignation letter as I told you to.' He clasped his hands behind him and turned to warm the back of his legs on the fire. 'You might think you're admired for your principles but I'll tell you this: there's not one person in the regiment, not one, who would regard Miss Davenport wrong to have broken the engagement. After all, what well-brought-up young woman would give up a comfortable life as a regimental wife to bury herself in some raggedy-arse school?'

'Father! Please,' Barbara remonstrated.

The colonel waved her objection away impatiently. 'All right, all right. But I speak as I find. So he sustained a wound—'

'Jonathan almost *died*, Father,' Barbara cut in.

'—and lost a couple of men. Who hasn't? It is the soldier's lot. Is that sufficient reason to dishonour the family's name or force me to suffer the pitying looks and condemnation of my fellow officers?'

Jonathan leapt to his feet. 'And I didn't let men in my command be led to slaughter because my commanding officer was too short-sighted to see the Russian guns on the ridge when he ordered the attack.' He stepped forward until his nose was within a few inches of his father's. 'What you describe as speaking as you find is in fact being opinionated, rude and boorish. Furthermore, if Louise Davenport's prerequisites for a husband are solely that he provides her with a social position and a luxurious living, then I am heartily thankful she is marrying Major Cruickshank!'

Jonathan glared at his father for a moment then strode to the window and stared blindly out at the frosted garden.

'This is *supposed* to be the season of goodwill,' Barbara said sharply. 'So for my sake and in *our* house, can you *please* try to observe it.'

Jonathan remained unmoved for a second or two longer then he returned to his seat. 'I'm sorry, Barbara.'

She looked pointedly at her father. For a moment the old man remained unbending and then with a grumbled oath flicked up his coat-tails and sat down again.

Barbara refilled their cups. 'There,' she said, picking up her own tea. 'Now we've all remembered this is the day when the peace of the Lord came to dwell among us, perhaps we can have some of it here.'

Joe wedged his feet against Bertie's rear and pushed for the third time in an effort to reclaim his share of the bed. Despite their protests, he and his cousin had been sent up to bed half an hour ago and had spent the time since trying to come to some agreement about how much room each should have.

Bertie turned over and elbowed him in the ribs. 'Stop shoving.'

Joe grabbed his pillow and swiped it at his cousin. 'Gis' some room then.'

His cousin retaliated, sending a couple of feathers fluttering above them as his pillow thumped into Joe's back. He scrambled to his feet and so did Bertie.

'You're too fat,' Joe shouted, thumping his cousin on the side of the head.

'And you ... you ... smell,' Bertie yelled, as he whacked Joe's shoulders.

The iron bed bars twanged and bonged as Joe and Bertie bounced on the mattress. Joe swung at Bertie. He teetered on the edge of the bed, winding his arms like a windmill before disappearing over the edge. Joe jumped after him and they wrestled across the floor.

Heavy footsteps clumped up the stairs. The boys sprang to their feet, grabbed their pillows from the floor and scrambled back into bed. They had just pulled the covers tight under their chins when the door clicked open and Uncle Pat strode into the room.

'Have you boys been larking about up here?' he asked, standing at the end of the bed and glaring at them.

'No, Uncle Pat,' they replied in unison.

'Well, what's all the noise then?'

'Joe had to use the gazunder and fell over,' Bertie replied.

Joe kicked him under the cover and Bertie kicked him back.

Uncle Pat's lips moved back and forth under his full moustache. 'All right then, but let's have no more of it. Do you hear?'

'Yes, Uncle Pat.'

Patrick walked back to the door and closed it behind him.

Joe and Bertie covered their mouths and giggled. A piano tinkled out the opening bars of a tune and Uncle Pat's deep voice picked up the refrain in the room below. Joe's eyes started to flicker closed.

'What did you like best: the cake or the plum pudding?' Bertie asked.

'Plum pudding, because it had custard.'

'Me, too.' Bertie grabbed his brightly coloured train that Aunt Josie had given him and tucked it under his arm. 'I think this is my best present *ever*.'

Joe reached under the long bolster and pulled out the sailing ship that Bertie's parents had bought for him. 'This is mine,' he announced, holding it up.

Bertie yawned. 'I wish it could be Christmas every day. Don't you, Joe?'

'Yes, it would be grand,' Joe replied.

Bertie answered with a faint snore. Joe looked at his cousin's open-mouthed silhouette then shoved him over with his hip. This time

Bertie didn't murmur. Joe punched his pillow and snuggled down.

The bed on the other side of the room was empty, waiting for the older boys who were still downstairs with their parents. Ella and the girls, Beth and baby Catherine had been tucked in to bed across the hall in the spare room, and Annie would have to squeeze in somewhere later on. Gran, Ma and Josie would sleep in Aunt Mattie's room at the back of the house while Uncle Pat and Uncle Nathaniel would make do with the sofas in the parlour. It was the same thing every year for as long as Joe could remember. The whole family eating too much, teasing each other and having the best time. Well, not the whole family. Pa should have been here.

Joe pulled his ship out from under the covers and held it up. He imagined his father sailing around the world like Uncle Pat had. Tears pinched the corners of his eyes but he bit his lip to stop them forming.

Why wasn't he here? When he asked Ma where Pa was she said he was working. Joe knew she was lying because her neck went red and Gran crossed herself. He also saw the look that passed between Uncle Pat and Aunt Mattie. Pa had said that Ma's family had a grudge against him but as he was always larking around, Joe hadn't taken much notice. But now he'd seen the way they all looked away when Pa's name was mentioned, he knew it to be true. But why?

It couldn't be Pa's fault – so it must be Ma's. She was never pleased to see him and always made him leave. And even he knew that wasn't right. Yes, it *was* her fault Pa wasn't here. Anger replaced his sadness.

'Don't worry, Pa,' Joe whispered. 'I'm *your* boy. And I don't care what Ma says. Now that you're home, I'm going to spend every Christmas with you for ever.'

Freddie rolled off Aggie and lay staring up at the ceiling with a satisfied smile across his face. Outside in the road the drunks sang and shouted good-naturedly. He scratched under his arm then pulled up his trousers to cover his essentials.

He raised himself up a little against the headboard and studied the pile of goods in the corner that he and Stefan had lifted from the draper's in Bishopsgate. Aggie shifted in the bed beside him and stroked her hand down his bare chest. She got herself on to one elbow, brushed the hair off her face and smiled down at him.

'Oh, Freddie,' she whispered, twirling the hair on his chest with her finger. 'You do know how to make a girl 'appy.'

'So I've heard tell.'

She kissed his chin. 'You were so late coming back I thought you'd forgotten all about me,' she said in a little-girly voice as her fingers inched downwards.

'How could I do that? And I told you where I was,' Freddie replied, nodding over at the dozen or so bales of silk and lace piled in the corner.

'I know, but ...' Her bottom lip jutted out. 'I thought as it was Christmas you might go home.'

'Go home! What, to watch a bunch of Micks scoffing beef and pudding? I'd rather hammer a nail through me foot. And besides ...' He reached out and fondled her breast. 'I wouldn't be getting this at home.'

Aggie giggled and snuggled into him. He had intended to drop home that morning, not for Kate or that cheeky girl of hers but to see his lad. Perhaps give him a penny or two. A warm feeling of contentment stole over Freddie as he thought of Joe. His boy. Despite Kate's fussing, he was shaping up to be a useful little chap. Sharp, too. Anyone could see that. His Joe would show them in that soft school what a bright spark he was. He shouldn't wonder if he didn't outshine them all and win himself some prize or something for being extra clever.

'Freddie ...?'

'Mmm.'

'What's your wife like?'

'What do you mean?'

'Is she blonde or dark?' Aggie asked, twisting out from under his arm and kneeling beside him.

'She's got sort of pale hair,' Freddie replied.

'And is she fat or slender like me?' Aggie asked, putting her hand on her hips and swaying from side to side.

Freddie's eyes flickered down to where the thin sheet was only just covering her breasts. 'She's a bit on the plump side.'

Aggie's expression lightened. 'But is she pretty?'

'She's all right.'

Her bottom lip began to tremble again. 'You think she's prettier than me?'

'I didn't say that.' Freddie tried to catch her but she wriggled away, the sheet slipping down to her navel. He tried to grab her arm.

'I bet you're thinking of her all the time when you're with me,' she wailed, as the rest of the sheet fell away.

Freddie lunged for her and caught her around the waist, pulling her back. She struggled against him, her breasts bouncing on to his chest as she did.

'Don't be daft.'

'You ... you tell me I'm your best gal ...' she sniffed, pressing herself against him.

'And so you are.' Freddie tilted her head up to face him.

Aggie's eyes shimmered with tears. 'Am I, Freddie?'

'Course,' he replied.

'I'm glad to hear you say that,' she said, breathlessly. 'I see the way that women look at you – like that slut Mary in the bar and the others who hang around in the Boy.'

Freddie leant back again and spread his arms along the headboard. 'Do you?' he replied, thinking of all the trollops who sent him inviting glances. Aggie was lucky he spotted her first.

'I know you'd only have to click your fingers to have the pick of them so I shouldn't tell you this but ...' She traced her finger around his navel and then down towards the open front of his trousers. 'I think I have lost my heart to you, Freddie Ellis.'

Freddie puffed out his chest as he basked in her adoration. 'Is that so?'

She nodded.

'Well, then get me another drink,' he said, slapping her bare bottom.

'All right but can we ...' Her eyes flickered onto his unbuttoned flies.

Freddie grinned. 'As soon as I've wet my whistle.'

Aggie scrambled off the bed and Freddie tucked his hands behind his head to study her as she walked naked across the room.

He didn't blame her for worrying. He'd always had a way about him with women. It was only sensible to keep a woman on her toes but if he were to tell the truth, he was more than a bit fond of Aggie. And did she have some tricks under the covers! Giving him an unexpected view of her rear, she bent down and picked up the half-empty bottle of brandy.

'Stay right there,' Freddie said.

Aggie looked around. 'Oh, Freddie, you've got some sauce!' She screamed then grabbed the loose end from a bale of silk. 'The things you ask me to do,' she laughed, wrapping herself with the fabric.

Freddie sat bolt upright and got off the bed. 'Leave the gear, Aggie.'

'But it's so lovely,' Aggie said, smoothing the shimmering fabric around her and gliding around on the dirty floor.

She swung around and brandy shot out of the bottle in her hand and splashed in a dark red stain across the silk. Freddie caught hold of the fabric to pull it from her but Aggie laughed and tugged at the other end.

'Don't I look like some duchess or something?' she asked, swirling around and crushing the costly material under her feet. It tangled around her ankles and she staggered back, knocking another bale of ivory-coloured lace onto the floor.

Freddie yanked the fabric from her. 'I said, leave it.'

Aggie stopped dancing. 'I was just having a lark. It is Christmas, after all,' she said, her lower lip jutting out once more.

Freddie picked up the cloth. 'You won't be having a lark when Mr Mac wants to know who ruined his stash,' he said rerolling the crumpled silk as best he could.

Aggie flicked the unravelled lace with her foot. 'Tell him it fell off the wagon.'

'I'll let you tell him yourself,' Freddie replied, trying not to think of Ollie Mac's expression if he turned up with half the haul covered in grease and dirt.

Aggie's eyes narrowed for a moment then she threw herself on him, winding her arms around his neck and pressing her body onto him. 'Oh, Freddie, don't be riled with me. It was only a bit of fun.'

'Perhaps,' he replied, trying to ignore her bare flesh and hold his stern expression.

'Say you'll forgive your little Aggie.'

Freddie swallowed. 'Well, all right, but you know as well as me that it don't pay to get on the wrong side of Mr Mac. So don't let me have to tell you again.'

'No, Freddie,' Aggie replied, looking suitably contrite.

'Good, because—'

'But I don't see why he has all the say.'

'He's the boss.'

'For now,' she replied.

'What do you mean?'

'The minute I set my eyes on you I said to myself, Aggie, there's a man who don't take no truck from anyone. I knew you were set to be top man when the old dog steps down.'

A worried look spread across Freddie's face. 'Leave it out, Aggie.'

She nudged him playfully in the ribs. 'I'm just saying, you've got brains and guts aplenty and I can see the way the others look to you when Ollie's not around.'

'Do they?'

Aggie let out a low laugh. 'I'd say, but you're just too loyal to notice.'

Perhaps she's right, thought Freddie.

He caught Aggie's chin and forced her head up. 'I wouldn't say such things out loud unless you want to find me lying in a gutter with my throat cut.'

Aggie looked up at him in horror. 'No, no I wouldn't, Freddie. Honest. It's just that,' she shrugged, 'well, who knows what's around the corner.'

He studied Aggie's face staring up at him, so loving, trusting and utterly devoted. She was right. He could see that now. He was the man to step into Ollie Mac's shoes but only if he kept his wits about him.

He kissed her mouth. 'You and me, Aggie, have to keep this between ourselves. You understand?'

'Of course, Freddie,' she replied seriously before a spark of mischief flashed into her eyes. 'But just for now,' her hand slipped down the front of his trousers and took hold of his old man, 'let me put a smile on the face of the next leader of the Black Eagle Gang.'

Chapter Thirteen

Jonathan stood in front of the hall mirror and Mrs Delaney held up his long black gown for him. He slipped his arms in the wide sleeves and shrugged it on.

'There you go, sir. All fit and proper.' She tilted her head and in the reflection Jonathan saw the now-familiar look creeping into her eye. 'It's a pity it's not a *lady* of the house to see you're looking your best before setting out,' she said, handing him the clothes brush.

'Thank you,' Jonathan said, taking the brush and applying it to the shoulders of his robe. 'That will be all, Mrs Delaney,' he said, keeping his tone and expression neutral.

'Very good sir,' she said, then lurched sideways in her usual way of curtsying. Jonathan positioned his mortar board so that the tassel was sitting over his eyepatch, picked up the school Bible, checked the time on his fob watch and then opened the door and stepped out.

From the top step he could see over the six-foot wall surrounding the playground and noted there was already a handful of boys there. There would soon be plenty more as the school was now full, with a dozen or so late applicants on a waiting list. Jonathan smiled to himself. Not bad for only a month in the post. Of course, that meant an influx of new faces to deal with but now he'd sorted out the curriculum, he was confident the new pupils would soon fit in.

The chill wind caught his gown, sending it billowing out behind him. He caught it around himself and trotted down the four front steps. Then he saw her. Kate Ellis.

The frost was stinging Kate's ears by the time she, Ella and Joe reached the gates. There were a couple of other mothers bringing their children to school for the first day of the new term. She could see a few of the boys in their playground and a handful of girls chattering in theirs. Kate's eyes moved to the side wall of the schoolhouse that abutted the girls' play area. She wondered if Captain Quinn was still in his house and if she'd catch a glimpse of him when school opened.

Yesterday at church was the first time she'd seen him since

Christmas. As she'd watched him escort Mrs Benson to her seat Miss Puttock fluttered into his path, all eyelashes and giggles.

'Ma, Joe's undone his collar again,' Ella said.

'For mercy's sake, Joe, will you leave it be?' Kate said, fastening his top button for the fourth time.

Joe squirmed. 'It's too tight.'

'It's new, that's all. It'll stretch as you wear it.' She straightened his cap. 'And remember to put your scarf on and button your coat when you are sent out to play.'

'Ma, I'm not a baby,' he protested, glancing at the boys in the playground behind him.

Kate held up the canvas satchel Mattie had bought Ella for Christmas. 'Now you've got bread and jam for break time and don't dawdle at dinner or you'll have to rush your meal and get hiccups.' Kate brushed the front of Ella's coat again. 'Now, I'm sure Captain Quinn will be ringing the bell any moment, so off you go. You don't want you to be late on your first day, do you? I want you both to come straight home and . . .' she said, looking pointedly at Joe, '*don't* scrape the toes of your boots. They have to last a few more months yet.'

Kate kissed Ella but Joe dashed away before she could give him a peck.

A door banged shut. Kate turned to see Captain Quinn in his schoolmaster's gown emerging from his house and then marching along the pavement towards her. His tassel swirled with each step he took. Kate's heart gave a little skip when he stopped in front of her and raised his mortar board. 'Mrs Ellis,' he said. 'What a pleasant surprise.'

'Good morning, Captain Quinn,' she replied. 'I've just brought Joe and Ella to school,' she added, inwardly scolding herself for stating what was plain to see.

'Will you be bringing them every morning?'

Kate laughed. 'No. I don't think Joe would be able to hold his head up in the playground if I did.'

Captain Quinn laughed then his expression changed. 'That's a pity – it means that we won't be seeing each other every morning.'

Jonathan wondered at himself as Kate Ellis's eyes, the sweep of her eyelashes, the curve of her cheek and the inviting shape of her lips suddenly pushed out every sensible thought in his head. He pulled himself together and nodded at Joe, who was dashing back and forth. 'It seems your son has found his feet already.'

Kate followed his gaze with a smile. 'Ella looks so grown up in her new uniform. It seems only yesterday that Joe cut his first tooth – now he's almost as tall as his sister.'

Other children were coming down the street now and out of the corner of his eye Jonathan saw Miss Wainwright step into the girls' playground.

'If you would excuse me, Mrs Ellis, I have to go,' he said, wanting nothing more than to stay right where he was.

'Of course, sir. And, I don't think I thanked you properly for giving Joe a place here,' she said, giving him another heart-stopping smile.

'It is my pleasure.' He touched his hat and marched into the yard.

An hour later, after drill, morning assembly, organising the new pupils into monitor groups and a start-of-term pep talk, Jonathan finally escaped to his office. He closed the door and threw his mortar board carelessly across his desk, scattering papers.

What on earth was wrong with him? He was supposed to be paying court to Miss Puttock but here he was paying compliments to Kate Ellis. Why had he done that? And why was he always thinking of her? He'd noticed a while back that he sought her out in church but had dismissed that as just habit. Now here he was trying to charm a smile out of her. He was becoming obsessed, which was utterly ridiculous.

Kate Ellis is just a woman, a beautiful one perhaps; but just a woman, he told himself firmly. *Apart from the fact she's married, we haven't the same family background or education or anything.*

For pity's sake it was *just* physical. Nothing more, nothing less. And it was hardly surprising considering he'd not been with a woman since he'd met Louise – it was little wonder he was acting like a raw recruit.

He turned from the window and picked up a copy of the *Illustrated London News*. Sitting down at his desk, Jonathan unfolded it and scanned down the page. But as he read advertisements for gentlemen requiring 'a quiet haven' or a 'listening ear', an image of Kate drifted back into his mind. He screwed up the journal and threw it into the bin beside his desk.

There was nothing for it. If the lack of female company was leading him to think too much about an already married woman then there was only one thing to do: ask Miss Puttock to marry him.

Mabel scribbled across the bottom of her note pad and looked up. 'There,' she said, smiling at Mrs Benson sitting beside her on the sofa. 'I think I can safely tell the church social committee that the plans for the summer fête are complete.'

'Splendid,' replied the older woman. She looked across at Jonathan. 'Don't you agree, Captain Quinn?'

'I do indeed,' he replied.

Mabel looked at him from under her eyelashes. 'Thanks mainly to you, Captain Quinn, for generously giving up so much of your time.'

He leant forward and put his cup and saucer back on the tray. 'Not at all. I am most grateful to your efforts on the school's behalf.'

'But it was *your* inspired idea to have the children parade in the native dress of Queen's subjects throughout the Empire that will be the highlight of the day,' she replied. 'I'm sure such a delightful spectacle will make this year's fête the most successful ever.'

Mrs Benson patted the young woman's hand. 'It will be the talk of the area, my dear, as will you.'

Mabel's round cheeks glowed. 'I work for the benefit of the dear children, nothing more.' Her eyes ran over Jonathan. 'And I'm sure it will be our most admirable headmaster who will command all the attention.'

Jonathan smiled politely.

'Well, now we have finished with the afternoon's business, shall I ring for some more tea?' Mrs Benson asked, as she lifted the lid of the teapot.

'Thank you,' Jonathan replied, settling back in the chair.

Mrs Benson looked at Mabel.

'I ought to get back but if Captain Quinn is staying then so shall I.' She smiled demurely at him.

Jonathan stood up and pulled the bell to save Mrs Benson the effort and to break free from Mabel's unwavering gaze. He enjoyed the admiration of the opposite sex as much as any man but after two hours, her unremitting adulation was beginning to cloy.

Mabel scanned her list again and her brows pulled together.

'What is it, my dear?' Mrs Benson asked.

'I've just added up the helpers again and with the addition of the hoops and peg game and the lucky-dip barrel there's no one to help me on the cake stall,' she said, looking a little forlorn. 'It's always busy and needs two people at least. How am I going to cope by myself?'

'Oh dear,' said Mrs Benson. 'I would offer to help but I'm overseeing the vegetable competition. What about Miss Clayton?'

'She's in the refreshments' tent.'

'Mrs Shrew?'

Mabel shook her head. 'Not after the incident with ... you know.'

'Of course.'

Mrs Benson studied her hands while Miss Puttock gazed at the wallpaper for inspiration.

'What about Mrs Ellis?' Jonathan said. They looked at him and Mrs Benson's face lit up.

'What a good idea! Kate would be the perfect person to help you, don't you agree, Miss Puttock?'

Miss Puttock hesitated for a moment and then gave him a dazzling smile. 'Kate Ellis, of course. What an excellent suggestion but ...' She looked thoughtful. 'But she has to run the chop house in the afternoons. I doubt she would be able to come.' She shrugged. 'What a pity.'

'Only during the week,' Jonathan replied. 'It's shut Saturday afternoons.'

Mabel's pleasant expression wavered. 'Does it?'

Mrs Benson grabbed the younger woman's hands and shook them. 'There you are, my dear, the perfect answer to your problem. Perhaps you should ask her on Sunday. What do you say?'

Mabel's eyes shifted from Mrs Benson to Jonathan and back again. 'Well ... I didn't want to rake up the past and as you know I'm not one to judge or condemn the weakness of others, but those who serve the church, in any capacity, should be beyond reproach.'

'I was suggesting Mrs Ellis help on the cake stall, Miss Puttock, not stand for churchwarden,' Jonathan said tersely.

'And if you're referring to what I think you are, it happened over seven years ago,' Mrs Benson added.

Mabel nodded solemnly. 'True. But it *was* the talk of every street corner for months.'

'So I understand,' Jonathan said with a hint of irritation creeping into his voice.

'Oh, please, Captain Quinn, do not condemn her completely,' Mabel said, in a flutter of righteousness. 'She is Irish, after all, and they have a very untroubled attitude towards chast—'

'Kate was only sixteen when Freddie Ellis set out to ruin her,' Mrs Benson interrupted, 'and too inexperienced to see through his deceit. Unfortunately, the moment he found out she was with child, Freddie abandoned her! What he stupidly overlooked was that she was Patrick Nolan's sister and you don't injure a member of his family and get away with it.'

'I would say the person shamed by this story is Freddie Ellis,' said Jonathan. 'I would certainly object to *him* selling cakes at the church fête but I can't see why anyone would complain if Mrs Ellis did.'

'Neither can I.' Mrs Benson turned to the young woman sitting beside her. 'So will you speak to her on Sunday or shall I, Miss Puttock?'

'That's kind of you, Mrs Benson, but as Mrs Overton has charged me with responsibility for the fair, I should be the one to ask dear Mrs Ellis to join our team.'

If Kate had known that it was compulsory to attend Mabel Puttock's weekly planning meeting, she would never have agreed to help on the cake stall. In truth, she should have said no straight away because it was being held on Saturday afternoon, which was the only time she had to take stock, properly scrub her baking trays, pie dishes and cooking trays, and simply rest. But when Miss Puttock mentioned that Captain Quinn would be opening the fair, all of Kate's reasons flew out of the window.

Stifling a yawn, and looking around the vestry table at the half-dozen young women of the parish who had also been recruited, Kate wondered if for once the meeting would finish on time. Somehow, with Miss Puttock presiding, she didn't think it likely, even though they had gone over the same lists at the previous meeting.

She smoothed a crease from her skirt. By young women of the parish, she didn't mean those who worked morning to night keeping their family business afloat or who laboured in the clothing sweat-shops and factories for ten hours a day. No – these were the chatty young ladies who helped Mama deal with the tradesmen, and took cabs to Cheapside to visit their dressmakers. Sitting among them in their brightly coloured crinolines, Kate felt her second best gown looked very drab.

Miss Puttock tapped lightly with the gavel to bring them to order. 'So if I can just read out the list of those helping with the main stalls to make sure there are sufficient troops to cover all areas,' she said, glancing down at her notes. 'Lottie will be in command of the flower stall and Miriam will be responsible for the preserves and pickles. I shall inspect the display to make sure they are all present and correctly labelled.'

The women around the table exchanged amused glances and suppressed their smiles.

Miss Puttock looked severely at them and they lowered their

eyes. Kate wondered if the grocer's boy had delivered tomorrow's vegetables to the shop yet.

'Ada and Eliza will garrison the . . .' Miss Puttock continued to list the home-craft stalls and the young women responsible for them and finally looked down the table at Kate. 'And I, as the overall commander, flanked by Mrs Ellis . . .'

There was another flurry of giggles. Miss Puttock's mouth pulled together disapprovingly.

'. . . will defend the cake table against all comers.'

The young women around the table tittered. Miss Puttock glared at them and tapped the gavel again.

'Do we all agree on who is to do what?' she asked. Six carefully coiffured heads nodded. 'Good.' She shuffled her papers. 'I expect you to carry out your orders to the—'

Ada's shoulders began to shake and Eliza spluttered.

'*What* is so amusing?' Miss Puttock asked crossly.

'We thought you were teasing us, Mabel.'

'Teasing!' Miss Puttock's face went red. 'Let me assure you, the success of this year's church fête is not something I would joke about.'

'It's just that you—' Ada started.

'You seem to be using a lot of military phrases,' Kate cut in. 'And I think they thought you were having a little joke. You know? A play on words.'

Mabel looked astonished.

Miriam nodded. 'Like garrison.'

'And present and correct,' added Caroline.

Eliza pulled a serious-minded face. '"Defend the cake table",' she said in a deep voice, then giggled. She cast her eyes around the table. 'It would seem that being in Captain Quinn's company has sent Mabel's head into a soldierly swirl.'

'I'm not surprised,' said Sophie. 'My head spins every time he walks past me.'

Mabel's demeanour went from tiger to kitten. 'I confess,' she said, looking demurely at them, 'when one is in the company of a man such as Captain Quinn, it is impossible not be affected by him.'

'I can just imagine him in his uniform,' sighed Lottie.

Kate's mind drifted back to the first time she met him. In fact it did quite often, although she'd never mentioned it to anyone, not even Mattie.

Miriam rested her chin on her hand and gazed upward. 'And the eyepatch is *so* dashing.'

Miss Puttock looked grave. 'I agree. The wound he received while defending our country does not detract from any part of him. He is a hero and gentleman and I greatly admire him.'

'But does *he* admire you, Mabel?' asked Sophie.

Miss Puttock's cheeks went crimson. 'You should not ask such things,' she replied, coquettishly. 'I cannot say.'

'Has he declared himself?'

'Is he going to speak to your father?'

'Has he held you in his arms?'

A sudden ache rose up in Kate. She studied the woman opposite her.

Miss Puttock placed one hand over the other on the table in front of her and looked coolly at them all. 'You will understand if I do not answer your question but I will say that whenever we have met, Captain Quinn has been a perfect gentleman.'

Kate let go of her breath. He hadn't and she felt oddly relieved.

'I agree with you, Miss Puttock. Captain Quinn pops in to my shop for a coffee at least three times a week and he is always extremely well mannered.' Kate rose to her feet as seven pairs of eyes stared at her. 'I hope you'll excuse me, Miss Puttock, but the children will be back from school soon.'

Miss Puttock forced a polite smile. 'Of course, Mrs Ellis, it was good of you to spare the time, and thank you for your generous donation of three cakes.'

'Not at all.' Kate tugged on her gloves. 'I'll make one of them a lemon cake. It's Captain Quinn's favourite.' She stepped out from her place at the table and walked to the door. She turned and looked at Lottie. 'And I can tell you, Miss Frances, he does look very fine in his red coat.'

Jonathan stifled a yawn as Mrs Puttock recounted a blow-by-blow account of her journey to her sister's house in Fulham on the paddle steamer. Mabel sat on the sofa beside her mother, with her hands folded demurely onto her lap and a pretty little expression on her lips. Her gaze shifted from her mother to him and Jonathan smiled admiringly. There was a light knock at the door.

'Come,' called Mrs Puttock.

The parlour door opened and the maid came in.

'Yes?' Mrs Puttock asked.

The maid bobbed a curtsy. 'I'm sorry to disturb you, ma'am, but

Cook said there's a problem with the butcher's order and càn you come to straighten it out?'

'Tell Cook I'll be down later,' Mrs Puttock replied, replenishing the teapot with hot water.

The maid bobbed another curtsy. 'Begging your pardon, ma'am, but Cook says it's urgent.'

Mrs Puttock sighed and rose to her feet. 'Please forgive me, Captain Quinn,' she said, smiling regretfully at him. 'It is most tiresome but I will have to attend to this.'

Jonathan stood up. 'Of course. I do hope you don't find too much of a problem in the kitchen.'

Mrs Puttock rolled her eyes. 'I'm sure it is something perfectly simple, but you know what servants are like.'

Jonathan didn't comment.

'I'm sure Mabel will be able to keep you entertained until I return.' Mrs Puttock gave her daughter a wide-eyed look. 'Why don't you show Captain Quinn your scrapbook, my dear?'

With a rustle of silk she swept out, closing the door behind her. Jonathan resumed his seat and smiled inwardly.

As a newly formed acquaintance of the family it would have been impolite of him to outstay his welcome, so Jonathan limited his afternoon visits to the Puttocks to just an hour. He was pleased to because, frankly, there was only so much upholstery and colour schemes a man could take. However, since Easter there seemed to have been a succession of domestic disasters requiring Mrs Puttock's immediate attention twenty-five minutes into his visit. Last week it had been the grocer's bill and the week before the coal delivery.

Mabel rose gracefully and glided across to the bureau to collect her leather-bound scrapbook. Hugging it to her, she returned to the sofa and set it on her lap.

'Why don't you come and sit beside me, Captain? You'll be able to see more easily.' She patted the vacant seat next to her.

Jonathan stood up and joined her on the sofa.

'You might have to sit a little closer,' she said, shyly.

Why not? After all wasn't it his intention to move things on so he could speak to her father? He shifted along.

'That's better.' She smiled beguilingly up at him then opened the book. 'I've collected four articles about the Queen this week,' she said, scanning her eyes over the page of pasted newspaper cuttings and snipped outline drawings.

'How interesting,' he said, trying to look as if he meant it.

'Yes. There are two from *The Times*. One about the Queen's working day and the other with her diary for the coming month. Another from the *Illustrated News* about her and Prince Albert's fondness for the Highlands and here' – she pointed a well-manicured finger at a pasted square of newsprint – '*The Lady's Newspaper* had two full columns about the royal children.'

Jonathan slid his arm along the back of the sofa behind Mabel. 'And what is that?' he asked, leaning closer and pointed at a picture of three women standing by a fountain.

'That's the latest fashion from Paris.' She turned and Jonathan found himself looking into her blue eyes.

Well, as blue as any eyes could be next to Kate Ellis's. He straightened up and removed his arm.

'I have a crick in my back,' he explained.

Mabel looked disappointed. Jonathan cursed himself. What on earth was wrong with him?

He smiled warmly at Mabel. 'Perhaps I'll move a little closer so I won't have to stretch.'

She brightened instantly. 'Yes, do.'

Jonathan shifted along until his thighs met the steel band of her crinoline. Mabel straightened the lace of her skirt and it fluttered against his trousers.

'This is my collection of puppies,' she said as she turned the page to reveal a dozen or so lapdogs with bows on their collars frolicking across the sheet. 'And these are things that are just pretty,' she said, turning the next leaf to show him the colour-prints of cherubs, flowers, children and birds glued to sugar paper.

Jonathan forced a smile and questioned the wisdom of keeping a girl cosseted with her mother beyond childhood. An image of Kate Ellis standing behind the counter and serving dinners popped into his mind. He tried to shove it aside but it wouldn't budge, and then his imagination added in her throaty laugh just to distract him further.

'Oh!' Mabel's hand went to her face. 'Something has flown into my eye.'

'Don't rub it,' Jonathan said, turning towards her.

'It stings.'

'Try to blink it out.'

She fluttered her eyelids a couple of times. 'It's still there.'

Jonathan took out his handkerchief and moved nearer. 'Let me see.'

Mabel tilted her head back.

'Which one?' Jonathan peered more closely.

'The left.'

Jonathan dipped his head. 'I can't see anything,' he said, putting his finger on her cheek and gently pulling down her lower lid.

Mabel blinked again. 'I think it's gone.' She swayed forward and smiled longingly up at him.

They were sitting very close together. All he needed to do was lower his lips on to hers. Wasn't that his intention and the reason Mrs Puttock left them alone in the parlour each week?

Jonathan's arm slipped around her waist and he pulled her closer. 'That colour becomes you very well, Mabel.'

'Oh, Jonathan,' she sighed, placing her hand on his chest.

Jonathan lowered his head and Mable closed her eyes.

He was just about to press his lips on hers when the door handle rattled. Her eyes flew open. Jonathan let go of Mabel instantly and moved away just as the maid walked in.

Although Mabel looked furious, Jonathan had an odd sense of relief.

The maid curtsied. 'Begging your pardon, miss. Cook told me to check the fires.'

'You're supposed to knock first,' Mabel said, tucking a strand of hair back in place.

'Yes, miss, but I didn't know you were in here with . . .' Her eyes darted from Mabel to Jonathan and back again. 'I'll come back later.' She bobbed again and fled.

Jonathan glanced at the clock. 'Is that the time?' He stood up. 'I ought to be getting back.'

Mabel's bottom lip jutted out. 'But you've only been here for forty minutes.'

'I know, but I shouldn't compromise your reputation by being alone with you. You know how servants talk,' he said, stepping away from the sofa.

'Your sentiments do you credit, Captain,' Mabel said, struggling to hide her frustration. 'But I'm sure my reputation is quite safe.'

'It certainly is, but if your mother had come upon us a few moments ago she might have thought otherwise.' Mabel was about to argue so Jonathan continued. 'I'm sorry, Miss Puttock, please give my regards to your mother and I look forward to seeing you both in church on Sunday. I'll see myself out. Good day.'

Chapter Fourteen

'So let me get this straight, Dermot, you are wanting me to supply a dozen beef and a dozen mixed-meat and onion each day,' Kate said.

They were sitting at the window table with the mid-afternoon sunlight throwing a dappled pattern on the scrubbed wooden surface. She'd turned the sign on the door to 'closed' and sent Sally off for her well-earned break. This was usually when Kate caught her breath before the children came in and the teatime onslaught began, but as Dermot Sullivan, the local baked-potato seller, wanted to have a word about business, this seemed the ideal time.

'That I do. With old Ruben selling a slice of your cake with his coffee, I thought I should offer a pie or two on the stall by way of a change. What price can you do me?'

'Two and three farthings for the meat-and-onion, a penny more for the beef,' Kate said.

Dermot pulled a face. 'Well, I know your fine Irish home cooking is the best to be had in the whole world,' his face creased in to an ingenious smile, 'but can you not see your way to shaving a bit more off for old times' sake, Kate, me darling?'

Kate lips twitched. 'I'll take off another farthing and wrap them for you, but that's my final price.'

Dermot paused a moment then grinned, showing his missing front teeth. 'A farthing it is then.' He shook her hand. 'Starting next week?'

'They'll be waiting for you to collect at ten. Park your cart in the yard and knock on the back—'

The door leading from the parlour flew open. It was Freddie. Kate's heart thumped uncomfortably in her chest.

Mattie used to call him Flashy Freddie and in his green and brown Worcester suit, high-crowned hat and polished leather brogues he certainly fitted that description now. His gaze flickered onto Dermot then back to Kate. She stood up.

'Who's the old man?' Freddie asked.

Kate stepped out from the table. 'Just a customer.'

Freddie strolled across and loomed over them. 'Sling your hook,' he said to Dermot.

The chair scraped on the floor as Dermot got up. 'Now look here—'

'No, you look here. Make yourself scarce before I'm forced to break something.' Freddie shoved him.

Dermot fell against the window.

Kate pushed past Freddie. 'Are you all right, Dermot?' she asked, helping him regain his balance.

He nodded.

'Perhaps you'd better go,' she added. He looked over her shoulder at Freddie and she smiled reassuringly. 'It's all right.'

Dermot gathered his cap from the table but as he left, he turned and jabbed his finger at Freddie. 'Mrs Ellis could have the law on you, walking into her shop as if you own it!'

Freddie laughed. 'I'm her old man, you stupid old sod, so I can walk in here any time I please and the law ain't got no way of stopping me.'

He stamped his foot and lunged forward. Dermot scurried out in a rush.

Freddie sneered. 'Gutless Paddy. They're only brave enough to stand up to their own kind.'

Kate spun around. 'You're the coward, picking on an old man twice your age.'

'Where's Joe?'

'At school.'

'Fucking waste of time,' Freddie said. 'I didn't go to school and I ain't book learned – a man needs but brains.' He tapped the side of his head.

Kate raised an eyebrow. 'Well then, it's a pity you haven't got any. If you did, you wouldn't keep showing up where you're not wanted.'

A mocking smile spread across his face as he looked down at her. 'I suppose cos I ain't been around, you hoped I'd disappeared again,' he said, reaching into the till.

'If I never saw you again until Judgement Day, it would be too soon,' Kate replied. 'But why did you have to promise Joe you'd see him on Christmas day? Have you got any notion how upset he was?'

Freddie waved her words away. 'He'll get over it.'

'If there were any justice in the world, Freddie Ellis, he'd have a proper father who would take him places and teach him things. Not a thieving wastrel like you.' Kate ran her eyes contemptuously over him. 'I suppose you think you look something special dressed up like an organ grinder's monkey waiting for a tune. And how did you pay for your showy togs? I'll bet by lifting goods from backs of wagons, breaking into warehouses and stealing from honest, hard-working people like me! Don't think I haven't heard you're thick with the Black Eagle Gang.' She placed her palm on her forehead in an attempt to ease the pounding. 'If you've got what you came for why don't you just—'

His hand grasped her jaw. 'You always did have a tongue to cut into a man's soul, Kate,' he said, squeezing her face painfully. His gaze ran over her, lingering on her breasts and sending a shiver of revulsion running through her. 'I remember a time when you couldn't get enough of me.' He seized her waist and walked her backwards. He slammed her against the counter and pressed his legs to hers so she couldn't knee him again. 'Do you remember?'

He grabbed the neckline of her gown and ripped it open. 'You were like a bitch in heat sniffing around me.'

Kate held his gaze. 'That's because I was too stupid to know what a lying bastard you really were.' She swung a punch at him but he caught her hand and twisted it behind her back.

A lecherous look crept into his eyes. 'Go on, fight me. I'd enjoy that.'

He grasped her breast and squeezed. Kate bit back a scream. She stretched out and groped along the counter to find something to defend herself with but Freddie dragged her away.

'Not this time.' He threw her on to a table and pressed down on her.

As if from far off she heard the parlour door click open. Kate swivelled her head and looked around Freddie's shoulder to see Ella peeking wide-eyed around the counter. She stood frozen for a moment then disappeared back into the house.

Kate tried to scramble out but Freddie forced her back and pulled her skirts up. She felt the cool air on her thighs and Freddie's hand tearing at her drawers.

'No!' she screamed, raking at his face with her nails.

'Bitch!' His fist smashed across her face.

Kate fell back as a thousand bells rang in her head and black spots started in the corner of her vision. Biting back the nausea threatening to choke her throat, Kate took a deep breath and forced herself to stay conscious.

Jonathan offered his hand to Ebenezer Drake, the master cooper. 'Thank you for agreeing to my proposal,' he shouted over the clang of metal.

Like most of the businesses along the Wapping waterfront, Black and Co. was cramped between the tall walls of the surrounding warehouses. Although the tubs full of oak planks lay soaking in the workshop at the far end of the rectangular plot, the business of making the barrels went on in the open yard where they were standing.

Drake wiped his hand on his ankle-length leather apron and took Jonathan's. 'Not at all. I'm sorry I can only take one apprentice,' he said as they walked towards the yard gate and past a burly worker hammering a ring over the belly of a tub.

'One will do.' Jonathan raised his hat. 'Good day to you, Mr Black.'

'And to you, Captain Quinn.'

When Jonathan pulled out his watch he saw that it was almost four. The direct route back to the school was left up Nightingale Lane, but Jonathan turned right in the direction of Kate's Kitchen knowing it would soon be open.

He crossed the road and turned the corner to see Ella Ellis tearing down the road with her plaits flying behind her. She spotted him and dodged between the dray carts, skidding to a halt in front of him. She grabbed his hand.

'Captain Quinn, you must come quick,' she said, dragging on his arm.

'What's the matter?' Jonathan asked, picking up speed.

'Pa's hurting Ma,' Ella replied.

With his heart pounding, Jonathan ran up the street with Ella close behind. Ignoring the shouts of warning from the drivers, he dodged around the afternoon traffic on the Highway. Scattering shoppers as he went, Jonathan lengthened his stride until finally he reached the shop. He grasped the handle and shook it, but it was locked.

He peered through the window and could see some kind of movement. Fury gripped him. He slammed his fists on the door frame, making the bell on the other side jungle frantically. He stepped back, preparing to kick it open.

Ella grabbed his sleeve. 'Round the back.'

She ran ahead of him. Jonathan overtook her as he shoved the rear gates open. Crossing the small cobbled yard he burst through the back door.

'Stay here,' he commanded Ella as he charged through the parlour and into the shop.

He saw Kate, with her gown ripped and skirts pulled up, struggling against the man pinning her to the table. Freddie had pressed himself between her legs but thankfully his trousers were still around his waist. As Jonathan swung around the edge of the counter Freddie looked up.

'What the—'

Jonathan crossed the space between them in two strides and wrenched Freddie away. Kate rolled off the table and hastily gathered her torn clothes to cover herself.

'Leave her alone, you bastard!' Jonathan bellowed as he threw Freddie across the room.

Freddie landed against the wall but recovered.

'I'm her fucking husband, you stupid one-eyed bugger,' he yelled, standing up again.

'I don't give a damn. I'll not stand by and see any woman abused.'

He glanced at Kate, who was trying to hide her face. Other than a red mark on her cheek and her torn clothes, she looked unharmed.

Jonathan studied Freddie dusting down his garish jacket, and his eyes narrowed.

'I'd leave if I were you,' he said, flexing his hands.

A venomous expression contorted Freddie's face. 'I'll leave when I'm good and ready.' He went for Jonathan, who jerked back so Freddie missed his target.

Jonathan retaliated with a right hook that smashed Freddie squarely on the chin. He followed through with another blow, this time to the stomach. Freddie doubled over. Before he fell Jonathan grabbed him and hauled him upright. He turned him, grabbed his collar and trouser-band and thrust him towards the door. Wedging Freddie's face against the window and jamming his knee in the small of his back, Jonathan threw back the bolts and pulled the door open. Still holding Freddie by the scruff of his neck Jonathan propelled him into the street, to the astonishment of those passing by. When they saw who Jonathan had hold of they started to cheer. He shoved Freddie forward. 'Only a coward forces himself where he's not wanted.'

Freddie tripped over his own feet and then righted himself in a last-ditch effort. He turned and launched himself at Jonathan, who caught Freddie by his fancy lapels.

'I warned you to leave,' he said, in a conversational tone. He then jolted Freddie towards him and smacked his forehead into the bridge of Freddie's nose.

There was a sickening crunch and another cheer from the crowd who'd stopped to watch. Jonathan released Freddie backwards into a pile of horse dung.

'That's where you belong, Ellis, in the shit,' someone shouted from the crowd.

'Crawl back into the rat hole you came from,' called another.

A docker shook his hook at Freddie. 'Yer, fuck off before Pat Nolan hears you've been using your fists on his sister again.'

Freddie scrambled to his feet as a clump of mud sailed through the air and splattered across his shoulder and face.

He jammed his muddy hat on his head and pointed at Jonathan. 'You've messed with the wrong man this time, Nelson.'

'So have you, Ellis,' Jonathan replied levelly.

Freddie glared hatefully at him then shoved his way through the crowd who taunted him all the while. Those who had gathered to see what the disturbance was started drifting away. Many of them tipped their hats to Jonathan before he went back into the shop.

Kate had managed to secure her blouse somewhat haphazardly by the time Captain Quinn returned. Her fingers trembled and her mind still reeled but now not so much from Freddie's attack but from Captain Quinn's decisive intervention. She still couldn't quite believe her eyes. A mixture of fury and relief crossed his face as he looked at her.

'Are you all right?' he asked.

She nodded.

'Thank God I got here in time.' He came forward and scrutinised her closely. 'You'll have a nasty bruise on your cheek for a few days but has he hurt you in any other way?'

'No, I'm fine,' Kate whispered, as a tear rolled down her cheek.

Just then Ella dashed out from behind the counter and threw herself into her mother's arms.

'I was so scared,' she said, hugging Kate's neck and burying her face into her shoulder.

Kate hugged her. 'It's over now.'

'Why can't he just stay away?' she cried.

Kate kissed her daughter's forehead. 'Perhaps he will this time.' She squeezed Ella. 'Pop upstairs and fetch me the shawl Aunt Josie gave me for Christmas.'

'Yes, Ma.' Ella slipped out of her arms.

Clutching her blouse, Kate tried to stand up.

'Let me,' Captain Quinn said, offering his hand.

Kate grasped it and stared down at his muscled hand, tapered fingers and the neat line of hair tracking from his wrist to the base of his little finger. She started to rise but her knees gave way. He caught her around the waist.

'Sorry, I'm a little shaky,' she said, enjoying the feel of him against her.

'Of course you are. It's the shock.'

Holding her steady, he walked her though to the parlour. As he settled her in her chair Ella reappeared carrying a broad paisley shawl with silken fringing. She draped it around her mother's shoulders.

Kate smiled at her. 'Thank you, sweetheart.' She tucked it around and tied it to make sure she was properly covered. 'Could you do me another favour and run around to Sally and ask her to come a bit earlier?'

Ella looked troubled. 'But what if *he* comes back again?'

'I don't think he will, Ella,' Captain Quinn replied. 'Not after the reception he got from your neighbours. Don't worry. I'll take good care of your mother until you return.'

'Thank you, Headmaster.' She dashed out of the back door.

'A cup of tea is what you need,' Captain Quinn said.

Kate went to rise from the chair. 'You've done more than enough already.'

'Nonsense.'

Kate sank back and he went into the kitchen where she heard him rattle around. He soon reappeared with a tray of tea, which he set on the table and then poured them a cup. He handed one to Kate.

'Thank you,' she said. 'It seems odd you making me a drink.'

'I hope it passes muster.'

Kate blew across the top and took a sip. 'Perfect.' She put the cup back in its saucer. 'I think, perhaps, I should give you an expl—'

'You don't have to explain. It's plain to see your husband's a brute.'

She looked at her hands. Embarrassment washed over her. Should she tell him the full story about Freddie? But then what on earth would he think of her?

She raised her head. 'But you don't know that—'

'Your brother had to drag him to the altar to face up to his responsibilities? That he left you and your children destitute?'

'But he's also—'

'Been in prison?'

Kate looked astonished. 'You know?'

'People talk.'

'Of my shame, no doubt,' she replied bitterly, looking away.

He pulled a straight-backed chair from the table. He set it next to her and sat down.

'A spiteful few, perhaps, but most talk with admiration of your perseverance and of how hard you work to provide for your family. Of your sunny disposition and kindly nature, and how as an innocent young girl you were seduced by a callous scoundrel who has treated you and your children disgracefully ever since.' Kate began to weep quietly and he gave her his handkerchief. 'The shame in this story is not yours but your husband's.'

Their faces were now only inches apart and she could see the late afternoon stubble on his cheek and chin. For a moment Kate thought he would take her in his arms. And suddenly she wanted him to. More than anything else she needed to feel his embrace and press herself into him. But she could not, should not.

'Thank you, sir,' she said. 'I shouldn't burden you with my problems.'

'You could *never* be a burden to me, Mrs Ellis,' he replied, staring deeply into her eyes.

Several seconds ticked by, then the back door opened and Kate looked away. Captain Quinn sat up.

Ella ran in. 'Sally said she'll be here soon,' she said, going to her mother's side. 'Are you better?'

'I am,' Kate replied.

Captain Quinn drained the last of his tea and stood up. 'I should be getting back. I'll leave you in Ella's capable hands.'

Kate smiled up at him. 'Thank you once again for coming to my aid.'

Ella bit her lower lip and looked fearfully at her mother. 'What about next time, Ma?'

Captain Quinn tapped his top hat into place. 'If there is a next time, Ella, just come and find me.'

Chapter Fifteen

Aggie pushed open the bar door of the Blue Coat Boy and strolled in. Several men looked her way, their eyes running slowly over her. She smiled professionally then swayed towards the counter.

The bar was full of the usual lunchtime drinkers but looking down the room she saw Ollie Mac holding court as usual, surrounded by Stefan and his other enforcers. Lilly was also there. Someone had brought a threadbare armchair and Ollie Mac's common-law baggage now sat enthroned and clutching a bundle of rags in her arms with a look of motherly contentment on her face.

Aggie's mouth pulled into a tight line. Much to her annoyance, Lilly and her brat had survived the rigours of childbirth. Unlike most girls in the rookery who were lucky to have a single day off after a birthing before they were back on the streets, Lilly had spent the last ten days with her feet up and stuffing her face.

The barmaid came over.

'Double muvver's,' Aggie ordered.

Mary pulled off the cork from the bottle with her teeth. 'Three-pence,' she said, pouring Aggie her drink.

'Put it on my Freddie's slate,' she replied, taking a large mouthful.

The door opened and a couple of navvies wearing dusty clothes came in, followed by Freddie. He was dressed in the suit he'd got himself after the raid on the tobacco warehouse in Moorgate the week before.

The bruising around his right eye and cheek had faded but his nose still sat at an odd angle. His face had looked like a piece of beaten meat a week ago. Somehow she'd managed to stay deadpan when he told her he'd been in a tussle with a *schoolmaster*.

'Hello, sweetheart,' he said, coming up to her and slipping his arm around her waist. 'How's my best girl? New gown?'

She smoothed over the midnight-blue satin skirt. The scooped neck was far too low for a day dress that fitted her like a glove. She felt it worth the three shillings merely for the number of heads she turned while wearing it.

'I saw it hanging in Cohen's window yesterday and I thought I'd treat myself. Do you like it?' She ran her fingers across the bare flesh of her breasts. Freddie's eyes followed their progress.

'I do – but that's three you've bought in the last week, as well as that fancy hat you got down the Waste,' he said, handing over a couple of coins for their drinks.

'Ain't I worth it?' she pouted.

'Course you are, ducks, but I'm just thinking, what with the extra rent for our new room and all . . .'

She put her index finger on his lips. 'Everyone knows I'm your gal, Freddie, and you don't want them thinking you can't keep me in style, do you? Not with you being Mr Mac's right-hand man and all.'

'Well, no, but . . .'

Aggie ran her hand over the front of his trousers. 'But what, Freddie?'

He drew a sharp breath and his irritation vanished. 'Oh, Aggie, you're a rare one and no mistake.'

'Freddie!' Ollie Mac's voice called above the noise. 'What you doing over there? Come and join us.'

'That's very kind of you, Mr Mac,' Freddie replied. He looked down at her. 'Come on.'

Aggie rolled her eyes. 'Do we have to? It's only to admire her stinking brat.'

Freddie squeezed her bottom. 'Just plaster a smile on your moosh and behave.'

Aggie slipped her arm through his and walked towards the crowd gathered around Ollie and Lilly.

'How's the lad?' Freddie asked, smiling jollily at his boss.

Ollie beckoned him closer. 'Come and see for yourself. Ain't he a right little man?' he asked, a simpering expression settling on his sharp features. 'Who do you think he looks like then?'

Freddie cocked his head. 'I can't rightly say.'

To Aggie's mind, Albert Mac, with his screwed-up face, bald head and squat neck, looked more like the pub mongrel than either Ollie or Lilly.

'I'd say he's the spitting image of you, Mr Mac,' she said, leaning forward to give Ollie an eyeful of cleavage.

Ollie puffed out his chest. 'Isn't he?'

'I thought you would have called him after yourself,' Aggie said, smiling sweetly at the proud father.

'I wanted to but the little woman thought otherwise.'

Lilly held the baby up. 'We called 'im Albert because he's our little prince. Ain't you?' she said to her sleeping son.

Another sentimental smile cut across Ollie's hard-bitten face as he looked down at his son. 'I tell you, Freddie, it's a fine thing to have a boy to follow in your footsteps.'

'I know,' Freddie replied, with the same soppy expression.

Aggie suppressed her annoyance and tried to pretend Lilly was holding the Messiah in her arms instead of a snotty infant in a whiffy bumrag.

Freddie nudged Ollie playfully in the ribs. 'There's something special about having a chip off the old block to carry on the name. My Joe's just li—'

'And how are you, Lilly, dear?' Aggie cut in. 'We were all *so* worried you might get child-bed fever or something dreadful.'

'I bet you were.'

'No, straight up. Didn't I ask every day, Mr Mac, how Lilly was faring?' She looked at Ollie for confirmation but he was talking to Stefan and didn't answer.

'Oh, Aggie,' Lilly replied. 'I know all the girls think you're a grasping bitch with no feeling but underneath I know you've got a heart of pure stone.'

The baby started to grizzle.

Ollie Mac's bullet-shaped head shot around. 'What's wrong with 'im?' he asked, tickling the child under the chin and fussing like an old spinster.

Lilly knocked his hand away lightly and shifted the child onto her other arm. 'He wants a bit of titty, that's all.'

'Don't we all?' Ollie chuckled, and the men around him joined in.

Lilly opened her blouse, heaved a pendulous breast sprinkled with flea bites out and pressed the fretting infant to it. Aggie suppressed a shudder.

As Albert gurgled away contentedly, Ollie's men started talking and Freddie turned to his boss. Aggie would have joined in the conversation but as Freddie would probably start on about his 'boy Joe', she thought better of it. Perhaps she'd leave them to it and take a stroll down Petticoat Lane. She might find a pair of gloves on a stall to match her new hat.

'Freddie.' He looked around. 'Don't forget I'll be waiting for you later.' Her eyes flickered onto his crotch and she blew a kiss.

He grinned at her then turned back to Ollie.

A crafty smile spread across Lilly's face. 'Ollie, 'as Aggie given you her ten bob this week yet?' she asked, raising her voice above the noise.

The men standing around them stopped talking.

'Not this week, she hasn't,' Ollie replied.

Aggie blinked. 'But ... but I'm Freddie's gal. Tell 'er, Freddie, that you won't have me turning tricks.'

Freddie's eyes darted from her to Ollie but he didn't speak.

'I'm not asking what Freddie wants,' Lilly cut in. 'I'm saying you ain't paid my Ollie for his protection this week and it's for him to say who pays what. Ain't that so, Freddie?'

Sweat glistened on Freddie's brow. 'Of course, everyone knows that,' he answered, without glancing at Aggie.

She grabbed his arm and pulled him around to face her. 'Freddie!'

He shook her off then gripped her upper arm painfully.

'You know *Mr Mac*'s in charge, Aggie,' he told her, his nose just inches from hers.

His fingers tightened further as his eyes bore menacingly into her for a moment then he let her go and turned back to Ollie. The low hum of conversation started again. A couple of the whores lounging on the bar who'd heard the exchange started giggling as they looked across at her. Aggie clenched her fists in the folds of her skirt.

'Oi, Lady Muck,' Lilly said, her eyes flickering on Aggie's low bodice. 'Get your titties out and go and earn my Ollie his money.'

Somehow Aggie managed to keep herself from snatching the bottle from the table, smashing the end and shoving it into Lilly's smirking face. She gave her a venomous look then turned and pushed her way through the bar. As she reached the door she looked back and caught a glimpse of Lilly settling the baby on to the other breast. *As the devil's my witness*, thought Aggie, *I'll not rest in my grave until I've ripped your poxy heart out, Lilly Bragg.*

Kate folded the white paper around the seed cake and tucked the ends in securely. She handed it to the man on the other side of the stall.

'There you go, Mr Williams, and I hope your mother enjoys it with her tea,' she said cheerfully.

'Thank you, Mrs Ellis. I'm sure she will.' He handed her threepence and walked off towards the tombola. Kate put the coin with the rest in the small tin then rearranged the cakes to fill the space.

It had rained at dawn but by the time the men of the parish had arrived to set up the stalls and booths the sun had dried up the puddles in the vicarage garden. Now there wasn't a cloud in the sky. Kate observed the crowds milling around between decorated trestle tables to where Miss Puttock stood bothering Miss Carter on the haberdashery stall. Would she run off in floods of tears as Miss Mosse on the pickle stall did after Miss Puttock's inspection? Kate smiled to herself.

The whole parish had turned out in their Sunday best for the annual festival and as the vicar wouldn't allow beer in the church precincts, there hadn't been any untoward incidents so far. Her gaze travelled over the tombola and bric-a-brac stall, over the coconut shy and finally onto the refreshment tent where Captain Quinn stood chatting to Mr Overton.

As if he sensed her eyes on him he glanced over. His gaze found hers and the space between them seemed to shrink.

He turned and ambled through the crowd towards her. Kate busied herself tidying stacks of wrapping paper.

'Good afternoon, Mrs Ellis,' he said, stopping in front of the stall.

Kate looked up. 'Good afternoon, Captain Quinn.'

'How are you?' he asked, with concern.

He'd been in for coffee three times since Freddie's attack the week before, and each time he'd asked her the same.

'I'm fine,' she replied, revelling in his nearness.

'He's not been back?'

Kate shook her head. 'Not after the drubbing you gave him. Now my brother's after him, too. I doubt he'll show his face for a while.'

She looked down and rearranged the cakes again. His hand closed over hers as she straightened the fruit loaf. 'I meant what I said, you know, about sending Ella or Joe to fetch me.'

She raised her head and found herself falling into his forceful gaze.

'Ma! Ma! Look what I won,' Joe shouted, running across the lawn, waving a Union flag above his head.

Captain Quinn withdrew his hand as Joe came to a skidding halt in front of them.

'And what was that for?' Kate asked.

'Second prize for my costume,' he replied, shaking it at her.

'Well, you certainly look as smart as any soldier I've ever commanded,' Captain Quinn said.

'Ma made it, Headmaster.'

Joe puffed out his chest to show off the bit of gilt braid Kate had sewn on as epaulettes and his cousin Mickey's spruced-up sailor's hat with a fancy shoe buckle fixed above the peak as a regimental badge.

'Ella's supposed to be an Indian princess,' Joe continued.

'Yes, I know. I saw her in the parade.' Captain Quinn smiled at Kate.

'Can I have a couple of farthings for another go on the hoops and pegs?' Joe asked.

Kate rummaged in her pocket and fished out two ha'pennies. She handed them to him. 'There's one for you and one for your sister. She's over by the trinket stall.'

'Thanks, Ma,' Joe said, taking the coins and then scooting off.

Something pink flashed into the corner of her eye and Kate turned to see Miss Puttock homing in on them.

'Captain Quinn,' she said, as she reached them. 'I haven't had a chance to tell you how wonderfully eloquent your opening speech was.'

'Thank you, Miss Puttock,' he replied. 'I was just admiring the delicious display of cakes.'

'Has anything particular taken your fancy?' she asked, coyly.

He glanced over the half a dozen remaining cakes then his gaze flickered over Kate's face. 'Possibly.'

Kate's pulse raced off.

Miss Puttock perused the table and her mouth pulled together. 'I see your three cakes have been sold, Mrs Ellis.'

Kate smiled sweetly. 'Don't worry, Miss Puttock, any latecomers will still buy yours.' She nodded at the four dense-looking fruit slabs with a sprinkling of burnt currants on the top.

'Miss Puttock, your cakes are certainly delicious – but there aren't many who could compete with Mrs Ellis when it comes to cake baking!' Captain Quinn said.

Kate cheeks grow warm. 'Go away with you.'

'It's true. Weren't you telling me on Tuesday that the grocer in Watney Street has asked you to supply him with a couple each week?'

'Well, yes, but—' Kate replied, enjoying his warm expression.

'Tuesday?' said Miss Puttock.

Captain Quinn glanced at her. 'I popped in for a coffee.' His gaze returned to Kate. 'And what about the potato seller?'

Her eyes opened wide. 'How did you—'

He laughed. 'Ella was cleaning the board when I came out of my office the other day and she mentioned the pies.'

'I thought you took tea at Mrs Benson's on Tuesday,' Miss Puttock chipped in.

'She was indisposed,' Captain Quinn told her. He tapped the table with his fingers. 'It seems to me, Mrs Ellis, that as people want *your* cakes and pies perhaps you should sell them with *your* name on them. Like the army-ration tins. They are labelled so the men know who's made them.'

Miss Puttock laughed. 'Miss Ellis may make the odd cake or two but she runs a chop house for dockers, not Fortnum and Mason, Captain Quinn.'

He shot her an irritated look. 'They started in a small way, just like Mrs Ellis. All I was suggesting was something to make sure that people know that the pie or cake they are buying is a genuine Kate's Kitchen product.'

Kate's brain whirled with several possibilities. 'I suppose the simplest way would be to get a ream of greaseproof paper printed up with my name across it. I could wrap the pies and cakes in that.'

He rapped the table lightly with his knuckles 'That is *exactly* what I mean! And you could seal them with a blob of wax after you wrap them.'

'What a good idea.' Kate laughed again. 'I've never known a man take such an interest in baking.'

Captain Quinn's good eye twinkled. 'Well, you know what they say, don't you, Mrs Ellis? The way to a man's heart is through his stomach.'

They laughed, then Miss Puttock's voice cut between them. 'Now, Captain Quinn, perhaps you'd like to chance your luck at the coconut shy.'

'Yes, I would,' he said, smiling pleasantly at her. He looked at Kate over Miss Puttock's shoulder. 'Good day to you, Mrs Ellis.'

Kate inclined her head and Miss Puttock led him away. Someone bought a jam sponge and the last four scones and Kate took the money, all the while keeping Captain Quinn in the corner of her vision. Miss Puttock fluttered around him as he sent half a dozen coconuts crashing to the ground and the man in charge handed him his prize, but then she noticed something that needed her attention on the second-hand clothes stall next door and walked on.

As Captain Quinn stood joking with the stallholder he noticed Ella standing by the side of the booth. He spoke to her and she shook her head. He dropped something into her hand and strolled after Miss Puttock.

Ella came trotting over. 'Did you see how the headmaster hit six coconuts in a row, Ma?'

Kate shook her head. 'I was tidying the stall.'

'Well, he smashed the lot!' Ella said with relish. 'He asked me if I'd bought you anything at the fair. I said I wanted to get you a blue ribbon but it had all been sold.' She put a small pink papier-mâché heart slung on a slender ribbon into the palm of Kate's hand. 'He said I could give you this instead.'

Hidden in the shadows of the bottling factory's main door, Freddie watched the back gate to Kate's shop.

For gawd's sake 'ow much longer? he thought, as a milk cart rolled slowly along the Highway at the far end of the passage.

He yawned and pulled his jacket collar up a little higher. He'd been up all night pinching gear out of the back door of Moses Brothers' warehouse in Shoreditch with Stefan and Ginger, so by rights he should be tucked up alongside Aggie. But needs must, and as Sunday morning was the only time he was sure Kate and the children would be out of the house for at least an hour, his bed, and Aggie, would have to wait.

St George's bell for the morning service sounded out across the rooftops and echoed around the peaceful streets. The yard gate creaked open a little. Freddie flattened himself against the solid door behind and held his breath.

Kate stepped out and Freddie's eyes narrowed as his gaze ran over her trim, dark blue skirt and jacket and matching bonnet. *Bloody jumped-up Paddy.*

She slipped her bag over her arm. 'Ella. Joe. We're late,' she called.

The girl appeared almost immediately and Kate fussed at her collar then stuck her head around the gate. 'For the love of mercy, will you come on, Joe?'

Joe scooted out and slammed the door behind him. Kate licked her hand and flattened a wayward tuft of hair before setting his cap straight. Holding Ella with her right hand and Joe with her left, she walked towards the main road.

Freddie's gaze rested on his son for a second or two, then he remembered why he was there. Glancing quickly up and down the alleyway to ensure the coast was clear, he darted through the back gate, closing it quietly behind him.

Freddie crossed the yard to the house, pulled the length of twine hanging from the small hole at the top of the door and the latch lifted. He shoved the door open, went through the house and straight to the till, but this time, instead of just filching coins, he grabbed the heavy iron key from the back of the drawer – just where Joe said it would be. He took the key and an old oil lamp, which he lit using one of the tapers in the jar by the oven. Quickly, he went back outside to the stable, wrenched the lock and opened the door to the cavernous, empty space as deep and wide as the chop house. The lintel over the double gates leading out to the street was high enough to let a good-sized carriage through.

He paced around to investigate. The walls were dry, if a bit crumbly, and the beams weren't completely riddled with worm holes, and despite a couple of missing slates the roof looked sound enough.

He pulled back a sheet of crumpled tarpaulin that covered some rotting tack, which he kicked aside to study the beaten-earth floor. It too was dry and more or less even. He found that an iron bar secured with a thick padlock fastened the gates. Freddie held the lamp to peer at the rusty bolts. Rusty but still strong. He straightened up and turned around. Perfect.

He walked out, locked the door, and slipped the key in his breast pocket. He extinguished the lamp and made his way back through Kate's tidy yard to the house. As he passed the chicken coop tucked into the lee of the house and the small vegetable patch with the first few shoots poking through the soil, an odd, low-spirited feeling that he couldn't name seemed to settle around him. He whistled a tune to shrug it off.

For some reason, instead of going straight into the shop, Freddie stopped in the parlour. The polished floor was offset by a brightly coloured rag rug in front of the hearth, the armchairs each had a clean antimacassar. The painted figurines on the mantelshelf may have come from a fairground but there wasn't a speck of dust on them.

An image of his and Aggie's room with the cracked window, unmade bug-infested bed and discarded plates and bottles flashed through his mind.

Freddie cursed under his breath and kicked the footstool aside. He marched into the kitchen to replace the lamp where he'd found it.

The range was still warm and the aroma escaping from it told Freddie that the Sunday joint was roasting in the oven.

Suddenly, from nowhere, images of a younger Kate smiling at him and the sweetness of her first responses flickered through his mind. He remembered the damp room in Salter Street that she'd scrubbed and furnished with second-hand bits to make a home. He thought about the hot meal each night and clean shirt every morning. Perhaps if he'd ... for one frightening moment a gnawing hole opened deep in Freddie's chest.

He punched the marble counter. Pain shot up his arm, driving out all other thoughts. Flexing his hand to ease the pain, Freddie lifted the lid of the pot on the back burner. He shook it and watched the meat and vegetables that would be on tomorrow's menu bob around for a moment, then hawked a mouthful of phlegm from the back of his throat and spat into the pan.

Chapter Sixteen

Ella picked up a length of orange thread and returned to her place. Because it was a fine day Miss Wainwright had moved the older girls into the playground for their afternoon's sewing lesson and they all sat in a circle in the sun. They were only just outside the classroom door so the teacher could keep an eye on them while she supervised the younger ones as they learnt their letters.

'Ella, could you unpick my stitches again?' asked Rose Spencer, who was sitting next to her.

'Give it here.' Ella took her friend's square of fabric and whipped her needle through the tangle. She handed it back. 'There you go. If you keep the cotton shorter, it won't catch in itself.'

'Ta.' Rose sighed. 'I wish I could sew as good as you.'

Ella smiled and smoothed her sampler over her knees. She completed the three small border rows of cross stitch in red, blue and green and now she was going to start the final one. She planned to stitch the alphabet and numbers one to ten as Miss Wainwright had told them to, but would leave enough space to embroider a special message in the centre.

She licked the end of the cotton and, holding the needle aloft, threaded it through. She was just about to start the next row when the schoolmistress stepped out of the door. She clapped her hands. The girls stopped their sewing and looked at her.

'I have a lovely surprise for you all,' she said, her sallow face flushed with excitement.

There was a flurry of activity as Miss Puttock and Miss Crompton squeezed their bell-shaped skirts through the doorway. Miss Puttock, in her flouncy grass-green gown and Miss Crompton, in her lacy blue one, looked like a couple of parrots from Jamrach's beside Miss Wainwright in her modest grey.

'Now, girls,' the schoolmistress said as the young women straightened their clothing and squared their bonnets. 'This afternoon we have two very special visitors to our school. Miss Puttock, whose father is churchwarden and a very important person, and Miss Crompton, daughter of Alderman Crompton, who owns one of the big warehouse on Wapping Lane. These fine young ladies have given up their valuable time to help you with your sewing. What do you think of that?' Her eyes darted sharply around at her charges.

'Thank you, Miss Puttock. Thank you, Miss Crompton,' a dozen voices chanted. Two of the big boys appeared through the door carrying chairs and stood waiting for instruction.

'Where would you like to sit?' Miss Wainwright twittered.

Miss Puttock's eyes skimmed over the girls and alighted on Ella. 'If you help the girls on the right, Caroline, I'll assist those on the left. I'll squeeze in between these two young ladies,' she said to the boy following her with the chair.

She smiled sweetly at Ella and Rose and they shuffled aside to make room. Miss Puttock sat down and practically covered the two girls with her voluptuous skirt.

'Now,' she said, straightening out the bows on her sleeves. 'Let's get to know each other.' She turned away from Ella. 'What's your name?'

'Rose.'

'How pretty,' replied Miss Puttock. She swivelled around to face Ella. 'And you're Elsie Ellis, aren't you?'

'Ella,' she corrected, noticing that the down on Miss Puttock's top lip was more visible in the sunlight.

'Of course. And what are you sewing?'

Ella held out her sampler.

'Very neat,' she said, grudgingly. 'And your stitches are surprisingly even.'

'My ma taught me to sew,' Ella told her proudly.

'Really,' replied Miss Puttock. 'And what are you going to put in the middle?'

'To Ma with love,' Ella said, imagining how pleased Ma would be when she saw it. Perhaps if she took it home secretly, she could ask Uncle Pat to put a frame around it so she could give it to her mother as a birthday present.

A sour look tightened Miss Puttock's face. 'You can't do that.'

'Why not?'

'Because it's not proper English. You should embroider "To Mother with deepest affection",' Miss Puttock said. 'That would be much more suitable.'

'Yes, ma'am,' Ella replied, looking coolly at her.

'Please, miss, I've tangled my thread,' Rose said.

Miss Puttock took her sampler and smiled serenely. 'Never mind, child. I'll have it unravelled in a trice.'

She plucked at the knotted threads for a moment then looked at Ella again. 'Your mother runs the chop house on the Highway, doesn't she?'

Ella nodded. 'She makes the best pies in the area. Everyone says so. And cakes.'

'How nice,' replied Miss Puttock stiffly. She made a play of unpicking the last of Rose's tangles. 'I believe your headmaster visits your mother's shop from time to time.'

Ella studied the young woman's controlled expression for a moment then a smile spread across her face.

'He's always popping in,' she said, artlessly. 'In fact, I'd say he was one of her most regular customers. He says he likes her coffee. But I know what he's really after.' Miss Puttock's eyebrows raised in consternation. Ella grinned. 'Her lemon cake.'

Suddenly Captain Quinn stepped into the playground. Miss Puttock's head snapped around and her cheeks flushed.

'Let me see how you're getting on, my dear,' Miss Puttock said, tossing her head and setting her ringlets dancing.

'Miss Puttock, how nice to see you,' he said.

'And you,' Miss Puttock replied.

'It's good of you to spare the time to help Miss Wainwright. I'm sure the girls will benefit greatly from your help.'

Miss Puttock laughed a little too loudly. 'I'm sure they will and we are having such fun, aren't we, girls?'

They nodded and Miss Puttock grabbed Ella and Rose's hands and squeezed them. 'Just girls together chatting about this and that.' She wrinkled her nose up in an odd way and grinned at them. 'The way girls do when engaged in homemaking tasks.'

Captain Quinn laughed. 'I'm afraid I'm more used to officers' mess chatter. I've absolutely no notion what young women talk about.'

'I can tell you, Headmaster,' Ella said, looking innocently up at him. 'Miss Puttock was just asking me how often you drop into Ma's shop.'

Miss Puttock's neck flushed crimson. 'Wh-what ... I ... I ...'

'And for what,' Ella added. She picked up her needle and stabbed it through her sampler. 'I said for coffee and cake.'

Captain Quinn's face darkened.

Miss Puttock plucked at the lace on her sleeve. 'I-I was asking how Elsie's mother—'

'Ella's mother,' Captain Quinn cut in.

'Of course,' Miss Puttock said. 'I was just asking how she was and *Ella* let slip that you had an occasional cup of coffee in her shop. Wasn't that so?' She looked at Ella.

Ella looked blankly at her.

'Good day, Miss Puttock,' Captain Quinn said. 'I trust you won't let any more chatter interrupt your visit?'

'Of course.'

Miss Puttock slumped into the chair and watched gloomily as Captain Quinn moved away to speak to Miss Crompton on the other side of the circle.

The Blue Coat Boy was heaving, as usual, after the factories and warehouses blew the end of day whistle. Aggie was there, too, as was Ollie and his crew but, thankfully, without Lilly or the poxy little prince.

'Afternoon, Mr Mac,' she said, giving Ollie her most inviting smile. 'How's the young 'un today?'

'He's grand,' Ollie replied, beaming at her. 'He smiled at me yesterday.'

'Did he?' replied Aggie, trying to look interested.

'You got something for me?'

'Haven't I always?' she replied, pulling a handful of coins from her pocket.

The door to Ollie's rooms flew back and Lilly strolled in. 'I'll take that,' she said, holding out a black-nailed hand.

Damn!

Forcing down her humiliation and loathing, Aggie handed over five shillings. Lilly counted the coins.

'It's all there,' Aggie told her.

'I'm making sure.'

'Lilly, ducks, where's my boy?' Ollie asked.

A scraggy lock of hair fell loose as Lilly shook her head. 'I've given him a couple of drops of Godfrey's Cordial. He's having a kip. I'll fetch him down later.'

'Will he be all right up there by 'imself?'

'Course he will. I've shut the window so the yard cat can't get in,' Lilly replied, squeezing her considerable rear end into the chair beside him. Her eyes flickered on to a couple of fresh-faced prostitutes who were lounging together at the far end of the bar. 'Oi, you! Get back to work.' The girls untangled themselves and hurried out of the room. She looked at Aggie. 'You, too.'

Aggie ground her teeth. Freddie had done bugger all about taking over the Black Eagle Gang. It couldn't go on. She wouldn't let it. If he didn't have the balls to bring Ollie and his fat sow down, she'd have to do it herself.

'Anything you say,' she replied, pointedly adjusting her neckline in full view of Ollie.

She made her way back outside and glanced down the narrow alley beside the pub. Thankfully, none of the girls were earning a shilling or two against its walls. Aggie sped down to the rear of the pub, pushed open the squeaky back gate and into the pub, tiptoeing up the back stairs.

The noise from the rooms below filtered up through the floorboards as she crept along the corridor to find Ollie and Lilly's room. She heard the baby grizzle lowly and pushed open the next door she came to. Her eyes fixed on the cradle beside the unmade bed.

She crept across the room and stopped beside the cot. She extended her index finger and stroked his cheek. The baby gave a little shudder and his budded lips made a little sucking noise. Now he'd grown out of his newborn redness, you could see his resemblance to his father. He lay there peacefully with his eyes moving back and forth under his almost transparent eyelids, dreaming no doubt of Lilly's milk-filled titties.

With precious little time to waste, Aggie slid open the window. The breeze lifted the curtains and the candle guttered. Aggie pushed the candle holder towards the fluttering drapes. The fabric ignited.

As the fire licked up the curtains Aggie skirted around the cradle back to the door. She paused and watched the breeze blow pieces of burning fabric on to the newspaper on the floor and the bed's straw mattress before opening the door and slipping out of the room. Fortunately, there was no one around when she slipped back down the corridor and into the piss-putrid air of the rear alleyway.

Lilly settled herself back in the chair and smiled. *That told the cheeky bitch*, she thought. *She might fool that idiot Freddie with her little act but she can't pull the wool over my eyes.*

She nudged Ollie. 'Pour us another, duck.'

He grinned. 'Get that down you, old girl,' he said, splashing a generous measure of brandy into her glass. 'You deserve it.'

He turned back to Stefan and continued jawing. Lilly took a sip.

She bloody well did. She'd survived the birthing, the milk fever and that slut Aggie trying to get her claws into Ollie. And now she had her little angel as well. Life was looking up. Perhaps she'd have a word with Ollie again about renting a little house down Bethnal Green Road. Somewhere with a bit of grass at the back for Albert to stretch his legs on when he started to tod—

The pub door crashed open and one of the butchers from across the road burst in.

'Fire!' he screamed, pointing at the ceiling. 'Fire!'

For a split second the room froze, and then erupted. People screamed and dashed for the door, knocking over tables and chairs in the scramble to get out.

Lilly sprang to her feet. 'Bertie!'

Ollie and his men ran towards the door. Lilly's heart crashed in her chest as terror gripped her.

'My baby! My baby!' she screamed.

Grabbing someone's jacket, she shoved them out of her path. One of the children who begged pennies from the drinkers got in her way and she sent him sprawling across the sawdust as she headed for the stairs.

'Water,' Ollie bellowed from somewhere behind her. His men crashed into the backyard towards the pump.

Lilly stumbled over an upturned stool. She put her hand on a broken glass to stop her fall but she didn't feel it slice her skin.

Ollie caught her arm. 'We'll get him out,' he said, his face ashen with dread.

Lilly shook him off and elbowed her way to the stairs; the smell of burning wood caught in her nose. Looking up, she saw grey smoke drifting out of her room and heard the crackle of flames. Ollie, Stefan and Jimmy thundered into the hallway behind her.

'Get up there,' Ollie shouted, thrusting his men forward with their buckets.

A tortured shriek pierced the air.

'Bertie!' screamed Lilly, as the sounds of her child's pain cut through every nerve in her body.

She pushed past Ollie and, blind to the flames and smoke, ran into their blazing room.

At that moment the oil lamp on the dresser exploded, flinging scorching oil across the room. The door frame blew out, throwing Ollie and his men back.

Albert's screams rose to a terrified, agonising pitch.

Lilly rushed forward. Ollie reached out to stop her but she punched him in the mouth without breaking her stride. The heat scorched her eyes and skin as she passed through the doorway but she didn't pause.

'Mammy's coming, my darling,' she called, and then, with her eyes fixed on the flaming cot, plunged into the inferno.

The mid-summer sun had just dipped behind the shops along White-chapel High Street as Freddie turned into Commercial Road. A dozen or so downtrodden individuals were already gathering on the steps of Christ Church waiting for the evening soup kitchen. Outside the Ten Bells next door, burly armed porters from the slaughterhouse in Brick Lane slaked their thirst with pints of cool ale.

Sidestepping a drunk sprawled in the gutter, Freddie crossed the road and entered Dorset Street. He stopped dead and his jaw dropped as he stared at the smoke floating skywards from the first-floor window of the Blue Coat Boy. The old wooden frame and criss-cross lattice work were no more than charred columns and the brickwork surrounding the windows was completely blackened. There was also a dreadful stench of cooked bacon mixed with the powerful smell of charcoal. The Black Eagle Gang were milling around outside while a couple of doxies huddled together in a doorway opposite and held grubby handkerchiefs to their noses as they stared red-eyed at the ruin.

Freddie was just about to walk over and join the rest of the gang when Aggie appeared at the far end of the street. When she saw the destruction she hurried over, looking horrified.

'Gawd luv us, what's happened?' she asked, clutching her hands as if in prayer. 'Isn't that Ollie and Lilly's room?' She pointed up at the burnt-out first-floor window.

'I think so.'

'Oh, my life, are they here?' Aggie glanced up and down the street. 'And where's their dear little baby?'

Freddie took of his hat and scratched his head. 'Look, there's Stefan.'

Ollie's second-in-command staggered out of the bar door. His shirt was torn and blackened. Sweat streaked down his dirty face and his trousers were wet from the knees down. He spotted Freddie and lurched over.

'We were too late,' he said, as he reached them.

'What happened?' Freddie asked.

'I'm not sure. We were all sitting in the bar when the butcher burst in. We all dashed up but the flames were already licking under the door of Ollie's room.' Stefan's face drained of colour. 'Then, God have mercy, we heard him. Little Albert! Screaming like a soul in hell. Lilly went wild and rushed into the flames. Ollie kicked and cursed us as we fetched water from the yard but we couldn't save them.'

Freddie's eyes returned to the gaping hole over the pub door but in his mind's eye saw Joe. Sympathy, an emotion that rarely troubled him, caught in his chest. Poor bugger. No matter how big a bastard Ollie was, he didn't deserve to listen to his child being roasted alive. Freddie swallowed hard.

Aggie slipped her arm in his. 'So poor little Albert *and* Lilly are dead,' she said quietly.

Stefan nodded. 'I tell you, Freddie, I've seen men with their faces eaten off by rats, bodies that have been floating in the river so long their mother wouldn't recognise them, all without turning a hair, but the screams of that poor child will haunt me until the day I die.' He covered his eyes with his hand.

'Where's Ollie?' Freddie asked.

'Still inside.'

The clatter of galloping hooves parted the gaping onlookers and the frantic clanging of a bell heralded the arrival of the police wagon. Six officers jumped out and went into the building. As the last of them disappeared, the ambulance cart trundled around the corner. The driver and his mate got down, unhooked the covering, lifted the canvas stretcher clear and followed the policemen into the pub. A few moments passed before the officers reappeared and formed up, their arms linked, in front of the crowd. The ambulance attendants walked through the door holding the poles of the stretcher. On top, wrapped in a sheet, was the form of an adult with a smaller bundle tucked in beside her. The onlookers surged forward and a combined sob went up from the whores. The crowd joined in. Ollie staggered into the street and stood staring at what had once been his Lilly and his son as they were secured on the cart.

Aggie and Freddie walked over. Ollie looked at them with hollow eyes. 'She said she'd closed the window but she couldn't have; the breeze must have blown the curtains on to the flame. They found her cradling 'im.'

'He was such a happy little chap,' Freddie said, as the image of his

Joe trotting along beside him floated back into his mind.

Aggie drew her handkerchief from her sleeve and dabbed her eyes. 'Can I see her, Mr Mac?'

Ollie nodded.

Aggie reached out and peeled the sheet back. Lilly was unrecognisable. The fire had burnt off her blonde hair and turned her face into something resembling a puffy roast chestnut. Freddie shuddered and looked away but Aggie stared down at Lilly for a few more moments then covered her face with her hands.

'Oh, God, why did you have to take sweet little Albert?' she wailed.

Freddie put his arms around her shaking shoulders. 'Come on, Aggie, don't take on so.'

She straightened up and dabbed her eyes again. 'I'm sorry, Mr Mac, but thinking of how your little lad must have suffered I can't . . .' she buried her head into Freddie's chest.

The attendants secured the cover after a word with Ollie and then climbed to the front of the cart. The police dropped arms, returning to their wagon, and both vehicles rolled on. The crowd drifted away.

As the vehicles disappeared around the corner, Ollie cleared his throat. 'Right, I want everyone to hear me now. I'm going to give my boy a right good send-off and I want you all there. Do you hear?'

Stefan went and put an arm around Ollie's shoulders. 'Come on, boss. Let's get a couple in the Ten Bells.'

Ollie wiped his nose and nodded then shuffled away.

Freddie turned to Aggie. 'You look like you could do with a drink, too, sweetheart.'

She put on a brave little smile and shook her head. 'I think I'll stroll along to the church and say a little prayer for poor . . . lit-little Albert and d-d-dear Lilly.' She put her handkerchief to her face and turned away.

Freddie watched her shaking shoulders as she walked back down the streets sobbing. Even the most hard-bitten of Ollie's whores cooed over a babe-in-arms and gave a little 'un the odd farthing for an aniseed twist, but Aggie had always seemed indifferent to children. Seeing her now, heartbroken over poor little Albert and Lilly's accident, he wondered if he'd misjudged her.

Chapter Seventeen

Jonathan took Mrs Benson's steps two at a time and tucked himself under the carved wooden porch to shelter from the rain. He knocked smartly on the door. Willamore opened it and ushered him inside.

'How is Mrs Benson?' Jonathan asked, handing over his soggy coat and hat.

'A little better but Madam doesn't complain.'

Like many in the congregation, Mrs Benson had taken a chill just after Christmas, but while others had shaken off the chest ague without too much trouble, Mrs Benson hadn't yet rallied. It was only to be expected at her age, but Jonathan was nonetheless concerned.

The butler led him towards the morning-room door. 'She'll be cheered to see you, Captain Quinn.'

Jonathan walked in to where Mrs Benson reclined, swathed in shawls, on the chaise longue. She'd always seemed frail but now the skin of her face seemed transparent, revealing the blue veins around her temples.

'Captain Quinn. You'll forgive me for not rising to greet you properly,' she said, extending a small hand.

'Of course,' Jonathan said, taking it gently. 'How are you?'

'Well enough for an old woman.' She covered her mouth with a lace handkerchief and coughed. 'I've got Harker trying to prescribe me all sorts of concoctions but I told him no.'

'Surely there must be something—'

She raised her hand. 'I'm too old to argue with, remember?'

Jonathan smiled and pulled a chair alongside her to sit down.

Mrs Benson tilted her head and studied him closely. 'Now, it's the duty of those visiting the sick to divert them from their troubles so let us talk of something other than my old bones.'

The housekeeper brought tea and cake and Jonathan told Mrs Benson how his plans for the school were progressing.

'Excellent! What with the new curriculum and books ...' she said with a twinkle in her eye. 'And what area are you going to tackle next?'

'Truancy,' Jonathan replied. 'It's lessening but there are still some children who never do a full week. I understand their circumstances – if the head of the household has no work or is on short time the children have to earn something – but I'm afraid that often means turning to petty crime. Of course Mrs Ellis's children are always in school. I saw her just yesterday,' he said, trying to sound casual. 'She asked me to pass on her best wishes.'

'That's kind of her.' She shifted position and winced.

'Am I tiring you?'

She shook her head. 'I'm quite all right. It's just a little stiffness from sitting. I'll be fine.' She smiled at him. 'But what about you? It worries me to think of you in that large schoolhouse with no one looking after you or keeping you company.'

'You sound like Mrs Delaney!'

Mrs Benson looked at him with impatience. 'Well, she has a point!'

'But—'

'But nothing,' she said, waving her hand dismissively. 'You've been with us for over six months now. I thought you and Miss Puttock were growing closer. She's a tendency to the dramatic, I grant you, but a household to run and a brood of children should keep her feet on the ground. You do want children, don't you?'

'I do, but—'

'Genesis chapter two, verse eighteen. "It is not good for a man to be alone." You can't argue with the Good Book.'

'I wouldn't dream of it,' Jonathan replied.

She sighed. 'And I would so like to see you settled and happy.' She studied his face again. 'Is there someone *else* who has caught your attention?'

An image of Kate Ellis on the cake stall floated into his mind. 'Of course not, but you can't rush these things.'

She scrutinised his face.

Jonathan pulled out his watch. 'Is that the time?' He stood up. 'I should be getting back.'

Mrs Benson studied him for a few seconds longer then put her cup down. 'It's good of you to call,' she said, ringing the small bell at her elbow.

'Not at all. I always look forward to putting the world to rights with you each Tuesday afternoon.'

'As do I.' She offered him her hand and Jonathan patted it gently.

The door opened and Willamore stood back so he could leave. Jonathan smiled down at her again then turned to go.

'Oh, Jonathan.' He turned. 'If you happen to see Kate Ellis as you take the air on your way home, would you give her my best regards?'

Freddie pressed himself hard against the wall and swivelled his eyes to the right to keep them trained on the police officer checking the doors at the end of the alley. The beam from the officer's bull-eyed lamp cut through the thick fog snaking up from the river. Freddie drew in a deep breath and held it. Ollie, Stefan and Inchy Pete, the gang's slip-in boy, did the same beside him.

Even though he stood upwind from Ollie, Freddie could smell the brandy he'd been consuming from the moment he woke. Since the fire, Ollie hadn't spent more than an hour sober.

'Right,' whispered Stefan. 'Once the bluebottle's around the corner we move. Freddie, do you know what to do?'

Hidden in the shadows, Freddie sent the large Swede a hateful look. 'Don't you worry about me.'

The officer rattled the lock of the last warehouse and then plodded out of sight. Stefan laid a massive hand on Pete's shoulder. 'Ready?'

'Yes, Mr Magson.'

Stefan cupped his hands and bent forward. Inchy put one bare foot in the improvised stirrup and Stefan lifted him on to his shoulders. The boy took a knife from his belt and clamped it between his teeth, then scrambled up the narrow window ledge before disappearing inside.

'He'ssss a good little lad,' Ollie slurred, looking balefully up at the open window. 'My little boy would have been just like him if the Good Lord had spared him,' he continued a little too loudly.

Freddie rolled his eyes. *Bloody fine fucking kettle of fish*, he thought. *Here we are outside a bonded warehouse with a dozen nabbers within spitting distance and our fucking boss man's blubbing like a sissy boy.*

'Now come on, Ollie man,' Stefan replied, in a soothing tone. 'Let's do business.'

Ollie wiped his nose on his sleeve and stood away from the wall. 'Yer right.' He spat on the floor then inched his way towards the door, hiccupping quietly as he went.

'Perhaps we should call it off,' Freddie said, watching Ollie stumble over a broken pavement slab. 'I was thinking, with Mr Mac being a bit under the weather, it might be best to—'

Stefan grasped Freddie's collar and tie, lifting him off the ground.

'Just see to the cart, Ellis, and leave the thinking to those who know how.'

Freddie twisted himself out of his grasp. 'Watch the suit,' he said, pulling the front of his jacket. 'I was just saying.'

'Don't,' Stefan hissed.

The warehouse door squeaked and Freddie and Stefan stepped back into the shadows. Ollie Mac wove his way unsteadily towards the entrance and then disappeared into the storehouse. Inchy padded silently across the cobbled street towards them.

'Good lad,' Stefan said, ruffling the boy's unkempt hair. 'Now nip up to the corner and give us a whistle if you spy anything.'

'Yes, Mr Magson.' The boy skipped off.

Stefan turned back. 'Me and Ollie will be out in no time so keep your fucking eyes peeled.'

He pulled his cap over his eyes.

Aggie was right, Freddie thought. Ollie's finished. It was only a matter of time before Stefan stepped into his shoes. The gang knew it and were already falling into line.

Bloody cheek. I ain't kowtowing to him.

It was all very well for Aggie to urge him to challenge Stefan but she wasn't the one who'd have to dodge the end of his blade. He remembered what happened to the last man who'd challenged Magson.

He glanced at the warehouse nervously. Where were they? The beat nabber would be checking in with his sergeant on the corner of Greenbank by now and starting back soon. If Ollie and Stefan didn't get a move on, they'd all be had.

Freddie's thoughts reeled as a dangerous but perfect solution to his problems popped into his mind. He shook his head to dislodge it. *No! He daren't.* But then Aggie's words floated back to him.

If you see a chance to do Ollie in, then take it, Freddie. Take it! That's what she'd said, and now that chance had presented itself. It was the perfect solution. Ollie and Stefan sorted in one blow ... Perspiration sprang out on his forehead and with the blood pounding in his ears and sweat dripping from his brow Freddie sprinted towards the Highway. St George's clock had just finished striking three when he spotted a cluster of nabbers gathered a hundred yards away on the corner of Ensign Street. He tucked himself into a doorway. *What was he thinking?* It was far too risky. He'd be dead meat if—

Take it, Freddie. Take it, Aggie's voice said again.

He stepped out from the shadows and the sergeant, a well-stuffed specimen of the constabulary with a bushy moustache, turned as he approached.

'Thank goodness,' he said, stopping in front of them. 'I'm just on my way to work and I saw a wagon tied up in front of Jones and Sons' warehouse down on Bostock Street and I think I saw a light in one of the upstairs windows.'

The sergeant's eyes flashed open. 'Constables Burton and Woolmer, you get yourselves down Broad Street, and Brooks, Almond and Grey, make haste down Pennington Street. Surround the warehouse and detain anyone who comes out. I'll fetch the wagon and reinforcements from the station.'

All five constables snapped to attention, drew their truncheons and ran off. The sergeant turned back to Freddie.

'And who are you?'

'Eddie Pollard. I'm a porter at Smithfield and live in Chapman Street. Number thirty-four.'

The sergeant studied him closely as Freddie fought the almost overwhelming urge to turn tail and run. After what seemed like hours the sergeant spoke.

'On your way, chum,' he said, flicking his head.

'Thank you, sir,' Freddie replied, touching the brim of his cap respectfully.

He shoved his hands in his pockets and sauntered down the street. He forced himself to maintain an unhurried pace until he turned the corner and then collapsed against the wall. Letting his head fall back on the rough brickwork, he shut his eyes. As the distant sound of police rattles broke the early morning silence, Freddie stood away from the wall and prayed that by the time he got back to the Blue Coat Boy, Ollie Mac and Stefan would be in a cell under Arbour Square police station.

Aggie lifted her brandy to her lips and studied the bar of the Blue Coat Boy over the rim. It was a bit quiet tonight but then it had been since the fire. Hopefully it would pick up again now that Lilly and her sprog were buried. And what a palaver that had been. Instead of just having the coffin carried on a handcart, Ollie had spent a fortune hiring a hearse with a black horse between the shafts and a plume stuck on its head like he was burying a nob or something, not Lilly Bragg who used to give hand jobs to sailors for tuppence. And if that weren't enough, they all had to traipse behind the procession for two miles to the burial ground and witness the sorry spectacle of Ollie blubbing all the way there.

Of course, she'd sniffed and dabbed her eyes along with the rest of them but wasn't best pleased when she couldn't get her shoes on the following day because of blisters. Still, she shouldn't be too put out by it all. After all, she'd only thought to spit on Lilly's strawberries by doing her nipper in but as luck would have it, she'd got rid of her, too. That left only Ollie to deal with, and as he'd been as drunk as a lord since they carted the bodies away that shouldn't take too long. Well, it wouldn't if Freddie got his fucking finger out and did something. Perhaps when Ollie finally sobered up, she'd try another crack at hooking him. If not, there were a couple of new men who might fit the bill. She swilled her drink and studied the unshaven dozen or so men around her. She would have considered Stefan himself but he seemed to be more interested in the Molly boys who lived over by the slaughterhouse than any of the whores.

Although she wasn't supposed to know, she'd wheedled out of Freddie that there was a raid on the bonded warehouse alongside the Mint. Ollie's men had drifted in during the past hour to await their governor.

She drained the last of her drink and was just considering whether or not to take a stroll upstairs to have another look around the burnt-out room to pass the time, when the door burst open. Freddie staggered in red-faced and sweating. There was terror in his eyes as they darted wildly around the room then fixed on her.

A shiver of excitement ran up her spine.

Well stone the crows! He's done it.

Freddie lurched towards the bar. 'Give us a drink,' he bellowed.

Mary started pouring one but Freddie snatched the bottle from her and took it to his lips. The gang jostled around and fired questions at him. Aggie got up and pushed her way through the press of sweaty bodies.

'For gawd's sake, let him get his breath,' she shouted.

She felt the tension in Freddie's body and saw the pulse in his neck galloping ten to the dozen. He drained the bottle and then wiped his mouth with the back of his hand.

'Are Ollie and Stefan here?'

The men looked at each other and shook their heads. Freddie tore at his hair. 'Don't say the fucking nabbers 'ave 'em.'

'What nabbers?'

'Hundreds of them. Big buggers, too. Swarming over the yards like ants in a sugar sack,' he replied. 'We didn't stand a chance.'

'Where did they come from?' asked someone.

'Didn't you see them coming?' another shouted.

'I reckon half of H division was there and by the time I saw them it was too late. I called out to Mr Mac but he and Stefan were too far away,' Freddie told them.

Jimmy stepped forward. 'So how come they didn't catch you?'

'They nearly did, I tell you. I could have got away clean as a whistle when I spotted them marching up the road but I couldn't just scarper and leave me mates, could I?' Freddie answered.

'So how *did* you get away?' he asked, suspiciously.

Freddie's Adam's apple bobbed up and down. 'I hid myself behind the door.'

Jimmy laughed. 'What, and these swarms of coppers didn't find you?'

'You calling me a liar?' Freddie barked.

Jimmy's eyes shifted. 'I'm just wondering how you managed to escape, that's all.'

'And I'm wondering if you've grassed him up to the nabbers for the half-crown in your pocket,' Aggie shot at Jimmy, raising her voice to make sure the whole bar heard.

Freddie's gaze flickered on to her for second then a crafty smile crept across his face. 'Yeah, maybe the coppers arrived because someone told them where to look,' he added.

A growl went around the room and Jimmy blanched. 'Well if someone did then on me muvver's life it weren't me.'

Harry Watson, a good-looking fella who'd recently joined the gang, pushed his way to the front. 'You were right smart hiding like that, Freddie,' he said, flashing a set of spectacularly white teeth.

'My Freddie *is* smart,' Aggie replied, giving the newcomer the appreciative once-over. 'And everyone knows how much Mr Mac relies on him, especially since he lost poor Lilly.' Aggie rolled her eyes upwards at the grubby ceiling and a couple of the gang members crossed themselves.

'What're we going to do now, Freddie?' Harry asked.

'The warehouse on Smithfield for a start.'

'What about the swarms of coppers?' asked Jimmy.

Freddie tapped his forehead with his finger. 'You dense or something? If Ollie and Stefan are in the cells and cartloads of pilfered stuff recovered, the local old bill will be slapping each other on the back in the cop shop all night, won't they?'

Harry laughed. 'You're right there.' The rest of the gang joined in.

'That's all very well and good,' Jimmy said, as he lounged against the bar. 'But now the lock-up's been found, what're you going to do with half a dozen barrels of stolen brandy, Freddie? Hide them behind the door?'

Freddie stepped forward. 'Don't you fret none. I've already got somewhere nice and snug marked out for those little beauties.'

Freddie lounged against the up-ended cannon with a ball wedged in its mouth and waited, along with a gaggle of children hanging on the chain railing of the towpath, for the tall rigged merchantman to glide through the narrow waterway from St Katharine Dock.

He drummed his fingers impatiently. Where on earth was he? Freddie wiped his damp palms down his trousers and tried to resume a casual stance. Strictly speaking, Knockfergus – the east end of Cable Street and the tangle of narrow roads running off it – was far enough north but it was still a little too close for comfort. It only needed one of the bloody bogtrotters to spot him and go running to poxy Pat Nolan. Thankfully, he spotted Joe trotting down the road. He and three other lads were whooping and shouting as they ran along. One of them whipped Joe's cap off and threw it in the air and Joe duly caught it and play-tussled with his friend until they broke from each other, mirthful and laughing.

Freddie stood away from the bollard. 'Joe!'

Joe looked around and his face lit up. 'Pa! Pa!'

He said something to the other boys and then ran over and hugged his legs. An odd soppy feeling started in Freddie's chest but he damped it down.

'That's enough of that,' he said, pulling down the front of his jacket. 'You don't want people to think you're a nancy boy, do you?'

Joe let go. 'No, Pa,' he said, lowering his eyes and kicking the toe of his boot on the kerb.

'I've been waiting for ages. Where have you been?'

Joe looked up and Freddie basked in his son's hero-worship. 'Have you come down specially to see me?'

'Well I had a bit of business down this way so I thought I'd hang about for you.'

Joe caught the edge of Freddie's new jacket and rubbed it between his thumb and forefinger. 'It feels so soft,' he said, feeling the velvet pile. 'It must have cost loads of money.'

'You know me, son, I won't have no rubbish. Watch out.' Freddie pulled the maroon fabric out of Joe's fingers. 'You'll make it grubby.'

Joe's hand dropped to his side. 'And are they solid gold?' he asked, looking in awe at Freddie's cufflinks.

'Yer,' Freddie replied, getting them to twinkle in the afternoon spring sunlight. They were plate really but Joe wouldn't know the difference. 'I thought I might wander down to the Tower and get myself a coffee. Do you want to come?'

Joe jumped up. 'Can I?'

Freddie smiled. 'Course.' He sauntered off towards the river with Joe trotting alongside him.

Freddie held his head up and caroused through the well-dressed crowd of men and women ambling along the riverbank. A couple of young Spitalfields fingersmiths working their art among the sightseers spotted him, tipped their hats respectfully as he and Joe made their way to the refreshment vendors by the ticket office.

'Can I have a lemonade?' Joe asked as Freddie ordered himself a coffee.

'I ain't made of money, boy, but here you go.' He handed Joe a tuppence. 'Run and get yourself a small one.'

Joe took the money and ran off. As he watched his young son queue for his drink a lump thickened in Freddie's throat. Joe paid for his lemonade and carried it back using both hands to hold it steady. He set it on the wall, then scrambled up and sat down. He smiled shyly at his father. The urge to take his son in his arms swept over Freddie. He made to raise his arm but then stopped himself.

'Are you all right, Pa?' Joe asked.

Freddie swallowed. 'Course I am. Never better. Why?'

Joe shrugged and picked up his drink. 'You just looked a bit funny, that's all.'

'I was just thinking of a pal of mine who lost his little lad a couple of weeks ago.'

'What, did he run off?'

'He died. In a fire.'

'Oooh. That's sad,' Joe said, taking a contemplative sip of lemonade. 'Pa, are you coming home?'

'You know your mother won't let me, boy. She's set her fucking tinker brother and half of Irish town after me – not to mention her sister's poxy husband.' He glanced down at Joe. 'Not that I couldn't take 'em both in a straight fight.'

'I know you could, Pa,' Joe replied.

'Good. And make sure you don't let anyone say otherwise, do you hear?' Freddie said.

'I'd bash them if they did,' Joe replied, putting up his fists and punching the air.

Freddie chuckled. 'Make sure you do.'

Joe's happy expression vanished. 'Is that why you didn't come around Christmas?'

'Christmas! Cor, that was months ago.'

'But you said you'd be there,' Joe persisted.

'Give it a rest, Joe. I've got things to do and can't hang around here all day. You'd better run along home.'

'When will I see you again, Pa?' Joe asked, looking up at him with tears shimmering in his eyes.

Freddie hesitated for a moment then bent down until his face was level with Joe's. 'I'll tell you what. If you promise not to tell a living soul, I'll meet you here next Thursday after school. What do you say?'

Joe jumped up and down with excitement.

Freddie grinned. 'OK. But when I say "don't tell a soul", I mean no one. Not your school chums, your sister, and *especially* not your ma. Do you understand?'

Joe nodded seriously and his cap slid off.

'Off you go then, son.' He ruffled his son's hair.

Joe looked surprised for an instant then scooped up his cap and dashed off home. As he got to the bottom of the road he stopped and waved at Freddie then disappeared. Freddie pulled the cigar out of his top pocket and lit it.

He shouldn't mollycoddle Joe of course – he had enough of that from his mother – but perhaps it was time he stepped in and steered Joe on to the right path.

Chapter Eighteen

The tip of Joe's tongue curled over his top lip as he concentrated on making the p in Joseph sit within the horizontal lines on his slate. All around him, the other twenty-five boys in the classroom sat hunched over their desks, concentrating on similar tasks. Having positioned the fifth letter of his name to his satisfaction, Joe turned his attention to the last letter. Repositioning his scriber, he started at the top, drew a line down, then tried to make it go up but it just squiggled off to the right. He kicked his boot against the leg of the desk. It was too hard! Pa said school was a waste of time and he was right. Why did he need to go to fucking school anyhow?

'Ellis,' Captain Quinn's voice boomed above him.

Joe stood up. 'Yes, sir.'

'You'll never master the art of writing by daydreaming out of the window.' He tapped the rectangular piece of board with Joe's name on it. 'Now start again.'

'Yes, sir.' Joe sat down.

Clasping his hands behind his back, Captain Quinn walked between the school benches to his desk at the front of the class. Joe poked out his tongue at the headmaster's back the way his father told him he used to.

He gripped his scriber firmly and finished his lesson. As he scratched the tail of the last s, Captain Quinn stood up and rang the bell on his desk.

The boys sat upright while the monitors collected the slates. Captain Quinn led the class in the end-of-day prayer and after twenty-six young voices said 'Amen' the row of boys filed towards the door where the headmaster waited to bid them goodbye.

'Good evening, Ellis.'

'Good evening, Headmaster.' He waited to be dismissed but Captain Quinn spoke again.

'You know, you're not without brains and with a little more effort, you could be one of St Katharine's star pupils.'

Joe puffed out his chest. 'Thank you, Headmaster.'

'I've also noticed you are very good at drawing. The copy of a fox you did in nature study was one of the best I've seen. Your mother might want to consider apprenticing you to a cartographer – that's someone who makes maps. How would you like that?'

Joe's eyes opened wide. Uncle Pat had lots of maps in his office and Cousin Mickey had let Joe trace the curves of the river last time he, Ma and Ella had visited.

He stood a little taller. 'That would be right grand.'

'Well then, Ellis. No map-maker will take you on unless you master the alphabet and arithmetic.'

Joe's shoulders slumped. 'Yes, sir. I *will* try harder.'

'Good. If you can complete your primer by the summer, then I might even consider making you a board monitor, but *only* if you put more effort into your lessons.'

'Thank you, sir,' Joe said, bobbing on to the balls of his toes.

'Off you go, then. And don't dawdle on your way home and worry your mother.'

Joe stood to attention and then walked tall into the schoolyard. At the far end, leaning against the wall, were a crowd of older boys. Joe's heart sank as he saw Chalky White in the middle of them. Chalky was just short of twelve but looked two years older and was leaving St Katharine's in the summer. Joe heartily wished he'd already gone.

Joe fixed his eyes on the school gate and, remembering Captain Quinn's story about St George facing the dragon, he marched across the yard.

Chalky peeled himself off the wall and sauntered across with his gang behind him, blocking Joe's escape. His guts churned, but Joe pulled his shoulders back and walked up to the group of boys.

'Oi, Teacher's Pet,' Chalky said, planting himself in Joe's path. 'What's old Nelson kept you back for?'

'Captain Quinn just asked me about the slate.'

'Captain Quinn. Captain Quinn,' Chalky mimicked in a high girly voice. The boys around him sniggered. Chalky stepped closer. 'I bet he was telling you what a good little boy you were.'

'I told you it was about the slates. Now let me pass.' Joe tried to walk between them but the bigger boy pushed him back.

'You're a fucking liar,' Chalky said, as he advanced towards Joe. 'A fucking liar. Just like your old man.' He lowered his face until his nose almost touched Joe's. 'Did you hear me, Teacher's Pet?'

Joe balled his fists but then remembered the possibility of becoming a board monitor. 'My pa's not,' he replied, trying to imitate the headmaster's measured tone.

Chalky's top lip curled. 'If he isn't, tell us where he's been for the last five years.'

'At sea,' Joe answered.

The boys standing behind Chalky held their stomachs, bent double and hung onto each other's shoulders, laughing.

'What's so funny?'

Chalky wiped his dry eyes. 'Did you hear that? Poor little bugger thinks his pa's been at sea.' His eyes narrowed. 'Your pa ain't been at sea, he's been in the clink for nicking a load of silver.'

Something thick seemed to crowd into Joe's mind and he shoved Chalky in the chest. 'You take that back, White!'

'Or what?'

Joe balled his fist and the bones cracked. 'I'll knock your block off.'

'What and have Nelson on at you for fighting in the—'

Joe's fist smashed into Chalky's protruding teeth. They split his knuckles but Joe hardly felt it. He punched Chalky again. This time on the nose, splattering blood across both of them. Joe's feet found their targets on the older boy's shins and the toe of Joe's boot caught Charlie just below the knee with a sickening crunch. Chalky groaned and his leg buckled. Joe leapt on him as he crashed to the ground and continued punching, kicking and gouging at his face.

A roar went up but to Joe it sounded a long way away. His fists smashed into his tormentor's face over and over. He felt hands on him trying to pull him away but he shook them off.

'My pa's not a liar,' he screamed.

Suddenly strong hands grasped his shoulders and Joe found himself punching air. He tried to wriggle free but was held fast.

'That's enough, Ellis!' a deep voice commanded.

Joe drew in a sharp breath and the fog in his head started to clear. His feet scraped the floor as he was set down. He shook his head and looked up into Captain Quinn's furious face.

'I said, that's enough!' Captain Quinn repeated, as he looked at the boys.

Joe followed the headmaster's gaze and gasped when he saw Chalky being helped up by two of his friends. He stared in disbelief at the boy's closed left eye, split lip and bloody nose.

'Run along home, White,' Captain Quinn said.

'Yes, sir,' mumbled Chalky through his swollen lips. He limped out of the schoolyard supported under the arms by two other boys.

Captain Quinn turned to Joe. 'Haven't I made it quite clear that I will not tolerate fighting in the school?'

Joe hung his head. 'Yes, sir.'

'Then why did you attack William White? I saw you arguing from my window. What's this all about, Ellis?'

'I can't tell.'

'Why can't you tell?'

'Because my pa told me that everyone hates a nark, so I'm not saying.'

'You can go home now, Ellis,' Captain Quinn said, in a disappointed tone that hurt Joe more than his cut knuckles. 'Ask your mother to come to my office tomorrow after school. We will discuss the whole incident then.'

Captain Quinn turned on his heels and marched back across the schoolyard. An odd feeling settled behind Joe's breastbone as he watched his headmaster's tall figure disappear through the door. He forced it away and turned his back on the school. Pa was right. School was a waste of time.

Kate sat dressed in her Sunday gown and best bonnet staring at Captain Quinn's study door, but instead of her heart thumping in her chest in anticipation, something akin to panic ran through her. She glared down at Joe sitting with two black eyes and his cap in his hands beside her. Sensing her furious stare he looked up at her with the same blasé expression she'd seen too often on Freddie's face.

The door finally opened. Kate's heart skipped a couple of beats as Captain Quinn stepped out.

'Mrs Ellis,' he said, his gaze warming a little as it rested on her. 'Would you care to step into my office?' He stood back from the door.

Kate took Joe's hand and walked through. The headmaster closed the door and indicated the seat in front of his desk. Kate sat and Joe stood beside her.

'Thank you for coming, Mrs Ellis,' he said as he resumed his seat on the other side of the desk. 'Joe has probably told you what happened yesterday.'

Kate nodded. 'Joe is very sorry about his behaviour, Captain Quinn. Aren't you, Joe?'

Joe gazed out of the window.

Captain Quinn's lips drew into a tight line. 'Joseph Ellis, your mother asked you a question,' he boomed.

Joe jumped. 'Yes, sir. I am very sorry,' he said in a flat tone. 'But Pa told me to hit them first.'

'Did he?'

'Yes.'

'But why did you hit William White? Was he bullying you? If he was, I would like to know as I will not tolerate such cowardly behaviour.'

Joe shifted his weight onto his other foot. 'I can take care of myself.'

Captain Quinn rested his arms on the desk and laced his fingers together. 'Why did you attack him?'

A truculent expression spread across Joe's face and Kate's temper boiled over. 'Joseph Patrick Ellis. Don't disgrace me by acting like you've never been taught manners and *answer* the headmaster's question.'

'But Pa said—'

'I don't care what your pa said,' Kate retorted, glaring at her son. '*I'm* telling you to explain why you beat another boy's nose into a piece of chewed meat!'

'He said Pa's been in prison. But it ain't true, is it, Ma?' he asked, looking pleadingly up at her.

A lump suddenly formed in Kate's throat and the floor tilted slightly.

Captain Quinn stood up and came around the desk to stand beside them. 'Master Ellis. People will say all sorts of things, hurtful things, but that isn't an excuse for the savage behaviour you displayed yesterday. Unless you learn to control your temper, it will land you in a great deal more trouble than a trip to my office.' Joe hung his head and Captain Quinn rested his hand lightly on his shoulder. 'How do you think I would have survived under fire from the enemy if I'd let my temper rule my reason?'

Joe looked up into Captain Quinn's face and so did Kate.

'I suppose I won't be a board monitor now,' Joe said, running his cap around in his hands.

'That depends on whether or not you learn from this lesson and I see an improvement in your attitude,' Captain Quinn replied, looking down at him severely.

Joe stood up straight. 'I promise you, sir, I won't fight in the playground again.'

'No, you won't.' Captain Quinn looked at Kate over her son's head and a warm feeling stole over her. He smiled and she smiled back. 'Now wait outside while I have a word with your mother. And remember what I've said.'

'Yes, sir.' Joe turned smartly and left the office.

Kate looked up at Captain Quinn. 'Thank you for being so understanding,' she said. 'I'm sure Joe has learnt his lesson but are you sure the other boy has? What if he picks on Joe again?'

Captain Quinn raised an eyebrow. 'I don't think any of the schoolyard bullies will be bothering your son after the drubbing he gave William White yesterday. But that's not the only reason I asked you to come and see me. It's because I'm concerned about Joe's attitude in class.'

'But Joe likes school,' Kate said. 'Why, only the day before yesterday he was showing me how he swung his arms like a soldier when he did drill.'

'Yes but sometimes after doing an excellent piece of work he'll deliberately do something that lands him in trouble. I'm sorry to have to tell you, Mrs Ellis, but young though he is, Joe is getting himself a reputation for being a jester. And it will do him no good. I've seen it too often in the barrack room. A man gets himself known as a troublemaker and it follows him wherever he goes.'

'But Joe's a good boy,' Kate said, trying not to imagine a grownup Joe wearing a flash suit and billycock hat.

'He is, and bright, too,' Captain Quinn replied. 'I think he could do very well if he applied himself. He might even win a scholarship to one of the new trade colleges. But in the past month his behaviour has become progressively worse.'

'I know ... I ...' Kate's voice started to falter and the fear that had begun to keep her awake at night rose to the surface.

Captain Quinn pulled up a chair and sat beside her. 'You can tell me, Mrs Ellis.'

Kate looked up into his face. 'I think Joe's been seeing his father.'

Captain Quinn's expression darkened. 'He hasn't been to the house, has he? He hasn't manhandled you in any way, has he? Because if he—'

'No,' Kate replied, warmed by the concern of his tone. 'There are too many people who'd tell my brother if they saw him hanging around. I think he meets Joe somewhere else.'

'What does Joe say?'

'When I ask him he denies it and then gets upset and goes into himself. But I'm sure he has seen Freddie because I've smelt tobacco on him a couple of times,' Kate said. 'And he's got cheekier recently. He's been sent to bed early twice this week for swearing in the house. I'm sure it's his father's influence but I can't prove it.' Kate pulled out her handkerchief from her bag but not quickly enough to stop a large tear from rolling down her cheek.

'I'm sorry,' she said, dabbing her eyes and forcing a smile. 'Please forgive me, for once again burdening you with my pro—'

He caught her arm. 'As I've said before, your concerns could *never* be a burden to me, Mrs Ellis,' he said gruffly.

'Thank you,' she said, forcing her voice to remain steady.

'Not at all. Good evening, Mrs Ellis, and, as always, I look forward to seeing you in church on Sunday.'

'Good evening, Captain Quinn,' she said, then left the office.

Joe jumped up from the chair when she emerged.

'I'm sorry, Ma,' he said, as he took her hand.

'I know you are, which is why we'll say no more about it,' Kate replied.

Ella skipped down the Highway swinging her satchel in one hand and holding her bonnet with the other. She circumvented the barrels of whale oil outside the dealers and jumped just in time to avoid being soaked by the bucket full of bloody water thrown out of the butcher's by his wife.

St George's clock struck four as she passed the church. School had finished an hour ago but Miss Wainwright had asked her and Rose to stay behind to help prepare the slates for the next day.

As Ma was taking Joe to have his hair cut before the shop opened for the evening trade she knew it would be all right if she agreed. In fact, Miss Wainwright had asked her twice last week and the week before and had even hinted that when the older girls left in the summer, she might become a monitor.

She was top of the class at sewing and Miss Wainwright said that if her mother could find the premium, one of the big couture houses in Mayfair might take her on as an apprentice. But Ella was beginning to think she might like to be a teacher, until she got married, of course.

Within a few moments she was outside the shop. The sign at the front was turned to 'closed' and the chairs were all pushed under the tables.

Waving hello to the draper's assistant rearranging his window display, Ella turned the corner and headed for the back gate. She was just about to lift the flowerpot to retrieve the back-door key when she noticed it was sticking out of the lock and that the door was ajar.

Cautiously, she pushed it open and crept along the hallway to the parlour. Everything was much as it should have been except that the dresser drawer wasn't closed properly. One of the china vases on the mantelshelf was also in the wrong place.

Ella heard movement behind the door leading to the shop and her heart thumped uncomfortably in her chest. She edged towards the hallway.

The door burst open and Freddie marched into the room.

He spotted her. 'Oh, it's you sneaking around,' he said guiltily.

'What are you doing here?' Ella asked fearfully.

He shoved his hands in his pockets and an innocent expression formed on his face. 'Just having a bit of a look around.'

'Are you pinching Ma's money again?'

He sneered at her. 'It ain't hers it's mine, you stupid girl, cos I'm her husband.'

'The vicar says stealing's a sin and you'll go to hell.'

'Tell the fucking vicar I'll see 'im there.' He shoved her aside.

The back door opened and Kate walked in. Ella ran to her. 'He's taken money out of the till again, Ma,' she said.

'I'm sure he has,' Kate replied, looking contemptuously at him. 'You're brave coming back here, aren't you, Freddie?'

Freddie's face darkened but before he could reply Joe threw his cap on the table and dashed to his father.

'Pa, you're here.'

Freddie shot Kate a hateful look then turned to his son. 'How are you, boy?'

'Glad to see you, Pa,' Joe said, beaming up at his father.

Kate opened the door to the hall and stood back. 'If you've got what you've come for I won't keep you.'

Joe tugged at his arm. 'I got all the names of the animals right on the chart, Pa.'

Freddie shook him off. 'Don't you fucking order me about, woman. The law says I can come and go as I please.'

'My brother and his mates in Knockfergus say different.'

Freddie clenched his fists and Ella prayed fervently he wouldn't lash out at her mother again. She wouldn't be able to run to Captain Quinn fast enough.

Freddie stood rooted to the spot for a second then snatched the milk jug from the table and hurled it at Kate. It whizzed within inches of her face and smashed on the wall, splashing milk everywhere.

Slowly, Kate picked up a tea towel and wiped her arm. She looked coolly at Freddie. 'As I said, don't let us detain you.'

Freddie kicked a chair out of his way and started for the door.

Joe caught his arm. 'Where you going, Pa?'

'To the pub,' he replied, glaring hatefully at Kate.

'Can I come?'

'No, you can't,' Kate said.

Freddie stopped. 'He didn't ask you.'

Kate grabbed Joe's shoulders but he twisted out of her grip and dashed to Freddie's side.

'Can I come then, Pa? Can I?' he pleaded beseechingly.

Kate came around the table and stood in front of Freddie. 'He's too young.'

'Rubbish. I was about his age when my old man first took me. I've had enough of you and that one-eyed schoolmaster stuffing my son's bonce with all sorts of toffee-nosed rubbish. It's about time he learnt how to be a proper man.' He rested his hand lightly on Joe's shoulder. 'And that's a father's job.'

Kate gave him a mocking look. 'What, to take him to meet drunks and whores?'

Freddie raised his fist. 'Watch your mouth.'

Kate stood her ground. 'Or what? You'll show him how to be a man, will you?'

Freddie's face turned scarlet and his eyes bulged. For one moment Ella thought he might hit her mother but then he shoved Joe aside and crashed out of the house, shaking the glass in the back door as he slammed it behind him.

Joe stood with his mouth open in dismay as he watched his father stride out of the kitchen. He spun around and glared at his mother. 'I want to go with Pa!'

'Joe, you're too young.' She guided him back to the table. 'Now sit up at the table and eat your supper. There're children in the workhouse who'd be glad of your stew.'

He twisted out of her grip. 'I don't care. You're *always* telling me no.' He crossed his arms across his chest and bit his lip until it hurt. 'You never let me have fun.'

'It's not like that,' his mother replied, trying to soothe him. 'The places your pa goes to are full of bad people.'

Joe just tucked himself in tighter and frowned at the floor. 'My pa's the best pa in the world and he wants to take me with him, just like Uncle Pat does with Mickey and Rob but *you* won't let him.'

'Joe, me darling.' She tried to catch him again but he shrugged her off.

'You hate him and me,' he screamed as tears ran down his face. He dashed at her and shoved her in the stomach. 'I'm Pa's boy, not yours.'

He ran across the kitchen and threw the door open. With the air burning his lungs he tore into the backyard to find Pa.

'Joe, come back, you'll catch a chill,' his mother's voice called after him.

'If you come in, Joe, I'll let you use my pencils,' Ella coaxed.

Joe tucked himself behind the water butt. 'I don't want to.'

There was some whispering, then his mother called again. 'All right, Joe. I'll put your supper on the stove but don't go out of the gates. It's dangerous.'

The back door closed and the yard was silent again. Joe kicked the barrel full of rainwater. Dangerous! Did she think he was a baby? It wouldn't be dangerous if she'd let him go with Pa in the first place.

He shoved his hands in his pockets as he'd seen his father do and marched to the gate. He pushed it open a crack and peered down the dark empty street.

He imagined himself walking alongside his father into the bar of the Blue Coat Boy. Everyone would know who he was because he looked the replica of his pa.

Joe crouched down and hugged his knees, suddenly aware of the cold night air on his bare legs. An unhappy lump wedged in his throat.

Something scraped on the other side of the yard and Joe looked up. He strained his eyes into the gloom and caught the glimpse of a faint beam of light flashing under the stable door.

Joe trotted over, opened the door and saw his father bending over something covered with ragged tarpaulin in the far corner.

'Pa!' he shouted, hurrying towards his father.

Freddie's head snapped around. 'What the—'

His father's fist smashed into his cheek. Joe flew backwards and hit the wall. He blinked and tried to think through the buzzing in his head. His legs felt like jelly and pain shot up his neck but he forced himself to his feet.

'It's me,' Joe said, as his eyes focused on his father standing half-crouched with a knife in his hand.

Freddie tucked the blade in the back of his belt and stood up. He clapped his hand over his heart. 'For fuck's sake. What you doing sneaking around?'

'I came to find you, Pa.'

'Did your mother see you slip into the stable?' Joe shook his head. 'Well, all right, but stay out of the way while I finish up.'

Joe stood back to let his father secure a loose rope hanging off a crate and looked around at the barrels and boxes stacked high.

'Why are all these barrels in the stable?' he asked, twisting his head and trying to figure out what the word was painted on the side.

'I'm looking after them for a friend,' his father replied.

'Can I help?' Joe asked, lifting up a lid on one of the crates.

Freddie grabbed his arm and dragged him away. 'No. Now leave be. You can help me another time.'

'Tomorrow?'

'Perhaps.'

'I can tell Ma that I'm here with you—'

Freddie grabbed him and hauled him off the ground. 'Don't tell your muvver nuffink, do you hear? Nuffink!'

'Yes, Pa,' he whispered, lowering his eyes from his father's angry face.

'Make sure you don't.' Freddie set him down.

Joe turned away from his father and leant against a cartwheel left over from the last occupant. He traced the rough wood of a spoke with his finger as his father finished what he was doing. His pa's hand plonked on his shoulder and Joe looked around.

'Look, son,' Freddie said. 'Perhaps I was a bit harsh with you but the thing is there's ... there're huge rats nesting in the back and I wouldn't want you to get bit.'

Joe flattened himself to the wheel and fixed his eyes on the far wall. 'Rats?'

Freddie crouched down beside him. 'Yeah, rats. Bloody hundreds of them. All squirming around and eating each other and if they get tired of ripping each other apart with their sharp teeth, they'll come looking for tender human flesh.' He squeezed Joe's upper arm. 'I should say they'd have a feast on you.'

Sweat broke out on Joe's brow and he suddenly had the urge to pass water.

'I tell you, straight up, Joe. I saw one just before you came in that was this big.' His father raised his hands and held them apart. 'He must have been gnawing on corpses in the graveyard to get so fat.'

Something tickled the back of Joe's leg. He jumped forward, grabbed his father and screamed. 'Don't let it eat me, Pa,' he sobbed.

Freddie chuckled, untangled Joe from his arms and set him on the floor.

'Don't come into the stable unless I'm with you, do you hear?' He lowered his face close to Joe's. 'Or else the rats might eat you.'

Joe shook his head vigorously.

Freddie picked up the lamp and snuffed out the wick. 'Good. Now follow me and don't make a sound. Now the light's gone you don't want the slimy buggers to know we're here, do you?'

Joe held on to his father's jacket and practically walked at his heels out of the stable. Freddie closed the door quietly then opened one of the yard gates. 'Time to wet my whistle.' He winked. 'I tell you, son, my stomach thinks me throat's been cut.'

'Can I come, Pa?'

Freddie glanced down at the front of Joe's trousers. 'Not like that you can't, you baby. Go and tell your mother to clean you up.'

He shoved his hands in his pockets and disappeared through the gate whistling. Joe listen to his receding footsteps then looked down to see a damp stain spreading across the front of his trousers.

Chapter Nineteen

As Aggie trotted over the iron swing bridge crossing the Shadwell Cut a two-tone whistle cut through the air. She turned, knowing it was directed at her.

'Oi, sweetheart, come over here,' called one of the bare-armed stevedores working the winch hoist on the dockside. 'This old jib,' he thumped the metalwork beside him, 'ain't the only thing rising with you wiggling by.'

His friends snorted and nudged each other.

One of the other dockers thrust his hands in his pockets. 'And if my mates ain't enough for you,' he flapped the front of his trousers. 'I've got a bigger one over there.' He nodded towards the huge steam crane hauling coal from a barge on the other side of the dock.

The yellow feather of her hat dipped over Aggie's face as she bent forward and lifted her skirts. Shaking off some imaginary dust, she made sure her admirers had a decent view of her calves.

The three dockers whistled and hooted louder and some of the other men on the quayside stopped work to watch her. She straightened her skirt, blew her audience an exaggerated kiss and sauntered on, content in the knowledge that at least a dozen pairs of male eyes were glued to her rear.

She stopped at Wapping Wall to get her bearings then continued past the Prospect of Whitby along Wapping High Street, dodging the wagons and carts as she went. Although she knew Spitalfields like the back of her hand she had only ventured south of Commercial Road a couple of times. Ginger had told her to head east along the Highway until she got to the big church and then follow the smell from the river to find Kate's fucking Kitchen.

Aggie tucked herself into a doorway and studied the jolly painted shop on the other side of the road. She was a stupid cow really for even bothering about Freddie's silly little Paddy wife, but curiosity got the better of her. She turned the corner, crossed the road, and then walked into the shop.

The bell tinkled and the low hum of conversation stopped. She looked around at all the men drinking their afternoon tea. A couple of them leered at her and nudged each other; the rest just stared. Automatically she arched her neck and gave them her I'll-make-you-smile look. She cast her eyes around. The place was clean enough and there was a faint smell of roast meat instead of boiled cabbage like in most of the eating houses in Spitalfields. Her gaze ran over the stack of white plates, trays of cutlery and upturned mugs and then alighted on the woman behind the counter. Aggie smiled.

No wonder Freddie looked for a bit of juicy elsewhere, she thought, studying the thin, pale-faced woman at the till.

She puffed out her chest and swayed over. 'I will have a coffee hif I may,' she said, lifting her skirts to sit on a high stool.

'Er . . .'

Aggie sniffed and looked down her nose at Freddie's mousy little wife. 'With two sugars. And don't take all day about it as I haf an important appointment, don't you know.'

Aggie tilted her hat so the feathers bobbed back and forth, thankful that she'd learnt to speak proper at the Sanctuary. She looked at the nondescript gown hanging over the young woman's flat chest. *What a drudge.*

Freddie's wife bit her lower lip and tucked a limp strand of hair behind her ear. 'Mrs E,' she called over her shoulder.

The door behind her opened. Aggie's jaw dropped when she saw the curvy young woman with a mass of silken blonde hair and clear blue eyes.

'What is it?' Kate rested her hands on her hips and eyed Aggie suspiciously. 'Yes?'

'I want a cup of coffee.'

'You'll not get one here,' Kate replied quietly. 'This is a respectable establishment and I'm not having the likes of you make it otherwise.'

Aggie's cheeks flamed red hot. 'The likes of me?' she screeched, putting her hand on her bare chest. 'How dare you? I'm . . . I'm just a young woman out for a stroll.'

'Out on the hook, you mean.' Kate's mouth lifted in a half smile. 'I don't know you, but I know what you're about. And let me tell you, I'm not having you touting for customers under my roof.' She lifted the counter flap and came through. 'There's a coffee stall along by Hermitage Wharf if you want a drink.'

She went over and opened the door.

Aggie balled her hands into fists to stop herself from springing at Kate.

If she were one of the girls in the Boy I'd . . .

Blood pounded in Aggie ears and a dart of pain cut across her head. A black cloud started to swirl at the edge of her vision somewhere and she heard a few of the customers snigger. She stared to quiver with rage.

Kate's voice cut through her fury. 'Are you leaving or do I have to call the police?'

Aggie lifted her head and took a deep breath. She forced her legs to work and stiffly walked to the door. As she came level with Kate she halted, looked her up and down.

'*You* might not know who I am but your husband Freddie does. *Intimately*.'

Kate's cool expression didn't falter. 'I'm sure he does, and many more like you. Now sling your hook.'

Aggie gave her a hateful stare and then sauntered out of the shop. The door slammed behind her and several people looked her way as Aggie straightened her shoulders and strolled back down the High Street. *Have a laugh today, all right, but like Lilly Bragg, you'll be laughing on the other side of your pretty face, Kate Ellis, when I've done with you.*

Aggie shoved open the Blue Coat Boy's door and pushed her way through the bar to where Freddie sat on his tatty throne.

He looked up as she approached. 'Hello, ducks,' he said, with the stupid grin she was beginning to despise plastered across his face. 'Where you been? Not spending my hard-earned money, I hope.'

The men lolling around him laughed and Aggie's fury boiled over. 'Your fucking wife threw me out of her poxy—'

'What do you mean "my wife"? Where have you been?' Freddie eyes took on a flint-like glint as he stood up.

Before she could stop herself, Aggie took a step back. There was a snigger from the men watching her.

She steeled herself and looked Freddie square in the eye. 'It's a free country, ain't it? Miserable cow.' She spat on the floor. 'Told me to sling me hook. *Me!* She was lucky I didn't rip her face off with me bare hands. She even threatened to get the cop—'

'Coppers!' He grasped her upper arms and shook her. 'You stupid bitch. I've got a ton of gear hidden in the stable.'

Aggie wrenched herself free. 'You're hurt—'

His fist smashed into her face and she crumpled onto the sawdust-covered floor. Bile burnt the back of her throat and stars popped in the corner of her vision.

'I'd be doing a whole lot more than fucking hurting you if the rozzers had stumbled on the stash.' He picked up the bottle and drained it in a couple of gulps. He wiped his mouth with the back of his hand.

Gritting her teeth, Aggie forced the blackness crowding her mind to flee. 'Why didn't you tell me?' she said, in her little-girl voice.

'Why should I? It's none of your business.' Freddie glanced at himself in the wall mirror and smoothed his hair. 'It's for the top man to say what's what and who's who. Ain't it, fellas?'

There was a chorus of 'Yes, boss' and 'Too true'.

Aggie's eyes narrowed. She'd like to tell him to go fuck himself and that if it hadn't been for her, he wouldn't be top man. It was her who put the ex-mariners to work the river, pick-locks cracking the warehouses and the creepers slipping into houses. It was her who walked miles fencing easily identifiable articles so the police couldn't find them. And wasn't it her idea to split the haul and store it in different places so even if the rozzers found one hoard they weren't out of pocket? And the infamous Black Eagle Gang! That was a bloody laugh. If it were up to Freddie, they'd spend all night drinking themselves insensible. But she daren't. There were a dozen trollops ready to jump into her place and then where would she be? Staring up at Moody's ceiling with a yokel jigging on her bones, that's where.

Forcing a tear, Aggie struggled to her feet. 'Oh, Freddie, don't be 'arsh with me.' She pressed herself into him and wound her arms around his neck. 'I've been such a silly girly, Freddie, but only cos I was afraid to lose you and if that happened, I'd throw myself in the river. Straight up, I would.'

'Course you would ... but as there was no 'arm done, I'll let it pass this time but,' he grabbed her face with his black-nailed hand, 'if you go snooping around the shop again you won't have to throw yourself in the river cos I'll sling you in myself. Do you hear?'

Looking as contrite as she could with her cheeks squeezed together, Aggie nodded.

'Good.' He let go of her and glanced around. 'Mary, gis' another bottle.'

Chapter Twenty

As Jonathan turned the corner the full force of the storm ripped his umbrella inside out. Although it was only nine o'clock in the evening, Cable Street was all but deserted. Usually, on his walk home from the bi-weekly meeting of the local Geographical Society, he had to weave his way through the drunks, hawkers and prostitutes that frequented the main thoroughfare; however, the storm had cleared the street more thoroughly than any police patrol ever could.

He closed his damaged umbrella, flipped up his collar and turned his face away from the wind. He managed to step over dirty torrents of water and avoid a waterfall from a broken gutter above but as he got to the top of Gravel Lane, he was drenched by a high arc of water thrown on the pavement by a hansom cab. Jonathan stepped back into a doorway just as the door opened. He turned and found himself looking at Kate Ellis.

She was dressed in her usual workaday blue gown, with a short jacket over it and a knitted russet-coloured shawl framing her face.

'Good evening, Captain Quinn, and if you'll excuse me the liberty, *what on earth* are you doing out on such a night?'

He raised his hat and a stream of cold water tipped down the back of his neck. 'Good evening, Mrs Ellis. And I could *very* well ask you the same question.'

'I just popped over to collect my pan,' she replied, holding up a battered pot.

'And I've just been to a very pleasant evening listening to a talk about the tribes of the Amazon but now,' he brushed the water from his shoulders, 'I feel as if I've swum across it.'

Kate gave a throaty laugh. 'It's raining fit to baptise you, that's for sure. But you're soaked through. The shop's only a step or two away – why don't you come and sit out the storm?'

'I couldn't intrude on you and your family,' he replied.

She waved away his protest. 'The children are asleep and I've only my own company. You'll not be putting me out.' She stepped closer to avoid the drips from the lintel above. For both their sakes he knew he should say no to her offer. There was an awkward pause.

'If you're sure it's no trouble,' he said finally.

'None whatsoever. Now come on before we're both washed into the Thames.' She lifted her skirts and tiptoed between the puddles around the corner to Kate's Kitchen. After a moment's hesitation, Jonathan followed.

Within minutes they were standing in the back hall of the shop with rainwater pooling around their feet. Jonathan removed his hat and slipped off his coat. He went to hook them up and noticed Joe's and Ella's school coats.

What was he thinking?

He turned. 'Thank you for your kind offer, Mrs Ellis, b—'

'Give them here,' she said, taking his coat and hat. 'They can dry by the fire while I make you a coffee, and there's a slice or two of walnut cake that needs eating before it goes stale.'

A burst of rain hit the quarter-glazed door behind him.

He watched her swish pleasantly towards the parlour door at the end of the hall. Jonathan slowly followed her.

'Rest your bones,' she said, nodding towards the chair by the parlour fire. 'I'll just pop up and check that Ella and Joe are all right.'

She reappeared a few moments later and went into the shop.

He rested back and watched her move to and fro through the open scullery door as she made his coffee and cut his cake. *This is how it should be,* he thought. *The woman you love looking after you at the end of a long day.* It was worth more than all the treasures of the Orient.

Kate returned carrying the blue-patterned mug she always gave him and a plate with two thick slices of cake. Jonathan stood up.

'There you go,' she said, placing the cup and plate on the three-legged stool beside his chair.

'Thank you,' he said quietly.

He waited to resume his seat until she had sat down in the chair opposite and placed a darning basket on the floor beside her.

He took a sip of coffee, unsure what to say next. 'If I'm to be a prisoner of the weather, would you help to pass the time by telling me about your family? Where did they come from in Ireland?'

Kate smile shyly, which accentuated the dimple in her cheek. 'Well, Mam and Pa came from Kinsale in the south – they came here a year or two after they were wed. My brother Patrick was born there but the rest of us, me, Mattie . . .'

Jonathan managed to grasp which children belonged to whom in her immediate family but lost track completely of the numerous

Bridies, Marys, Pats and Mickeys scattered around the globe. But it didn't matter. He was content to watch her eyes flash with mirth as she spoke.

'So you see, no matter where you roam, Captain, you'll be sure to bump into a Nolan from the old country in your travels.' She sat back in her chair. 'What about yours?'

'Mine are very dull,' he replied.

Kate's eyes twinkled. 'Now, Captain Quinn, you don't think I'll be letting you get away with that, do you?'

Jonathan smiled. 'I have only one sister . . .'

He skimmed over his father's animosity, told her about his time in the army and found himself telling her little stories he'd all but forgotten. He enjoyed the sight of her breathless amazement as he described the sunrise over the Himalayas, the ancient stone temple deep in tropical forests and the white palace built by a prince as a tomb for his beloved wife.

'What an exciting life you've had,' she said, when he'd finished.

'It was, but hard, too. I can't tell you the times I've slept rough and eaten tinned food.'

Kate laughed. 'But you loved every minute of it, didn't you?'

'You have me there,' he chuckled. 'I did. Every blooming moment except seeing good men slaughtered.'

Her eyes flickered on to his patch. 'It must have hurt something fierce,' she said tenderly.

'The devil it did,' he replied. 'The surgeon had to keep me drunk and strapped to the bed for five days while I was out of my mind with the pain.'

'How did it happen?'

'Our company had just waded across the Alma River when we came under attack from a gun emplacement on a small hillock. Our commander ordered us to attack and we surged up the hill. The gun was stoutly defended by a dozen or so Russian artillery soldiers, and within minutes of cresting the hill we were engaged in close hand-to-hand fighting. I wrestled a grizzly-looking chap to the ground and was just about to disarm him when he wrenched his gun free. He aimed at my head and I only just knocked the barrel away as he fired. The powder ignited against my left temple. All I remember was a flash of light then a heat like the fires of hell. I managed to stay conscious long enough to finish him off with my bayonet. The next thing I remember was waking up in Scutari Hospital with my eyes swathed in bandages.'

Kate crossed herself. 'Sweet Mary.'

'The surgeon said I was fortunate. And that the heat from the exploding gunpowder seared the flesh to stop it corrupting.'

She looked horrified. 'But another inch and ...'

'I never would have met you,' he said quietly.

Kate looked confused and Jonathan took hold of himself. He was being reckless. He should go before he did something foolish. He drained the last of his coffee and rose to his feet. 'How rude of me to stay so long. You've been up since first light and must be tired.'

Kate stood up in front of him. It would take just a dip of his head for him to kiss her. Instead he held out his empty cup.

'Thank you. I think it's easing up,' he said, ignoring the rain still driving against the window.

'Your coat should be dry,' she replied, still staring up at him.

'Yes.' He made no move to retrieve it.

She took the cup and their fingers touched. She looked up at him from under her lashes and he caught his breath.

Leave, Jonathan. Now!

She went to walk past him but he caught her arm and she turned. He slid his arm around her waist and drew her to him. She looked surprised but didn't pull away.

He smiled down at her and studied her face for a moment then pressed his lips onto her. She raised her hands and placed them on his chest then her mouth opened under his. He kissed her deeply, savouring the feel of her in his arms, then he lifted his head. 'I've wanted to do that for a long time, Kate.'

Somehow, Kate managed to override the pleasure of being in Jonathan's arms and forced her mind to work. She pushed him away.

'You shouldn't because —'

'You're married?' His expression softened as he stared down at her. 'It's wrong, I know, but I can't help myself. Being close to you makes me lose all reason.'

'Captain Quinn, I ... I ...'

He went to kiss her again but Kate held him off.

'You mustn't,' she said.

For one moment she thought he would brush aside her protest but then he released her.

'Forgive me.' He snatched up his coat and hat. 'I should go before I forget myself again.'

He turned and Kate caught his arm. 'Jonathan.'

Their gazes locked for two heartbeats then he threw his coat on the floor and took her in his arms. Kate melted into him, pressing her breasts into his hard chest as her hands slipped upwards and around his neck.

'Say my name again.'

'Jonathan,' she whispered.

He ran his fingers lightly along her jaw, through her hair and then gripped the back of her head. Kate's mouth opened and his closed over hers in a demanding kiss.

He lifted his head. 'Oh, Kate, it's madness, I know, but day and night I can't keep you from my mind. I want you. I—'

Kate stopped his words with her lips. He lifted her off her feet, pressing her to him. She clung to him. He kissed her brow while her lips grazed the rough squareness of his chin. He walked her backwards until they reached the table set against wall. He laid her gently on it and arched over her. Kate slid her hands under his jacket and ran them up the contours of his chest.

Jonathan shrugged off his jacket, undid his cravat and top buttons then covered her with his body again. His fingers fumbled with the fastening at her neck. Kate twisted her head aside to help him release it. His lips found the base of her throat.

'I need you, Kate,' he said, opening the front of her blouse and kissing his way across the swell of her. As his hand cupped her breast, Kate sighed and her head rolled to one side. Her half-opened eyes focused on Joe's school cap sitting on the sideboard. She felt as if someone had thrown iced water over her. What was she doing? She pushed Jonathan away.

'Stop. Please. This is wrong.'

'I know,' Jonathan replied, working his way down her bare shoulder. 'But I can't help myself. It's like a raging fire burning in my chest.' He tried to capture her lips again but Kate twisted out of his embrace and stood up.

'Sweet Mary, I made a solemn vow before God that I can't break.' She balled her fists until the nails dug into her palms. 'Please understand – I can't!'

Jonathan stared, unseeing and breathing heavily, for a few moments before his focus returned.

'You're right. Forgive me. I let my own needs cloud my judgement. But is there no hope for us?' he asked quietly.

Tears sprang into Kate's eyes and she bit her lip to hold them back.

'What hope can there be?' she replied, flatly. 'I'm married and there is nothing to be done.'

He raked his hands through his hair. 'But if you weren't?'

Kate looked away. 'Then perhaps we . . .'

He strode over to her and took her hands. 'We could go away. I have money. We could start afresh with Ella and Joe.'

'And what if Freddie found us? He'd take the children from me and no one would think him wrong to do so. And if he didn't catch up with us, what about any children we might have? They'd be labelled bastards and suffer their whole lives because of our folly. I tell you, I've learnt the hard way how a moment's pleasure can cause a lifetime of pain. I'm sorry – I'm so sorry – but you should leave.'

Jonathan's shoulders slumped. 'Of course.'

He turned and headed for the door. Kate watched him cross the parlour and forced herself not to follow him. The back-door latch clicked.

'Jonathan!' Kate dashed after him but the yard was empty. She staggered out into the open space where she stood, hollow-eyed, then slowly sank to her knees among the pools of water left from the rain.

She hugged herself and imagined it was his embrace. She ran her fingers over her lips, remembering the feel of him. But it could never be. She'd made her loveless bed with Freddie seven years ago and now she had to lie in it. She buried her face in her hands and sobbed.

The organ struck up for the last hymn and the congregation rose to their feet. Jonathan did the same and although he'd promised himself he wouldn't, he glanced across at Kate. She was looking at him. They stared at each other for a moment then she turned away.

As the vicar and choir processed out Jonathan sang the last chorus then knelt and bowed his head.

Hadn't he learnt his lesson? First Louise and now Kate Ellis. He should have stuck to his original intent and avoided becoming emotionally embroiled yet again. But he was in command of his emotions, wasn't he, and would stand firm until the madness had passed.

Jonathan crossed himself, stood up and made his way to the end of the row.

'Oh, Mr Quinn!' Mabel's shrill voice called from behind him.

Jonathan turned and forced a smile. 'Miss Puttock.'

She put her hand on her chest. 'Wasn't that a wonderful service?' she said breathlessly.

'Indeed.'

Over Mabel's head he saw Kate was talking to an elderly woman.

'And I thought the choir were on fine form, too.' Mabel edged closer and her lacy skirts brushed against him. 'Especially those dear little boys in the front.'

'It's true. They were in fine voice.'

Kate finished her conversation and was walking towards them.

'I do so love children,' Mabel continued, smiling up at him shyly and blushing.

'Good morning, Mrs Ellis,' Jonathan said, stepping around Mabel and into Kate's path.

Kate halted. 'Good morning, Captain Quinn.' She glanced at the young woman beside him. 'And to you, Miss Puttock.'

She started to walk on.

'And how are the children?' Jonathan asked.

'Very well, thank you.' Kate regarded him steadily.

They stared at each other for a moment then Kate looked away. 'If you'd excuse me, I have to get home.'

'Of course,' Mabel replied, smiling benevolently at her. 'Don't let us detain you any longer.'

'Miss Puttock. Captain.' Kate's eyes flickered over his face once again then she walked away.

'Good day, Mrs Ellis,' Jonathan called after her as she hurried towards the back of the church.

Miss Puttock sighed. 'It's so sad to see Kate Ellis looking thin and old, especially as she was once considered a local beauty. But Annie and Jim are *such* sweet children and—'

'Ella and Joe,' Jonathan corrected.

'Yes, of course.' Mabel's lower lip stuck out petulantly.

Kate stopped, had a couple of words with Mr Overton and left the church.

'If you'd excuse me, Miss Puttock,' Jonathan said. 'Mrs Delaney will have dinner ready so I ought to be heading home. Good day.'

Without waiting for her to speak Jonathan strode down the aisle and out of the church.

Mabel's fair eyebrows pulled together tightly as she watched Jonathan stride down the centre of the church. How rude. She ought to be very cross with him for such ungentlemanly behaviour, but then why wouldn't he furious at being accosted like that?

Why on earth couldn't that insufferable Kate Ellis just give him a deferential nod, as she should, instead of striking up a conversation? And just as *she* was about to ask him to dinner.

Of course, Jonathan was too fine a gentleman to cut Kate Ellis dead as she deserved. Perhaps commanding riff-raff in the army had made him a little too affably disposed to the lower orders.

She sighed, pulled on her gloves and swept down the aisle towards the main doors. She commended Mr Overton on his sermon and walked out of the church into the bright early summer sunlight where many of the congregation were still milling around.

She adjusted the brim of her bonnet to shade her face and was just about to start for home when she caught sight of Jonathan heading for the back exit from the churchyard.

Perhaps all was not lost. If she cut along the path to the rectory, she would be able to reach the side gate ahead of him.

Gathering her skirts, she sped around, emerging on the other side of the church. Her shoulders relaxed. Jonathan hadn't arrived yet.

Mabel dusted herself down and, assuming an air of quiet contemplation, she gazed down at an old headstone. After she'd read Bridget Shanahan's inscription for the third time, she ventured a quick glance around.

Where on earth was he? She took a couple of steps along the path before she stopped dead in her tracks. He was there standing behind the solid square column of Raine's monument. Alongside him stood Kate Ellis. He was holding her hand and she gazed up at him. They were clearly not talking about the service.

Mabel's blood turned to ice. She jumped back and took a deep breath to steady her pounding heart and throbbing temples.

For a moment she stood motionless as fury gripped her and then, making sure they couldn't see her, Mabel picked her way through the graves towards the family memorial. She pressed her back against the opposite side of the square column from Jonathan and Kate and held her breath.

'Please, Kate?' Mabel heard Jonathan say.

'No matter how I feel, Jonathan, I cannot break the vows I made before God.'

'We could go away . . .'

'Oh, Jonathan.'

'I don't care where or how far, Kate, but . . .' There was a rustle of clothing.

Mabel clenched her fist as she imagined the passionate embrace taking place an arm's reach from where she stood.

'Please, Jonathan. I must go,' Kate said, breathlessly.

'But, Kate, I need you I—'

'The children will be looking for me. I'm sorry.'

There was a crunch of gravel. Mabel flattened herself against the rough stone. She stayed there, holding her breath, until they both walked away.

Jonathan, her Jonathan and Kate Ellis . . . A painful lump lodged in Mabel's chest. *How could he? And with her!*

Her most cherished dream of walking down the aisle on her father's arm to become Mrs Quinn danced before her eyes and then vanished. Grief flooded over her and for a couple of moments a sobbing hysteria gripped her, shaking her body and drenching her face.

Mabel stumbled out of the graveyard and ran home. She dashed up the three steps to her front door and hammered on the knocker. Mrs West the housekeeper answered and Mabel strode into the hall. She ripped off her bonnet and threw it on the side table. Mrs West bobbed a quick curtsy and beat a hasty retreat to the kitchen.

Mrs Puttock came out of the front parlour. 'What on earth is the matter, sweetheart?' she asked.

Mabel turned her tear-stained face away and hurried up the stairs. 'Nothing, Mama, it's just a headache, that's all.'

'Shall I bring you some camomile tea?' her mother called after her.

'No, Mama, I just need to rest,' she replied, hoping her mother wouldn't hear the tremble in her voice.

At the top of the stairs she rushed along the landing to her bedroom. Staggering in, Mabel collapsed on her bed and sobbed.

It had puzzled her why he'd been so distant of late. And now she knew.

Because of her! she thought as her mind conjured up images of Jonathan and Kate Ellis entwined in each other's arms. *She runs a common chop house. For goodness sake!*

Mabel rolled onto her back and stared up at the lacy canopy over her bed. Eliza and Caroline had managed to secure a husband each and had already set the date for their weddings. Even Lottie, who had a nose like a boxer, was betrothed. And until an hour ago Mabel was sure she too would soon be leaving spinsterhood behind.

Tears welled up again and rolled down her face into her hair.

Of course, she didn't blame him. It was *her*, that Irish Jezebel. It wasn't his fault and if *she* hadn't clouded dear Jonathan's thinking Mabel knew he would have declared himself. But now *she* was ruining Mabel's last chance of marriage. The sound of Jonathan's voice swearing his undying love for Kate echoed around Mabel's mind.

She clenched her fists as fury coursed through her. She sat up and wiped her eyes.

Jumping off the bed she went to her writing bureau and sat down. She pulled out a sheet of paper and picked up a pen. She jabbed it in the inkwell.

Kate Ellis might be set to spend eternity in Hell but while there was breath in her body, she, Mabel Puttock, wouldn't let her take dear Jonathan with her.

Chapter Twenty-One

Kate sat in the pew nearest to the vestry in the deserted church looking straight ahead; she forced herself not to fiddle with her skirt fabric. Although it was an ordinary working day she had spent the best part of an hour that morning brushing her Sunday clothes and steaming her hat back into its proper shape. Her outfit now looked as good as new but it didn't make her feel any better.

The vestry door opened and Mr Puttock stepped out. He looked her over. 'We are ready to see you now.'

With her heart practically lodged in her throat, Kate stood up and followed him into the church's office. At the far end, ranged behind the desk were Mr Overton, Mr Puttock, Mr Wendover and, on the far right, Jonathan.

Automatically her eyes fixed on him. She didn't need to, of course, as his image and his touch lived with her day and night. Although it was dangerous, as others might see her true feelings in her eyes, Kate couldn't deny herself the pleasure of gazing at him.

He was looking at her with a mixture of love and pain on his angular face. An unreadable expression flitted across his face and Kate's heart ached.

'If you would take a seat, Mrs Ellis,' Mr Puttock said, cutting through her thoughts and indicating a straight-backed chair in front of the table.

Kate sat and rested her hands on her lap.

'Thank you for arriving promptly, Mrs Ellis,' Mr Overton said.

Kate smiled pleasantly as she fought to quell her disquiet. 'Your note said you wanted to see me on a matter of some importance, sir,' she said, in as even a voice as she could muster.

'It is indeed,' Mr Overton replied in his best pulpit voice. 'I think you know everyone here.' He waved at his fellow school guardians.

'I do.' She looked at Mr Puttock – he lowered his eyes but Mr Wendover smirked.

'Unfortunately, Mrs Benson is unable to be with us this afternoon,' continued the vicar, 'but Captain Quinn has kindly given up his valuable time to attend in her stead.' He spread his smooth white hand on the table before him.

The knot in Kate's stomach tightened.

'Mrs Ellis, a very grave matter has been brought to the attention of the school guardians which may, if it proves to be true, oblige us to expel your children from the school.'

'Expel Ella and Joe!' Kate gasped. 'But why? What have they done?'

Mr Overton peered over his glasses. 'Your children have done nothing. It is your conduct that has caused us to convene this extraordinary meeting, Mrs Ellis. We are here today to investigate a most grievous matter which came to light four days ago when I received this.' He picked up a folded sheet.

Kate stared dumbly at the flimsy paper in the vicar's hand.

'Excuse me, Mr Overton,' Jonathan cut in before the vicar could continue. 'I would like Mr Puttock to enter into the minutes my strongest objection to this meeting taking place at all.'

'Your objections are duly noted,' Mr Puttock replied tersely.

'If I may continue, Captain Quinn?' Mr Overton said.

Jonathan nodded sharply but his disgruntled expression remained.

The vicar turned his attention back to Kate. 'The letter states that you, Mrs Ellis, are deeply embroiled in an adulterous relationship with an unnamed man. Is this true?'

The floor seemed to shift under Kate's chair. 'I . . . I . . .'

'So you don't deny it?' Mr Puttock's voice barked from a long way away.

Kate forced down her panic. 'Of course, I do. It's a lie. Who sent it?'

'Someone too cowardly to sign their name,' Jonathan replied.

Mr Wendover glared at Jonathan. 'Someone who takes the moral welfare of the children in our charge as seriously as we do.'

'But who does so in an underhand way, to prevent Mrs Ellis from facing her accuser,' Jonathan said.

'But I'm sure you'll agree we have to question Mrs Ellis,' Mr Puttock said.

'Question her about what?' Jonathan replied.

'We need to discover the truth,' Mr Overton chipped in.

'The truth is, I have not broken my marriage vows,' Kate said forcefully.

'And, as far as I can see, other than a piece of malicious gossip, there is no evidence that she has,' Jonathan added, fixing the vicar with an unwavering look. 'I further propose that as Mrs Ellis has refuted the allegation the whole matter should be dismissed.'

Mr Overton fiddled with his signet ring. 'I don't know ...'

'While I applaud your sense of fair play, Captain Quinn, you don't know all the circumstances,' Mr Wendover said.

'And what circumstances might that be, Mr Wendover?' Kate asked, as her anger overtook her fear. 'Haven't I already said the letter's a pack of lies?'

'You have, but it is our duty to weigh up all the facts.' He gave her an oily smile. 'For example, it is common knowledge you were raised as a follower of Rome and that you were with child when you wed. However, like the true Christian he is, Mr Overton overlooked your lack of virtue when he recommended that your daughter be given a place in St Katharine's. And of course Captain Quinn, not knowing about your moral frailty or – how can I put it delicately – your husband's wayward nature, offered your son a place in the school. I'm sure if he'd been aware of the full story he would have come to a different decision.'

Jonathan's mouth pulled into a hard line. 'I'd advise you not to judge me by your own standards, Mr Wendover,' he replied icily.

'In my experience, there's no smoke without fire.' Mr Wendover looked back at Kate and his piggy eyes roamed slowly over her. 'Who is the man?'

Although her heart pounded in her chest, Kate managed to maintain her unruffled expression. 'There *is* no man,' she replied firmly.

'Will you swear to that?' Mr Overton asked, eagerly.

Kate nodded.

The vicar's shoulders relaxed. 'Well, if you're prepared to lay your hand on the Good Book and assure us that you are innocent of any wrongdoing, Mrs Ellis, then I for one am prepared to let the matter rest. What say you, gentlemen?'

Mr Puttock and Mr Wendover muttered their agreement.

'Captain Quinn?'

'I see no need for Mrs Ellis to swear anything,' Jonathan said, looking at her. 'As, like every other man and woman living under English law, Mrs Ellis is innocent until proven guilty. And I tell you this: one spiteful anonymous letter would be thrown out as evidence in any court in the land.'

Jonathan glared furiously at them and the three men shifted uncomfortably in their seats.

'Thank you, Captain Quinn,' Kate said, quietly. 'I have nothing to hide.'

Their gazes locked for a heartbeat and then Kate looked away.

Mr Puttock went to retrieve the church Bible from the altar. He returned in a few moments and placed it on the table in front of Mr Overton.

Kate stood up, walked to the table and placed her hands on the embossed leather Bible. 'I swear by almighty God I have known no other man except my husband since the day I married.' She crossed herself and all four men did the same.

Kate stepped back. 'Is there anything else you require of me?'

'No,' replied Mr Overton. 'I believe we can draw a line under this matter.'

'And there will be no more talk of my children being expelled from St Katharine's?'

'Not while I'm headmaster,' replied Jonathan.

Mr Overton shuffled his papers together. 'Well, good day, Mrs Ellis, and once again thank you for your prompt attendance.'

'Not at all,' Kate replied, icily. 'I know you are all busy men.'

Jonathan rose and came out from behind the table. 'Let me see you out,' he said, as the vicar and the other two guardians started to discuss different matters.

Kate turned and headed towards the door. Jonathan was already there holding it open. As she reached him Kate paused. Standing so close she could feel his breath on her cheek, resisting the almost overwhelming urge to throw herself in his arms, Kate looked straight ahead and walked back into the chilly church and her empty existence without him.

Mrs Benson lowered herself carefully back against the cushion on the chaise longue. The ache on her left side threatened to take hold again but then it subsided. She breathed out. She eyed the foul-tasting medicine, which was four-fifths laudanum, topped up with cherry cordial. She would have to take it later but she could do without it for now.

She had picked up her Bible and started to flick through the familiar pages when someone hammered on the front door. It opened and closed and then there was a light knock.

'Come.'

Willamore appeared. 'I'm sorry to disturb you, madam. It's Captain Quinn. He seems very unlike himself.'

Mrs Benson sat up. 'Show him in.'

The butler stood back and Jonathan entered. 'I'm sorry to—' He saw her and stopped. 'You're unwell. I'll come back when you're better.'

'No, you won't, young man,' she said, in her firmest voice. 'You'll stay and tell me what has brought you hot-foot to my parlour.'

For a moment she thought he was going to argue but then he strode to the window and stared out with his hands clasped behind his back. Mrs Benson nodded at Willamore and he left.

Jonathan turned. 'The vicar's wife told me it was still just a mild chill so I am shocked to see you so unwell.'

'It was, but unfortunately it allowed the malignancy within to finally get the upper hand.'

A look of genuine grief flashed across his face and she loved him for it. Yes, God taketh away but sometimes he giveth back, too.

'Don't look so melancholy, my dear,' she said. 'We have to die of something. Now tell me what happened at the guardians' meeting. As I know that's where you've come from.'

Jonathan clenched his fists. 'Blasted gossip-mongers. No court in the land would give credence to such a letter. It's against the rules of justice but that didn't stop them quizzing Mrs Ellis.'

'Well it's their duty to investigate anything that might tarnish the good name of the school.'

'But this was clearly a malicious allegation from someone too cowardly to sign their name.' He balled his fists as he struggled to master his temper. 'I suppose if they'd only dealt with the matter at hand it wouldn't have been so bad, but they dragged up all the dirt surrounding Mrs Ellis's marriage and her husband's prison record – which has nothing to do with her. They even asked her to swear her innocence on the Bible.'

'Did she?'

Jonathan looked indignant. 'Of course she did. I'm just thankful I insisted on attending, or goodness knows what might have happened.'

'It must have been very difficult for you, seeing Kate treated so,' Mrs Benson said, quietly. 'Especially as you are the unnamed man in the letter.'

Jonathan looked astonished. 'But . . . how?'

She laughed. 'My dear Jonathan, I have seen young men fall in love for over fifty years. I know the signs. And I'm not at all surprised.

Kate is a very beautiful woman. And I can see by the way she looks at you that your feelings are reciprocated.'

'But aren't you going to remind me she's married?'

'I will if you like, but will it stop you pursuing her?'

'No.'

'Then I won't waste my breath. But have you any idea who wrote the letter or how they found out?'

He shook his head. 'I can only think that someone must have seen us in the churchyard last Sunday. I caught Kate after the service and asked her to come away with me. She refused and we parted. But surely if they saw us together, why didn't they accuse me too?'

'Because I suspect that the author of the letter isn't so much interested in upholding morality as separating you from Kate,' Mrs Benson said.

He looked at her bleakly for a moment then turned and walked back to the window.

'My poor Jonathan,' she said quietly, as she studied him staring out of the window.

'This is a mess,' he said, turning to face her. 'If someone has tried to destroy Kate because of my feelings for her, then I must leave.'

'There must be some other way,' Mrs Benson said, as panic fluttered in her chest. 'And if you and Kate are innocent of any wrongdoing then why go? Surely, your sudden departure would only set tongues wagging as people put two and two together.'

'Possibly, but they will soon forget. Don't you see it's for Kate's sake I have to go because I'm just not strong enough to see her every day and not want to make her mine. This time she was able to swear her innocence in good conscience but if I stay . . .' He raked his fingers through his hair as a tortured expression twisted his face.

Ignoring the dull throbbing in her side, Mrs Benson beckoned him to the chair beside her. He hesitated for a moment then walked back and sat down. She reached out and moved a stray lock of hair from his forehead the way she'd done a hundred times before from Christopher's, then took his hand. 'You must hold on to hope, Jonathan.'

He looked into her eyes then lifted her hand to his lips and pressed it there. 'Loath as I am to argue with you, my dearest Mrs Benson, I fear that in this case there is none.' He kissed her hand again then stood up. 'Thank you for your offer of tea but you must conserve your strength so I'll leave you to rest. I'll tell Willamore on my way out.' He walked to the door. 'I'll call on Tuesday as usual, if I may?'

'I shall look forward to it as always,' she replied, knowing she would never see him again in this life.

Mrs Benson sank back and closed her eyes. He was right, of course. While Freddie stood between them there was very little chance of Jonathan and Kate being together. If he stayed he might become reckless and that would ruin them both. A feeling of frustration swept over her. Jonathan needed her and here she was, a useless old woman with no more than a day or two left to her. It was so unfair. *Why couldn't I have another year or so? Why couldn't ...* She pressed her hands together on her chest. *Forgive me, Lord, your will be done.* The gnawing pain was spreading towards her spine and building momentum. She opened one eye and looked at the bottle of medicine. She closed it again. *Lord, if it be your will, grant Jonathan his heart's desire.*

A warm breeze passed over her and she looked up, thinking the window had been left open, but the lace curtains hung limply from their poles. She shivered and her Bible fell open. She read the passage and then rang the small hand bell on the table beside her furiously. Willamore appeared immediately.

'Send a message to Mr Gillespie and ask him to call on me in an hour, no later. And tell him it's urgent.'

From the pulpit at the far end of the church, Mr Overton drew a deep breath before launching himself into the next part of his sermon. Kate shifted in her seat but kept her eyes on Mrs Benson's black-draped coffin in the centre of the nave. The front pews of St George's were filled with members of the parish council and local dignitaries. Behind them were the employees from the various companies she owned. The local tradesmen and St George's congregation were packed into the remaining seats. Sitting alone in the front pew sat Mrs Benson's only surviving relative, Mr Rogers, the son of her cousin. Throughout the service he'd tried to look suitably mournful at the loss of a dear relative but the fact that he'd inherited all of Mrs Benson's considerable fortune couldn't help but lift his expression from time to time. Jonathan sat straight-backed in the third pew, and even at this distance she could see the pain in his face.

The vicar finally concluded his doleful address, made the sign of the cross and climbed down from the pulpit. The congregation rose while the pallbearers took up their positions and, in one swift movement, gracefully heaved the coffin to their shoulders. The vicar moved to the front and the procession started slowly towards the church door. The mourners peeled off row by row and followed. As Jonathan passed the end of her pew their gazes met. He gave her a bleak look and then walked by.

Kate filed out with the rest of the congregation and stepped out of the church as the hearse arrived, drawn by a pair of black horses. The pallbearers carefully placed the coffin in the back, with sprays of flowers around it. The crowd started to drift away and Kate made ready to leave but saw that Captain Quinn was heading towards her.

'Good day, Mrs Ellis,' he said, raising his hat.

'Good day, Captain Quinn.'

There was a pause as they stared helplessly at each other, then Jonathan looked away.

'It was good of you to come.'

'Mrs Benson was so kind to me – to everyone – I wanted to pay my last respects.'

'As did many,' Jonathan said, indicating the throng of people milling around the church doors.

'I'm not surprised. She did so much for those in need, like organising the church wives to distribute baby clothes to new mothers. She even delivered Ella and Joe's clothes herself. I remember she picked Joe up and he was sick down the skirt of her beautiful gown. I was red with embarrassment but she shrugged and said it would sponge.'

'That sounds very like her,' Jonathan said, with an echo of a smile. 'At least now she will be at peace with her husband and son.'

'God bless her and keep her, so she is,' replied Kate. 'There wasn't a dry eye in the neighbourhood when we heard Master Christopher had been killed. I don't know how she carried on after such a loss.'

Jonathan watched the coaches rolling through the church gate. 'Mrs Benson had such faith in the Almighty and firmly believed that everything happened for a purpose.' He looked down at Kate. 'I only wish I had her faith.'

'Yes. She was an example to us all,' Kate replied, softly.

Jonathan's gaze travelled slowly over her. 'You are looking very well, Kate.'

She looked away. 'Jonathan. Please I . . .'

'I'm sorry but when you're near I can't help myself,' he said.

'Oh, Captain Quinn,' a trill voice cut between them.

They looked around to see Mabel dashing towards them, her black mourning silks rustling as she moved between the gravestones.

'Thank goodness I found you,' she said, stopping breathlessly in front of them. 'Mrs Harrison's invalid chair has become jammed in the church hall doors and I wonder if you could help free her?'

'Of course,' Jonathan replied.

'I had better get back to the shop,' Kate said, retying her bonnet ribbon.

Miss Puttock gave her a haughty smile. 'Of course you must.' She started back across to the hall. 'Captain Quinn, Mrs Harrison would be most grateful for your assistance.'

Jonathan raised his hat again. 'Good day to you, Mrs Ellis.'

Kate stared up at him, unable to speak. He again looked bleakly at her for a moment, then turned and strode off.

With her heart feeling like a lead weight in her chest, Kate watched him walk away with Miss Puttock beside him.

Chapter Twenty-Two

Aggie blew on her hands to warm them as she studied the muted light in the window above Kate Ellis's chop house. If she'd known she'd still be standing around this long she would have put her coat on. Who'd have thought a woman who was up at dawn would still be burning a candle at this time of night?

Something brushed against her skirt and Aggie looked down at Inchy Pete, standing beside her. Although he was seven years old, the top of his head barely reached her elbow, and with sticks for legs it looked as if a strong breeze would carry him off. She wondered in passing what happened to his mother.

Aggie had been about ten when her mother sobered up enough to stagger out of the hovel she, her younger sister Suzy and brother Arty lived in to 'get a bite of something' and disappeared for ever. After her mother vanished, Arty had told her he'd look after them. He walked them all the way from Hoddesdon to London and then sold her and Suzy to the house in the Haymarket for five pounds. After which Aggie decided she'd look after herself.

A gust of wind disturbed the river fog floating just above the cobbles and the boy shivered. Aggie whacked him around the head.

'Stop fidgeting,' she hissed.

He rubbed his ear and glared up at her in the dim glow from the street lamp. ''Ow long we going to be here then?'

'Until I tell you otherwise.'

'What we hanging about for, anyhow?'

'Belt up.'

'Does Mr Ellis know—'

Aggie grabbed his ear, twisted it and then pulled him to her. 'Never mind Mr Ellis, you poxy little runt.'

Terror shot across Inchy's face and he nodded rapidly.

Aggie twisted his ear again and he whimpered. 'Remember I'm someone you don't want to cross.'

She let go of him. The boy gave her another hateful look then, covering his injured ear with his hand, huddled further into the doorway. Just then the light in the upstairs window disappeared. A church clock nearby struck eleven and on the last chime the beat constable appeared around the corner. Automatically, Aggie and Inchy pressed back into the doorway and watched him turn away from them and plod off down the street.

She jabbed Inchy and he turned. 'We ain't got much time so listen and listen good. You're to slip in to the kitchen and find the pot that's got that Paddy muck they eat for breakfast and put this' – she pulled out a small green glass bottle and shoved it in his hand – 'in, then stir it around.'

'What is it?'

'Never you mind.'

'It ain't going to do 'em in, is it?' Inchy asked, turning the vial over in his hand.

'Course not, it's just something to send them to the privy, that's all. But if you get it on your fingers don't lick it off.'

'I thought you said—'

'Get a move on.' Aggie shoved him out of the doorway.

Inchy slipped the bottle into his pocket and crept silently across the road.

Aggie watched the boy disappear down the side of the house and a satisfied smile crept across her lips. By this time tomorrow Kate Ellis would be in no position to sling anyone out of her shitty little shop because her and her brats would be lying on a slab in London Hospital's morgue.

Kate yawned and smoothed the hair from her eyes. Although the clock across the road said a quarter to seven she'd already been up for an hour. It took that long to light the stove, set the water to boil and collect the eggs from the chickens in the yard. Added to which it was Thursday and she had the midweek grocery deliveries arriving.

The smell of bacon, toast and fresh coffee already floated in the air as Sally served up the first few breakfasts. Something thumped on the floor above.

'Your Joe's up then,' Sally said, flipping over a slice of bread sizzling in the frying pan.

Kate looked up and smiled. She reached for the small saucepan with the family breakfast in and pulled it onto the heat. The working men she catered for turned their noses up at oats, preferring a plate of eggs and sausages, but as porridge had been Kate's first meal of the day since as long as she could remember, she made a small pot of it for herself and the children each morning.

The edges started to bubble so Kate stirred it to stop it sticking to the sides. A faint bitter smell drifted up but it vanished before she could identify it. She lifted the spoon to her lips and swallowed a little.

It was slightly tart so she reached for the sugar jar, stirred in two large tablespoons and then replaced the lid.

'I'm just going to sort the children out for school. I'll be back as soon as I can,' Kate said, wiping her hands on the tea towel.

'Don't worry, I'll manage and Bette will be here soon,' Sally replied.

Kate filled her small teapot from the kettle then carried it and a jug of milk back into her small parlour. Ella was already sitting at the table fully dressed with her books beside her.

'Morning, sweetheart,' Kate said, setting the teapot and jug down on the table. 'Did you sleep—'

The floor shifted and Kate grabbed the nearest chair to steady herself.

Ella jumped up and put her arm around her. 'Are you all right, Ma?' she asked, looking uneasily at her.

'I'm fine,' Kate replied, as the room stopped spinning. 'I've just been rushing around. Now give Joe a call.'

Ella gave her another anxious look and then went to the bottom of the stairs. A dull pain started in Kate's head. She took a deep breath to clear it.

'Joe, Ma says to get yourself down here,' Ella called, her voice echoing in Kate's ears.

Joe thumped down the stairs, still struggling into his school jacket.

Kate pulled herself together. 'About time too, young man.'

'Sorry, Ma,' Joe said, as he took his place opposite his sister.

'All right,' Kate said. 'Now button your shirt properly while I fetch our breakfast.'

She went back into the kitchen.

'You look very pale, Mrs E,' Sally said, looking her over. 'Are you sure you're all the ticket?'

'I don't feel all that good,' Kate replied. 'But I'm sure once I've got breakfast down me I'll perk up.'

She stirred the porridge again then, wrapping a tea towel around her hand, picked the saucepan up and carried it through to the children.

'Here we are, something to stick to your ribs until dinner time,' Kate said.

The children giggled and picked their spoons up in readiness.

Kate's vision wavered and she lurched forward.

'Ma!' shouted Ella from what seemed like a long way away.

Blackness swirled around and a wave of nausea swept over her. The pot slipped from her hand and clattered onto the floor. Kate forced herself upright and, clutching onto the furniture and walls, staggered into the backyard. Without warning, her stomach turned, and she vomited. She put her hand out against the wall to steady herself as she retched up the contents of her stomach onto the flagstones.

She felt her knees buckle and she tried to stay upright but she must have passed out because she opened her eyes to find herself lying on the floor with Sally waving smelling salts under her nose. She coughed.

'Take a couple of breaths to clear your head,' Sally said, helping her to sit up.

Kate did and felt a tad better.

Ella and Joe crowded around her. Ella hugged Kate tightly around the neck and Joe leant against her with his thumb in his mouth.

'There, I said she'd be all right,' Sally said. 'Now let's get you in.'

She helped Kate to her feet and steered her along the passage and into the parlour.

'You sit there and I'll see to these two,' Sally said as she lowered Kate into the armchair. 'And don't you try and clear that up.' She indicated the porridge sitting in a congealed mass on the rug with the saucepan on top. 'I'll see to that when Bette gets in.'

'Thank you,' Kate said weakly, resting her head back.

Sally smoothed a stray lock out of Ella's eyes. 'Now you and Joe come with me and I'll do you a proper fry-up.'

Joe's eyes lit up but Ella lingered alongside Kate's chair. She gave her daughter a hug. 'I'm fine now. You go with Sally and then get off to school.'

'Yes, Ma.' Ella gave her a quick kiss on the forehead and then went into the shop.

Sally came back carrying a mug. 'Here, get that down you,' she said, handing it to Kate. 'It's baking powder and it'll settle your stomach.'

'Thank you,' Kate said, taking a sip.

'Now you put your feet up for a minute of two and I'll sort out the shop,' Sally said, and then she left.

Kate let her head fall back and closed her eyes. She must have drifted off to sleep because Sally's return made her start.

'You feeling better?' she asked as she closed the door to the shop behind her.

'Yes. What's the time?'

'Half past eleven.'

Kate sat up. 'What? The dinner bells ring in half an hour.'

Sally placed her hand on Kate's shoulder and pushed her back gently. 'And Bette and me can sort it out. You've had a nasty turn.'

'I've never felt so sick even when I was breeding,' Kate replied. 'I must have eaten something yesterday that didn't agree with me.'

'Maybe so, but if you ask me, it was that 'orrible pong from the river the other day – it's given lots of people the heaves.'

'Perhaps you're right,' Kate replied. 'I do feel very dizzy.'

'Well, better out than in, as my old mum used to say.' Sally looked her over. 'Your colour's come back, so do you want me to bring you a cup of weak tea?'

'Please.'

Sally went into the shop. Kate relaxed again. Maybe it was the smell from the river. After all, the children, Sally and Bette, and at least fifty men a day ate what she had the day before and they were still on their feet.

The clerk led Jonathan up the polished staircase and knocked quietly on the half-glazed door at the top.

'Come,' came the muffled reply. The young man turned the brass handle and ushered Jonathan in.

The lawyer's office was very much as Jonathan expected it to be, lined with shelves, stuffed with books and smelling musty from old paper. The busy hum of legal chatter drifted up from the floor below.

'Captain Quinn for you, Mr Gillespie,' the clerk said and then withdrew.

The solicitor looked over his half-rimmed glasses.

'It's good to meet you at last, Captain Quinn. I wish it were under happier circumstances.' Mr Gillespie tottered out from behind his desk to greet him.

Jonathan gripped the offered hand. 'Indeed. I didn't know Mrs Benson for very long but I greatly miss her.'

'As does everyone. Please.' Mr Gillespie indicated the leather-upholstered chair in front of the desk.

Jonathan sat down and crossed his legs.

'It's good of you to come at such short notice,' Mr Gillespie said, resuming his seat.

'Not at all, but I must confess I was a little surprised by your letter. I thought Mrs Benson's estate had already been settled.'

'The majority has but Mrs Benson added in a late amendment, just a few days before she died. It concerns you and the school. Now, before I get to the main reason for this meeting I am instructed to give you this.' Mr Gillespie handed Mrs Benson's well-worn Bible to Jonathan. 'And also this.' He picked up a sealed letter.

Jonathan stared down at his name written in the familiar hand and sadness washed over him. He was thankful she'd allowed him to unburden himself to her about Kate but he was even more grateful for her lack of censure.

Mr Gillespie opened the leather file sitting in front of him. 'Now, to the main change,' he said. 'In addition to the money she has already bequeathed to St Katharine's Foundation, Mrs Benson charged me with setting up a trust fund with the specific purpose of providing a hot midday meal to all pupils. It is to be administered by you or your successors. As there are no cooking facilities on the school premises, Mrs Benson leaves you free to commission whichever provider you feel best. The trust will be audited by the guardians with the school accounts each year.' He looked over the will at Jonathan. 'I trust you are agreeable?'

Jonathan nodded.

'Have you anyone in mind for the job?'

Jonathan smiled. 'Indeed I have.'

'Good. It will take only a couple of weeks for me to sort out the details.'

Jonathan rose to his feet. 'Thank you for your time.'

Mr Gillespie gripped the arms of the chair and stood up. He took Jonathan's hand and kept it. 'I've looked after Mrs Benson's affairs for almost thirty years and one thing I've learnt in dealing with her is that nothing she does is without purpose. She told me herself how fond she was of you, and although this late addition will greatly benefit the children at St Katharine's, I know she would have added it in the manner she did with you in mind.'

Jonathan smiled. 'I know, and I bless her for it.'

Kate had just started busying herself with the preparations for tomorrow's lunch when the doorbell jingled. She looked up and held her breath as Jonathan stepped through the door. He removed his hat, ran his fingers through his hair and smiled at her.

'Captain Quinn,' she said, shaken to see him standing in her shop after so long.

'Good afternoon to you, Mrs Ellis,' he said, looking at her anxiously. 'I hear you've been unwell.'

'I had an upset stomach, that's all.'

He studied her face closely. 'But you're all right. I mean, you've fully recovered.'

Kate smiled. 'I have. Completely.'

His rigid stance relaxed.

'Can I get you a cup of coffee?' she asked, trying to keep her voice steady.

'Please.'

Kate turned and with nervous hands uncorked the earthenware jar and spooned an extra portion of ground beans into the percolator.

He handed over his money and her fingers brushed his. Their gazes locked for a second before she pulled her hand away.

She poured the coffee, splashed the cream to float on the top and slid it towards him. 'There you go, one cup of very strong coffee. And it was good of you to come to enquire after my health.'

He took a sip. 'Actually, Mrs Ellis, that wasn't the only reason for my call,' he said, as she studied his fingers curled around the mug.

'I hope Joe isn't giving you trouble again.'

'No he's not but I would like to talk to you privately, if I may.'

Kate's heart started to flutter expectantly but she controlled herself. 'I don't think that would be a good—'

'It's school business,' Jonathan cut in. 'Something you might be able to help with. Perhaps we could sit by the window to discuss it?'

'Oh, yes. Of course,' Kate replied, not quite sure if she was relieved or disappointed that Jonathan had not come to plead with her to leave again.

She wiped her hands on her apron. He lifted the hinged section of counter for her to walk through. As she did Kate found herself passing disturbingly close to him.

'After you.' He indicated for her to go ahead of him.

Kate's heart hammered wildly in her chest as she wove her way to the window table knowing he was only a step behind. He waited for her to sit then took the chair on the other side and put his coffee cup down.

'I had a meeting with Mrs Benson's solicitor three days ago. He informed me that in addition to her other bequests to St Katharine's she also made a provision in her will for the children of the school to receive a hot midday meal.'

'How generous and so like her to think of something practical,' she replied.

'And,' Jonathan smiled in the way that always sent her pulse racing, 'the choice of supplier is mine so I would like to ask you if you would be able to supply the school with forty-five hot meals each day?'

Kate's eyes opened wide. 'You want me to . . . but how? There's no kitchen in the school.'

'I know, but we can do as the army does. Cook all the food in one place and then transport it to the mess, or in this case the school. I will send Mr Delaney with the handcart to collect the meals just before noon each day. Bear in mind though that the amount allocated for each pupil is only threepence a day and payable at the end of each week.'

Three times five times forty-five! Two pound, sixteen shillings and threepence a week! I'd need a couple of bigger pots but I'll be able to haggle a better price out of the butcher and grocer.

'Threepence a day, you say. Well, I tell you, Captain Quinn, those children will have a feast for that. No less.'

'I know they will.' His gaze flickered over her face for a moment then he stood up abruptly. 'That's settled, then. I'll call by next week to finalise the menu. Good day, Mrs Ellis.'

A weight settled on Kate as she followed him to the door.

'Thank you for thinking of me,' she said as he opened it.

Jonathan stopped and looked down at her. 'I'm always thinking of you, Kate,' he said softly, then strode out of the shop.

Chapter Twenty-Three

Kate sat up on one elbow, plumped the bolster then lay down again. She stared at the ceiling and listened to the faint sound of Joe and Ella sleeping in the room opposite. It was no good. Try as she might, she knew that she would still be wide awake when the knocker-up started his round in an hour or so. It had been the same last night and the one before.

Day and night she relived Jonathan's every word, gesture and expression. She let her imagination conjure up images of them entwined in each other's arms, making love and sometimes, when her need for him was almost overwhelming, Kate wished she'd let her desires have their way. But then she remembered where her passion had led her the last time.

She rolled over and, trying not to dwell on the fact that she had to get up in two hours, started to count imaginary sheep.

Something scuffled outside her window and she sat bolt upright.

It's only the yard cat, she told herself as her heart thumped painfully in her chest. *Just the cat.*

She strained her ears but could only hear the low boom of the barges knocking together on the river. After a moment or two she lay back and shut her eyes again.

She began to drift off when a crash outside snapped her fully awake.

She threw off the bed covers and went quickly to the window. In the pale moonlight she saw someone moving about in the stable.

To her astonishment the double gates leading out to the road creaked open and a man's head poked out. He looked sharply up and down the road then opened the gates so that another man could push a loaded cart out to the street. They closed the gates and, taking a shaft each, pulled the cart away.

Fear and anger twisted together in Kate's chest. She didn't know who they were or what they were doing but she knew as sure as there were saints above it had something to do with Freddie.

She shrugged on her dressing gown as she ran downstairs and with trembling fingers lit a lamp, went through to the kitchen and rummaged around in the money drawer for the key to the stable. It wasn't there.

With blood pounding in her ears, she dashed through the parlour, collecting a poker on the way. She unbolted the back door and opened it an inch to look out on to the silent yard. Satisfied that she was alone, Kate dashed across to the stable, jammed the tip of the poker between the door frame and leant on it to force it open.

What on earth ...?

Kate squeezed her way between crates and barrels stencilled with:

PROPERTY OF GOSWELL BONDED WAREHOUSE
WEST INDIA DOCK

She used the poker again to prise open a couple of crates, revealing tobacco leaves, bales of silk and lace, silver plate, sacks of coffee beans and tea. There was even a pair of curled ivory tusks covered by a tarpaulin in the far corner.

Kate stared at the stash of stolen goods knowing it could send her, and Patrick, to prison for upwards of fifteen years. Her grip on the poker tightened. For the first time in six years, she couldn't wait to see Freddie.

Kate tucked the greaseproof paper with *Kate's Kitchen* printed in pale blue across it around the fruit cake, then placed it in the basket with others ready for the grocer to collect in the morning. Thankfully, it was half-day closing so she was able to shut up shop as soon as the last lunchtime customer had departed.

She glanced out of the back window and prayed once again that Freddie had picked up the message she'd left him at the Sword, where she knew he still had a pint each evening.

She looked over at Ella sitting with her head bowed over a book and Joe marching his soldier along the table top. Her resolve stiffened. She suffered enough at Freddie's hands but this time he'd gone too far.

But when – and if – he arrived, what would she do? She knew what she was going to *say* right enough, but, sweet Mary, let her keep hold of her temper.

Suddenly the back door opened and Freddie strolled in with his hands in his pockets and his hat cocked on the back of his head.

'Pa! Pa!' Joe shouted, dashing towards his father.

Ella looked up briefly then returned to her studies.

'What's all this about?' Freddie asked.

'Ella, Joe. Will you go to your room, please?' Kate said, firmly.

Ella closed her book and headed towards the stairs; with a reluctant pout, Joe followed her.

Kate waited until the door clicked shut then turned her attention to Freddie. 'I want your stolen haul out of my stable by morning.'

Freddie looked unabashed. 'It ain't stolen – I'm storing it for someone.'

'I want it moved or I'll be going to the police.'

He jabbed his finger at her. 'I *said* it ain't nicked.'

'You're a bloody liar, Freddie Ellis, and always have been,' she shouted. 'But this time you've gone too far. You'll not use my home to stash your pilfered goods.' She looked him up and down contemptuously. 'You're a sorry excuse for a man if ever there was one. What with your cocky swagger, fancy suits, and dirty tarts you're nothing more than a small-time crook.'

'Now you listen here, I—'

'No, you listen, Freddie,' Kate cut in. 'Get that stuff moved or, as God is my witness, I'll be banging on the police station door at—'

Freddie's fist smashed into her left cheek, sending her staggering backwards to fall against the table.

'Go to the police, will you?' he snarled, as she backed away. 'You won't be going anywhere when I'm finished with you.'

Kate put her hand to her nose and felt something sticky. She looked down to see the bloody tips of her fingers.

'Don't you hit my ma!' screamed Ella, running back into the room with Joe scrabbling along after. But while she grabbed the broom leaning against the wall to swing it at her father, Joe cowered in the corner with his hands over his face. Freddie dealt his daughter a glancing blow with the back of his hand. She landed on the floor in a heap.

He then turned back to Kate, who'd curled herself into a ball. He kicked her then dragged her up by her hair and punched her again. She staggered but shook her head to clear the ringing in her ears as she tried to stand. Somehow she grabbed the poker from the hearth and as Freddie lunged at her again she smashed it down on his forearm. He shrieked and clutched his arm.

'You fucking bitch! You've broken my arm.'

'And I'll break your head if you touch Ella again,' Kate yelled back.

Ella crawled behind Kate and put her arms around Joe, who still had his face turned away.

'Ella, get up,' she said, without taking her eyes off Freddie. 'Take Joe and fetch your Uncle Pat. Go now!'

Ella scrambled up, and gripping Joe by the hand, dragged him out. Kate heard them running through the yard and out of the gate.

'I'd make myself scarce, if I were you, before my brother arrives with the whole of Knockfergus behind him.'

Freddie's face contorted with rage. 'I'll get you for this, you bitch,' he ground. Nursing his injured arm, he lumbered out the back door.

Kate, still gripping the poker, followed him and threw the bolts across. She leant on the door for a moment then crumpled to the floor.

Aggie looked up as Freddie crashed through the Boy's door clutching his right arm. He stomped towards her with a murderous expression on his face and threw himself into the chair.

'Fucking Paddy bitch.'

'What's happened to her? Is she ill or sumink?' she asked and wondering, not for the first time, why Kate wasn't mouldering in her grave. She should have been after all, she'd given her enough poison to kill an ox. 'No, more's the pity.' Freddie grabbed her drink and downed it in one. 'It's the stash in the stable. It's lost.'

'What do you mean "lost"?'

Freddie took a gulp from the bottle. 'The nabbers'll have it by now . . .' He recounted the whole story.

'But if she gave you till the morning to shift the gear, why are the coppers crawling all over it now?'

'Cos I belted her one and she sent the kids to fetch her poxy brother. He'll get the rozzers down for sure.'

Aggie sneered. 'So you could have moved the stuff but you smacked her about instead and lost the lot.'

'But she almost broke my arm.' He raised it for her to see.

Aggie rolled her eyes.

'Well, what was I supposed to do?' Freddie shouted. 'I weren't going to let her talk to me like that.'

'You could have *moved* the gear first and *then* gone back and shown her what's what. You should have finished the job, so then she couldn't tell anyone anything. Now the coppers will be wanting to ask you a few questions about what they've found.'

Freddie signalled for another bottle. 'No one crosses Freddie Ellis and gets away with it but now she's gone running to her fucking brother, I'll have to lay low for a bit.'

'Surely you can deal with a bloody bogtrotter.'

'Of course I can.'

Freddie jumped to his feet. 'I'm top man around here and don't you forget it.' He raised his fist to her and winced.

'Of course you are, Freddie,' Aggie said. 'Everyone knows you're the boss.'

'Don't you worry, Aggie,' he said, as Mary arrived with the bottle. 'I'll deal with her and her poxy brother, but only when I'm good and ready.'

Chapter Twenty-Four

When Mattie turned the corner, her heart nearly stopped. She gathered her skirts and dashed across the road.

'What's happened?' she demanded, gripping the officer's arm. 'Is my sister all right?'

'Sister?'

'Mrs Ellis. This is her shop,' Mattie replied, with a rising sense of panic. 'Tell me nothing's happened to her.'

'Mrs Ellis has had a bit of a shock but she's well enough,' the constable replied.

Mattie crossed herself rapidly. 'Thank God! May I . . .' She pointed at the house.

'Well . . . I'll have to check with the governor. Come with me.'

They went through the gates into Kate's backyard to find two constables rolling barrels from the stable and stacking crates of tea and all manner of other things. As she looked on in amazement, she heard Kate call her name.

'Mattie!'

Kate was standing in the door frame and although she was neatly dressed in her usual dark blue gown and a crisp white apron, her face was the colour of a Victoria plum and her left eye was swollen shut.

'Me darling girl,' Mattie said, rushing towards her sister. 'You shouldn't be walking about like that. You come with me right now.'

She put her arm gently around Kate and led her back into the parlour and to her chair. She pulled over the small footstool and lifted Kate's legs onto it then covered her in a knitted blanket from the back of the chair. She tucked it around her sister's legs.

'There, that's better. Where are the children? Are they all right?'

Kate nodded. 'I thought it better if they were out of the way at school while the police were here. Ella didn't want to leave me . . .' Her eyes filled with tears.

'Now, you keep your rear fixed on that seat while I make you a nice cuppa. Have you eaten?'

'No, I can't face it.'

'Yes, you can.' Mattie put her hands on her hips. 'I'll be right back with a cup of sweet tea and scrambled eggs.'

For a moment she thought Kate was going to argue but then her sister smiled feebly. 'Thanks, sis.'

Mattie bent to kiss Kate lightly on her cheek then went through to the shop. The heat from the range hit her as she stepped in. Sally, who was clearing away the last of the empty plates, returned to the serving area.

'If you'll excuse my French, Mrs Tate, that Freddie Ellis is a proper bastard, and no mistake,' Sally said as Mattie moved the kettle back onto the hotplate.

'Sally, I couldn't have said it better myself,' Mattie said, spooning tea into the pot. 'And may the devil take him.'

Mattie quickly made the tea and eggs and took it back to Kate.

'So what happened?' she asked, lifting the teapot lid and stirring the leaves.

Kate told her about the events of the previous night. 'How much was there?' Mattie asked.

'Hundreds of pounds' worth the sergeant said, but they won't know until they've done a full inventory.' Kate covered her eyes with her hand. 'Oh, Mattie, if the police had discovered the stash themselves, Pat and I would have been answering questions at the Old Bailey for handling stolen goods.'

'But I thought you kept the stable locked?' Mattie asked.

'He took the key from the cash drawer.' Kate clenched her fists. 'When I think of the danger he's put us in, well . . . it makes my blood fair boil. I tell you, Mattie, if Freddie had been standing in front of me when I opened the stable door, I would have put him in his grave myself.'

'You'll have to wait your turn behind Pat and me,' Mattie replied.

Kate gave the best smile she could muster with a fat lip. 'What would I do without you both?'

Mattie patted her sister's hand. 'You'll never have to. Now have some of your egg and drink your tea.'

Kate finished her egg and then laid her head back on the cushion Mattie had placed there and closed her eyes. Mattie sat down quietly and studied her sleeping sister, bruised and battered. She crossed herself and pleaded with the Virgin that this would be the very last time Freddie's fists would find their mark on Kate's beautiful face.

*

Jonathan was chewing the end of his pen as he reread the weekly school's report when a knock on the door roused him from his task.

'Enter.'

Miss Wainwright opened the door and ushered Ella into the room. 'I'm sorry to disturb you, Headmaster, but Miss Ellis has been beside herself all morning and I can't seem to get to the bottom of it. I thought perhaps you might ...'

'Of course,' Jonathan replied, standing up and coming around the desk. 'Come now, Ella, this is not like you,' he said in a friendly voice. 'You're normally one of St Katharine's jolliest pupils. What is all this crying about?'

Ella looked up at him and Jonathan saw the echo of Kate in the young girl's bruised face.

'It's ... It's ...' Her chin started to wobble uncontrollably and she covered her face with her hands.

Jonathan looked over her head. 'Thank you, Miss Wainwright, I'll deal with this. You continue with your class.'

The schoolmistress left.

Jonathan placed his hand lightly on Ella's shoulder and led her to the chair. 'Come and sit here,' he said, pulling up another chair beside her.

She took out her handkerchief from her pocket and blew her nose.

'Are you unwell at all, Ella?'

She shook her head.

'Has someone been bullying you?'

She shook her head again.

Jonathan ran his fingers through his hair. 'Are you having trouble with—'

'It's my ma,' she said, as tears spilled over again.

'What wrong with your ma?' he asked, suddenly alarmed.

'Last night Pa came home.' Ella recounted the tale. '... and then Joe and I ran all the way to Uncle Pat's. When I told him what had happened, he and Mickey ran back to the shop. Aunt Josie wanted me and Joe to stay with her but I was afraid that Ma might be hurt so Rob walked us back. When I got there the police were already in the stable with Uncle Pat but when I saw what he'd done to Ma ...' She blew her nose. 'Her face is swollen and she can't chew,' Ella went on. 'Uncle Pat got the doctor from Chapman Street to see her and he said there were no bones broken and that she'd be all right in a day or two but ...' She clutched her hands. 'Oh, Headmaster, I was so afraid Pa had killed her that when I saw she was alive, I just started crying and I can't seem to stop.'

Jonathan patted her shoulder lightly. 'Don't worry, Ella, it's just shock. I've seen grown men crumple after witnessing such terrible things. It's perfectly normal and you'll soon be yourself again.'

Ella looked up at him with a strangely grown-up expression on her young face. 'I don't care what the Sunday school teacher says about honouring your father and mother, I hate *him*.' She clasped her hands together. 'Why couldn't he have stayed away?' she sobbed. 'All he does is take Ma's money and hit her.'

'Now, now . . .'

'I wish you'd been there.'

'So do I,' he said, gently. 'Would you like to collect your brother and go home?'

'Yes, sir.' Ella blew her nose again. 'Thank you, Headmaster.'

When she'd gone, Jonathan strode to the window and blindly looked into the empty schoolyard. He slammed his hand against the window frame, nearly shattering the glass. He turned, snatched his hat from the stand then tore open his office door and marched out.

Kate sat back in the chair and watched as Mattie folded the last of the washing into a neat pile on the table.

'Thank you for doing all that,' she mumbled through her swollen lip.

'I had to do something while you were snoozing.' Mattie straightened the blanket over Kate's legs again. 'Is your headache easing?'

'A little.'

In truth, what with weeks of broken sleep and the drama of the night before, Kate had been dozing in and out of sleep all day.

Mattie placed her hand on her forehead. 'Well, there's no fever. But don't forget to take another dose of the medicine Doctor Ives left you.'

'Do you think Sally will be able to cope with the supper rush?' Kate asked, looking at the closed door that led to the shop.

Mattie nodded. 'Your old neighbour Peggy and a couple of others dropped by while you were asleep to see if they could help.'

'What time did the police leave?' Kate asked, shifting in her seat to ease the throbbing in her hip where Freddie's boot had landed.

'About midday,' Mattie said. 'And they are as keen as mustard to have a word with Freddie about it all. So that should stop him slipping back to bother you again.'

The back door opened and Ella and Joe came in. They ran over to her and Kate did her best to hug them.

'You're home early,' Kate said, trying to give a sunny smile.

Ella took her hand. 'I couldn't stop crying so Miss Wainwright took me to the headmaster. I . . . I told him what happened and he sent us home.'

'That's kind of him,' Kate said, looking up at Mattie.

'Well, now you've seen your ma's all right, what about coming back to my house for supper to let her have another few hours' rest?' Mattie said, as Joe and Ella started to unbutton their coats.

The children didn't seem so keen.

Mattie slipped her arms around the children's shoulders. 'It only for a couple of hours and Uncle Nathaniel can bring you back on one of the wagons.' They still looked unsure. 'There's jam pudding for afters, Joe, and you can help me bath Grace, Ella.'

'But what if *he* comes back?' Ella asked.

'He won't,' replied Mattie. 'Not with the streets crawling with coppers and your uncle Pat after his blood.'

Ella hesitated for a moment longer and then nodded.

Mattie kissed Kate on the head. 'You rest up and I'll see you tomorrow.' Her eyes flickered over Kate's bruised face. 'Come on, you two, give your ma a kiss, *gently*,' she said, looking pointedly at Joe, 'and let's get back.'

Kate settled down when they'd gone and must have dropped off to sleep again as a light knock on the door woke her. She opened her eyes to see Sally ushering Jonathan through from the shop.

He stopped dead with a look of horror on his face. 'My God!' The brim of his hat buckled in his grip as his expression turned from shock to fury. 'Ella told me you were injured but I . . .'

Sally shut the door.

'Jonathan,' Kate whispered, as tears began to slip down her cheeks.

He threw his hat aside and knelt down beside her. Slipping his arm around her he carefully cradled her in his arms. 'My darling.'

She rested her head on his shoulder and closed her eyes. 'I didn't want you to see me li—'

His lips touched hers gently, stopping her words.

'Shhh, sweetheart. What did the doctor say? Are there any broken bones? Who is looking after you?'

'Once the bruising has subsided, I'll be as good as new,' she replied. 'My sister, Mattie, will be dropping by each day to make sure I'm all right. You've just missed her.'

'And the children?'

Tears welled up in her eyes. 'Oh, Jonathan, I . . . I . . .'

He gathered her into his arms again and held her as she wept quietly.

'Tell me where I can find him,' he said in a controlled voice, once she'd stopped crying.

Kate froze. 'What are you going to do?'

'Find him, of course.' Jonathan started to rise. 'If the brute thinks he can—'

'You mustn't.' Kate clung to him. 'He's probably hiding in the Spitalfields rookery and even the police don't venture in there unless a dozen go together.'

'I damn well can and I will.'

'But if you do anything, then he and everyone else will know about us.'

Jonathan clenched his fist. 'When I get my hands on him, I'll . . .' He looked at her for a moment then returned to her side. '*Us?*'

Kate nodded.

He returned to her side and gathered her gently into his arms. 'Oh, Kate,' he said, as his lips lightly pressed onto hers. 'I love you.'

Kate rested her head on his chest. 'And I you but what are we to do?'

'We have to go away as far as possible,' he said, kissing her forehead. 'To Australia.'

'Is there no other way?' she asked, already knowing the answer – she wasn't rich enough to hire lawyers for a divorce and anyway, in Knockfergus you were married for life.

'Kate, I understand what I'm asking you to do but we can be Mr and Mrs Quinn with no one to say otherwise there. Ella and Joe can grow up in a country with endless possibilities. And it would be the same for our children, too, Kate.'

But what a scandal! thought Kate. *A wife throwing aside respectability and absconding with the schoolmaster.* She would be the talk of the neighbourhood for years to come. And what of Jonathan? He would be labelled a scoundrel and blackguard. And then there was Ella and Joe – would they thrive in this faraway land? And what about Patrick, Mattie, her ma and the rest of the family? How could she possibly leave everyone she loved behind? Her gaze moved slowly over his face, taking in its details. She reached up and released a strand of hair sitting over his eyepatch.

'When can we go?'

He grasped her hand and pressed it to his lips. 'We should leave before the end of September to avoid the Atlantic storms.'

Panic fluttered in Kate's chest. It was mid-August now so they would be leaving in just six weeks.

'So soon?'

Jonathan kissed her hand again. 'The sooner I get you out of reach of that brute, the better. Just get well and leave the arrangements to me.'

'I understand but, Jonathan, the person who wrote that letter to the guardians is still watching us and might find out our plan,' Kate said.

Jonathan raked his fingers through his hair. 'We will need to be extra careful to act completely normal. We must be safely on the ship in the middle of the Atlantic before anyone realises we've gone. I promise you'll never regret it, Kate.'

Kate pushed aside the knot of unhappiness about her family and smiled up at him. 'If we're together, Jonathan, I know I never will.'

'There you go, Polly,' Kate said, handing over two bowls of mutton and dumplings. 'I've put an extra couple of potatoes in your lads' bowls as I know the young 'uns have hollow legs.'

'Thank you, Mrs E,' Polly replied. 'What do you say, boys?'

'Fank you, Mssss E,' said the two lads, clinging to their mother's skirt.

Kate stepped through the gap in the counter and bent down so her face was level with theirs. 'That's all right but mind you eat it all up,' she said, handing them a spoon each, 'because if you do, I might just have a bit of custard for you both.'

The youngsters' eyes lit up. Kate stood up as their mother led them to the back of the shop. The doorbell tinkled. Kate looked around and saw Miss Puttock squeezing her immensely wide skirts through the door. She was surprised to see her as she'd never been to the shop before.

'Good day, Miss Puttock,' said Kate, wiping her hands and walking over to greet her.

'Mrs Ellis,' Miss Puttock replied, trying to negotiate her way through the tightly packed tables and chairs without knocking the furniture over.

'I confess I am a little surprised to see you here,' Kate said, as the young woman stopped in front of her.

Miss Puttock looked around disdainfully. 'No more than I am to be here, I assure you.'

A navvy pushed past, forcing her to step closer to the counter. The back of her skirt rose up and knocked a mug of tea off the table behind. A whoop went up from the men in the shop and Miss Puttock's tightly drawn lips pulled in further.

'Is there somewhere we could talk privately?' she asked, looking condescendingly at Kate.

'Of course,' Kate replied. 'Come through to the parlour.'

Miss Puttock side-stepped between the open part of the counter and swept into Kate's back room.

Sally put a handful of bowls on the worktop. 'We must be going up in the world if Lady Muck's dropping in for afternoon tea,' she hissed.

'That will be the day,' Kate replied, before she followed Miss Puttock. Quickly she untied her apron and tucked a stray curl of hair behind her ear. Miss Puttock was standing with her hands clasped in front of her and a resolute expression on her face.

'Please, take a seat.' Kate indicated the chair by the fire.

Miss Puttock pulled out a straight-backed chair from the table and perched on the edge.

'Would you like a cup of tea?'

'Thank you, no. This isn't a social call.'

Kate pulled out another chair from the table and sat down. 'If it's about Joe's behaviour at Sunday school, I can only—'

'It's not your son's conduct I have come to discuss, Mrs Ellis.' She glared at Kate. 'Perhaps I should come straight to the point. I *know* about you and Captain Quinn.'

Kate's heart lurched. 'What about Captain Quinn and me?' she asked, praying only she could hear the tremor in her voice.

'About your sordid liaison,' Miss Puttock replied, her face contorted with venom.

'I . . . I don't know what you are talking about,' Kate stuttered, feeling her cheeks grow warm.

'Don't try to play the innocent with me. I overheard you talking in the graveyard.'

'It was you who sent the letter to the school guardians.'

Miss Puttock's neck flushed a deep crimson. 'I don't know to what you are referring. I was merely strolling in the graveyard contemplating Mr Overton's fine sermon when I spotted the two of you together and—'

'Sneaked behind the monument and spied on us.'

'I did no such thing.' Miss Puttock's gaze shifted. 'But I couldn't help but hear your shameful conversation.'

'Then you no doubt heard me turn him away,' Kate replied, as the memory of Jonathan's agonised expression cut her heart again.

Miss Puttock gave a mirthless laugh. 'You may have feigned reluctance but only to enflame his emotions and entangle him further.' Her gaze ran slowly over Kate. 'After all, that's how you caught Freddie Ellis, wasn't it?' She straightened an imaginary crease on her skirt. 'Of course, I do not blame Captain Quinn. Even godly, righteous men are still men and their fallen natures make them susceptible to the lures of women like you. But the Lord tells us to forgive the transgressions of others and I shall most willingly pardon Captain Quinn. However,' her eyes narrowed, 'if he refuses to see the error of his ways, I'm afraid it would be my duty to inform the school guardians of this deplorable situation. Do you understand?'

Kate studied her hands resting in her lap and counted backwards slowly from ten. She raised her head. 'Yes.'

Miss Puttock scrutinised her closely. 'I'm relieved to hear that.' She stood up. 'It would be a pity if Captain Quinn were to throw away his position and blight his good name with a woman like you.'

Kate stood up and looked her squarely in the eye. 'Have you finished?'

'I think so,' Miss Puttock replied, pulling on her gloves.

'Good.' Kate crossed the room and flung open the parlour door. 'Don't let me detain you.'

With an indignant toss of her head, Mabel stormed across the room to the door. As she came level with Kate, she paused.

'You may have hoodwinked the guardians, Mrs Ellis, but you don't fool me. I shall be watching you very closely indeed and if I hear Captain Quinn's name even whispered in the same sentence as yours, I *will* destroy his good name. Do you understand?'

'I do,' Kate replied, fighting the urge to slap the smug, condescending expression off the young woman's face.

Miss Puttock smiled sweetly. 'I'm glad you do. After all, we can't have a man in charge of the moral welfare of our dear children embroiled in an adulterous relationship, can we?'

She swept out. Kate stood there for a moment to regain her composure before walking back into the shop.

Sally was up to her elbows in suds, washing plates, but looked around as Kate appeared. 'By the look on her face when she stormed through, I'd say you won the battle with dragon Puttock good and proper.'

Kate forced a smile. She wished it were so but she had the feeling that unlike St George's defeated dragon, Miss Puttock would rise up and finish them both.

Chapter Twenty-Five

Kate straightened the curtains and looked out at the leaden sky. A few heavy raindrops had begun to patter down and it looked as if there were more to follow. She glanced anxiously along the street but there was no sign of Jonathan. She put her hand on her forehead to ease her throbbing headache. Although she'd recovered completely from Freddie's brutal attack, two sleepless nights thinking about Miss Puttock's visit had left her mind battered and bruised.

She pushed vacant chairs under the tables and made her way back to the counter. To stop herself jumping each time someone walked past, Kate busied herself with the preparations for tomorrow's lunch. She'd just put the last of the plates into the drying rack when the doorbell jingled.

Kate turned as Jonathan walked into the shop. He looked anxiously at her.

She dried her hands on her apron. 'Good afternoon, Captain Quinn. I see you received my note about the school menu,' she said loudly so the handful of customers in the shop could hear.

'Yes, I did,' he replied, in the same clear tone. 'Perhaps we could discuss it now if you're not too busy.'

'No, that would be fine,' Kate said. 'Bette, will you look after things for a few minutes while I speak to Captain Quinn?'

Bette looked up from wiping down the tables. 'Right you are, Mrs E.'

Jonathan went and sat at the table by the window, drew out his pocket book and opened it. Kate took down her order pad from the shelf and went to join him. She set it down and took her place opposite.

'What's happened?' he whispered.

Kate leant over the table, tilting her head as if to see the page better. 'I had a visit from Mabel Puttock.' She told him about their conversation. 'I know I should have waited until you came on Thursday to tell you but I was so worried I had to—'

'Shush, sweetheart,' he said softly, pretending to look at the books on the table. 'It's all right.' His expression became grim. 'So it was

Mabel who sent the anonymous letter to the guardians.'

Kate nodded. 'She denied it but I know it was her. Oh, Jonathan, what are we going to do? If she gets even a whiff of our plans she'll destroy you,' she said, as panic threatened to take hold again.

'Don't worry, Kate. I'll deal with Mabel Puttock.'

Kate shoulders relaxed a couple of notches. 'I'm certain no one else knows.'

'So am I, but even so, we'll have to be careful. It won't be for much longer as I've started making the final arrangements. I've instructed the bank to send my annuity to the British and Colonial Bank in Melbourne every six months from January.'

'And I'll get Patrick to send my money to us once we are settled.' Kate looked up from her order book. 'Jonathan, I have to tell my family that I'm leaving.'

He gave her a little smile. 'I know you do, darling, and I am going to see my sister, Barbara, too.'

'And your father?'

Jonathan chewed his lip. 'I haven't decided.'

'Well, you've got time enough yet to make up your mind,' Kate said.

Jonathan shifted in the chair and looked intensely at her. 'Kate, I've been to the shipping office, too. There's a ship, the *Charlotte Anne*, sailing for Melbourne on the thirteenth of September.'

'That's only two weeks away!'

'I know it's sooner than you expected and I'd understand if you're having second thoughts but—'

'I'm *not* having second thoughts.' She slid her fingers across the page of the order book and brushed them against his. 'I love my family but our future together is more important now.'

He scribbled *mince, onion and potato* along the top line. 'Then shall I reserve four berths on the *Charlotte Anne*?'

Although Kate's heart thumped uncomfortably in her chest, she smiled at him. 'Yes.'

Jonathan closed the dinner ledger and rested his hands on it. 'I love you, Kate,' he whispered.

Kate shut her order book too. 'I thought we were being careful.'

'I am being careful. If I were not, I'd kiss you here and now and to hell with the consequences.'

They stared into each other's eyes for a moment then the doorbell rang. Kate looked around and saw her niece standing in the shop.

'Annie?' she said. 'What are you doing here?'

'Pa sent me to fetch you, Aunt Kate, because Gran's taken a tumble.'

'Is she all right?' Kate asked, jumping up and untying her apron in one swift move.

'She's just a bit shaken. The doctor said she has to stay in bed for a few days. I'll stay with Ella and Joe until you get back.'

'Ella's in the parlour but Joe's out – he should be back before supper.' Kate put on her bonnet hurriedly.

'Would you allow me to accompany you to your mother's, Mrs Ellis?' Jonathan asked, rising to his feet.

'Oh, yes, I would, Captain Quinn,' Kate replied.

Patrick opened his front door to find Kate standing on the doorstep. 'That was quick. I only sent Annie to fetch you half an hour ago.'

'She arrived when I was discussing the school dinners with Captain Quinn. He kindly brought me here,' Kate replied, with a slight blush on her cheeks.

Patrick looked over his sister's head at the man paying the hansom cab.

'This is my brother Patrick,' Kate said, stepping inside when he joined them.

'It is a pleasure to meet you, Mr Nolan,' Jonathan said, offering his hand.

Patrick accepted and found his grip evenly matched. Also, somewhat unusually, he didn't have to look down to meet Quinn's gaze. 'Thank you for bringing my sister.'

'It was my pleasure,' Quinn replied, glancing at Kate who smiled shyly up at him.

'Kate!' Josie called from the top of the stairs. 'Come up. Ma would like to see you.'

'Thank you again,' Kate said, quietly.

'Not at all – I hope your mother makes a full recovery. I'll drop in at the end of the week to finalise the school meals, if I may.'

Kate nodded and smiled hesitantly then went up to join Josie and her mother.

Captain Quinn's gaze followed her as she climbed the stairs.

'Please let me offer you a drink,' Patrick said. 'It's the least I can do.'

'That's very kind of you but I'm sure you've got things to attend to.'

Patrick stepped back from the door. 'No, please. I insist.'

Jonathan removed his hat and stepped in. 'And how is your mother?'

'Remarkably well, considering she's almost eighty and fell down the four front steps,' he replied. Patrick went to the sideboard and picked up the Jameson's. 'Can I offer you ...' He held up the bottle.

'Thank you, but it's a little early for me.'

'Me too.' He put it down. 'There's some lemonade in the pantry if you'd prefer.'

'I'm not really thirsty actually,' Captain Quinn replied. 'And I should return to St Katharine's before the end of the school day.'

They stared at each other for a moment then Captain Quinn dusted the crown of his hat. 'I really should get back to the school. Please give my compliments to your wife. You have a very welcoming home,' he said, putting on his hat on.

'Ah, well now. That is indeed her doing. You should look to find yourself a woman if you want a homely touch at the end of the day,' Patrick replied, studying his face intensely. 'I wonder ... Do you often find yourself at my sister's shop?'

Something like amusement flickered across the schoolmaster's face. 'From time to time. Fortunately I was there today.'

'Indeed and I am obliged to you.'

'Say nothing of it.'

'You'll allow me to reimburse the cost of the fare.'

'I could not.' Jonathan's pleasant expression didn't falter. 'Good day to you and I hope to meet you again in more pleasant circumstances.'

Patrick opened the front door. 'Good day.'

Jonathan jogged down the whitened front steps and turned towards the river. Patrick watched him stride down the street for a moment then shut the door.

Josie came down the stairs. 'I've left Kate with Ma while I make us a cup of tea.' She looked into the empty parlour. 'Has Captain Quinn gone?'

'Yes, he said he had to get back.'

Josie sighed. 'That's a pity. Mattie said Kate is always saying how marvellous he is at St Katharine's. I would have liked to have found about more about him.'

Patrick raised an eyebrow. 'So would I, my dear. So would I.'

There wasn't an inch of Sarah Nolan's face that wasn't either purple, grazed or swollen after her tumble down the steps.

Kate stroked her mother's hand. 'Are you sure you are all right?'

'I'll be better when you all stop fussing over me,' Sarah replied. 'I'm not made of glass, you know.'

Kate laughed. 'Just as well, by all accounts.'

'I tripped, that's all,' her mother replied. 'And I'll have a word or two to say to Patrick when I'm up and about for dragging you all the way over here for nothing.'

Kate straightened the covers. 'And I would have had a word or two with him myself if he hadn't.'

Sarah wrinkled her nose and smiled. 'And glad I am, my sweet darling. When you get to my age, having your family close is a blessing worth having.'

Kate lowered her eyes and studied her mother's work-worn hands. Leaving Patrick and Mattie would be bad enough but Ma ... Before she could stop them, tears welled up in her eyes.

Sarah looked worried. 'For the *love of Mary*, is there something the doctor's not told me?'

'No, no. He said you'll be back to your old self in days. It's just ...' Kate twisted the fabric of her skirt.

'Katharine Ellen Nolan, tell me what's bringing tears to those lovely eyes of yours.'

'I can't tell you.'

'Of course you can. I'm your mother.'

Kate took her mother's hand. 'You must promise not to tell Patrick and Mattie.'

'It's not that bastard Freddie again, is it?' She groped for her walking stick at the foot of the bed. 'Cos I'll tell you, Kate, as God is my witness, if he's touched another hair on your head, I'll crack his worthless skull myself.' She shook the cane at the window.

'No. It's not Freddie. He hasn't been near – and he's not likely to with every policeman in H division out looking for him.'

'Well, what is it then?'

Kate drew a deep breath. 'I'm in love wi—'

'Captain Quinn.'

Kate's mouth dropped open. 'But how did you know?'

'Well, hasn't he been the topic of conversation each time I've seen you for months now?' She tilted her head. 'And what has he to say on the matter?'

'He loves me, too.'

'Well, why wouldn't he?' Sarah replied. 'And you plan to go away together?'

Kate looked astonished. 'But . . .?'

Sarah rolled her eyes. 'While that devil Freddie's still drawing breath, what choice do you have?' She folded her arms across her chest. 'You know you'll be the topic on every street corner.'

'I've been that before, Ma. At least this time I won't be around to hear it.'

Sarah studied her for a moment then nodded. 'Let them talk, I say. Where are you and your schoolmaster going?'

'Australia,' Kate replied. 'Jonathan says the government is virtually giving away land. He showed me an article in a newspaper all about it and there was a picture of the countryside. It looks like the painting you have downstairs of Ireland. He has money enough to get us started and the children would have room to grow.'

'You must go,' Sarah said firmly.

Kate took her mother's hand. 'But, Ma, I can't leave when you're so . . . so . . . unwell.'

'So old, you mean.'

Kate lowered her head and her mother squeezed her hand.

'There's no doubt that I'll soon leave the troubles of this world behind me. And, my darling girl, don't you think it will be easier for me knowing you've found happiness after all the trials you've been through? Look at me, child.' Kate raised her head. 'Me and your pappy, God rest his soul, left Ireland forty years ago with empty stomachs and only the clothes on our backs to make a better life for our children, and now you must do the same for yours. You *must* grasp this chance with both hands. If it were Ella sitting where you are and you were in my place, what would you say to her?' Sarah rested back and folded her arms again. 'Well, then?'

A fat tear escaped and rolled down Kate's left cheek. 'I don't know how I'll manage without you, Ma,' she said.

'Nor I you, but do it for me, Kate. I'll bear our parting better if I know you're happy. And you must tell Mattie and Pat. It would break their hearts if you go without a farewell.'

Kate nodded. 'I will, but only a day or two before we sail.'

'That's probably wise. You know Mattie was in a similar situation with Nathaniel. She'll understand. And Patrick will try to do something so you won't have to go. He's still cursing himself for forcing Freddie to marry you in the first place.'

'I know, and I'm afraid that if he does interfere he might unwittingly tip off Freddie. I can't take the chance of him taking the children.'

Sarah's brow furrowed. 'Why do you think he would?'

'To spite me for one, although he'd probably abandon Ella on the steps of the first poor house he passed, but Freddie's got it in his head that Joe should grow up like him.'

'God forbid.' Sarah crossed herself. 'We'll keep it as our secret but you must promise to write and tell me how those darling children are.'

'Every week without fail, I promise,' Kate replied, feeling tears welling up again.

Sarah held out her arms and Kate hopped on the bed beside her mother. Sarah embraced her. Kate rested her head on her mother's shoulder as she'd done so many times before. 'Now, as we have a minute or two before Josie brings the tea I want you to tell me *all about* this schoolmaster of yours.'

Chapter Twenty-Six

After shaking the vicar's hand Jonathan stepped out of the church and spotted Mabel talking to an old woman on the church path. He'd argued long and hard with his conscience but although it went against every honourable bone in his body Jonathan knew there was no other way. He had to wrong-foot Mabel because if she exposed him to the school guardians, as she threatened to, then any hope of him and Kate having a life together would be lost for ever. Buttoning down his scruples, Jonathan strolled towards her.

She spotted him and her expression became frosty. The old woman went on her way and Jonathan walked over.

'Good morning, Miss Puttock,' he said, smiling warmly at her.

Her eyes darted over him. 'Captain Quinn.'

'Lovely day, isn't it?' he said, looking towards the sky.

'Fair.'

'I see your mother didn't accompany you to church this morning. I trust she is well,' Jonathan asked, maintaining his friendly tone.

'She has a summer chill and thought it best to stay at home,' Miss Mabel replied. 'Now, if you'd excuse me, Captain Quinn. I am needed at home.'

She tried to walk past but Jonathan stepped in her path.

'Miss Puttock. May I speak to you for a moment?' he asked.

Mabel tugged her glove on further. 'I don't think—'

'Please?' He damped down his integrity and forced a look of mute desire onto his face.

She hesitated. 'Very well. Just for a few minutes; no longer.'

'Miss Puttock,' he said. 'I am ashamed to admit that for these past months I have not been myself and I fear my thoughtless manner has cost me your good opinion.'

Mabel looked him over and her chilly expression melted a little. Jonathan continued. 'I will not try to excuse my behaviour but perhaps you will not judge me too harshly if I explain that Miss Davenport's rejection hit me harder than I at first imagined and has clouded my thinking.'

'I can understand that,' she said, with a slight tremor in her voice.

'Having one's affection rebuffed is hurtful and apt to twist one's view of things.'

Jonathan let out a long breath. 'Indeed, which is why, before school resumes, I'm travelling to Scotland for a month.'

She looked dismayed. 'A month!'

Jonathan nodded. 'I intend to tour the Highlands and then visit my aunt in Edinburgh. I feel walking the hills will set my mind aright and bring me back renewed.' He took a step closer to her. 'Miss Puttock, after my oafish behaviour I have no right to ask this of you, but when I come back could we return to our former cordiality?'

Mabel's lips remained tight for a moment then they spread wide. 'I should say no and tell you that you have lost my esteem for ever but . . .' She sighed, and held out her hand.

'You are a woman of great compassion,' Jonathan said, reluctantly taking it.

Mabel looked coyly at him. 'Perhaps now we are friends you would like to take tea with Mama and me on Thursday as we used to.'

Remembering that his and Kate's happiness hung in the balance, Jonathan forced a smile. 'Will three o'clock be all right?'

Aggie studied Freddie as he stared into the bottom of his brandy glass and hate rose to the boil. If Inchy had done what he ought to, Freddie's bogtrotter wife – God rot her – should be mouldering in her grave, not serving fucking Paddy stew. But perhaps it wasn't all bad. After all, if the truth were told, she'd been a tad disappointed that Lilly had died in the fire – Aggie had been looking forward to enjoying Lilly's broken-hearted grief.

Aggie had found early on that if she wanted the most out of her revenge, it paid to bide her time. And she'd never been disappointed. It would have been easy enough just to slash the bitch Rosie's face, but how much more satisfying to smell the flesh burning off and leave puckered, disfigured skin. And even after Old Madame Tootle had slung her out, her only real regret was that she wouldn't be there to see the old baggage squirm in agony when the acid she'd laced the old crone's gin with ate through her gut.

Freddie drained the last of the brandy into his glass.

'Mary,' he bellowed, waving the empty bottle at the barmaid.

That would be his second tonight and it wasn't yet ten o'clock, but it suited her plans because he'd be in no position to interfere when the gang gathered an hour later and she allocated the night's work.

The few members of the crew who didn't have sawdust for brains realised that it was she and not Freddie who set up the jobs with the greatest haul. They continued to string Freddie along, calling him 'boss', but they now looked to her for leadership.

'Are you going to take a look at that bed Tubby Barrel is offering you or not?' Aggie asked.

He turned his bleary eyes on her. 'I said I'd go tomorrow.'

'You said that yesterday.'

'Stop yakking, woman.' He shoved the table away. 'Ain't it good enough for you that you've got half the fucking furniture in London crammed upstairs?' he shouted, jabbing his finger at the ceiling and swaying precariously. 'Why do you want another bed?'

Aggie grabbed his arm and put on her sugary smile. 'This one's got cherubs and stuff carved on it, nicked from some duke's house up west.' She slid her free hand over his crotch. 'Just think, Freddie, when we're having a bit of how's-your-father, I could be on me back with me arse in the exact same spot as a duchess. And we could move into the front room.'

Freddie's face clouded. 'You know I can't do that.'

'For gawd's sake, Freddie, they've been dead for months,' she cried.

Freddie shook his head. 'It don't seem respectful, somehow, sleeping in a room where poor little Albert died. When I think about that little lad ...'

Here we go. Aggie signalled for another bottle. *Joe's a chip off the old block.*

'Did I tell you my Joe's a right chip off the old block?' Freddie said, refilling his glass.

'I remember you saying.'

When I look at him, it's like looking in a mirror, Aggie chanted in her head.

'When I look at my little lad, it's like looking in a mirror,' Freddie continued.

'I think you mentioned it yesterday.'

And the day before and the one before that, too, thought Aggie, clenching her jaw to stifle a yawn.

The bar door swung open and Ginger loped in.

'Mr Ellis! Mr Ellis!' he shouted as he pushed through the drinkers towards them.

Freddie looked up.

'What is it?' Aggie asked.

'It's Inchy Pete. He's been took.'

Freddie looked confused. 'Took?'

Ginger nodded. 'He was caught robbing a baker in the high street.'

'Bloody nabbers!' Freddie shouted. 'Nick a lad cos he fancied a mouthful of bun.'

'It were the weekly takings he was caught with, Mr Ellis,' Ginger replied. 'What are we going to do? We'll never get into that big house in Hackney without him.'

Aggie slipped her arm in to Freddie's. 'Don't you fret, Mr E's already got a lad. Ain't you, Freddie?'

Freddie looked puzzled. 'Have I?'

'Don't lark around.' She nudged him playfully in the ribs. 'You've got your little lad Joe, of course.'

Jonathan strolled into the officers' lounge in the newly built Victoria Barracks. With its enormous paintings of long-dead officers and regimental silverware behind glass cases, it could have been any one of the dozens of army salons he'd been in. Clustered around low tables were leather button-backed chairs cradling an old field marshal or general, snoozing within their sheltered wings.

'Can I help you, sir?' asked a young footman.

'I'm here to see Colonel Quinn,' Jonathan replied, looking through the haze of cigar smoke.

'It he expecting you?'

'Not as such.'

The young man's Adam's apple bobbed up and down. 'Well, I'll have to enquire if he is at liberty to—'

Jonathan handed his hat and cane to him. 'I'm his son, Captain Quinn.'

'Very good, sir.' The servant saluted and stepped aside.

Jonathan marched down the long room and spotted his father reading a copy of *The Times*. The colonel looked surprised but quickly recovered. He put aside his paper and looked him over.

'You're a long way from your scraggy-arse school, aren't you?'

'And good day to you, too,' Jonathan replied. 'I have come to tell you something.'

His father slapped his thigh. 'I knew you'd come to your senses and take up your commission again. I was putting out enquires – discreetly, mind you – just in case—'

'I am *not* taking up my commission,' Jonathan cut in. 'It's something much more important.'

His father picked up the paper and shook it out. 'There's nothing more important than family honour.'

Jonathan stared down at him. He had lost count of the number of times he'd vowed never to see his pig-headed father again. But when he'd visited his sister Barbara yesterday to tell her his plans, she reminded him that no matter what, his father *was* his father and he had a duty to him. It was for that reason, after booking the tickets for Australia in Lower Thames Street that morning, he'd crossed the river and walked the two miles to Waterloo station to catch the ten forty-five to Windsor.

His father sighed. 'I suppose as you're here you had better get whatever it is off your chest.' He signalled to the waiter. 'Two whiskies.'

Jonathan settled in the chair opposite as the drinks arrived.

'The Queen's health,' the colonel said, raising his glass.

'The Queen,' Jonathan echoed. They both took a mouthful of spirit. 'Barbara sends her regards.'

His father raised a bushy eyebrow. 'It must be important if you've been to see your sister.'

'It is.' Jonathan took another mouthful and told his father about Kate. 'We sail in two weeks.'

His father sat motionless for a second or two as his face grew florid. 'Damn you. It wasn't enough to make me a laughing stock in Horse Guard's. You're now going to drag our name through the mud by setting up home with a married Irish woman who runs a chop house!'

Jonathan threw back the last of his whisky and stood up. 'I knew it was a mistake to come.'

'Indeed, why did you?'

Jonathan bent forward until his face was inches from his father's. 'Because when that ship casts off there is a very real chance we will never meet again in this life. Stupidly, I had the odd idea I should see you before I leave. I can see now I was mistaken.'

He straightened up and started walking away.

'I read the account of your stand on the hill at Alma in the despatches,' his father called after him.

Jonathan turned.

His father studied his face. 'If you'd listened to me and ripped up that damned letter you'd have been Major Quinn by now. Still, at least in Australia no one will know you're my son.' He jammed his monocle back in place, picked up the newspaper again and shook it out.

Jonathan clenched his fists and stared down at his father for a moment then turned again and marched out.

Chapter Twenty-Seven

Lifting her skirts to avoid a particularly pungent swirl of dog dirt, Mabel stepped off the pavement and crossed the Highway. In her tartan crinoline and maroon velvet jacket she was probably a little grand for strolling around the docks, but no matter. Ducking to avoid coils of rope hanging from an awning, she turned into Cartwright Street. It wasn't the most direct way home from the church and she preferred it.

She spotted the schoolhouse at the far end and longing welled up in her as she imagined herself welcoming Jonathan home after school each day. She adjusted the bow at the side of her bonnet and walked on.

Lessons had finished half an hour ago so the boys' gate was open. Nonchalantly, but with her heart beating furiously in her chest, Mabel glanced into the playground. Jonathan wasn't there. She bit her lip. Was he still in his office or had he already returned to the schoolhouse?

She noticed a handful of girls still hanging around their playground entrance. Thankfully, that impertinent Ella Ellis wasn't among them.

Adjusting the basket on her arm, Mabel strolled over. Mindful that Jonathan could come upon her at any moment, she smiled kindly at them.

'Good afternoon, children,' she said, making sure they didn't come too close to her with their grubby hands.

'Good afternoon, miss,' they muttered, standing up straight and looking nervously at her.

'And what have you been doing today?' she asked.

'Miss Wainwright asked us to . . .' One of the bigger girls began.

There was a movement in one of the school windows and Mabel's stomach fluttered. She tried to make out who it was but couldn't. She noticed the girl had stopped speaking.

'That's nice,' she said, automatically.

The children looked puzzled.

''Scuse me, miss. Dolly asked if you've been on a steam boat?' one of the taller girls said.

'What? A ship? Yes I—'

The schoolhouse door started opening.

'Run along home now,' Mabel said, practically knocking them aside with her skirts. She hurried towards the schoolhouse as fast as she decently could but slowed to her normal pace as she reached the end of the playground wall. She hoped the exertion had left her with a pleasing blush rather than red in the face. The schoolhouse front door opened a little further.

Mabel slowly strolled past until she heard footsteps coming down the steps behind her and then with a look of complete surprise on her face, she turned.

'Oh, Captain Quinn, I didn't ...'

Her face fell as instead of Jonathan's tall figure gracing the top step her eyes rested on the scruffy old caretaker Delaney who had just dragged a hefty trunk out of the front door. He took his cap off and wiped his forehead.

'Af'renoon, miss,' he said, as he spotted her.

'And to you, Delaney,' Mabel replied. 'I thought you were Captain Quinn.'

'Naw, you'll not see of 'imself today. He's gone off somewhere.' He spat on his hands, heaved the trunk on his back and lumbered down the steps.

'Is that for Captain Quinn's holiday?' Mabel asked, as the caretaker set the well-travelled piece of luggage upright on the pavement.

'That it is, miss. Although the Lord only knows what he's got in there.'

'A gentleman has to pack for all eventualities,' Mabel replied.

'If you say so, miss.'

'I suppose you're taking it to King's Cross to store it in the left luggage.'

Mr Delaney shook his head. 'He ain't going by train. He's catching a paddle steamer to Edinburgh from Brunswick Docks, which is where I'm taking this.' He thumped the trunk.

Mabel's jaw dropped. 'But he told me he was catching the train. Why would he do that when he was going by boat?'

'That I can't say. All I know is I've been left instructions to take 'is chest to the British and Colonial Shipping Company. Now if you'd excuse me, I had better get on before her indoors gets on at me.' Mr Delaney heaved the trunk off the floor and onto his shoulders.

The luggage label tied to the handle fluttered in the breeze. Mabel sprang forward.

'Let me help you get your balance,' she said, steadying the case with one hand while with the other she turned the label and read it.

'God bless you, miss,' Mr Delaney said as he shrugged the weight into a comfortable position on his shoulder. Mabel let go of the ticket.

He touched his forehead. 'Good day.'

Mabel stared after the school caretaker as he staggered off. An image of Jonathan sitting on the sofa next to her as he told her about his trip to Scotland floated into her mind.

No, she wasn't mistaken. He *had* said he was taking the train.

A mixture of pain and anger twisted together in Mabel's chest. Slowly her hands clenched into two tight fists and then, with a fearsome expression on her face, she turned and marched home.

Having spent a sleepless night fretting over the matter, Mabel still walked past the front door of the British and Colonial Shipping Company three times before she finally plucked up the courage to push it open and walk in.

The booking office was a sectioned-off corner of the warehouse and there was already a handful of customers talking to the clerk. Mabel ambled over to the far wall and studied the notices plastered on the wall. She scanned the list of ships, their cargo and destination but couldn't find the *Charlotte Anne* name among them. She let out a long breath, feeling very foolish indeed. If dear Jonathan said he was catching the train then he was; the luggage label was probably from a previous trip and had been left on by mistake. And if that daft old fool Delaney had had to make a double trip then it served him right for getting it all about-face.

Mabel turned to leave

'Can I help you, miss?' the fresh-faced clerk asked as the last of the scruffy individuals he'd been attending to left the office.

'No, it's quite all right, you've not got the ship I'm interested in listed.'

'And which one would that be?'

'The *Charlotte Anne*,' Mabel replied.

The clerk's face lifted into a knowing smile. 'That's because the *Charlotte Anne* doesn't set sail for Australia until the twenty-seventh.'

Australia!

'We never post the full itinerary and notice until a week before,' the clerk continued. 'Is there a reason for your enquiry?'

'Yes, my husband, Captain Quinn, has booked passage on the *Charlotte Anne* and is concerned that our servant didn't deliver his trunk as instructed. As I'm catching the ten-thirty ferry to Westminster I said I would call in to make sure it had arrived,' she replied, astonished at her inventiveness.

The clerk turned and peered over his spectacles at the ledgers on the shelf behind him then pulled down a leather-bound volume and opened it on the counter.

He ran his finger down the column of names. 'I can see no Captain Quinn on the passenger list.'

Mabel's heart gave a little happy tremble as hysterical laughter rose up in her chest.

'But there's a Mr and Mrs Quinn. Could that be your booking?'

Something akin to iced water washed over Mabel. 'Yes,' she croaked. 'He doesn't always use his army title.'

The clerk beamed at her. 'Well then I can assure you that your husband's luggage has arrived and is safe and sound.' He glanced down at the entry again. 'And I see that you will be bringing the remainder on the day of departure.'

'Indeed.' Mabel forced a brittle smile. 'Thank you, you've been most helpful.'

With the sound of her blood pounding in her ears, Mabel turned and headed towards the door.

'Oh, Mrs Quinn?' She looked around. 'Will your children have any luggage of their own?'

Mabel shook her head and hurried out of the door. She stumbled blindly through the throng of people queuing for the river ferries. On reaching the dock wall Mabel collapsed on it and stared blindly out at the grey river.

So when he stood there and told her that he was going away to 'set his mind aright and bring him back renewed', he had already set in motion his plans to sneak away to the other side of the world with Kate Ellis.

Tears of anguish sprang into Mabel's eyes but she blinked them away and concentrated on her rage. She'd warned him but it seemed he was willing to throw away everything, even her, for Kate Ellis's base-born charms.

Mabel's hands clenched until her nails bit into the palms. A tear escaped but she rubbed it away before it reached her cheek.

She would stop them by telling her father. But tell him what? That she had read Jonathan's luggage label when she had no right to and then lied that she was his wife? No. She could write another letter to the guardians. But saying what? That Jonathan was running off with

Kate Ellis? They would probably just screw it up and throw it in the bin. And even if they didn't, by the time they had the evidence to expose Jonathan he and Kate would be halfway around the world and then it would be too late.

A sly smile crept across her face. She knew someone who would make certain they never got on board the ship.

Mabel could hardly hear the carts and wagons rolling past the Aldgate Pump for the blood pounding in her ears. Something brushed her skirts and she jumped. It was only a flea-bitten dog dashing along but it was enough to set fear coursing through her again.

As it was midday the street was bustling with people so she should be safe enough, but although she was dressed in her old gown and jacket, she could feel the dozens of pairs of eyes watching from the dank alleyways running between the shops, waiting for the chance to steal the clothes from her back.

If her parents ever found out she'd ventured along Whitechapel High Street alone there would be hell to pay. Her father would stop her allowance for a year and lock her in her bedroom for a month, and poor Mama would need the smelling salts, but it didn't matter.

In fact, since the awful moment in the ticket office the day before, nothing mattered except destroying Jonathan's dreams of happiness the way he'd destroyed hers.

There was a low laugh from a man propped up in an empty doorway drinking gin from a broken-necked bottle.

'Lost your way, missis?' he said, eyeing her up and down.

Mabel stepped away from him, taking a deep breath to control her terror. Ignoring the curious glances of the rogued-cheeked women loitering outside the public house, Mabel set her sights on the square tower of St Botolph's church and hurried on.

She stopped on the corner of Jewry Street and looked across at the barefooted lad leaning on an old birch broom on the other side the road.

She'd seen him a couple of times as she and Mama trotted by in a hansom cab on their way to their dressmakers. Although he was dressed in filthy rags like the rest of the urchins who hung around outside the churches, he had a lively look about him so he might just be her salvation. He spotted her and dashed into the road.

'My lady!' he shouted as he swerved out of the path of a meat wagon, coming to a halt in front of her. 'Clear for you?'

Mabel nodded.

Walking backwards, the boy swept aside the pungent slurry of waste so she could cross. Mabel followed him to the other side and handed him a threepenny piece.

The boy looked astonished.

'Cor, fank you, miss,' he said, staring at the little silver coin in his hand.

'Well, you did a good job,' she said, brightly.

The boy slipped the money in his pocket and touched his forehead. 'Any time, miss.'

Mabel smiled sweetly. 'What's your name, child?' she asked in her best Sunday school voice.

'Toby.'

'Well, Toby, would you like to earn this?' She fished a shilling from her purse.

Toby's nodded. 'Sure fing I would'

'Do you know a man called Freddie Ellis?'

A guarded expression stole over the boy's face. 'Might do.'

Mabel pulled out a note from her jacket pocket and offered it to him. 'I want you to give him this.'

'What's it about?' Toby asked, regarding the letter warily.

'Something that he should know,' Mabel replied. 'You give it to him and I'll give this to you.' She held up the shilling again and twisted it so the sunlight glinted on it.

Toby glanced around. 'How do I know you ain't a stooge for the nabbers and this ain't a trap to catch Mr Ellis?'

'Have you heard about Jesus?'

Toby looked affronted. 'Course I 'ave.'

'Well, then.' Mabel crossed herself. 'I swear by Jesus that I have nothing to do with the police.'

Toby still hesitated.

Mabel closed her hand around the shilling. 'Of course, if you can't do it I'll find a boy who can.'

He snatched the letter and shoved it in his shirt then held out his hand.

Mabel handed him the coin. 'Make sure you take it to him straight away.'

'And what if he asks who gave it to me?' he asked, pocketing the money.

'Tell him "a friend".'

Toby regarded her thoughtfully for a moment then shouldered his broom. 'Right you are, miss. Consider it done.'

'I hope that's true because if you take my shilling and don't give him my note' – she pointed at the sky – 'St Peter will write "thief" in black letters next to your name and then give you to the devil on Judgement Day.'

Fear flashed across Toby's face and he swallowed. 'I'll give it to him, miss. Promise.' He turned and dashed off.

As she watched the boy disappear into the crowd a sly smile crept across Mabel's face. She'd like to see the look on Freddie Ellis's face when he read about his wife's little secret, but more particularly she would relish the look on Jonathan's when he realised all his hopes were destroyed.

Freddie sat on old Ollie Mac's armchair in the corner savouring a fat cigar he'd lifted along with three gross like it from a warehouse the night before. There was a low hum of conversation as the Boy settled into the after-lunch lull. Other than a couple of the gang sitting on the other side of the room and a handful of people at the counter, the bar was empty. Aggie had gone for a stroll down Petticoat Lane to 'catch a bit of fresh air' and Freddie wondered, in passing, how much it would cost him.

He picked up his glass and swallowed a mouthful of brandy. Settling his shoulders into the leather padding he leant back and closed his eyes. The hum of voices faded as he started to doze off. The door swung open and Freddie jumped awake.

Aggie walked in and glanced around. The two trollops chatting to the landlord finished their drinks and hurried out. Her gaze rested on Freddie and her mouth pulled into a tight line.

Freddie sat up. 'Hello, ducks. Bought something nice for yourself, have you?'

Aggie collected a glass from the bar and strolled over. 'I thought you were going to take those barrels of salt pork over to Tommy the Top,' she said, pouring herself a drink.

Freddie drew on his cigar then puffed smoke circles towards the ceiling. 'I'll do it tomorrow.'

Aggie smiled. 'I tell you what,' she said, conversationally. 'Why don't you leave them until Saturday? After all, they've only been sitting there for two weeks, and so in a day or two they'll walk themselves to Club Row.'

'I'll get Harry to take 'em over in the morning.'

'And have you taken a shufti at Lipton's warehouse yet?' Aggie continued. 'Cos I'm thinking if you don't do it before they dole the wages out on Friday the safe will be empty.'

'Give your jaw a rest, Aggie.' Freddie stretched and linked his hands behind his head. 'And remember, I'm the one who does the brain work around here.'

Aggie shot him a withering look and threw herself on the chair beside him. She studied him for a moment and then spoke again. 'So when are you going to fetch your boy then?'

He rolled his eyes. 'Not that again.'

'When?'

'Soon. Next week.' Freddie buried his nose in his glass.

'You said that last week.' She gave him a mocking look. 'If I didn't know better I'd say for all your talk about him being a "chip off the old block" you know 'e's too soft to take Inchy's place.'

Freddie glared at her. 'My boy's as sharp as they come.'

'Well, then.' Aggie swirled the drink in her glass. 'Perhaps you're too afraid of *her* family to fetch your own son.'

Freddie slammed the bottle on the table. 'For fuck's sake, Aggie, give it a rest.'

The bar door opened again and a boy carrying an old broom over his shoulder rushed in.

'Mr Ellis,' he shouted, dashing across the bar towards him.

Aggie's hand shot out and caught the boy by one skinny arm as he reached them. 'What you after Mr Ellis for?'

The boy snatched his arm from her grasp and rubbed it. 'Some toff bit of skirt told me to give him this.' He handed Freddie a crumpled piece of paper.

Freddie opened it and he scowled.

He could scratch out his name, if pushed, and recognise tobacco, brandy and tea written on a crate but that was about his limit. His lips moved silently as he tried to sound out the letters in his head.

'What does it say?' Aggie asked, impatiently.

'If you stop yapping for a minute I'll tell you,' Freddie replied, trying to decipher the first word.

'Give it here,' Aggie said, snatching it from him.

She scanned the document and chuckled. 'It seems that your Joe won't be taking Inchy Pete's place after all.'

'Wot you talking about?'

Aggie waved the paper at him. 'It seems your wife's been making

239

jiggy-jiggy as well as pies down at 'er shop. Her and the one-eyed schoolmaster who gave you a pasting are planning to run away to Australia and taking your "little lad" with them.'

Freddie snatched the note back and stared down at it. But instead of the squarely printed words he saw Joe's tousled hair, pale blue eyes and crooked smile that was so like his own. The pulse in his temple started to throb. Fury and an unfamiliar painful emotion caught in Freddie's chest as Aggie's words sank in. He stood up.

'You're not going to let her take your Joe, are you?' Aggie asked, from what seemed like a long way away.

Freddie's eyes narrowed as he screwed the note in his fist. 'She and that poxy schoolteacher can go to hell for all I care, and good riddance to them, but take my Joe? Not fucking likely.'

Joe repositioned his satchel on his back and stepped through the school gate. Ella was already outside talking to her friends and when she saw him she came over.

'Are you ready?' She held out her hand.

'I'm not a baby,' he said, looking defiantly up at her from under the peak of his cap.

Ella shrugged and started off and Joe fell into step beside her.

'It's oxtail stew tonight,' Joe said as they turned the corner.

'Don't you think of anything else but your belly?'

'Not really.'

Ella rolled her eyes in the same way that Ma did. She stopped in front of the haberdasher's and studied the frilly girly things in the window. Joe shoved his hands in his pockets and nudged a stone back and forth with his toe.

'Don't do that, you'll scuff your boots,' Ella told him, walking on.

Why couldn't I have an older brother like Mickey instead of a bossy-boots sister? Joe thought, looking at Ella's pigtails swinging back and forth.

Dodging under the display of buckets hanging from the iron-monger's awning Joe trotted after her. As they reached Bird Alley, Joe stopped.

'Let's cut through,' he said, glancing down the walkway between the high walls of London Docks and Rolfe's warehouse.

'Ma doesn't like us going that way,' she said, trying to grab him.

Joe poked his tongue out at her and danced backwards. '*Ma doesn't like us going that way*,' he repeated in a falsetto voice as he started down the alley.

'Joe! You come back here,' she shouted.

'Ella's scared, Ella's scared,' he chanted.

Ella hesitated for a moment then caught up with him.

'Cor, it stinks,' she said.

Joe was already breathing through his mouth to avoid drawing in the acrid smell of urine. 'I can't smell anything,' he replied, blinking to relieve his stinging eyes.

They had just reached the halfway point when, out of the corner of his eye, Joe caught a glimpse of someone hiding in the shadows.

'Ella,' he whispered, taking her hand.

'I told you not to come this way,' she whispered back, quickening her pace.

Footsteps sounded behind them, raising the hairs on the back of Joe's neck.

'Joe!'

Letting go of his sister's hand, Joe spun around. 'Pa?'

Joe started forward but then the image of his mother lying beaten and bruised on the floor flashed into his mind. He hesitated, his heart torn between both parents.

The look of love and pride, that Joe craved above all others, crept into Freddie's eye. 'I've missed you, son,' he said, tenderly.

Something burst in Joe's chest and he launched himself at his father. 'Oh, Pa, I kept watch for you every day, Pa, hoping you'd come back.'

Freddie's eyes narrowed. 'And I've been keeping watch for you too, boy.'

Ella grabbed Joe's hand. 'Ma's expecting us for supper. Come on, Joe.' She pulled him away.

Freddie caught his other arm. 'Joe's coming with me.'

Joe wrenched his hand out of Ella's and stood next to his father.

'Where are we going?' he asked, hopefully.

'You're forever pestering me to take you to pub, so now I am.'

'But Ma's expecting us,' Ella replied.

'Your mother can go to hell!' Freddie's face contorted with fury. 'Clear off,' he yelled, swiping at Ella with the back of his hand.

She backed away. 'Come with me, Joe,' she pleaded.

He looked back and forth between the two of them then shook his head. 'I'm going with Pa.'

Ella hesitated for a second then ran off. Joe stared after her and felt oddly alone. If the truth were told he was a little afraid of his father, but if Pa was especially looking out for him ...

'Now Miss Sour Face has gone, it's just me and my boy.' Freddie shoved his hands in his pockets, turned and walked off. 'Well, let's go.'

Joe glanced behind him and an image of his mother preparing supper flashed through his mind. *Me and my boy*, he heard his father's voice say again in his head.

Joe turned. 'Pa! Pa! Wait for me,' he yelled.

He was so happy to finally be allowed into his father's world that it was only when he almost tripped over a scar-faced old woman lying in a doorway that he realised they weren't in Wapping any longer.

'Where are we, Pa?' he asked, stepping closer to his father.

'Whitechapel.'

Joe looked fearfully around. Although he dashed around the streets of Wapping without a care, he'd never crossed to the other side of Commercial Road alone. To suddenly find himself in an area full of robbers and murderers set fear churning in his stomach. He looked up at his father, who seemed to know almost every ragged man and woman they passed. Grey, hollow-eyed people huddled in doorways or squatted on the dirty pavement. To Joe, they looked older than his gran but many of the women held limp infants in their arms and had skinny, hollow-eyed children clutching at their skirts.

At last, he and Freddie reached the Blue Coat Boy, a pub he'd heard his ma and Uncle Pat whisper about in connection with his father when they thought he wasn't listening.

Joe's eyes watered and burnt from the thick tobacco smoke, which swirled around him as he walked in after his father. He drew a sharp breath when he noticed the rough men leaning on the bar and the young women with very red lips and untidy hair who were clinging on to the men. Joe pressed in behind his father as Freddie strolled between them.

'What you drinking, boss?' one pock-marked man asked.

'The usual, Tommy.'

A young woman with a sore on her top lip slipped her arm in Freddie's. 'Hello, guv,' she said, giving his father a noisy kiss.

Freddie grinned, took his drink and strolled on. Dodging a drunk and a sleek speckled dog with chewed ears, Freddie came to a halt at the far corner, where Joe tucked himself behind his father's legs.

'Did you get 'im?' a woman's voice asked.

'Course I did.' His father stepped aside.

Joe's eyes opened wide as he stared at a young woman sitting on a sofa. Her red hair was scooped up on the top of her head and held in place with a blue-feather pin, which reminded him of the picture of the peacock on the school chart. The dark green gown she wore was much too tight and wouldn't do up at the front. She leant forward until her nose was within a couple of inches of his. He could see the small red veins on her nose and cheeks and was overwhelmed by the proximity of her bosoms and the heady smell of her cologne, which barely cloaked her foul breath.

'Where's your manners, boy?' Freddie snapped.

Joe took off his cap. 'Good evening, miss,' he said, trying not to look at the nit crawling up a strand of her hair.

She slapped her thigh and laughed. 'Did you hear that?' she shouted at the men loitering around them.

They joined in laughing and Joe looked at his father. Freddie stepped forward and placed his hand on Joe's shoulder. 'Didn't I tell you he was the replica of me?'

Aggie lifted the corners of her mouth but the smile didn't reach her eyes. 'You're a bit skinny, ain't you, boy? Don't your muvver feed you?'

Joe looked at his toes.

'Wot, cat got your tongue?' she continued.

Joe raised his head. 'My mother's the best cook in the world, isn't she, Pa?'

A couple of men behind his father looked away and smiled while Aggie's neck went red.

Joe's stomach rumbled and his father laughed and reached into his pocket. 'Oi, Ginny,' he called to a girl sporting a black eye, standing against the bar. 'Go and fetch me a pie-and-potatoes supper.' She took the money and ambled off. 'And you,' he jabbed his finger at Aggie, 'watch yourself.'

She smiled lovingly up at Freddie. 'I was only wondering if he's too little,' she said, in girly voice.

'Course 'e's not.' Freddie looked down at Joe. 'You're not too little to help your old man out, are you?'

Joe beamed up at his father. 'No, Pa.'

Freddie squeezed Joe's shoulder. 'Listen here, you lot. This is my boy and I don't want any of you to forget it.'

The men around them called 'No, boss' and 'Right, Mr Ellis' and Joe thought his chest was going to burst with pride.

Aggie caught Joe's cheek between her black-nailed finger and thumb. 'He's your Joe and I'll look after him as if he were my own.'

Chapter Twenty-Eight

Kate tied the last bundle of old clothes and put it alongside the others. It wouldn't fetch more than ten shillings but she could only take what she and the children could carry, which wasn't much for a four-month voyage. Jonathan had assured her they'd be able to buy cotton, linen and other goods in the African ports along the way, so Kate was taking her sewing box, too.

Jonathan had arranged everything so well. To allay suspicion, he'd told the board of guardians that he was going to Scotland for a holiday two days before the *Charlotte Anne* sailed from East India Dock. In reality he was booking into the Brunswick Hotel alongside the berth, where he would be waiting for her and the children. He'd wanted to collect them from the shop in the early hours but Kate thought it better to avoid any scene with the children until they were safely aboard. In two weeks they would be off to a new life, and although she was excited, she knew it would be a great shock for Ella and Joe. She intended to present the journey as a big adventure and hoped that once they saw how happy she and Jonathan were they'd be happy too, although she was prepared for some tears.

Pulling open the ill-fitting drawer she slipped her hand under the lace-trimmed nightgown and lifted it out. She ran her fingers over the narrow ribbon gathering the neckline together and then held it up so the light from the window behind filtered through the finely woven lawn cotton. She closed her eyes and hugged it to her.

Fourteen days! How was she going to keep her excitement in check? But she *had* to hold back, just for a short while longer until they were safely beyond Freddie's reach. Then she could slip on Jonathan's ring and become Mrs Quinn in fact, if not in law. Although it went against every honest grain in her body, Kate planned to tell the children that she'd been able to divorce Freddie and marry Jonathan in secret.

The back door slammed shut downstairs. Kate refolded the nightgown and returned it to the drawer.

'I'm up here,' she called.

Ella came banging up the stairs and swung around the doorpost into the room. 'Ma! Ma! Pa stopped us on the way home and Joe's gone with him to the pub.'

Kate's heart lurched. 'When was this?'

'About half an hour ago. I tried to get Joe to come with me but he pulled him away.' Her chin started to wobble. 'I'm sorry, Ma.'

Kate put her arms around her daughter and kissed her forehead. 'It's not your fault.' She gathered up her skirts and went downstairs with Ella following. She snatched her coat off the hook and went through to the shop where Sally was serving the first teatime customers.

'Sally, would you keep an eye on Ella for me? I have to go somewhere.'

'Sure, Mrs E. She can help me clear the tables.'

Kate shrugged on her coat then kissed Ella on the forehead. 'I won't be long, sweetheart, and don't worry. If I have to tear down every pub in the area I'll find Joe and bring him home.'

With a tea towel wrapped around her hand, Mrs Delaney picked up the flat iron from the range and spat on the plate. Satisfied with the result, she plopped it on the tail of the shirt.

'How many's that?' her husband asked, knocking his pipe out on the grate.

'Eight.'

'How many shirts does a man need for two weeks?'

'Captain Quinn ain't like you, changing on Sunday and then making do with the same all week,' she replied, turning a sleeve to start on the cuff. 'The headmaster's a gentleman.'

'Gentleman or no, eight shirts still seems six too many to my way of thinking,' he replied, refilling his pipe. 'Not to mention that chest packed with all manner of things he had me lug down to Brunswick Dock. I mean, ain't they got books up north?' He stood up and took a taper from the mantelshelf and held it to the flames. 'If I didn't know better, I'd have thought 'e was going to Timbuktu, not Scotchland.'

Bridget Delaney looked irritated. 'I don't see how it matters to you what Captain Quinn puts in his trunk.'

'It does if I have to carry it down the stairs.' He drew on the pipe.

Bridget lifted the iron from the cloth and stopped. 'Shouldn't you be seeing to the playground instead of cluttering up my kitchen?'

'In a bit,' he said. 'Himself won't be back for hours yet. But it seems if I want to give me ears a rest from your clacking, I'd better get myself into the yard.' He put on his cap and left.

Mrs Delaney put the iron back in the hotplate then folded the shirt and put it with the others. She had offered to pack Captain Quinn's clothes for him but he'd smiled and said that after ten years in the army, he was more than able to do that for himself, which was a pity because she'd like to have peeked inside that chest. She shouldn't, of course, but after she spotted a pair of lacy women's gloves poking out from a parcel he'd brought home the week before, she was desperate to know if there were any other such items tucked away. Perhaps Captain Quinn wasn't picking up one ticket to Scotland but two. She smiled at the thought.

The bell on a coil above her head tinkled. She took off her apron, trundled out of the kitchen and into the hall. She shuffled to the front door and opened it to find Kate Ellis on the top step.

She and Fergus had lived across the road from Kate's parents, Paddy and Sarah Nolan and their half a dozen nippers in Cinnamon Street, and had known Kate since she was a toddler.

'Good afternoon to you, Mrs Delaney,' said Kate, trying to look around her. 'I need to see Captain Quinn. Is he at home?'

Bridget looked her up and down. 'Captain Quinn isn't the butcher or baker. He's not here for people to just pop by when they feel like it. If you want to see the headmaster, you should make an appointment in the proper way.'

Kate twisted her fingers together. 'Please, is he at home?'

'Not at present.'

Kate covered her eyes with her hand. 'Of course. It's Thursday. He's gone to see—' She stopped. 'When are you expecting him back?'

'I don't see it's any business of yours, Kate Ellis,' she replied, drawing herself up. 'I don't know . . . You come around here demanding to see—'

'For the love of Mary, I'm only asking you when he's back, Bridget, not to give me the keys to the house.'

She crossed her arms. 'Not until late. And it's Mrs Delaney to you.'

Kate's shoulders sagged. 'Thank you. Will you tell him I called?'

'What do you want him for?'

'It's personal.' Kate linked her fingers together to secure her gloves. 'And if you could tell Captain Quinn as soon as he returns, I'd be obliged. Good day.'

She turned and trudged down the stairs.

Jumped up madam, thought Bridget, as she watched Kate dash back along the street. She slammed the door. *Coming up to the front door as bold as you like, full of airs and graces. Demanding to know*

the inside and out of the headmaster's business as if she was someone.
She straightened the picture on the wall. *And if she thinks I'll be
worrying Captain Quinn as soon as the poor man walks in the door,
then she's got another think coming.*

Suddenly the image of Kate's threadbare lace gloves sprang into
her mind. She stared open-mouthed at her reflection for a moment
then chuckled and ambled back along the hall towards the kitchen
door. *Silly old fool y'are, Bridget Delaney. Silly old fool.*

The breath tore out of Kate's chest as she dashed along Commercial
Road. Blindly, she crashed into people and narrowly missed being
mowed down by a milk cart, but with fears for Joe's safety screaming
in her mind she barely noticed.

Finally, with her legs feeling like lead and her heart fit to burst
from her chest, Kate turned into Belgrave Road. Holding her side in
an effort to ease the razor-like pain cutting through her and with her
skirts flying, she sprinted the last few yards to her brother's house.

Leaning on the door to stop herself falling, Kate grasped the
knocker and hammered relentlessly.

After what seemed like an eternity Patrick opened the door. 'What
the—'

'Freddie's taken Joe,' she gasped, stumbling into the hallway and
collapsing into his arms.

'What? When?'

'I ... I ...' Blackness swirled around Kate's head and her knees
gave way.

Patrick's arm went around her waist as he half-walked half-carried
her to the sofa. 'Josie!'

Josie ran down the stairs followed by Annie. 'Get her a brandy,
Pat,' she said, sitting next to Kate and rubbing her hands. 'There,
there, my pet, you're safe with us now. Wha—'

'Freddie's taken Joe,' Patrick said before Kate could.

Horror flashed across Josie's face. She put her arm around Kate's
shoulders. 'Don't worry, we'll find him.'

'Too damn right we will,' Patrick said. 'And when we do, that
bastard will wish he'd never been born.' He turned to his daughter.
'Annie, run to Mattie's and fetch Nathaniel and any men he can
spare. Tell them to meet us at the Town.'

Annie shot out of the room and Patrick followed her into the hall.
'Rob!'

There was a clatter of feet and Patrick's second son swung around the doorpost. 'Go down to the pier and tell Mickey that Freddie's got our Joe. Get him to round up some men for a search and let him know we're assembling at the Town.'

Pat came back into the room and poured Kate a large glass of brandy.

'Get that down you,' he said.

Kate took it but she trembled so much that Josie had to close her hand over hers to guide the glass to Kate's lips.

Kate's mother walked into the room. 'For the love of mercy. You'd think it was the second coming with all the galloping up and down the stairs.' She saw Kate and hurried over as fast as her knees and walking stick allowed.

'Dear God. What's happened?' she said, looking anxiously at Kate's face.

Tears stung the corners of Kate's eyes and her chin wobbled. 'Freddie's gone off with Joe, Ma.'

An image of Joe waving goodbye as he walked off to school that morning flashed into her mind. Kate covered her face with her hands and sobbed.

Her mother sat beside her and cradled her in her arms. 'We'll get him back, never you fear,' she said, stroking Kate's hair. 'Now quieten yourself, child, and tell us what happened.'

Kate pulled herself together and looked up. She told them about the children's meeting with their father, and Ella running straight back to the shop.

'And you came here,' Patrick concluded.

Kate shook her head and felt the effects of the brandy. 'I . . . I went to the school first. Just to find Captain Quinn but he's gone to see his father about . . .' She glanced at her family's fearful faces and took another large mouthful of drink.

Patrick's brow furrowed. 'Why did you go there first? What could he do?'

The brandy was making her woozy but Kate forced her gaze to remain steady. 'I . . . I . . . don't know. I just thought he . . .'

'She was in shock, weren't you, my sweet.' Sarah patted her hands. 'She probably thought Joe might have changed his mind and gone back to the school, didn't you, Kate?' Her mother's bright eyes glared at her.

'Yes, yes,' Kate replied.

'But surely,' persisted Patrick, 'Joe would have—'

'Quit badgering your sister, Pat,' Sarah said, looking fiercely at him. 'And shouldn't you get yourself to the Town?'

He raked his fingers through his hair. 'I should.' He went over to Kate and kissed her on her forehead. 'Put your mind at ease, sis. We'll get Joe back.'

He marched out of the room, snatched his jacket from the coat stand, and slammed the door on his way out.

Kate stood up. 'I ought to get back just in case Joe comes home.'

Josie rose to her feet also. 'Perhaps you should. Mattie will be here soon.'

'I can't help wondering why he decided now to ...' She thought of Jonathan booking passage for them only the week before.

'Don't you fret, me girl,' Sarah said, patting her hand. 'You get yourself home quick sharp, case Joe comes back. Josie, do you think you could spare a shilling or two from the housekeeping so Kate can take a cab home?'

Joe trotted down tree-lined gravel avenues with his father on one side and a man called Harry on the other. Both men carried empty sacks over their shoulders.

'Are we almost at the market, Pa?'

'Market?'

'Where you work.'

The other man sniggered.

'We're not going there,' his father replied without breaking his stride.

'But I thought I was coming to work with you,' Joe said, as they reached a narrow alleyway running along the back of the big houses set back from the road.

'Rozzers,' the other man hissed.

His father grabbed Joe by the scruff of the neck and hauled him into the shadows.

'Why are—'

His father's hand clamped over his mouth. Moments later a police officer strolled into view and stopped close by; a beam of light from his lamp narrowly missed the toe of Joe's boot. It went dark again and Joe heard the rhythmic crunch of the constable's footsteps as he continued on his beat. His father removed his hand.

'Why are we hiding from the police, Pa?'

'Don't that fucking kid of yours shut up?' hissed Harry.

Freddie glared at him.

Harry shrugged. 'I'm just saying he's done nought but jabber on since we left the Boy. And with a copper creeping about, you know ...'

'All right, all right.' Freddie hunkered down in front of Joe. 'Now listen to me, boy. If you don't want me to send you home you'd better keep this shut.' He poked Joe's lips. 'Understand?'

Joe nodded.

'Good.'

The two men started off again. Joe trudged behind them with his head hung low and his stomach rumbling. He'd tried to eat the pie the scruffy girl had given him but it was mostly gristle and the potatoes were cold and gluey. He hoped Ma would save him some of the stew for when he got home and not send him to bed without supper as she threatened to last time.

They reached the back gate of a house and Freddie stopped. 'This is it.' He turned to Joe. 'Right, son. You want to be my best pal, don't you?'

'Yes, Pa,' he whispered, pleased that his father's cheeriness had returned.

'Course you do, cos you're my boy, ain't you?' Joe nodded again and his father hooked his hands under his arms and hoisted him in the air. 'Right. See that window above the back door?'

Joe peered over. 'Yes.'

His father set him back on the ground. 'I want you climb through that window, creep down the stairs as quiet as a mouse and open the front door for me.'

'Are we breaking into someone's house?' Joe asked.

His father grinned. 'Course not, son. The bloke who lives there's a mate of mine and 'e's away. He asked me to keep an eye on it but I've lost the key. If you don't think you can ...'

Joe puffed out his chest. 'I can.'

Freddie looked at Harry lounging against the wall. 'Didn't I tell you he'd do fine?'

'He ain't in there yet,' was the scornful reply.

His father lifted Joe on to the wall. He wobbled a bit as he found his balance then, with his heart thumping in his chest, he lowered himself down the other side as far as he could before falling on to the soft earth of the flowerbed. His cap fell off so he picked it up, shoved it in his pocket and then darted across the garden. It didn't take him long to clamber up the sweet-smelling shrub, climb around the door and slip through the window on to a carpeted landing. As he ran past the portraits on the wall and down the main stairs, Joe wondered fleetingly why, if the house was empty, he had to be quiet. He gripped the stout brass bolt and eased it back to open the front door.

His father and Harry almost knocked him flying as they dashed in. Joe shut the door and followed them into the grandest room he'd ever seen.

It was filled with pictures on the walls and large polished dressers and glass-fronted cabinets. There were also gold clocks, porcelain figurines and silver statues which his father and Harry were throwing into their sacks as fast as they could. Joe's arms fell limp as he watched them rifling through the drawers and realised why he'd really been told to climb into the house.

God said that stealing was wrong. He'd learnt that at Sunday school. 'Thou shall not steal.' Was he as guilty as Pa for helping him?

An image of his mother smiling at him flashed into his mind and suddenly he didn't want to be in Pa's dirty world of red-lipped women and unshaven men. He wanted to be snug and safe with Ma.

'I want to go home, Pa,' he wailed.

'Shut your fucking kid up,' Harry snarled as he tipped the cutlery from the sideboard into his sack.

Freddie crossed the room in two strides and gripped Joe's collar. 'I told you to button it!' he snarled, shaking the boy.

'Who's there?' a man's voice shouted.

For one second his father and Harry froze, then they threw their sacks over their shoulders and, tramping over discarded china, crashed towards the door. Joe shot after them but stared in wild-eyed horror as his father and Harry frantically grappled with the handle.

'Your fucking kid's let the bolt drop.'

Freddie swore and yanked at the brass handle. It didn't budge.

'Stop thief!'

Joe's head snapped around to see a large man dressed in his nightgown and carpet slippers standing at the top of the stairs. He was holding a fire poker and, on seeing the intruders, he shouted, 'Esther, call the constabulary!' at the woman who appeared on the landing behind him.

'No, Isaac, let them go!' she screamed.

Her husband ignored her and ran down the stairs, setting the tassel of his nightcap bouncing across his forehead.

'Stop, I say!'

Harry ducked away from the swing of the poker and managed to tug the bolt from its housing to release the door. He scooped up his bag and shot out into the street. Freddie tried to follow but the man lunged at him. Joe screamed and the man looked around in surprise. Freddie leapt forwards and wrenched the weapon from his hand.

Time slowed for Joe as he watched his father swing the two-foot-long rod of iron in a wide arc and smash it across the man's head. His eyes bulged and his mouth contorted as the poker crushed his skull. Blood splattered across the delicately flowered wallpaper, the plush carpet and Joe's face. His gaze locked with the man, who sank to his knees and crumpled to the floor. Nausea choked the back of Joe's throat as the dying man's eyes rolled upwards and lost their focus.

'Isaac, Isaac!' the woman shrieked. 'Murder! Murder!'

'Come on.' Joe heard his father's voice from somewhere far away.

He trembled and his knees started to buckle. Just as he thought he would pitch into the sticky pool of blood spreading across the floor, he was lifted off his feet and carried through the air. Then his feet found the ground again.

'Run, Joe!'

Joe couldn't move. A hand slapped across his face in a stinging blow. His eyes flashed open. He blinked and looked around. A police rattle sounded out a few streets away, followed by another. Lights came on and windows were thrown open.

His father grabbed the back of his jacket and dragged him along the cobbles. 'Run, you bugger!'

He released Joe and tore off down the street. Joe stumbled, tripped a couple of times then found his stride and ran after his father.

Chapter Twenty-Nine

Jonathan tapped his nib down the column of figures as he added up the school's weekly expenditure. Although he awoke each morning knowing that he was a day closer to being with Kate, their abrupt departure sat uncomfortably on his shoulders. There was nothing for it, of course, and he had resolved to put the school in good order so that Mr Rudd and Miss Wainwright could keep it ticking over until a new headmaster was appointed. To that end, he'd ordered the necessary supplies for the autumn term and drafted out the report for the guardians' October meeting and finished the last report for all forty-five children. Finally, he needed to write to Reggie Braithwaite to apologise and explain his reasons for leaving.

He knew their lives would be a struggle at first but he was sure that once he found work they'd soon find their feet. He'd given a great deal of thought to starting a school, especially as the new regional government was keen to encourage families rather than just prospectors. Kate wanted to set up a chop house but Jonathan was determined that she shouldn't have to.

He shut the account book and opened the school-attendance register to double-check his figures but was interrupted by a light knock on the door.

'Enter,' he called.

The door opened and the girls' mistress slid through the gap.

'Good morning, Headmaster,' she said, two splashes of crimson colouring her pale cheeks as she smiled at him.

'Good morning, Miss Wainwright. Is that today's roll call?' he asked, glancing at the long slate she clutched in front of her.

She nodded and offered him the board. 'Just nine missing today. Three girls and six boys but two of those are the Potter twins who have measles.'

Jonathan looked impressed, glanced down the list of pupils and then returned to a name near to the top.

'I see Master Ellis isn't in school today?'

'No, Headmaster, but Ella brought a letter explaining his absence.' Miss Wainwright handed him the note.

He took it, laid it on the blotting paper and placed his hands over it. 'Thank you, Miss Wainwright. Would you tell Mr Rudd I will be out presently to conduct the history lesson.'

She inclined her head and left.

Jonathan unfolded Kate's note and read it. *Dear God!* He jumped up and ran into the boys' classroom.

'I would be obliged, Mr Rudd, if you could please cover Hannibal's traverse of the Alps. I'm afraid I must go out unexpectedly urgently,' Jonathan said, marching past the back of the class and not waiting for a reply.

Kate shut the door to the shop, collapsed on to the chair and closed her eyes to ease her throbbing temples. Mattie had come to sit with her earlier but had to leave when Nathaniel came to fetch her at ten. He, Patrick and dozens of men from Knockfergus had been to every pub and dive from Limehouse to Whitechapel searching for Freddie but with no luck. She was now beside herself with worry.

The latch on the back door clicked and her eyes flew open. She jumped up.

It was Jonathan, who strode into the parlour with his hair blown back from his face and mud splashed on his trousers. He crossed the space between them and gathered her into his arms.

'It's all right, sweetheart,' he said, holding her tightly and kissing her hair. 'We'll find him. What happened?'

Kate told him.

'I know we are being careful but why didn't you come to—'

'I did. But I realised when you didn't come last night that Mrs Delaney hadn't told you. That's why I sent the note with Ella.'

'I'll be having a word with Mrs Delaney.'

A tear rolled down Kate's cheek.

Jonathan hooked his finger under her chin and lifted her head. 'I promise I'll find Joe and bring him home. Even if we have to delay our plans.'

She began to protest but then he kissed her.

There was a noise behind them. They turned to see Patrick standing in the doorway.

'So, Kate? What's going on here?'

Jonathan released her. 'Good morning, Mr Nolan.'

'Let's forget the niceties, shall we?'

'I'm sorry you had to find out about us like this, Nolan,' Jonathan said, stepping closer to Kate.

Patrick sent him a caustic look then turned to Kate. 'What plans?'

'We're sailing to Melbourne in two weeks.'

'Australia!'

The hurt in his voice cut deep into Kate's heart. 'I was going to tell you and Mattie a few days before but we had to keep it secret in case Freddie found out.'

Patrick looked at her starkly. 'And Ma?'

'She gave her blessing.'

Jonathan cleared his throat. 'I'm sorry, Patrick. But —'

'Sorry, are you?' Patrick spun around to face him. 'You bloody will be when I've done with you, thinking you can take our Kate away.'

He swung at Jonathan who dodged the blow.

Kate squeezed between them. 'For the love of God, Patrick!'

'Get out of my way, Kate,' he yelled back. 'While I give your schoolmaster a lesson he won't forget.'

Patrick punched out but Jonathan sidestepped and grabbed him by the lapels. He shoved him backwards and pinned him to the wall. 'Perhaps we can discuss this *after* we've found Joe —'

There was a knock on the parlour door. They looked around to find a policeman staring at them. His eyes flickered from Jonathan to Patrick and back again.

'You'll forgive me for interrupting a family moment,' he said, taking off his hat and walking into the middle of the room. 'I'm Sergeant Groves, from Arbour Square Police Station, and I would like to speak with the parents of Joe Ellis.'

Kate's legs buckled and she fell back into the chair. 'What's happened to Joe? Where is he?'

Jonathan let go of Patrick and the two men placed themselves protectively on either side of her.

'I was about to ask you the same question, Mrs Ellis,' the officer replied. 'I take it you don't know where your lad is?' Kate shook her head. The officer pulled a cap from his pocket. He held it out. 'Is this your son's?'

The floor seemed to tilt as Kate reached out for Joe's school hat. 'Yes. Where did you get it?'

The sergeant's eyes narrowed. 'Could you tell me when you last saw your son?'

Kate nodded but couldn't speak.

'Before you distress Mrs Ellis further, Sergeant,' Jonathan said, 'perhaps you'd be kind enough to tell her *why* you have her son's cap?'

'There was a burglary in Mare Street, Hackney, last night,' the sergeant replied. 'Two men gained entrance to the premises by getting a boy to climb into an upstairs window and open the front door. Unfortunately, the householder awoke and surprised the criminals. One escaped but Mr Cohen cornered the other. There was a tussle and he was killed with a blow to the head, after which the second murderer and the young boy with him escaped. The whole thing was witnessed by Mrs Cohen and this,' he indicated the cap Kate clutched in her hand, 'was found at the scene.'

Kate's looked at Joe's cap. 'You don't think . . .'

Sergeant Groves fixed her with a hard stare. 'I certainly do. The description of the man who bludgeoned the jeweller to death fits that of your husband Freddie Ellis. He and his gang are wanted for a dozen similar burglaries. I have reason to believe that your husband was the second robber and that the young lad seen running away after him was your son. So I ask again: when did you last see him?'

'When I sent him off to school yesterday morning,' Kate said. 'His father stopped him – and my daughter Ella – on the way home and took him away. We've been desperately looking for him since. Joe's a good boy, Sergeant. He's never been in trouble before.'

Groves pulled a sour face. 'Well, he's in trouble now, all right.'

'Well, *if* Joe was the boy who broke into the house then it was only because his father forced him to,' Jonathan said.

'That's for the magistrate to decide.'

Kate jumped up. 'The magistrate! My son's only six.'

'The magistrate at Worship Street sends nippers of that age to reformatory schools each day. Your son is complicit in a murder.'

Black spots danced at the corner of Kate's vision then started to merge together. She felt Jonathan's arm around her.

'Sit down, Mrs Ellis,' he said, quietly.

Kate allowed him to guide her back to the chair.

'I must tell you, Sergeant, that if you persist in bullying Mrs Ellis, I will be seeking an interview with your superior to complain about your conduct.'

Sergeant Groves's moustache twitched and his gaze flickered. 'I am gathering information.'

'What, by browbeating innocent women? If this is the way the Metropolitan Police go about things, I'm surprised you bring anyone before the law.'

Patrick rested his hand on Kate's shoulder. 'Apart from sending my sister out of her mind with worry, what do you intend to do to find her missing son?'

Sergeant Groves picked up his hat. 'We are making enquiries and will inform you of any developments in due course. Good day to you, Mrs Ellis. Should you hear of the whereabouts of your husband, do tell the police immediately.'

'Of course,' Kate replied. 'But my son is innocent.'

'Be that as it may, I don't need to remind you that aiding a felon is also a criminal offence.' He nodded to Jonathan and Patrick. 'Gentlemen.' He flipped his hat on his head and showed himself out.

Kate clutched Jonathan's arm. 'We have to find Joe before the police do.'

Chapter Thirty

Joe wedged himself behind the chair in the far corner of the Blue Coat Boy's bar and wrapped his arms around his knees. The images of the night before played over and over in his mind.

He crossed himself three times and then clasped his hands tightly together. *Please, Jesus, if you let me go home I promise I'll be good*, he mouthed wordlessly.

Heels clipped across the floor and Joe started to shake.

'So that's where you're hiding,' Aggie said, pushing the chair away.

'I'm waiting for Pa,' Joe said, crawling out from his hiding place.

'Well, he ain't back yet and until he shows his face, you can come downstairs with me so I can keep an eye on you.' She grabbed his arm and dragged him towards the cellar door.

The Blue Coat Boy's basement was only just high enough for a man to stand upright and the roughly plastered walls were blistered with damp and thick with cobwebs. A battered oil lamp hanging from the ceiling cast a harsh light over the two dozen or so scruffy men crammed into the suffocating space. In the centre of the room was a pit, dug from the bare earth and lined with planks of wood, and on the far side a fat man wearing a tight suit, flowery waistcoat and a tall top hat was chalking numbers on a blackboard.

Aggie brushed past Joe and swept across the room, picking up dirt and mouse droppings on her skirt. She settled herself onto the bench and clicked her fingers at him.

'Drink.'

She turned to talk to someone and Joe gave her a hateful look as he weaved his way between the men to the improvised bar. He picked up a bottle and a dull pewter tankard and turned to see his father standing at the bottom of the stairs swaying.

'Pa!' Joe shouted.

His father glanced at him briefly out of red-rimmed eyes then, shoving him aside, made his way to Aggie. Joe grabbed onto his coat tails.

'I'm glad you're back, Pa.'

Freddie belched, releasing a wave of sour breath. 'Wotcha, son,' he said, tousling Joe's hair roughly before sprawling in the chair next to Aggie.

She snatched the bottle from Joe. 'Give it here before you drop it.'

Splashing half of it in the mug for herself, she handed the bottle to Freddie, who put it to his lips and gulped it down.

'Any word?' she asked.

Freddie shook his head. 'Nabbers ain't got nuffink except the dead geezer's old bird but it were so dark and I doubt she'd recognise me if I went up and kissed her. If I keep my head down for a week or two, I'll be in the clear.'

'Well good gawd, but,' Aggie swiped Joe across the top of the head, 'no thanks to this snotty little bugger.'

She grabbed his arm and pulled him towards her until her nose was just an inch from his. 'If you ask me, your pa should have bashed *your* brains out for being so fucking stupid.' Joe started to shake. 'Maybe 'e's dim-witted cos his ma dropped him on his bonce when he was a baby.'

Joe balled his fists. 'Don't you talk about my ma.'

'Leave 'im alone, Aggie,' Freddie said, half-heartedly as he wiped his mouth with the back of his hand. 'Oi! Jolly. When you going to get this fucking show going?' he shouted, waving the bottle in the air.

The bookmaker tipped his hat. 'Right you are, Mr Ellis.'

He stuck his fingers in his mouth and let out a two-tone whistle. The stairs creaked as men dressed in garish checked suits and holding barrel-chested dogs with chewed leads came down the stairs.

Freddie thumped on the table with his fist. 'Let's have a look at them then, before old Jolly starts calling the odds.'

The crowd pressed back as the owners paraded their dogs and then unleashed a couple into the pit. The dogs ran around snarling and snapping at each other as the men above placed their bets.

'D'you want a flutter, sweetheart?' he asked Aggie.

She shook her head. 'I ain't wasting my money on counting rats.'

Rats! Joe's pulse raced off.

The bookmaker whistled again and Joe's eyes opened wide with terror as two men trudged down the stairs carrying a wicker basket between them. They tipped the contents into the pit.

Rats of all colours and sizes tumbled out, shrieking and twisting. The dogs were on them immediately, grabbing their squirming bodies between their powerful jaws. Some of the rats tried to claw their way up the side but were kicked back to the dogs, who had blood smeared across their noses and flanks from tearing the rodents apart.

'D'you want a better look, boy?' Aggie said, grinning. She pushed him forward.

Joe sprang back and tucked himself behind the upright beam. Aggie laughed.

Harry Watson burst in, thumped down the stairs and dashed over.

'You'd better scarper, boss, and quick,' he said, gasping to catch his breath in the smoky atmosphere. 'The peelers are on their way.'

Freddie rose unsteadily to his feet. 'What, here? Why . . .?'

Aggie grabbed Harry's arm. 'If someone's grassed, I'll—'

Harry shook his head. 'The rozzers found 'is cap.' He pointed at Joe.

Aggie's hand shot out and she grabbed a clump of Joe's hair. 'You left your fucking cap!' she screamed as she dragged him towards the pit.

Joe wedged his toes against the wooden edge. 'Please, Miss Aggie,' he whimpered, trying to prise her fingers open. 'I didn't mean to – it just dropped out of my pocket.' His eyes fixed on the squirming rats desperately trying to claw their way out over the other bloody, half-chewed bodies. 'No!'

She twisted her hand and sharp needles of pain pricked his scalp. 'You know what you've done, don't you?'

'I don't—'

'Only put a noose around your pa's neck, that's all.' She thrust him over the pit edge.

Joe flailed his arms, trying to grasp hold of something. His right foot slipped and he closed his eyes as he tried to remember what Captain Quinn had said about how soldiers faced death.

A police rattle sounded in the room above their heads.

'It's the filth!' someone shouted.

Bottles smashed on the floor as the audience upturned tables to shove their way to the stairs with dogs snarling and snapping at their heels.

Freddie grabbed Joe's free arm and yanked him back.

'Aggie, sort the girls. Harry, do the same for the fellas. I'll be in the usual place.'

'What about 'im?' Aggie asked, jabbing her finger at Joe.

'He's coming with me.'

Freddie shoved him towards a corner of the cellar then kicked open one of the panels to reveal a narrow passageway.

'Get in,' he shouted, throwing Joe to his knees. His father's boot connected with his rear. 'Move!'

Joe crawled blindly over sharp stones and puddles and just when he felt he could go no further a light cut through the darkness and the stench of stagnating sewage clogged his nose. He climbed out and found himself behind an overflowing privy in someone's yard.

Freddie heaved himself up from the escape tunnel and dusted his coat down.

Joe gripped his father's trousers and looked up. 'I thought you were gonna leave me behind, Pa.'

His father plonked a heavy hand on his shoulder. 'I wouldn't do that, would I? Not to my boy. Besides, you're the only other person who saw me whack the bugger over the head.'

With his cane firmly in his hand, Jonathan turned into Neptune Close. His boots squelched through the slurry trickling down the central channel as he made his way towards the collection of hovels at the far end. Stepping over the drunk sprawled in the gutter, Jonathan pushed open the bare wood door and strolled into the Two Feathers.

Like the last four public houses he'd visited, the bar was little more than the bare bones of a building with distempered walls. The counter, if you could call it that, was a rough plank of wood resting on two barrels above which, hanging from a low beam, were a collection of battered tankards. Behind the bar was a keg turned on its side and supported by an X-shaped rest. Beer dripped from the tap.

The colourless drinkers slouched over the bar looked up as he walked in then quickly returned to their drinks. One person stood out: a dark-haired man in a tailored, broad russet-striped suit. Jonathan took in the angle of his hat and the knife handle just visible beneath his jacket. He let the door close and walked to the bar. The landlord broke off from talking to a scruffy trollop and sidled over. He planted his hairy hands on the bar.

'We don't know nuffink about no boy.'

Jonathan stowed his cane under his arm. 'I thought it traditional to ask a customer what he wanted to drink.'

'Don't try that old shit with me, Nelson. You ain't no poxy customer, you're that headmaster that's been nosing around.'

A couple of the men close to them threw back their drinks and shuffled towards the door. The rest of the drinkers tucked themselves further into the shadows.

'Then there's no need for introduction,' Jonathan replied, keeping the flashily dressed man in his sight.

'Mr Ellis don't like people poking about his business,' the landlord said, polishing a pewter tankard with a grubby cloth.

'Ah. Mr Ellis – just the man I'm looking for. Where is he?'

'I 'spect he's left the area.'

Although he seemed to be chatting to the girl in his arms, the flashily dressed man at the end of the bar cocked his head.

'The police don't think so, do they?' Jonathan said, raising his voice. 'There's a poster plastered outside the station offering a *reward* and they've got patrols out looking for him.'

'And even if 'e is hereabouts, and I ain't saying he is, mind, if the rozzers can't find Mr Ellis, then you and that fucking bogtrotter Nolan won't either.'

The landlord continued. 'You might want to be a bit careful, you do. Asking questions about Mr Ellis might be dangerous to your 'ealf.'

Jonathan leant forward. 'I'm not interested in Freddie Ellis, he can go hang for all I care, and probably will when the police catch him. It's his boy I want to find. No questions asked,' he said, loud enough for the whole bar to hear. Several pairs of eyes met his gaze briefly. The chap at the end of the bar banged his empty glass down.

'That's me done,' he said. 'If anyone comes looking for me tell them to catch me later by St Mary's.' He stared at Jonathan for a moment then shoved his hands in his pockets and sauntered out.

Jonathan watched him go and turned back to the landlord. 'So, you don't know anything about Joe Ellis.'

'Not a thing,' replied the landlord coolly.

Jonathan left the pub and as casually as possible glanced down the road, quickly spotting the nattily dressed drinker lounging outside a tobacconist. When he saw Jonathan he stood away from the wall and strolled off. Jonathan waited for a couple of seconds then followed at a discreet distance.

Harry Watson greeted a couple of the stallholders with his customary jaunty smile and a nod as he sauntered along Brick Lane towards Whitechapel High Street. The black-faced clock high on St Mary's tower struck three as he dodged between the empty hay wagons heading east and turned down Church Lane. Casually, he stopped in the granite arch of the church entrance, pulled out his pipe and made a play of refilling it. He waited until a couple of women carrying sacks on their backs passed him and then slipped into the churchyard. Shoving the unlit pipe back into his pocket, Harry tucked himself behind the solid stonework and peered behind him down the road.

Where was the one-eyed bugger? he thought, looking through the afternoon crowd at the end of the road. *He couldn't have been more than twenty steps behind me.*

He wiped his moist hands on his trousers and scanned the street again. *Surely he couldn't have got hi–*

Harry froze as ice-cold metal slid across his windpipe. He swallowed, hearing his bristles scrape across the blade as his Adam's apple rose and fell.

'That's not very friendly, mister,' he said, in his broad Essex accent.

'After the landlord's warning you can't blame me for being cautious,' came the reply. 'Now drop the knife you've got tucked in your belt and I'll take my blade from your throat. Slowly. Any sudden movements and my hand might slip.'

For a second or two Harry toyed with the idea of whipping out his blade and sinking it in the other man's chest but the hand holding the blade was too sure and the voice too calm. He reached into his jacket, fished out his weapon and let it clatter to the flagstones.

Quinn removed the razor-sharp steel from his throat and Harry turned to face him.

He dusted down his lapels. 'You were dead lucky to get the drop on me like that.'

A mocking expression crept across the other man's face. 'I've stolen up on Bedouin tribesmen without them hearing a peep. Creeping up behind you crunching over the gravel wasn't much of a challenge, chum.'

Chum! Resentment flared in Harry's chest but he held it in check. There was still a blade between them and he wasn't the one holding it.

'Now, about Joe Ellis?'

'Is he a little lad about this tall?' Harry held his hand out at hip height. 'With blond hair, sort of cut short? A bright kid with blue eyes?'

Quinn nodded.

Harry lifted his hat and scratched his head. 'Well, now, I may have seen him.'

The tip of Quinn's blade flickered. 'Don't try to be clever with me.'

'You said something about a reward?' Harry said, trying to keep the tremor from his voice.

'Where is Joe Ellis?'

'With his pa somewhere.'

Quinn's inflexible stare sent a chill down Harry's spine. 'You're wasting my time.'

'B-b-but I know how you can find him, and the boy. There's this woman, see. Red Aggie. She's Freddie's bit of knock-knock. She knows where he is.'

Although the blade remained poised, Quinn's stance relaxed a little.

'I suppose you know this because you're one of Ellis's gang,' Quinn said, studying him closely.

'What, me?' he asked, with a hollow laugh. 'No, you have me wrong. I only come to the Smoke twice a week to deliver hay.'

Amusement flickered briefly across Quinn's face. 'You've been most helpful.' He eyed Harry's tailored suit, the ivory-and-jet pin anchoring his silk cravat and his beaver-skin top hat. 'I won't detain you further as I'm sure you'll be wanting to hitch up your wagon and head off back to the farm.'

Kate pulled her nightdress down from the rack over the fire and placed it on the top of the pile of clean washing on the table.

Despite not having slept properly for a week, she'd somehow managed to drag herself out of bed that morning at five o'clock, cook breakfast for forty and complete the tradesmen's orders for the following week. Sally and Bette, who had been saints since Joe's disappearance, arrived together just before seven and had brought their other sister, Lynnie, along to help. With the kitchen packed to the rafters all day, she could afford to increase Sally's wages and have Bette in for an extra two hours each day. They had gone home now for an hour or two while the shop closed for a mid-morning break but they would be back at eleven to prepare for the lunchtime onslaught.

The back door clicked open and Kate spun around. Her heart thumped uncomfortably for a couple of beats then Patrick trudged into the room. His expression said everything.

'Is there no word at all?' she said, leaning on the table to steady herself.

Patrick shook his head. 'I've been in every beer shop north of

Flower and Dean Street and got the same response.'

Kate collapsed in a chair at the table. 'So no one knows where he is.'

'A lot of people know where he is but none of them are saying,' Patrick replied, taking the seat next to her.

'I know at first we didn't want the police to find Joe but now I wish they had,' Kate said. 'He must be scared out of his wits by now. I just pray he's all right.'

Patrick slipped his arm around her shoulder and squeezed. 'Now, come on, sis. We'll find him. I promise.'

'Perhaps Jonathan has had better luck.'

Patrick straightened up and looked away. 'Maybe,' he replied in a tight voice.

Kate closed her hand over her brother's forearm. 'I wish you'd try to understand, Patrick.'

He turned back. 'I'm trying, Kate, but I can't bear the thought of never seeing you or the children again.'

'Oh, Patrick, you know from the moment I wed Freddie my life's been nothing but a living hell. I thought I'd squandered my chance of love but then Jonathan came and everything changed.' Her brows pulled tightly together. 'Don't I deserve a chance at happiness, too?'

'Couldn't you wait a bit longer and—'

'Wait for what? I've waited long enough already, Patrick.'

His eyes narrowed. 'But you won't be his wife, will you?' He sat back and folded his arms. 'I don't understand how Quinn can say he cares for you in one breath and then shame you in the next.'

'That's fine coming from you,' Kate replied, matching his unyielding expression. 'Perhaps you've forgotten that you didn't know you were a free man until after you and Josie set up home together and she was six months in the family way.'

'Yes, well ...' Patrick pulled down his waistcoat. 'At least wait until the police catch Freddie.'

'And what if they don't?'

Patrick raised an eyebrow. 'Perhaps I should do what I should have done long ago and dropped Freddie overboard at Barking Creek.'

'Patrick!'

'Yes, well.' His gaze flickered briefly across her face. 'It would be no more than the bastard deserves. But I tell you, Kate, as much as I'd like to see you settled happily, as head of the family I can't agree to you running off with Quinn to some godforsaken land.'

'For goodness sake, Patrick – enough. Can't you see I'm near mad with worry? Will you have some mercy and let the matter rest until Joe's home safe?'

Patrick expression softened. 'Very well, but—'

The back door clicked and they looked around.

It was Jonathan. 'I think I've found Joe.'

Chapter Thirty-One

Joe lay staring up at the blackened ceiling of the attic and listening to the early morning sounds outside. The eye-watering smell of turpentine from the paint factory next door was already seeping into the eaves of the lodging house where he and his father were hiding. Soon the fires would be lit and the steam pump would chug into life, adding the smell of rotten eggs and ammonia to the stench as the dye in the vats heated up.

It had been over a week since he'd proudly trotted behind his father into the Blue Coat Boy, and now his life was full of drunken foul-mouthed men and half-dressed, red-lipped women.

Instead of a bed with clean sheets and a patchwork cover he slept on a damp and stained straw mattress under a ragged, bug-infested blanket. That was when he could block out the grunts and squeals from below and the hunger in his belly and get to sleep. He'd washed around his neck each morning at the back yard pump but his clothes and person were now as dirty as everyone else's.

Something nipped his arm. He thrust it out from under the cover and scratched furiously. A drop of blood smeared across his skin and the itch settled. He studied his dozen or so flea bites for a moment then turned his head to look across the room at his father. Freddie lay sprawled on another mattress on the far side of the room, fully clothed and with an empty bottle in his right hand. Thankfully, he slept alone.

Joe watched his father's chest rise and fall a couple more times then rolled off the damp mattress. He crept across the floor and collected his shirt and jacket from the back of the chair, which scraped on the bare boards. Joe froze but Freddie only grunted.

Joe slipped on his shirt. He'd lost the button from the collar but fastened it as best he could, then picked up his boots and tiptoed out to the landing.

Watching where he placed his feet to avoid the squeaky boards, Joe inched his way towards the stairs. Someone in one of the rooms below hacked out a chest-ripping cough. As he expected, the communal room on the ground floor was empty as the superintendent was asleep and the doors were still locked. Joe slipped his boots on and placed a stool under the tiny window that overlooked the backyard.

He clambered up then carefully lifted the latch and swung it open. Stretching as tall as he could, Joe hooked his hands over the sill and pulled himself up. Kicking his legs for momentum he heaved himself through the narrow frame and then on to the outside ledge before lowering himself to the cobbles.

Joe ignored the cold morning air and fixed his eyes on the gate. He dashed across, slipped the top and bottom bolt clear before turning his attentions to the one in the middle. He gripped the rusty bolt and tried to waggle it free. It wouldn't budge. Sweat broke out on his brow. He curled his finger tighter and tried again. It moved a little then jammed. Taking a deep breath, he tugged at it once more and it slowly slid out of its housing but when he lifted the latch a hand clamped on his shoulder.

'Where are you going?'

Joe turned and looked up at his father.

'Home,' he replied flatly.

A look of disappointment spread across his father's unshaven face. 'I thought you were my boy, Joe?'

A lead weight settled across Joe's chest. 'I am, Pa, but ...'

Freddie's sorrowful expression deepened. 'When I was away at sea I used say "when I get back my boy will be so glad to see his old pa he'd do anything just to make him 'appy". Ain't I right, Joe?'

Joe's chin started to wobble. 'I ... I ... want my ma. I want to go home.'

His father tightened his grip and pulled Joe back from the gate. 'Stop snivelling, you jessie. The nabbers are after us so you can't go home.'

'Never?'

'No,' Freddie replied, shooting the bolts back in place. 'We'll have to scarper for a bit. Leave town. I ain't decided where yet but we'll go together, eh!' He nudged Joe in the ribs. 'You and me. What'd yer say?'

'I want to go home, Pa. Let me go home,' Joe cried, tears streaming down his cheeks. 'Please. I won't tell anyone where you are. Promise.' He grabbed his father's arm. 'Please, Pa, please.'

Freddie shook him off. 'You're a right fucking mammy's boy, ain't yer?'

He grabbed Joe by the scruff of the neck and marched him towards the back door. 'Get back to the room before everyone wakes up,' he said, as he shoved Joe up the stairs. 'And think yourself lucky I don't take my belt to you for cheeking me like that.'

With leaden feet Joe tramped up the wooden steps, to his prison at the top of the house.

'Stay put until Aggie arrives with breakfast. And you better take that look off your face before I wipe it off.'

Joe glared at his father and Freddie's hand smacked across his cheek. Joe flew backwards and landed with a thump on the floor. His ears were ringing and strange white lights popped at the edge of his vision. He shook his head to clear them.

'I'll give you worse than that if you lip me again,' Freddie told him as Joe cradled his throbbing cheek. He jabbed a finger at Joe. 'You stay put while I find meself something to take the dust from me throat. Do you hear?'

He nodded then wished he hadn't as it set his head pounding.

Freddie looked him over again and left the room. Joe curled up in the corner and quietly sobbed as he realised he'd never see his mother or sister again.

Kate stepped back further to avoid a drip from a broken gutter and tugged the knitted shawl tighter around her head. She blew on her hands to ward off the chill of the autumnal morning. Although Kate's first instinct was to dash to the dosshouse and tear it apart brick by brick until she found Joe, she knew they wouldn't have a hope in hell of getting within a mile of Freddie except at first light when he, and the rest of the low-lifes living in the area, would be sleeping off the excesses of the night.

As the dosshouses along Dorset Street were clearing out their customers she guessed it must be nearly eight-thirty, halfway through the working morning for the coffee vendors, road sweepers and porters who'd been awake since first light or earlier. It was still the middle of the night for the Spitalfields public houses, gambling dens and knocking shops.

The early morning damp was seeping through her old gown but Kate barely noticed it as her whole focus was on the Blue Coat Boy's front door across the street. Huddled alongside her in the dank doorway were Jonathan and Patrick. Concealed in a shop entrance on the other side of the road were Patrick's son Mickey and Mattie's husband Nathaniel.

Something flickered in one of the pub windows and Kate's heart raced. An image of Joe trotting into the school gate flashed into her mind and she started to tremble.

Sweet Mary, let me find him alive and well.

The thick, muzzy fog clogging her mind threatened to close in again but she blinked her dry, sleepless eyes a couple of times and forced them to refocus. She looked up at Jonathan, who was leaning against the door frame wearing an old military greatcoat. A battered homburg half covered his face. On the other side of him stood Patrick dressed in a scruffy mariner's smock. They were both unshaven and had rubbed dirt on to their faces to blend in with the early morning crowds.

Sensing her eyes on him, Jonathan turned and looked over his upturned collar at her. 'We'll get him back,' he said, giving her a reassuring glance.

Kate prayed that the saints above would hear his words.

'I wish you'd stayed at home, Kate,' Patrick said. 'Or at least do as I ask and fetch the police with Mickey.'

Kate shook her head. 'I'm staying right here. While you're dealing with Freddie, I'll be finding Joe.' She pointed across the road.

'There,' she said, as the door opened a couple of inches.

They held their breath. A woman slipped out with a basket hooked over her arm. She too wore a ragged shawl but everything else – from her crimson jacket to her purple button boots – were distinctive, if grimy.

'That's Red Aggie,' said Kate.

Aggie crossed the road, popped into the baker's for a couple of moments and then walked towards Commercial Street. She turned left into Commercial Street and Kate and the four men raced after her.

As they reached the busy thoroughfare, Nathaniel dodged behind a dustcart while Patrick and Mickey crossed through Christ Church graveyard. Jonathan took hold of Kate's elbow. 'This way,' he said, guiding her behind the costermongers' stall.

Aggie disappeared from Kate's view. 'I can't see her,' she said, craning her neck and frantically searching the throng.

'I have her,' Jonathan replied, pushing a shop awning aside. 'Quick, she's going down Ten Bells Path.'

Kate dodged through the carts and wagons and into a filthy alley-way with Jonathan just half a step behind her. They joined the others who were already at the corner. Jonathan peered around it then dodged back.

'Blast! It's empty,' he said. 'If we go marching down there, she'll spot us.'

'Let me go and have a shufti,' Mickey said.

Patrick gave a sharp nod. 'Watch yourself.'

Mickey shoved his hands in his pockets and strolled down the unpaved passage as if he was going to work. The moments ticked by and Kate had just started her second Hail Mary when her nephew reappeared.

'She's gone into the dosshouse next to the paint factory halfway down,' he said. 'There's a gate and a small courtyard at the front and a garden at the back.'

Patrick slapped his son on the back. 'Good work. Now quick sharp to the nabber's shop.'

Mickey ran off towards Commercial Road Police Station.

Jonathan looked up and down the alleyway then scanned the rooftops. 'I'd put a pound to a penny that there's a tunnel out in the cellar.'

'How do you know?' Patrick asked.

'I've never been in a hideout or bolt-hole that hasn't but we're here to find them, not flush them out. We just have to make sure they stay put until the police arrive.'

'But if they do make a run for it they're likely to bolt out the back, so me and Nat will take the rear if you and Kate cover the front,' Patrick said.

Kate and Jonathan watched them go. He squeezed Kate's hands. 'We *will* get Joe back, Kate. I promise.'

Kate mustered a half-smile. 'I hope so.'

Aggie stopped on the small third-floor landing to catch her breath for a second. *Bugger this*, she thought. She repositioned the basket in the crook of her arm and headed for the door at the end of the landing leading to the attic.

When she arrived at the room she marched over to Joe and crouched in front of him.

'Good morning, Joe,' she said, sweetly. 'And how are we this morning?'

'All right,' he mumbled, shrinking back.

She raised her hand. He flinched and turned from the expected blow.

'I'm all right, Miss Aggie,' she crooned, smoothing her finger down his cheek.

Her hand slid down and then closed around his throat. Joe's eyes flew open and she smiled.

Freddie rolled over and farted.

'What . . . who?' he muttered as he struggled on to one elbow.

Aggie straightened up. 'It's fucking lucky I ain't a troop of coppers or they'd be marching you down to the hurry-up wagon in cuffs by now.'

Freddie slipped his hand through the opened buttons of his vest and scratched his chest. 'Have you got something for me belly or have you just come to nag?'

Aggie held out the basket and he snatched it from her. He rummaged around and pulled out a loaf of bread, a pie wrapped in newspaper and a quart stone bottle.

'Is this it?' he asked, incredulously.

'What do you expect?'

'Something better than this pigswill,' he replied, tearing at a chunk of bread to throw at Joe. 'There you are, boy, get your chops around that.' Freddie sank his teeth into the pie.

Aggie's eyes narrowed. *Bloody idiot*, she thought, watching the grease drip on his shirt.

She folded her arms. 'What's the plan?'

Freddie looked up. 'I'm still thinking on it.'

'Well, you'd better get a move on because if you think I'm spending the rest of my life ferrying your grub up four flights of stairs each day, you've got another think coming.'

He looked up. 'I thought you said you'd do anything for me.'

A sharp retort sprang to Aggie's lips but she bit it back. She looked contrite. 'And I would. Oh, Freddie, I've tried to keep things going but there's no one to step into your shoes.' She fluttered her eyelashes at him. 'They want their guv'nor back and so do I.'

'Stop fretting. I said I'd come up with something.' Freddie grinned. 'After all, ain't I the brains of the Black Eagle Gang?'

Joe whimpered and her attention moved to him, causing her temper to erupt.

'It's a fucking pity you didn't think things through when you took 'im with you.'

'Don't start, Aggie.'

'Don't start! I'll give you "don't start, Aggie".' She marched across the floor and dragged Joe to his feet. He tried to pull away but she tightened her grip, shook him and he stumbled.

'It's because of this poxy little brat that we've had the police crawling all over the Blue Coat Boy for the last four days. The men are sitting around drinking all day instead of earning their keep and the sluts can't wander the streets for fear of being nicked. And all because of 'im.' She smacked Joe across the side of head. 'Your "little lad", who's a "chip off the old block", leaving his fucking cap behind.'

She slapped him again. Joe kicked her and snatched his arm back.

'I hate you,' he screamed, flailing his arms and booting her again.

She hobbled after him. 'You little bastard.'

She lunged to catch him but he dodged out of her grasp.

'You're ugly and old and you stink like dog shit and when my ma finds you, she'll smash you good and proper,' he screamed at her.

Aggie ran at him but he feigned left and dodged right. Aggie crashed into the wall.

Freddie laughed. 'My boy's too quick for you, Aggie.'

She put her hand on her hip, grimaced and then limped over to pick up her shawl. As she stooped Joe turned his head and she sprang at him. Her nails sank into his neck and fear flashed into his eyes. He yelped as she tightened her grip.

'Not so brave now, are we?' she said, thrusting her face in his.

'Leave him be, Aggie!'

'Fuck off.' She dragged Joe across the floor to the window. 'I've had a bellyful of your fucking "little lad".'

Freddie rose unsteadily to his feet and stumbled towards them. 'No.'

Joe gagged as Aggie's stench surrounded him. He tried to dig his feet in but they skidded over the dirty floorboards. His heart pounded as panic and fear twisted in his chest. He pulled together every ounce of strength to brace his feet against the brickwork. She punched him in the ribs.

He crumpled.

'Pa!' he gasped as Aggie heaved him up and pitched him out of the window.

Joe screamed as he tumbled over the wet tiles. The slates snagged his clothes and cut his cheeks and hands as he skidded over them. Colours and images sped through his mind so swiftly they barely registered. He grabbed wildly for anything that would stop him toppling towards the edge but his hands found nothing. Joe shut his eyes, expecting to fly into thin air but then he crashed into something.

He blacked out momentarily and when he came to he found himself looking up at puffy white clouds scuttling across a very blue sky. In the distance a clock chimed. He swivelled his eyes and looked at the low wall running around the edge of the roof. With shaky hands he gripped the top and pulled himself to his knees. Pressing his face against the rough brickwork he peered over the edge and looked down to the cobbled courtyard below.

He spotted his mother and headmaster running across the yard and could hardly believe it was true – he resisted a sudden urge to throw up. Cupping his hands around his mouth he leant over the edge. 'Mammy!'

Chapter Thirty-Two

Joe's cry ripped through every nerve in Kate's body. 'Joe!' she screamed, shading her eyes to scan the dosshouse roof.

'Can you see anything?' Jonathan asked as he did the same.

'No, but it came from up—'

'Mammy!'

'My God, Jonathan. He's on the roof,' she shouted.

'I'll fetch him down,' he called over his shoulder as he sprinted towards the house.

Kate yelled up. 'Don't move, Joe. We're coming.'

She gathered her skirts and with her heart bursting in her chest, she dashed after Jonathan. By the time she reached the hallway, he was already halfway up the stairs. Kate elbowed her way through the crowds and caught up with him on the third-floor landing.

'Where are the stairs to the roof?' she asked, looking at the landing.

'I don't know. They must be here somewhere.'

They began trying the doors, all but one of which opened on to fetid scenes of unwashed bodies and rows of coffin-sized cots.

They rattled the handle of the locked door but it wouldn't budge.

'Stand back,' said Jonathan.

She stepped aside and he threw his weight against the door. It crashed open to reveal a flight of narrow stairs. Jonathan rushed in with Kate at his heels.

'Joe!' Freddie yelled, running to the window.

Relief flooded through him as he saw Joe clinging to the low buttress.

'Don't move, boy,' he shouted, swaying from side to side, the effects of the early morning brandy still muddling his brain. 'I'll fetch you.' He turned to Aggie.

'What do you think you're playing at?' he shouted. 'If the wall hadn't been there, my boy would have gone over the bloody edge.'

Aggie looked puzzled. 'What wall?'

He roared, lurched across the room and punched her in the face. There was a sickening crunch as his knuckles hammered her nose.

She staggered back and put her hand on the wall to steady herself, then worked her jaw from side to side before touching her lip.

'You great bastard. You've loosened my front tooth,' she shrieked, and picked up the smashed bottom of an empty bottle. 'Touch me again and I'll gut you,' she said, swiping the jagged glass back and forth between them.

'You think you can face up to the top man, do you?' he yelled, sidestepping to keep his balance.

She gave a hard laugh. 'Top man? Look at you. Top joke, more like. You ain't got the brains to run a fucking whelk stall let alone the Black Eagle Gang. If it weren't for me, you'd still be Ollie Mac's boot rag. I've done with you,' she said, edging towards the door. 'The rozzers can hang you, for all I care.'

He sprang forward and grabbed the bottle. It sliced across his left palm as he twisted it from her hand.

'You double-crossing slut!' He thrust the bottle into her throat and blood spurted out, cutting off her reply in an instant.

Her eyes flew open in astonishment and her hands groped at the glass stuck in her windpipe. She gurgled, then blood spewed from her mouth, drenching the front of her as her lips moved wordlessly and her eyes rolled up. She sank to her knees and fell back.

Freddie looked down at her and kicked her head. 'Bitch.'

The cut on his hand smarted so he ripped a strip off her petticoat to bind it around the wound.

The door handle rattled and he looked up to see the door being forced open against the weight of Aggie's body jammed against it.

'Joe!' screamed Kate's voice through the gap.

Freddie ran to the window. Putting his foot on the sill and gripping the edge, he heaved himself out. Police rattles rang out and swarms of policemen and spectators filled the courtyard below.

Freddie pressed himself flat on to the slates and skidded down next to Joe.

'What's happening, Pa?' he asked.

Freddie leant into the pitch of the roof and stood up in the narrow gutter. 'Don't worry, son,' he said, hauling Joe to his feet and setting him in front. 'Me and you are going on a nice little journey far away, but first we have to get off this roof.'

Kate added her weight to Jonathan's in an effort to open the door.

'It's moving,' he said, squaring his shoulders to give it an almighty shove.

The gap widened by a few more inches and Jonathan squeezed through. Kate tumbled in behind him. They crossed to the window to see Freddie slipping and sliding over the wet tiles, dragging Joe behind him.

'Joe!' she screamed, as her son stumbled.

He turned and she could see the fear in his eyes. 'Mammy! Mammy!' he sobbed.

Freddie shoved Joe forward.

'Don't worry, me darling, we're coming for you,' Kate screamed, her voice carrying over the chimney tops.

'He's heading towards the far end of the roof,' Jonathan said.

'What good will that do?' Kate asked, frantically. 'They're trapped.'

Jonathan pulled her back from the window and jumped on to the sill.

'Maybe there's another way down. I'm going after him. Go down to the police, Kate.' She hesitated. 'Go, Kate!'

Sweet Mary, protect him, she prayed. She touched his cheek then turned back into the room and saw Aggie.

The trollop's body was half hidden behind the door and her blood had flooded across the floorboards. Her neck was bent at an unnatural angle, revealing a large piece of brown glass protruding from a gash in her throat. Kate crossed herself again, lifted her skirts and stepped over Red Aggie's lifeless body.

Forcing his gaze not to drift over the edge of the roof to the hard ground fifty feet below, Jonathan edged his way along the guttering after Freddie.

The narrow space between the low wall and the lead flashing was only just wide enough for him to place his feet toe to heel. This, coupled with his one-sided vision, meant he had to concentrate to maintain his balance. He was still more sure-footed than Freddie, though, who swayed dangerously but kept a tight hold on Joe.

The sun was fully up now, bathing the cramped tenements and the city buildings beyond with a warm autumnal glow. Squinting into the sun, Jonathan leant into the pitch of the roof and hurried towards Freddie as fast as he dared. Just as he got to within a few feet, Freddie turned.

'Keep back!' he shouted.

Jonathan stopped and looked around for any means of escape.

Although the flashing around the roof was now wide enough for him to stand properly, the wall had gone. If Freddie slipped or fell, there was nothing to prevent him from tipping over the edge and taking his son with him.

Joe craned his neck around and his terrified eyes fixed on Jonathan.

'It's all right, Joe,' Jonathan said quietly, giving the boy a reassuring smile.

Freddie's right foot skidded a few inches. 'What are you doing up here?'

Jonathan stretched out his arms. 'I just want to talk,' he said, calmly.

'About what?'

'About your son. I want you to let him go.'

'My boy's staying with me, aren't you?'

Joe nodded stiffly. 'Y-Yes ... P-Pa.'

An oddly emotional expression stole over Freddie's hardbitten face. 'You're a good son, Joe. No man ever had better. You wouldn't turn your back on me like ...' Freddie sniffed and wiped his nose on his sleeve. 'Ain't he a chip off the old block?' he asked Jonathan.

'Joe *is* a son to be proud of, Ellis,' Jonathan replied, edging forward and dislodging a tile, which hurtled to the ground. Sweat sprang out between his shoulder blades and his heart hammered painfully at the back of his breastbone.

'That he is,' Freddie replied, with a crack in his voice.

'Then why don't you let him go?'

Freddie's belligerent expression returned. 'No!' He swayed again and tightened his grip on Joe.

Jonathan tried to gauge the distance between himself, Joe and the edge of the roof. If he were quick, he could snatch Joe safely but if his restricted vision caused him to misjudge the space, they'd all plunge to their deaths.

Freddie lumbered to the edge and looked over at the factory ten feet away.

Alarm shot through Jonathan. *Surely, he's not ...*

'Don't do it, Ellis,' he yelled, as Freddie teetered dangerously on the guttering. 'Think of Joe! He can't jump that far. You'll kill him.'

Freddie laughed, grabbed Joe and hurled him into the air.

Joe screamed and Jonathan lunged forward instinctively. His boots lost traction and he tried to walk up the slates to regain his footing but kept dislodging tiles instead. As he slid towards the edge, an image of Kate standing in the courtyard below flashed into his mind. He threw himself down on the tiles, praying it would halt his descent. Mercifully, it did.

He heard Joe land with a thud on the paint factory roof. He rolled a couple of times and then came to rest by one of the chimneys. Relief swept through Jonathan. At least if Freddie did pitch over the side he'd crash to the ground alone.

'Hold on, Joe,' Jonathan shouted, rising up and planting his feet as firmly as he could on the slanted roof.

Joe pressed his face to the brickwork and wrapped his arms around the stack.

'Can't you see it's over, Ellis?' Jonathan bellowed.

Freddie looked scornfully at Jonathan, took a couple of unsteady steps backwards and then ran to the edge. As he jumped, the tile under his right foot snapped and broke his stride.

Flailing his arms and legs like a disjointed windmill, Freddie crashed into the side of the factory, half on and half off the roof. He hung there for a long moment then began to slide slowly down.

'Help me, boy,' he bellowed, kicking his legs frantically to push himself upwards.

'Stay where you are, Joe,' Jonathan shouted.

Joe nodded, closed his eyes tightly and hugged the brickwork again.

Jonathan stood up. Pushing all thoughts of the hard cobbles below from his mind he sprang onto the balls of his toes and ran across the tiles. He launched himself into the air and landed soundly next to Joe.

Straightening up from his semi-crouched position, he looked at Freddie clinging to the guttering for dear life. He'd slipped further and now had only his elbows anchoring him above the edge.

'Hurry up, you bugger. I'm slipping,' he shouted, his eyes wild with fear.

Jonathan flattened himself on the tiles.

'Stay where you are, Ellis, and don't move,' he shouted, edging forward.

Freddie unhooked his left arm and grasped at Jonathan, but he couldn't keep hold.

'No!' Jonathan shouted.

Freddie's head disappeared. Jonathan lunged forward over the jagged edge and caught his right hand.

'For fuck's sake, pull me up,' screamed Freddie, swinging wildly as he tried to grasp Jonathan with his free hand.

As Jonathan gazed down at the man dangling beneath him, the image of Kate's beaten face floated into his mind. It would be easy just to let him fall. With Freddie dead, there would be no need for him and Kate to be fugitives in Australia, have their children born as bastards, or live with the fear of discovery and disgrace.

Why did he even have to justify himself? How many better men had he killed in battle that he should now be troubled by putting an end to the likes of Freddie Ellis? In truth, Freddie was as good as dead anyway for there was no doubt he'd be hanged for murder when he faced the judge. Perhaps he'd just save everyone the trouble.

Something moved at the edge of his vision. Jonathan turned his head. As he looked at Joe huddled against the chimney, he shuffled forward until his shoulders were clear. He clasped Freddie's wrist with his other hand. 'I've got you. Just hold on until help arrives.'

Something banged behind Jonathan. He craned his neck and saw two policemen climbing through a skylight.

'Over here,' he yelled, as Freddie's weight tore at his shoulder muscles.

The officers inched their way across the slippery roof.

'I can't hold on,' screamed Freddie, thrashing about madly.

Jonathan summoned every bit of strength and tightened his grip but Freddie's hands suddenly slipped from his.

A scream rose up from the spectators.

Freddie spread his arms and plummeted. His limbs flopped like a rag doll as he hit the ground and then he lay still. The police in the yard gathered around him to cordon him off from the crowd.

Jonathan rose to his feet.

'It was a brave effort, sir,' said one of the constables standing behind him.

Jonathan climbed up the roof to Joe, who hadn't moved and continued to cling to the chimney with his eyes tightly closed.

Jonathan hunkered down beside him and gently placed his arms around the boy's trembling shoulders.

'It's over, Joe,' he said, softly.

For a second Joe didn't move but then he flung his arms around Jonathan's neck and buried his face into his chest. Jonathan held him as he sobbed uncontrollably for a few moments before raising his head.

'Pa?'

'I'm sorry, Joe, but your pa is gone,' Jonathan replied.

Joe's lower lip wobbled and he let out a hiccuppy little sob.

Jonathan moved a strand of hair from the boy's eyes. 'Shall we go and find your mother?'

Joe nodded.

Tucking his arm under his legs, Jonathan lifted Joe and carried him towards the open skylight, where the two policemen were waiting to help them down. As he ducked his head under the window frame into the paint-factory attic, Joe looked up.

'Captain Quinn, I was so afraid,' he said, his arms still tightly clasped around Jonathan's neck.

Jonathan smiled down at him. 'So was I, Joe, so was I.'

As Kate re-emerged into the yard, she met Patrick at the head of a dozen or so policemen. They had divided into two groups and while half the patrol rounded up the dosshouse lodgers for questioning, the others had stormed to the roof.

It was only Patrick's strong arm that had stopped her fainting when first Joe and then Jonathan flew across the space between the two buildings.

Barely able to breathe, she'd fixed her eyes fixed on the paint factory's green door.

Suddenly Jonathan stepped out with Joe in his arms.

'There they are,' Patrick said.

But Kate was already halfway across the yard.

'Joe!' she shouted, dodging past two burly policemen herding the women and children to one side.

Joe twisted in Jonathan's arms. 'Mammy!' he cried, stretching for her.

Kate scooped him into her arms and hugged him to her. She closed her eyes and pressed her lips on to his soft hair.

'Thank you,' she said to Jonathan, wanting to say so much more.

He smiled down at her tenderly and caressed her back.

'Excuse me.' They looked around to see the sergeant in charge of the patrol standing behind them. 'You'll pardon my intrusion into your grief, Mrs Ellis, but I will need someone to formally identify Mr Ellis.'

Joe's arms tightened around Kate's neck and he buried his face into her shoulder.

'Couldn't it wait for a few moments?'

The officer's moustache moved for side to side. 'Well, we'd like to move the bo—'

'My sister's been through enough this morning, officer. I'll do it,' Patrick cut in.

'Very good, sir,' the sergeant replied. 'If you would follow me.'

Kate caught Patrick's arm. 'Thank you, Pat.'

His eyes briefly flickered over her and Jonathan and then he followed the officer.

Kate looked up at Jonathan.

'Are *you* all right?' he asked, his deep voice rolling over her like a protective blanket.

'I am now.'

Their gazes locked as unspoken words, thoughts and emotions passed between them.

'Mammy.' They looked down at Joe. 'I was frightened on the roof.'

'I'm sure you were.'

'Well, I'll tell you, son, you were as brave as any soldier I've ever commanded.'

Joe basked in the praise for a moment then looked up with a shimmer of tears on his eyelashes. 'Captain Quinn tried to pull Pa up to the roof but he couldn't.'

A lump caught in Kate's throat. 'I know he did.' She kissed his forehead then raised her eyes to Jonathan's face. 'Captain Quinn wouldn't have done anything else.'

Jonathan's expression softened for a moment, then he looked over her head. Kate turned to see Patrick striding towards them followed by his son, Mickey, their brother-in-law Nathaniel and the police sergeant.

'Is everything all right?' she asked.

'Yes, thank you, Mrs Ellis,' the officer replied. 'They can't move—' He looked at Joe. 'You know, until the police surgeon arrives. We discovered a woman's body when they were searching the dosshouse so he'll have to look at her, too. We don't know who she is as yet.'

'Her name's Red Aggie,' Kate replied, feeling Joe tremble.

The policeman eyebrows rose. 'So *that's* Red Aggie, is it?'

Patrick cleared his throat. 'Well, sergeant, if there's nothing else, perhaps I can take my sister and her son home?'

'I don't see why not,' the policemen replied. 'I think no one would doubt that Master Ellis was an unwilling party to his father's doings but we will want to speak to him in a day or two when he's recovered. I'll release him into your custody, Mr Nolan, if you'd come to the station and sign the paperwork.'

'Gladly.'

The officer studied Kate for a moment and then his gaze drifted up to the man beside her. 'I shall need a statement from you also . . .'

'Captain Quinn. And I'll present myself at the station after lunch, if that is convenient.'

'Thank you.' The officer looked Jonathan over again. 'And you are the boy's headmaster, you say?'

'I am.'

'And you are also a close friend of the family?' the officer asked, scrutinising him closely.

'Mrs Ellis supplies the meals for the school and I am acquainted with Mr Nolan through her,' he replied, holding the officer's enquiring gaze.

The sergeant's heavy eyebrows rose to the middle of his broad forehead. 'Well, your actions are to be commended. I can't say I've ever heard of a headteacher racing across rooftops to rescue one of their charges.'

'The welfare of the children in my care is my overriding concern, but I hope not to repeat the experience again.'

'Shall we leave the police to their duty and allow Captain Quinn to return to the school?' Patrick said, looking hard at Kate.

'But ...' Kate's eyes darted from Jonathan to Patrick then back again. Then a sense of calm settled on her that it was over. Joe was safe and so was she, held and cherished by Jonathan. And now they had the time and freedom to order the rest of their lives.

'Yes, we should, Patrick.' She shifted Joe in her arms. 'Thank you, Captain Quinn.'

The tender look she knew so well flitted briefly across Jonathan's face. 'Not at all, Mrs Ellis,' he said, touching her shoulder. 'And please accept my condolences for your loss.'

'Thank you.'

Patrick stepped forward and thrust out his hand. 'On behalf of my whole family I'd like to thank you once again, Captain Quinn, for rescuing Joe. I'm sure you'll understand that my wife and I will be caring for my sister and her children until after her husband's funeral.'

Jonathan shook his hand. 'Of course. I would not expect it to be otherwise.'

'And perhaps, Captain Quinn,' Patrick added as he slipped his arm around Kate, 'if you should find yourself in Stepney tomorrow you might like to call in and enquire after my sister's health.'

Chapter Thirty-Three

Kate guided her mother up the three stone steps to Patrick's front door and into the hall. Despite her thick coat, bonnet and knitted gloves, Sarah's wrinkled face was white with the cold. She, Kate, Mattie and Josie had squeezed into a hansom cab to come back from Christmas-morning Mass while Patrick and Nathaniel walked the children home.

'If you settle Ma in the parlour, Kate, we'll check on the roast and start the vegetables,' Josie said, as she and Mattie removed their outdoor clothes.

'Of course.' Kate hung her mother's coat alongside her own on the stand then hooked the old woman's hand in the crook of her arm.

'Come and warm yourself by the fire, Mam,' she said, leading her into the snug parlour.

Like last year at Mattie's, there was a large spruce tree decked in paper chains and sweetmeats along with new glass baubles and tinsel garlands. There were also a number of small candles wired onto the branches ready to be lit when Kate's large cake, decorated with dried fruit and nuts, was set on the table. As she settled her mother in the chair, Josie came in carrying a tablecloth.

'Do you want any help?' Kate asked.

'No, we're fine.' She exchanged an odd look with Sarah then dashed from the room.

'They'll manage fine enough without you for this once. Now tell me. Has Patrick sorted out the bank yet?'

Kate smiled. 'Yes. We are proper partners at last. All signed and sealed. And I have an account in the East London Mutual Bank with *money* in it and to celebrate I bought Ella and Joe a whole new set of clothes, a rug for the parlour and this for myself.' She smoothed her hand over the new moss-green gown with delicate amber flowers printed over it. 'I've *never* had a new dress before, Ma. And you know, when I handed over the seventeen shillings my hand shook.'

'And grand you look in it. I'm sure there's a special someone else who'll think so, too.' Sarah said, with a twinkle of devilment in her eye.

Kate lowered her eyes.

Although she could barely hold herself back from falling into his arms each time they met, for both their sakes, she dare not, especially with Mabel still circling like a vulture and waiting for a chance to expose their love. They contrived to meet almost every day, however briefly, but for propriety's sake they had to ensure it was where everyone could see them. Even when they discussed the school menu, they did so at the window table at the shop, not in her parlour. After the reports in the papers about how Jonathan rescued Joe, the merest hint that she and Jonathan were involved with each other before Freddie died would have destroyed Jonathan's reputation. He would have been dismissed from St Katharine's. And although there wasn't a soul in Knockfergus who would have shed a tear at Freddie's passing, the conventions had to be observed. After all, Nolan and Sons was one of the most prosperous haulage companies on the river, and Maguire's had just bought a second coal yard in Stratford. Kate couldn't disgrace her family by refusing to wear widow's weeds for at least three months. The reports in the national newspapers had also brought an unexpected letter from Jonathan's father and she'd urged him to accept the olive branch. After some deliberation he replied and they planned to meet at his sister's house again before school resumed.

She'd been so taken up with helping Joe through the inquests and police inquiries that her own desires took second place but recently, lying alone in her bed, the need to have Jonathan's arms around her had become almost too much to bear. It was only last week that she'd been able to cast off her mourning garb which meant soon, very soon, she and Jonathan could start to plan their life together.

A life with Jonathan! A proper life, as his wife without shame. Only a few months ago that had been an impossible dream but ... perhaps this time next year she would be holding his child in her arms!

The parlour door burst open and Patrick and Nathaniel, followed by the children, stomped in, filling the hallway with snow and laughter.

'Mattie and Josie are in the kitchen and I think the kettle just boiled,' Kate called through the open door as she tucked a blanket around her mother's legs.

'Kettle!' Patrick said, shrugging off his coat. 'I can think of something better to warm us. Can't you, Nat?'

'I certainly can.'

Ella and Beth came in and squeezed themselves onto the chair in the far corner, then huddled together whispering and giggling.

Joe dashed into the parlour, his cheeks glowing with the frosty air. 'Ma, Bertie threw a snowball at me but I dodged it like this.' He leapt sideways almost knocking over Josie's prized aspidistra. 'I chucked one back and it hit him right on his nose.'

Sarah caught hold of Joe's hand and pulled him closer. 'I could eat you, me darling boy, so I could,' she said, kissing him on the cheek.

Joe rubbed his cheek vigorously. 'Grrrrran!'

Kate and her mother laughed.

Patrick and Nathaniel went to the sideboard to pour themselves a drink each.

'I wouldn't say no to a small one,' Sarah said. 'Just to ease me joints.'

Patrick smiled at his mother. 'Kate?' he asked, lifting the bottle.

She shook her head. 'I'll wait for a cup of tea.'

'There you go,' he said, handing Sarah a brandy. 'Get that down you, Mam.'

Sarah took a sip. Patrick went to warm the backs of his legs in front of the hearth alongside Nathaniel. When Mickey came in, he helped himself to a tankard of beer from the barrel set up at the end of the dresser under the watchful eye of his father.

Josie popped her head out of the kitchen door. 'Go and play upstairs, boys, so you don't get underfoot.'

Joe twisted out of Sarah's embrace and clattered upstairs after his cousins.

'It fair warms me to see Joe back to his old self,' Sarah said, watching him go.

Kate followed her gaze. 'I know.'

For two months after Freddie's death there wasn't a night that went by that Joe didn't wake screaming. It was only in the last few weeks that she hadn't had to stay with him each night until he slept.

Josie bustled in with her sleeves rolled up past her elbows, wearing an apron over her best gown.

'Beth and Ella. Will you get the plates out and put the cutlery in order while Annie and I set the vegetables boiling?'

'Yes, Aunt Josie,' the girls said in unison as they jumped up and went to the oak dresser at the far end of the room.

Josie bit her lower lip. 'I hope we have enough food for all fifteen of us.'

Kate looked puzzled. 'Fourteen, you mean.'

Josie's neck flushed. 'Oh ... oh ... yes, what am I about? Fourteen, of course.'

She shot a furtive look at Kate and then dashed out to the kitchen again leaving Kate and Mattie chatting with their mother. After a few moments Nathaniel looked at the clock and finished his drink.

'You'd better call the boys, Pat,' he said, taking up position behind his wife. Patrick pulled his watch out of his fob pocket. 'You're right.' He drained his glass, too, then crossed to the parlour door and opened it.

'Josie!' he shouted.

'We're coming,' she shouted back from the kitchen.

'Beth, Ella, leave what you're doing and join us.' The two girls came back in. Mattie ushered her daughter over and Ella came and stood next to Kate.

'Why is Uncle Pat calling us down?' Ella asked. 'The table's not even out yet.'

Sarah's wrinkled face lifted into a girly smile. 'Just wait, sweetheart,' she said, hugging her granddaughter.

Patrick went to the bottom of the stairs. 'Tidy yourselves and come down, lads,' he yelled up.

There was a great deal of thumping as the boys ran down and into the parlour. Josie and Annie came in without aprons and Josie checked her hair in the mirror before sitting in one of the fireside chairs. She signalled for Rob to join her.

'Is dinner ready?' Joe asked.

Kate shook her head and looked around at her family. 'What's happening?'

Josie's eyes darted to Patrick. He glanced at Mattie and she shot a look at Nathaniel, just as the clock struck the first note for one o'clock. There was a knock at the front door.

'I wonder who that can be?' said Mattie, beaming at her sister.

Josie put her hand over her mouth. 'I've no idea, Mattie.' She giggled.

Nathaniel's eyebrows rose innocently as he struggled to suppress a grin.

'Shall we see?' Patrick said, striding across the room and to the hall.

Everyone's eyes fixed on Kate. The door clicked open and a male voice sounded in the hall. It couldn't be ...? Kate's heart did a double beat then galloped off.

The door opened and Kate stopped breathing as Jonathan walked into the room.

It had been twelve weeks and three days since Jonathan had last held her in his arms and kissed her, and his need to do so again was growing more urgent with each passing day; however, as much as he wanted to post the banns, they could not, just yet, for a number of reasons.

Firstly, there were the school guardians who had demanded a full explanation as to why, instead of overseeing the school, Jonathan had been chasing a criminal across a dosshouse roof. They raised their collective eyebrows in astonishment when they found out that the criminal was not only the father of a pupil but the husband of the woman whose morals had already been enquired into by the board of guardians. As if this wasn't enough to give the guardians dyspepsia, Jonathan's revelation that Aggie's body was found in the same premises as Joe had them all reaching for their medicinal hip flasks. Thankfully, his argument that his swift, if somewhat unconventional, actions had saved the school's good name carried the day.

Then there was Joe, who had been abused and put in fear of his life at the hands of his own father. He had needed Kate's undivided love and care to restore him.

Lastly, there was Kate herself, who needed time to adjust to her new circumstances. Jonathan swept his gaze around the room to acknowledge the members of the Nolan family who all smiled at him.

'I know some of you have already met him but to those of you who have not, this is Captain Quinn.' Patrick led him further into the room. He walked Jonathan around the parlour and introduced him formally. The boys shook his hand and the girls curtsied. Joe stood up and bowed as if they were in school but Ella looked at him knowingly.

Finally, he reached Kate.

'My sister, Mrs Ellis, you already know, of course,' Patrick said, with just a trace of amusement.

'I do,' Jonathan said, gazing down at the woman he would love into eternity.

She raised her head. 'Captain Quinn,' she said softly.

Jonathan nearly lost himself in her lovely blue eyes.

'And this,' Patrick said, 'is my mother.'

'Mrs Nolan,' Jonathan said, offering her his hand. 'It is a pleasure to meet you at last.'

'And delighted, I am, to meet you, too, Captain Quinn,' she said, gripping his hand more firmly than he expected. 'Patrick, will you fetch a chair so our guest can rest his bones.'

Patrick did as his mother asked and set it down beside Kate.

'A drink, Captain Quinn?' Patrick asked.

'Perhaps after dinner,' Jonathan replied, taking his seat. His leg brushed against Kate's skirts.

'That colour becomes you, Mrs Ellis,' he said, in a low voice.

'Thank you,' Kate replied, her arm pressed against his.

They exchanged a look and Jonathan only just managed to stop slipping his arm around her waist. He glanced around again.

'You have a lovely home, Mrs Nolan,' he said.

'Thank you,' Josie replied, glowing with pride.

'And I noticed you've had a daguerreotype taken,' he said, motioning towards the framed portrait perched on the table mantelshelf.

'Yes. There's a studio next to the Hoop and Grapes in Aldgate. They have painted scenes to stand against, pot plants and all sorts. We went with Mattie and Nathaniel and they had their likenesses taken, too,' Josie said.

'And I tell you, it's the devil's own job to keep the children still for the image to set, Captain Quinn,' Mattie added.

Jonathan laughed. 'I can believe that.' He turned to Kate. 'Didn't you want a picture of you and your children, Mrs Ellis?'

Kate's eyes flickered over his face. 'Not just at the moment. Perhaps in a month or two.'

'Are you visiting your family at all over Christmas, Captain Quinn?' Nathaniel asked.

'I am catching the train to St Albans to visit my sister the day after tomorrow but I will be back on the first of January' – he looked at Kate – 'as I have some plans to put into place for the New Year.'

'So your second year at St Katharine's will have everyone talking, too, Captain Quinn,' Josie said.

'I hope so. In fact, as it will be common knowledge soon, I can tell you that the guardians have agreed to use Mrs Benson's bequest to enlarge the school. It will mean that I shall be moving from the house as the builders will be making the ground floor into the girls' classroom. Mr and Mrs Delaney will stay in their quarters above and I'll need to find somewhere else to live.'

'Have you settled on where?' Kate's mother asked.

'I'm not sure exactly but perhaps a house around here might suit me very well. It's a brisk walk to the school but away from the docks.' Jonathan gave her a crooked smile. 'So who knows, Mrs Nolan, in a month or two we may be neighbours.'

A look of delight flashed into the old woman's eyes.

Josie stood up. 'If you'll excuse me, Captain Quinn, we have to see to our dinner.' She signalled to Annie, Beth and Ella who jumped off their chairs.

Jonathan and the other men in the room rose to their feet as they left.

'And we should set the table up,' Patrick said.

'Captain Quinn,' said Sarah. 'Kate tells me that in your travels you've been to my old home town of Kinsale.'

'Indeed I have.'

'We have a painting of the old place in Patrick's office across the hall.' A mischievous look crept into her eye. 'Perhaps you'd like to show it to Captain Quinn, Kate.'

Kate rose to her feet. 'Of course, Mother,' she said, giving Jonathan a look that set his pulse racing.

He stepped back. 'After you, Mrs Ellis.'

Kate brushed past him and walked to the door.

'Can I come, Ma?' Joe said, scooting around from the other side of his grandmother.

Sarah caught him. 'Not just now, Joe, but if you help me up I'll go and see if there are any marbles in the jar.'

Kate entered her brother's study and turned to face Jonathan, her senses and emotions reeling from having him so near. He closed the door then his arm encircled her waist, drawing her to him. Kate melted into him, her hands running up his chest and around his neck. She looked up into his face, hardly believing that she was in his arms again.

'Jonathan, I—'

His mouth pressed on hers in a demanding kiss. Kate closed her eyes and gave herself up to the pleasure of feeling his body against hers and his lips caressing her mouth, her cheek and her neck.

'I've been wanting to do that every day for the last three months,' he said, as they broke from a breathless embrace.

Kate ran her hand over his face. 'I couldn't believe my eyes when you walked in.'

He kissed her nose. 'I dropped in on your brother last week and told him that now your mourning was over, I intended to marry you.'

'What did he say?'

'Nothing at all for a moment, then he said, "I can see you're not a man to be deterred, Captain Quinn, so why don't you join the family for Christmas dinner?"' Jonathan replied, in a passable Irish accent.

Kate laughed and his arm tightened around her. 'What about an April wedding?' he said.

'What's wrong with March?' she asked, shamelessly nudging his leg with hers.

A look of desire flashed across his face. 'February it is, then.'

'We will be the talk of every street corner.'

'We will.'

'And we'll have to be good until then.'

'Of course.'

There was a light knock at the door.

Jonathan raised his head. 'I love you,' he whispered.

'And I you,' she replied. 'We ought to go back to the parlour.'

He kissed her again and Kate lost herself once more in the heady pleasure of his embrace.

There was a second knock.

'We're dishing up dinner,' Mattie called through the door.

'We should go through,' Kate said, gently pushing him away.

He sighed. 'February seems a very long way away.'

'That's true but,' Kate looked up at him from under her lashes, 'you could always call in for a coffee on your way home from the Geographical Society.'

He took her hand and kissed each finger individually. 'I most certainly will.'

He stared down at her for a moment then straightened the front of his jacket as Kate repositioned a couple of curls that had been dislodged.

'Oh, and that,' she said, giving him a quirky smile and pointing to the landscape over her brother's desk, 'is the picture you're *supposed* to be looking at.'

'Beautiful,' he replied, not glancing at it.

The extended table was already loaded with tureens of potatoes, turnips and carrots with a joint of beef at the centre flanked by jars of mustard and pickles. The plates were set out and Patrick was already at the head of the table. As Kate walked into the room with Jonathan beside her, everyone stopped what they were doing and turned.

On the other side of the room Mattie slipped her arm in Nathaniel's and smiled fondly at them. Josie took Patrick's. Sarah had tears in her eyes, which brought a lump to Kate's throat.

'I thought you might like to sit between Kate and Ella, Jonathan,' Patrick said, as everyone took their seats.

'Thank you, Patrick,' Jonathan replied, pulling out the chair for Kate.

As he took his seat he moved it fractionally nearer to her and pressed his knee against her under the table.

Joe scrambled onto the chair beside Kate.

'Are you enjoying yourself?' Kate asked.

He nodded. 'Christmas is the best day of the year!'

'I am inclined to agree with you, Joe,' Jonathan said, his gaze flickering onto Kate. 'Particularly this one.'

Patrick rose to his feet. 'If we could bow our heads before we start. And *no* peeking,' he said, casting his eyes around the younger children.

Everyone lowered their heads as Patrick gave thanks for the meal and other blessings. After the 'amens' he began to carve the meat, piling it high on each plate. There was a small skirmish between the children over the crunchiest potato and the gravy jug but soon conversation quietened as the family tucked into their feast. When everyone had had another slice of meat, a second helping of turnips and the men had been persuaded to finish off the remaining potatoes between them, Patrick leant back in his chair and patted his belly.

'Well, my love, you've done us proud yet again.'

There was a chorus of approval and Josie inclined her head modestly.

Mattie dabbed her mouth with her napkin then placed it on the table. 'I shall be hard-pressed to match such a spread next year.'

'Well you won't have to, Mattie,' Kate said, beaming at her family, 'because I think it must be my turn.'

Her mother, Mattie, Josie and Nathaniel smiled at her and Patrick rose to his feet and held up his glass.

'I'll drink to that,' he said, and everyone raised their own glasses in agreement. He turned to Josie. 'Now, Mrs Nolan, where's the plum duff?'

Josie stood and began to clear the plates.

Jonathan's hand found Kate's under the table. She looked up at him and smiled as she remembered how miserable she had been only twelve short months ago. Now, against all the odds, she was sitting in the midst of her family with Jonathan, the man she loved, beside her. She had been taught some hard lessons and lived through tough times on her way to happiness. And she wasn't foolish enough to think that life would always be smooth sailing but whatever the future held she knew she would always have Jonathan.

Acknowledgements

As with my previous three books, *No Cure for Love*, *A Glimpse at Happiness* and *Perhaps Tomorrow*, I would like to mention a few books, and authors to whom I am particularly indebted.

As before, I have drawn on Henry Mayhew's contemporary accounts of the poor in *London Labour and the London Poor* (edited by Neuburg, Penguin, 1985). His painstaking reporting of the worries, concerns and language of the people he interviewed have helped me set the scenes for all my books. Millicent Rose's out of print *The East End of London* (The Cressent Press, 1951) which gives an account of east London before the slum clearances in the late 1950s early 1960s and provides a tantalising glimpse into the tight-knit communities clustered around the London docks.

I again use several photographic books of old east London including *East London Neighbourhoods* by Brian Girling (Tempus, 2005), *Dockland Life* by Chris Ellmers and Alex Werner (Mainstream Publishing, 1991), *London's East End* by Jan Cox (Weidenfeld & Nicolson, 1994) and *East End Past* by Richard Tames (Historical Publications, 2004). To get Jonathan's army career right I drew on the comprehensive *The Oxford History of the British Army* (Oxford, 2003), *The British Officer* (Clayton, 2007), Lambert and Badsey's *The Crimean War* (Alan Sutton, 1994) and Philip Warner's *Army Life in the '90s* which is a reprint of an article from *Navy and Army Illustrated* which gives a snapshot of the British army at the height of the Empire.

Kate's menu came from *East London* by Walter Besant (1899, reprinted 2005). It also helped me understand the school day at St Katharine's, as did *Victorian Life: School* by Nicola Barber. I made use of the BBC's excellent website http://www.victorianschool. co.uk/ and http://www.bbc.co.uk/schools/primaryhistory/victorian – britain/. Mayhew (cited above) gave me an excellent description of the Blue Coat Boy and Fiona Rule's comparative and detailed study of Dorset Street in *The Worst Street in London* (Ian Allan, 2008) helped me fill in the details. Lastly, I would like to mention once more Lee Jackson's brilliant website *The Victorian Dictionary*: http://www.victorianlondon.org/

As ever no book is a single person's effort so I'd like to thank a few more people. Firstly my husband Kelvin, my three daughters, Janet, Fiona, Amy and my best friend Dee for their unwavering support. My good friends and authors Elizabeth Hawksley and Jenny Haddon who encourage me on when the muddle in the middle seems almost irresolvable. My fellow author and chum Fenella Miller who is always at the end of the phone for a natter. Once again my lovely agent Laura Longrigg, whose encouragement and incisive editorial mind helped me to see the wood for the trees. Finally, but by no means least, a big thank you once again to the editorial team at Orion, especially Natalie Braine, for once again turning my 400+ pages of type into a beautiful book.